The Shameless Game

A Suspenseful Political Thriller

THIS BOOK INCLUDES

Something Soon

Craving Redemption

Slowly We Rise

Never Nothing

Twisted Truths

Keep the Faith

Table of Contents

Something Soon

CHAPTER ONE 3

CHAPTER TWO..12

CHAPTER THREE.. 30

CHAPTER FOUR... 50

CHAPTER FIVE.. 72

CHAPTER SIX 86

CHAPTER SEVEN 98

Craving Redemption

CHAPTER ONE 109

CHAPTER TWO..125

CHAPTER THREE..138

CHAPTER FOUR..160

CHAPTER FIVE..173

CHAPTER SIX 181

CHAPTER SEVEN 197

Slowly We Rise

CHAPTER ONE 207

CHAPTER TWO 226

CHAPTER THREE 234

CHAPTER FOUR 247

CHAPTER FIVE 268

CHAPTER SIX 295

Never Nothing

CHAPTER ONE 309

CHAPTER TWO 320

CHAPTER THREE 343

CHAPTER FOUR 364

CHAPTER FIVE 373

CHAPTER SIX 394

Twisted Truths

CHAPTER ONE 407

CHAPTER TWO 435

CHAPTER THREE 456

CHAPTER FOUR 467

CHAPTER FIVE 482

CHAPTER SIX 491

Keep the Faith

CHAPTER ONE 505

CHAPTER TWO... 527

CHAPTER THREE.. 543

CHAPTER FOUR 563

CHAPTER FIVE... 570

CHAPTER SIX 583

Something Soon

The Journey to the Start

CHAPTER ONE

Seditionists HQ

Los Angeles

Daven sat back in his chair and tented his fingers thoughtfully. The dreaded first contact had gone exactly as badly as he expected, but now all he could do about the Bancroft boys was wait for Lester to cave in to his curiosity and call him back to open a more fruitful dialogue.

In the meantime, there were a hundred other things to manage. As he was began sifting through his long-neglected mail, Rupert walked in the office and sat down noisily in the huge couch off to the side, so that Daven was forced to turn around to talk to him.

"Where have you been?"

Rupert made a face. "Conference call with the PR team. You know, the one you are supposed to join every day but keep neglecting, so maybe I should be the one asking where *you've* been?"

"On the phone with Lester Boyd."

"Well, well. So that's the mystery man. Sleeping with the enemy at last, eh?" Rupe grinned.

Daven looked startled. "Absolutely not. How did you come to that conclusion?"

"Never mind, that's not what…forget it. I suppose you told him we know our man was framed, even though I said we shouldn't let that cat out of the bag just yet?"

Daven stood up and looked out the window, gazing to the far reaches of the Pacific Ocean. "I did tell him, and his reaction indicated he was shocked to hear such an accusation. Honestly…now I don't think he's as closely connected to the party as we thought he was. Perhaps my entire theory has been misguided."

"So if he's a nobody, why did he get assigned to babysit Hank's kids, then? That doesn't make any sense, Dav."

"I know. I'll work it out. We have time. Anybody on the team have more guesses as to why Hank rolled over so easily?"

"Said it before, but we still think he was out of his goddamn mind is all."

"I don't think he lost his mind. You know him, he was up to something big. I just wish he had told us what it was before he got himself killed."

Rupert sighed heavily. "Taylor's theory still might hold water: Harmon's minions threatened his kids and forced him into a confession."

"I thought of that, too. But Hank had the option to have me assume guardianship, and he didn't take it. They could've been safe in my home in a heartbeat, but he *willingly* had them taken away and then died for it less than a week later. For nothing. Not only that, but whatever we think about Harmon's party on other issues, their leadership wouldn't abide threatening children. I just don't understand any of this!"

He threw his notebook onto the chair in frustration and went to make another espresso, the third one of the day so far. It wasn't doing anything for him at this point but making him more agitated; he shouldn't have another and ignored his colleague's raised eyebrows that said exactly the same. But Rupe kept his mouth shut; everyone who knew Daven had at some point learned the hard way not to comment on his caffeine addiction.

"Well...at the very least, Hank really threw the Urbanes out of whack. They ousted more aides today, and I've heard more heads are on the chopping block."

Daven nodded. "It does seem strange that we're getting all the good press considering only the two of us know Hank's a martyr and not a traitor. And donations are going through the roof. If I believed in karma, this case would be a prime example for study."

Rupert nodded solemnly. "Absolutely. And what about his sons?"

"I don't know if we can get them back, and I can't afford to focus on them right now. Finding out what Hank was up to has to take precedence." He drank down the espresso in a single gulp and picked up the notebook again, tapping it irregularly as he decisively plotted his next move.

"Rupe…I'm really going to need your help finding out everything there is to know about this Lester Boyd."

Undisclosed location, Virginia

The first week at Bonded Retainer Training School for Minors passed almost without incident. Sure, Theo was highly prone to childish outbursts over small things, but Floyd fought to remember that it occurred precisely because he *was* still a child and understandably upset that life had changed so drastically, virtually overnight.

The humble, diligent, and endlessly dutiful 16-year old Floyd had never been spoiled by Hank Bancroft's power and lifestyle. He didn't care about material things, and was kind to the servants and butler almost to the point of obsequiousness. Their quiet loyalty and devotion to him helped him stay out of trouble. He was well known for sneaking them money and forbidden items, and secretly throwing birthday parties for them in the expansive basements that served as their quarters.

Floyd was already keenly missing them after just a few weeks of being apart.

Theo had always been nice to the servants, but aloof. He didn't dare gift them anything after being caught just once. However, he loved the lavish Bancroft lifestyle. Relished it. At twelve, his precocious imagination had already conjured up a veritable timeline of pleasure and indulgence that he was insistent upon being able to experience. But he also wanted to go to college, to be married, to have a different car to drive every day of the week, to have season tickets for a sports team. The list was endless. He wanted his *own* servants.

He hadn't come to terms yet with the fact that none of the goals would ever be achievable now - except perhaps marriage once he was freed. Floyd needed to make him understand, but Theo wasn't ready for that talk yet. He was still asking when they were going to go home, when they were going to see dad again, when he would be able to reunite with his dogs. So far Floyd had deflected the questions, even knowing he deserved answers...which would most likely never satisfy him.

After all, how do you explain to a 12-year old that the next 20 years of his life belonged to the enemies of your father, and that he had to do well with the opportunity he was given -

which wasn't much, admittedly - or else he would suffer even more? Considering the seriousness of the accusations that had taken down Hank Bancroft, they were lucky they had any chance at all for a halfway decent life. And being a house servant wasn't nearly as terrible as some of the other options.

Without that talk, things escalated quickly and Theo went into a crisis on the first day of week two, when half the class was busy preparing lunch for the entire class. First, he refused to do anything except stare at the wall and hum. Floyd talked him out of that, but then, as they were learning how to pluck birds and check the temperature of meats, when Theo threw down the thermometer and yelled, "this is why we have a chef!" At first Floyd thought he was joking, but that was not the case. He bent down to pick up the wand and quickly handed it back to Theo, fearful of what their temperamental kitchen trainer was going to do.

"Quiet, Theo!" he barked in a low tone. "You know we don't have Chef anymore."

"Yes we do, and he's waiting for us. Probably has lunch on the table right now! I want to go home!" And with that, Theo shoved everything off of the kitchen island onto the ground and ran out the door. Blood and juices from uncooked steak and pheasants splattered everywhere, along with broken glass from all goblets that had been waiting to be filled with (fake) wine.

Floyd didn't dare chase him; he couldn't afford another warning. He raised a hand and waited for the trainer to look at him, and then blurted, "May I go and get him-"

"No," said the trainer icily, as he turned to retrieve a box of gloves from a shelf and set it down on the counter. "Clean this mess up, now. All of you. Then you can let everyone know who to thank for missing lunch today."

"But we can still make all the sides," Floyd insisted. "They don't have to go without, please, sir."

He gestured around the room. "We don't have the time. The kitchen and floor needs to be thoroughly sanitized. This is a good lesson, actually. Almost a case study. In real life, you see, Theodore would lose his job immediately and the rest of you would have to clean it up for him anyway. This is-"

"I'll clean it up myself if you'll just let them make something for-"

"Have you forgotten this morning's penalty for speaking out of turn? If so, I'm happy to repeat it for clarification."

Everyone now turned to gape at Floyd in shocked silence, so he flushed, took the gloves, and bent down to start cleaning, first taking a moment to study his aching palms that were criss-crossed with raised welts. Sliding the blue gloves on was agony. His throat suddenly swelled with grief; Dad was a strict disciplinarian, too, but he would never dream of doing such a cruel thing to his boys. Floyd missed him terribly and was counting down the days until it was time for yearly visitation. Only 350 days left...

While working on mopping up the rest of the blood from Theo's tirade, Floyd calmed himself and resolutely decided to stop delaying and have *the talk* with his little brother. But first, he needed to talk to their guidance counselor and see if he could offer some advice.

CHAPTER TWO

MAYFAIR FEDERAL PRISON, PENNSYLVANIA

"Jesus Christ, Hank," muttered Lester as he plopped down on the other side of the visitor's booth, slapping down a thick file folder onto the counter. "What a bloody mess you've gotten yourself into."

"Lester?" Hank queried in disbelief as he squinted his eyes, reached forward, and hooked his fingers into the wire partition that was separating them. "Is that....is that you?"

"In the flesh. Been a long time."

"Holy shit. What...how... *what the fuck are you doing here?*"

"I got asked to be here. Calm down, let's talk like gentlemen. It's just you and me, and we have a lot to cover."

Hank was so taken aback that he literally could not get the mechanisms in his throat to work in order to enable to him to respond - had he anything to say, that is. For now, all he could do was stare and gape. So Lester dived right in.

"Harmon has appointed me as the negotiator for this discussion, prior to the arraignment tomorrow. You do know that's happening tomorrow, right? I don't know what they've told you."

Hank continued to stare, and Lester gave it right back to him. Several long moments passed.

"What. *the fuck.* are you doing. *here*," Hank repeated, having almost recovered from the shock. There was no anger in the question, although there should be, considering what happened the last time they saw each other.

"As I said," Lester repeated calmly, although he felt like passing out from anxiety, "I'm a pre-arraignment negotiator. Appointed by Harmon himself."

Hank stood up and walked away, pacing his little booth fruitlessly, hoping to exit. There was no guard to let him out, though, and after pounding on the door a few times without response, he stood against the back wall as far as he could go, glaring daggers at his former friend.

"Yes, I know the arraignment is tomorrow, to answer your question. But this makes absolutely zero sense. I repeat: *why are you here?* I heard you were a teacher and that you left the Urbanes. Turns out you're still Harmon's little bitch, huh?"

"Never was his bitch. If anything, he was mine. I'm actually here to talk about Theo and Floyd…more specifically, to discuss their future when you're found guilty. Harmon chose me for obvious reasons, but if you need me to spell them out, I will."

Hank said nothing. Harmon of course knew that Lester had loved the boys once, so…yes, this made sense now. But that didn't mean it was acceptable.

"Are you going to talk to me, or just stare at me like I have three heads?" Lester asked harshly. "Sit down, Hank. We have one hour."

Hank growled, "So Harmon has some fucking balls, after all. Who knew. Sending you, of all people, to threaten my sons in the same breath you claim to still love them. I'm perfectly happy to just stand here and stare at you for 54 more minutes."

"You see me threatening anyone? I'm here to help them."

Hank snorted. "Right. Help. What do you want, exactly?"

"To be precise, I want you to sit down in front of me and talk about old times for a minute or so. Then we'll talk about the future. There will be no more arguing from my end, but you're welcome to it if it makes you feel better. Just don't expect me to reciprocate. Now sit the hell down."

Lester watched as Hank gauged his expression critically, then crossed the room and sat down heavily. He smiled sardonically and pitched his tone up to an excessively cheerful tenor.

"So, Lester, old friend. How have you been? Life treating you well? Divorced yet? Got kids? Been on vacation? Do tell."

Lester sighed. "Fine. Not really. Widower. No kids, she miscarried twice. Forgot what the word vacation even means. Anything else?"

"Not for the moment," Hank replied in a much gentler tone, feeling like total shit suddenly as the lump in his throat doubled. "I'm very sorry to hear about Karen. What happened?"

Lester ignored that. "Listen up, Hank. These charges...if you plead not guilty against the evidence, the trial is going to be an absolute shit show. Even without it, you must know the jury will be heavily prejudiced against you, especially with your recent tirade against your own constituents."

"It wasn't a tirade, it was a...forget that! I thought you were only here to discuss the boys," Hank replied sharply, pounding the counter as he did so.

"In a minute." He picked up the file. "Bribery of state officials. Abuse of the public trust. Corporate espionage...that's the one that allowed Harmon in the game when he decided to bring criminal charges. Blackmail. I'm not here to discuss your guilt or innocence, but-"

"I won't be found guilty of anything," Hank responded confidently. "These charges were only brought three days ago, but-"

"Yes, you will. That's why I'm here."

Now Hank looked at him like he really *did* have three heads. "What are you saying?"

Lester took a deep breath and lowered his voice. "I'm saying…look, it's really difficult to say this to you, but I have to. Hank, this is so bad that *your own party* decided to lock you up, not us. This is their doing. I'm not the enemy. Harmon's not the enemy, at least not right now. I'm just wondering how the hell it was *you* that finally brought down the Seditionists? I mean, perhaps I should be saying thank you, but damn, I'm just as confused as everyone else. This is unprecedented. It's sensational."

"My own party turned me in, huh? Jesus, you got to stop listening to Hailey. If you're already convinced of my guilt, why are you here?"

"As I said, to help-"

Hank interrupted furiously, "If Harmon really thinks I'm done for, he should be doing handstands and throwing a party right about now, not sending in a negotiator. I would appreciate if you would get to the point."

Lester's eyes narrowed. "What part of *I'm here to help your sons* are you not getting?"

Hank grinned. "I can still read you like a book after all these years, Lester. You're threatening them because a trial could prompt me to expose things my double agents found that would bring down Harmon, should I decide to bargain with the government instead of you. This is such an obvious ploy that I'm almost disappointed at the lack of suspense."

Lester hesitated for the first time, and felt unsure of his own footing for a few moments. Hank wasn't wrong about the party's motives where Harmon was concerned, but no one was threatening the boys. Lester would never have agreed to such a tactic, and neither would Harmon - who, ironically, was the one with the more humane constituents and party policies.

"Alright, Hank. Let's put emotions aside and talk facts instead for the moment. If you are found guilty by trial on or after April 1, your boys will be deeded to the state for life. And that's whether you spend 48 hours or 48 years in jail. It's automatic, no negotiation. You know that already, I assume?"

Hank nodded wordlessly. He was pale and sweaty all of a sudden.

Lester softened his tone, hating himself for what he had to say next. "The Urbanes can propose a plea deal in which that does not occur, but you must plead guilty and agree to immediate execution. Before you decide, I'll remind you one last time that your conviction on at least one count is certain."

Lester reached over to the tape recorder and hit play. Hank listened to himself blackmailing Harmon, then sat stone-faced and said nothing, even long after the recording ended. He'd had no idea that tape existed until a few days ago. Those remarks to his chief rival had been sarcastic, joking even, made in a moment of anger...but no jury in their right mind could say it was anything but outright blackmail. *Fuck.*

Lester cleared his throat harshly. "Hank, the deal is simple. You plead no contest, agree to execution, and the boys will be taken care of."

"I am *not* negotiating," Hank fired back. "The answer is no. Go fuck yourself."

Lester shrugged and stood up as if to leave. "Fine. Then you have zero chance of wrapping this up before April 1, and the deeds to the boys will go to the state. If you're fine with that, I'll just take my leave now."

Hank's expression could have set the world on fire in its intensity. He leaned forward, thankful for the wire barricade that would stop him from adding homicide to the long list of charges against him.

"You son of a bitch," he growled dangerously. "Don't you walk away from me again."

Seditionists HQ, Los Angeles

It was 9pm, and Daven hadn't even sifted through half of his much-despised email for the day yet. It seemed like for every one he answered, two more would appear in his box to take its place. How was this technology supposed to make life easier? he wondered for the hundredth time. All it did was create more work in a shorter time span.

The desk phone rang. Dav leaned over to press the speakerphone button and dumped half a cup of espresso into his lap at the same time.

"Fuck," he blurted as he leaped up to snatch a handful of napkins from the sideboard.

"Not right now, honey, I have a headache," Hank retorted with a snort.

"Oh. Sorry to hear that. I have ibuprofen and Aleve."

Hank rolled his eyes and sighed. "Hey, call it a night already, would you? Your office light is keeping me awake down here."

Daven leaned all the way over his desk and looked out the door down the hallway. Hank was doing the same from his office, but the lights were off.

"You're sleeping in the office? Did something happen at the house?"

There was a bark of laughter from the dark office. "No, I'm actually heading out. Floyd isn't feeling well. Hang up, I'm coming over."

Hank gathered up his coat and briefcase and strolled into Daven's office.

"Look, I know you don't celebrate Christmas and all, but I wish you'd reconsider for once. You've never come once in 6 years. It's going to be a hell of a party."

Daven dabbed feverishly at his slacks with a comically large stack of cocktail napkins. "I'm not sure I would enjoy a party described as *hellish*, Hank. Please forgive me for passing it up."

Bancroft Manor, Christmas Eve

Daven went to the party, of course. He wasn't nearly as immune to his boss's charms as he wished he could be; the man could get literally anyone to do anything he wanted. After giving his coat to a house servant and heading to the bar for a glass of water, his phone rang noisily.

Unknown number.

Daven never answered unknown numbers, and he proceeded to ignore it the next five times it rang with a call as well. On the seventh time, however, his curiosity got the best of him and he pulled it back out of his pocket and decided to answer. Since his voice as the speaker of the party was so well-known and constantly mimicked, he pitched it up a bit to avoid the caller identifying the number as his.

"Yes?" he answered. "Who is calling?"

"Do you have a moment to speak in private, Daven? It's important."

Daven moved outside to a quiet corner of the patio, interest now greatly piqued. "I think you have the wrong number," he tried hopefully. "But if you tell me what it's about, maybe I can point you in the right direction."

"I am calling on the emergency line with some information that you personally need to hear. Immediately. And I know this is Daven, so please don't keep pretending I have the wrong number."

Daven's blood went cold. That's why the caller got directed to this phone; the emergency number that was given to all undercover agents was diverted to an unlisted office line, which was currently forwarded to his cell. He had never actually received one of these calls before.

"I'm listening. Please proceed."

"Only if you promise to look in this immediately. I'm risking everything to call you right now. But I trust you with my life to do what you'll say you'll do."

"I promise I will address it immediately. Tell me what's going on."

"Political treason, Daven, plain and simple. Four days ago Hank Bancroft paid a leader of the Urbanes to plant an agent within the government, who would be working on behalf of the Urbanes. I was there, because I happened to be the particular agent that was chosen for the task. The problem is, I already work for you guys. For us, rather. So I'm bugging out, and I'll need you to send me relocation and restart compensation. *Without* getting Hank involved, obviously."

Holy shit. There were almost 50 agents working undercover in Urbane territory, and it was absolutely certain this man's cover would be blown fairly quickly, if not the very instant he set foot in the capital. That's why his career was over, and the party would have to pay for it no matter what happened next.

Daven cleared his throat and tried to sound unconcerned. "Look, I know you have a verification code that can prove your identity, but I'm not in my office and can't cross-check it. You have to call me back tomorrow at 8am Pacific, okay? Don't say anything else until then."

"Will do. I can explain further, but got to run now. They're making my arrangements to leave for the Capital and I'll go, but somehow on the way there-"

"I can't say anything more until you're verified. I have to end this call now. You must call me tomorrow at 8am and no later. Be careful."

He disconnected the call and carefully set his face expressionless as Hank approached him and offered a glass of champagne, which Daven reluctantly took.

"Merry Christmas, Dav. You're standing under the mistletoe, so that means I get to kiss you now. Always wanted to do that, actually," he joked easily. A little alcohol always loosened him up enough to flirt with just about anybody.

"Maybe later, Hank. We need to talk. Can we go somewhere private?"

"Ooh, moving so fast. I hope we'll be doing more than talking," Hank teased again, although there was absolutely nothing meant by it other than to make his subordinate blush.

"I'm serious, boss. I just received an emergency call that you need to know about immediately."

That sorted Hank out; he led the way to his first floor library, far from the opposite wing of the house where the party was taking place.

Hank was no longer interested in his wine and set it down on the sideboard as he closed the door.

"What's up, Dav? You've got my adrenaline going, so let's hear it."

"The Urbanes are about to make one of our agents. I don't know who he is yet, but he's going to call me back."

"Well, shit. Get Taylor to start the relocation process, then. That's unfortunate. What exactly did he say?"

Daven took a deep breath and tried not to let his nervousness show.

"He said...well, it was about a meeting you had on Tuesday. He is deeply concerned that you were misled about the man's identity and motives. Seems the outcome of that meeting was this agent being chosen for a mission for the Urbanes which he cannot undertake or decline without being exposed."

It wasn't the whole truth... but it wasn't a lie, either.

"Jesus," Hank breathed heavily. "I had five or six meetings that day. Did he say which one?"

"No." *Here goes nothing*, Daven thought. "But if you get me a list of who you met with, I'll look into them immediately. We should be able to pin it down quickly."

Hank looked a little startled. "Did you verify this agent's identity?"

"Uh, no. Not yet."

Hank looked annoyed. "Oh come on Dav, you know better than to talk to unverified callers on that line! Do that first, and then I'll get you the list. For all we know, he was captured and is calling under duress. The code he gives will tell us."

"But we should get started right away-"

"No. There's also the possibility he got cold feet and wants to disappear on our dime. When's he going to call back?"

Daven had never lied to Hank before - even when he probably should have - and wasn't about to start now. "Tomorrow at 8am."

"Christmas day? Nice."

"Hank, don't you think it's best if we start to check up on those names right now? Why wait?"

"Dav, I *think* we should enjoy this party. It's Christmas eve. Come on."

Hank swept his wine off the sideboard and disappeared without another glance at his colleague and friend. Daven watched him go, his heart suddenly heavy with uncertainty. If Hank insisted on joining him to hear the agent's call, things were about to get *very* complicated.

Merry Christmas, indeed..

CHAPTER THREE

Bonded Retainer Training School for Minors - Virginia

Lester Boyd made his way to his office and glanced at the day's agenda that his secretary prepared for him every morning. He was incredulous upon seeing Floyd and Theo Bancroft's names on his visitor list for the day, for the third time in ten days. The boys could not stay out of trouble if their lives depended on it. If he didn't get them under control fast, everything he had done to keep them safe would be ultimately pointless. It was time to lay down the law.

"Theo was freaking out in kitchen class, sir, and he....I just went after him about it and we-"

"What do you mean, *went after him* ?"

Floyd swallowed his resentment at the whole affair and kept his tone level. "I don't think he's taking our situation seriously enough. I got mad and yelled at him in front of everyone, and then I hit him. I don't regret it and would do the same thing all over again to keep him safe. He has no idea what's going to happen to us if we don't finish this training, because I keep....I just...I need your help. Please."

Lester groaned inwardly; had he known this, he wouldn't have been so harsh in his lecture. It was clear there was a lot more going on than he bargained for with the young Bancrofts.

"I see. Floyd, you're out of verbal warnings already. The next one's written. Seven written warnings means you're deeded to the state, and no one besides me is going to care what your excuse is. I've been force to eject students in week 25, and that could happen to you if you don't keep yourself under control, immediately. You have a long way to go and need to choose your battles wisely. Do we understand each other?"

Floyd looked absolutely crushed. What battles could be more important than those he fought to protect Theo? "Yes, sir, but-"

"No buts. We're still in week two. I had high hopes for you, but to be honest, right now I'm really disappointed at your lack of common sense and control. I have 60 students to handle and just the two of you have taken up all of my time since you arrived. Your brother is waiting outside. Call him in to stand with you, and you're not to say a single word until I address you directly. I mean it."

Floyd froze, his increasing panic not allowing for any verbal response.

"Go get your brother," Mr. Boyd repeated, a little more gently this time.

Floyd propelled himself out the door and spotted Theo standing dejectedly by the water fountain on the other side of the hall and called him over. To his credit, Theo hurried to his side without hesitation and looked sufficiently abashed.

"I'm so sorry, Floyd. Are you okay?"

"For now. But if you mouth off again, I swear to-"

"I won't!"

"Then get in there, and behave yourself." Floyd gave vent to his frustration by shoving Theo through the doorway as they passed through, a movement that caused Lester to raise his eyebrows in dismay. Floyd looked at the floor, feeling ashamed of himself.

"Floyd," Lester said in a warning tone, but then turned to Theo without further comment. "Theodore. I'm going to repeat what I just told your brother. Seven written warnings of any kind and you're automatically deeded to the state. Period. Do you understand what that means?"

"I'm sure I'll find out soon enough," was the mumbled reply.

"I'm going to pretend you didn't say that. Now, not only did you damage property and ruin the food, I also have a report here of you fooling around the day before and carving 'anatomical pictures' into fruit with a melon baller. Shockingly enough, you're not the first genius to have thought of that. Just wait to see what happens when you all advance to cucumber canapés."

Floyd glanced at Theo, fearing he would start laughing all over again.

Theo was not in the mood for comedy, however. He wanted to argue. "That was harmless. I can't believe I got in trouble for that."

"Anything you get in trouble for is designed to protect you. When you're placed as a house servant, behavior like that will cost you your job. And that, in turn, will mean you're automatically reduced to the lowest tier of service for the state. For life. No second chances. Do you even know what the lowest tier is, Theodore?"

Floyd answered quickly, "Manual labor."

Lester sighed and reached into his desk. "You're speaking out of turn, Floyd. Lucky for you, I don't give warnings for that. Hold out your hands."

Floyd complied, eyes wide, while Lester stepped around the desk and quickly laid down one stripe across each palm with a thin cane. It was shockingly painful over the existing welts, and Floyd hissed and immediately began rubbing his hands together while tears sprouted unchecked from both eyes. Mr. Boyd considered this "lucky?"

Theo was staring agape at them, turning white as a sheet. Neither of them had any experience with this particular form of discipline, as Hank Bancroft openly considered corporal punishment on anything other than spanking the backside of children to be barbaric. It was part of the reason he had been so openly in conflict with his own constituents, who wished to bring back public floggings and were very close to succeeding in getting a measure drawn in the House.

Lester replaced the implement in his drawer and Floyd could see he clearly regretted having to take the action, but it was better than using up another warning. Floyd reminded himself to thank him later...maybe it was lucky, after all, but it sure didn't feel like it right now.

"Now, let's try this again. Theodore, do you know what the lowest tier is that you can be assigned to?"

"You just hit my brother!" Theo blurted out hotly. Floyd almost told him to shut up, but held back at the last millisecond and swallowed down his emotion. He wasn't resentful, or even remotely angry, about what had happened. He was just scared out of his wits for his brother.

"Theo, *answer him* ," Floyd whispered.

Theo looked like he was about to answer, but then he set his shoulders in *that* way that had always made Floyd and his father want to scream.

"Can you repeat the question?" he replied with a smirk.

"Do you know what the lowest tier of indentured servitude is that you can be assigned to?"

"Yes. And I also know you've now ended a question twice with a preposition."

"Yes, I did. But you started a sentence with 'and.' I'm not sure what is worse."

"*Which* is worse."

"That should be phrased as a question," retorted Lester lightly.

"Whatever. This is stupid," complained Theo bitterly.

It was taking everything Floyd had not to leap over and throttle his brother. He had kept himself occupied during this bizarre debate by wringing his palms together to help stave off the increasing pain, but it wasn't working.

"Stop being a fucking idiot, Theo!" Floyd turned and growled, being completely unable to hold his tongue any longer.

"Floyd, be still," Lester said sharply as he glanced over at him, although there was a definite glint of amusement in his expression. "Your brother and I were just discussing proper grammar techniques, everything's fine."

"Yeah. Shut up, Floyd, unless you can contribute something to the conversation."

Floyd and Theo immediately erupted into the petty bickering that young teenage boys do. So much for employing humor as a disarming tactic. Far from that, it had backfired spectacularly; Floyd was visibly ready to tackle the brat and beat him senseless, and there wasn't much holding him back any longer.

"Boys!"

They stopped their arguing abruptly and looked down at the floor.

"You're obviously intelligent enough to grasp what you're doing wrong, so I won't spell it out. I just have one question: can you get your shit together before I'm forced to replace you with new students from the waiting list? I assure you, at this rate I'll be making that decision in less than a week."

"Let them in. It's a stupid program anyway," Theo responded petulantly. "Melon balls? I mean, come on."

"I'm so sorry," blurted Floyd desperately, in tears again. House servitude was the only program that guaranteed them both placement together in the same workplace if they successfully passed it. They were lucky to be here, and he was furious at Theo for not seeing that. "Can we just...can I call my dad and have him talk to Theody? He will set him straight, I promise. Please don't kick us out."

Lester's heart dropped, and he had to take in a long, deep breath to steady himself.

"You know you can't call him," he responded gently. "Neither can I. Theodore, I'm not your enemy. Do you understand that?"

"Right," he huffed, almost to himself. "That's why you can just beat us on the spot whenever you feel like it. Go ahead, seize the *opportunity*."

Emphasis on the last word, just to throw it in his face that they were not cut from the same cloth.

Theo held his palms out and glanced at Floyd, expecting and perhaps looking forward to another round of swearing, but he was ignoring them and absently picking at the buttons on his coat. Already defeated. Depressed. Lost.

Lester saw it, too. "Put your hands down. I understand your situation is unusually tough, and I'm willing to let your attitude slide until you adjust. But you must answer a question before you can go. I want to remind you that your indenture as a house servant is for 20 years. If you fail with this behavior, which is imminent...meaning, you're on the path to fail in just a few days...you will be deeded to the state *for life*. You have no other options, period. So I have to ask: are you going to try and get through this program, or not?"

"Yes, sir. I'm sorry," Theo replied quietly, without any trace of rancor. Floyd was pleasantly surprised at how quickly he became compliant - especially after being threatened, which was usually the fastest route to a massive temper tantrum. He did not realize that was Theo had seen Floyd's grief and was really apologizing to him, not their mentor.

"Floyd? How about you?"

"Yes, sir. Please forgive us, we've...it's been..."

"Forgiven. One last thing. It was a mistake to have you room together. I'm going to split you up-"

"No, wait-" sputtered Floyd.

"I don't want to hear it. Theo, dismissed. Go pack your bag and get ready to move."

Theo left wearily, wisely refraining from spouting off again as he went, and Floyd did all he could not to dissolve again in front of his counselor.

"Floyd, don't start that puppy dog eyes crap with me. A blind fool could see that you're spending too much time together and all he's doing is entertaining himself by pushing every button you have. I'm going to put him in a room by himself and that's the end of it. If and when I'm ready to reconsider, I will let you know. Clear?"

“I don’t understand why you’re doing this,” Floyd muttered. “Please tell me why.”

“Why I’m being so nice to you, you mean?” Lester responded calmly. "You asked me to help your brother, and this is part of how I'm going to do it. He needs his space for the time being. You can visit him during the free hour each evening. There's nothing more I want than to see the two of you *not* thrown into state custody. For now, you're the one causing the most trouble, not him. So keep it together and behave yourself."

Floyd immediately got the point, took a deep breath, and looked him straight in the eyes. “Thank you for what you’re trying to do, Mr. Boyd. I’m sorry my brother doesn’t appreciate it, but I do.”

“No one ever does. You’re a rare one. One last thing: Theo’s discipline is not your job, it’s mine. If you ever manhandle him again on my watch, you won’t be able to sit down for a week. Clear? Good. Dismissed.”

He watched Floyd trudge out, hating that he had to be so harsh with him. He still wasn't sure whether to be grateful or hurt that neither of the boys yet recognized their “Uncle” Lester from so long ago. It certainly did make things less complicated, but Floyd's plea for Lester to call his father to help Theo nearly broke his heart in a hundred pieces.

The boys did not know Hank was already dead, and Lester was under strict orders not to tell them until Harmon gave him permission to do so.

Christmas Day

Seditionists HQ, Los Angeles

Daven arrived at the office at 7am, eager to hear back from the agent regarding the intel he had passed along during Hank's Christmas party. First things first - he had to identify the agent. There were five individualized codes that the man had to memorize upon his first day of work, and each of them had a separate purpose to be used to calls to their superiors or the emergency line:

1 - agent reporting normally

2 - agent reporting under duress, information is accurate

3 - agent reporting under duress, information is false

4 - agent is made, attempt a rescue

5 - agent is made, do not attempt rescue

Depending on what code the man gave, Dav would know the situation immediately and be able to act accordingly. His predecessor had been the one to take these calls; this was his first, and the anxiety was almost unbearable for several reasons.

Obviously, the first reason was because of the reason for the call. Number 3 in this case would be the best scenario in regards to what he had said about Hank. Number 1 would be the worst case.

Then, there was the problem about him having honestly told Hank the time that the agent was going to be calling. He wished he had lied. As a preventative measure, he had pulled Rupert aside at the Christmas party and asked him to help get Hank as drunk as possible. The man's hangovers were few but epic, and if anything could prevent him from showing up at the office at 8am, that would be the thing to do it. Rupert hadn't asked questions, and Daven watched him bring glass after glass to their boss.

The last thing causing him such anxiety was the idea that he might have to go behind Hank's back to get the full story, and that was the worst part. In ten years they had worked together, neither of them had expressed any desire to be dishonest towards each other for any reason, for better or worse. And sometimes it was for the worst, but it never caused any longstanding friction between them.

Daven had never lied, not once, and he believed it was the same with Hank. At least, he hoped it was so.

At 7:50am Daven laid the book of identifying codes out in front of him, then stood at the window to watch the parking lot while he was on the phone. If Hank did show up, at least he would get advanced notice and could perhaps warn the agent.

A moment later his phone rang, startling him enough that he jumped away from the window and nearly fell over the horrible fluffy chair that he had been unsuccessfully trying to get removed from his office for as long as he could remember.

"Good morning, Hank," Daven answered, trying to sound completely normal.

"Ugh. Don't talk so loud."

"Sorry."

"Just got to the office, but I forgot my badge. Can you come downstairs and swipe me in? I'm at the backdoor."

Shit. Shit. Shit.

"Sure. Be right there. Should I get an espresso going for you, too?"

"Yeah. Thanks."

Daven hung up the phone and pressed the button to pre-heat the water, then made his way to the elevator with a pounding heart.

He should have lied. *God damn it.*

As they entered his office and Hank draped himself across Rupe's chair, flinging an arm over his face to shield his eyes from the sun, Daven prepared the espresso for his boss without speaking. He didn't know what to say, in any case, there was no time. It was almost 8am.

He handed the cup to Hank, who blew on it for some time before asking, "You think he's going to call? Hope he's alright."

"I hope so."

"Hmm. Sorry to ask, but do you mind closing the blinds?"

Daven nodded and closed them wordlessly.

"Thanks. You okay, Dav? You seem nervous."

Nervous. If you only knew.

"I am. Listen, Hank, he...he wants to talk to me alone. I'm not sure he will agree to say a word if you're listening. Apparently he knows me and trusts me, but it doesn't appear he knows you."

"Or trusts me, maybe. That's fine. Don't tell him I'm on the line, then."

"But what if-"

"This isn't negotiable. Dav, please don't ask me such a thing ever again. I'm the goddamned leader of the party, in case you forgot."

Daven clamped his mouth shut. Hank rarely pulled rank, but when he did, he meant business.

"And while I'm at it," Hank continued sternly as he peered at Dav through half-closed eyelids, "I will nail your ass to the wall if you ever converse with an unverified asset again, do you hear me?"

"You are right on both counts, of course. My deepest apologies."

Hank leaned back and threw his arm over his eyes again, and fell silent. It was an expected and well-deserved chastisement, and Daven was relieved to get off so easy.

But he still couldn't shake the deep feeling of dread that had darkened his thoughts since first hearing the agent's intel. At 7:59 Daven lifted his cell phone, made sure Hank wasn't looking, and discreetly toggled the satellite connection to OFF.

Then he sat down to wait for the call that could never come.

CHAPTER FOUR

BRTSM, Virginia

"I need your help again, Olivia," Lester said gently into the phone. "I got to start finding a place for two brothers for five months. A good one, no history of abuse or a bunch of turnover in the household. If you have any ideas, please let me know. They'll be ready to enter service on December first. Can you ask around and see who's looking for new servants? You have my number, call me back when you can. Thanks a ton."

He hung up and turned to the next phone number of his list of closest friends within the party. "Hey Hailey, it's Lester Boyd. Listen... I need your help with some more of my boys. I've got two good ones, 12 and 16, who need to be placed together. I know you're connected to the Hannigans, so can you poke around with them and see if they need anyone in one of their estates, or if they know anyone who does? Call me back as soon as you can, thanks so much."

There was one more number in his contacts with no name attached. As usual, he stared at it thoughtfully for a while and debated calling it just to see who would answer, but set it aside for the hundredth time. The boys were due any minute now for their weekly review, and he was as nervous as a wet cat. Floyd had been giving him strange looks lately, and it was possible he had figured out who Lester was, or maybe not. Not that it would mean anything had to change if he did, but it would make it a lot harder to keep threatening to kick them out; the fact that they just might put two and two together and call his bluff was always in the back of his mind.

The phone rang a minute later at the exact same time as they knock on the door. Lester yelled "come in!" at the same time he lifted the receiver, fully expecting it to be one of the school administrators to remind him of some faculty meeting or another. His phone didn't have caller ID, though, so pretty much every call was a surprise.

"Hello."

There was a long pause.

"Hello?" he repeated.

"Who is this, please?" said the gruff voice on the other line. "Just want to make sure I have the right number."

Theo and Floyd shuffled in, eyes darting about warily. Lester held a hand up to stop them from saying anything, and focused on the caller.

"Nice try. Who are *you* ?"

Another long pause. "I see we are at an impasse. Very well. I received your number from Hank Bancroft some time ago, but I was not in a position to call until now. Can you talk? It's important."

Holy smokes. *What the hell...*

"I'm in a meeting. Let me take your number and call you back."

"Not possible. When is a good time to call you back?"

Lester looked at Theo and Floyd, who seemed just as intensely curious about the caller as he was. Then a light bulb went off and he grabbed the notebook he had recently set aside, and looked at the last number without really needing to. It was all but seared into his brain.

"Okay, let me read that back to you," Lester said slyly. It was a big gamble, but there was no other reasonable explanation. "310-758-5100. Is that right?"

A brief pause, now. "No. I'm not sure who's number that is. When would be a good time to call you back?" the voice repeated, a little more tension evident than before.

"Actually, I'm not interested. Please remove my number from your database. Have a good day."

He hung up the phone with numb hands and tried to remember to breathe normally. This kind of subterfuge was a thing of the past, better left there, and an unshakable feeling of ill-omen gripped him hard. He couldn't think for a few moments, and cursed Hank silently for putting him in the middle of god knows what.

"Damned telemarketing calls," he muttered as he reached behind the phone to unplug the cord, then changed the subject as quickly as he could get away with. "Theodore, I heard you made another ruckus in kitchen class yesterday. I'm supposed to give you grief about it, so what happened?"

"If I wanted to be a chef, I could have gone to cooking school. This is stupid!"

"We're not training you to be a chef!" Lester blurted impatiently. "You're a house servant, and nothing more. If you don't behave yourself, you won't even be that. If you haven't grasped that concept yet since our last conversation, maybe I should just kick you out now and save all of us the time and grief."

Theo and Floyd both looked absolutely crushed by this outburst, and Lester realized he had completely lost his grip on his temper and unfairly taken it out on the boys. The mysterious call had rattled him a lot more than he would be willing to admit. He calmed himself down, but decided not to apologize. Theo was acting stupidly and it wouldn't hurt to call him out on it.

"Speaking of which, I fully expect that you both did the research I asked you for on exactly what it means to be deeded to the state. What did you learn, Theo?"

"I..." he was still shocked from Lester's outburst and couldn't respond.

"I'll get back to you. Floyd? Same question."

"I learned that I would rather die, sir." He had unshed tears in his eyes; perhaps from Lester's outburst, but most likely caused by the fact he had discovered that siblings were always separated into different facilities and were extremely unlikely to find each other again.

"Good takeaway. Discouragement was the point of the exercise, after all. Theo, back to you."

"Same answer, sir," he managed to choke out.

Lester had almost forgotten about the mysterious caller at this point, since both boys were now fighting back tears and looked as guilty as beagles caught raiding a trash can. But now the man's voice came back with frightening clarity, and suddenly he couldn't focus on anything else.

"Then we'll consider this review over and lesson learned. Onward and upwards. Dismissed."

They practically ran out, and Lester plugged the phone back in and before the door had even closed he began dialing the number Hank gave him. He needed to know who this man was. But then he stopped himself abruptly and slammed down the phone. The call logs were closely monitored, and he would have an awful lot of explaining to do if someone noticed him calling Los Angeles from his work office. Not if... *when* they noticed.

The number was for a close friend of Hank's family, presumably. Lester had memorized it ever since Hank dictated it to him in their final moments together and made him promise to let the boys call it when they were ready to hear of his death. Lester told Harmon about the exchange, and the party leader agreed to honor the request, but only when he personally gave the go-ahead. That caveat irked Lester to no end, but they weren't ready yet anyway.

At any rate, the strange call had to be reported, even if he couldn't confirm where it came from. He sighed, went to lock the door, said a short prayer, and reluctantly dialed up Colbert.

Floyd was perfectly silent as they made their way back to quarters, but Theo was bursting with excitement.

"Shut up, Theo. Don't say a word. I mean it."

"I can't help it. You heard the number, too, didn't you? Uncle Dav knows where we are! He's going to get us out of here and back to-"

Floyd turned around and pushed him up against the wall, pinning him there in a tight hold.

"Shut. UP. I swear to god I will rip out your throat myself if you ever mention him to me again."

Theo pushed Floyd off of him and wriggled away. "What the fuck are you doing, Floyd?" he whined. "Are you nuts? Aren't you happy he wants to help us?"

Floyd grabbed him roughly and pinned him again, harder this time. "No! Daven is the one who turned in dad!"

"What?!" Theo gasped.

"So you're going to forget about him, and Rupert. Forget that they exist. And besides, the whole world probably knows where we are by now. That call meant nothing, understand? This doesn't change a damned thing. You and I need to fend for ourselves now, and lay low and get through this fucking training before we get separated. You're all I have, and if you-"

"Okay, okay. Stop it, Floyd! I didn't know. Get off me, please."

He had stopped fighting, and his face was ashen.

Floyd choked back a sob. "I'm sorry I didn't tell you before. But now...well, now you know. So don't get your hopes up."

He let go, and then pulled his little brother into a tight hug as they both dissolved into long-overdue tears of grief and loss.

"I'm so sorry. Forgive me, Theody..."

Seditionist HQ, Los Angeles

Christmas Day, 1994

8am.

8:30am.

9am.

9:30am.

The phone never rang, of course, and Daven had not said a single word the entire time except to offer Hank another cup of espresso.

10am.

"I don't think he's going to call, Dav," Hank said sleepily. "We should give it another hour, though."

"As you wish," Daven replied curtly, without taking his eyes off of the code book. To say he was on edge was a massive understatement. Every minute that passed by felt like a lifetime in itself.

10:30am.

Daven suddenly bolted noisily upright and dived a hand into his desk drawer, which startled the dozing Hank into complete wakefulness, and not a little bit of confusion.

"What the hell, Dav-"

"Shh! Someone's in the building."

They listened for a good 30 seconds and heard nothing, but then the unmistakable sound of steady footsteps on the metal stairway confirmed Dav's worst fears.

They looked at each other askance; the safe room was in Hank's office and there was no possible way to dart across the long hallway and get into without being seen - or possibly intercepted - by their unauthorized visitor.

Daven cocked the gun that he always kept within arm's reach in a hidden drawer. "Hank, lock yourself in my restroom," he ordered in a whisper.

"What? No!"

The footsteps came closer, and there was the sound of something falling over or being dropped.

"Hank! Get in there!"

"Dad?" came a high-pitched tentative voice from the hallway.

"Floyd?" they both cried out, and a few seconds later the boy appeared around the corner, then gasped and dived back again when he saw Daven's gun.

Hank collected himself quickly and then barked, "Floyd! Get your ass in here." Then, to Dav as he was calmly uncocking his gun and putting it away, "Thank you for not shooting my son, considering I would very much enjoy the satisfaction of doing it myself."

Floyd trudged in, holding Hank's badge that he had forgotten at home. "You're not picking up your phone, so I got in with this."

Hank strode over to him and snatched the badge out of his hand, drawing on every ounce of willpower he had left to stop himself from spinning the boy around and giving him the belting of a lifetime. He would never dream of doing it here in front of Dav, but at home? Different story.

"What *exactly* are you doing here, and how did you get here?" he asked with that kind of dangerous tone that invariably sent Hank's employees, friends, and even family instantly scurrying for cover. But never Floyd; he was either braver or more reckless than most.

"I drove. Dad, Theo hasn't stopped crying for hours. I couldn't stand it anymore. Can you come home?"

Hank was stunned. "*Drove?* Are you serious? Nobody's dying or anything, right? Just checking, because there could be no other acceptable reason for you to-"

"It's Christmas day!" Floyd protested, and water droplets started to form in his eyes. "You said you would never miss another one." And then, absurdly, he looked to Dav and smiled as if nothing was wrong. "Hi Uncle Dav. Merry Christmas."

Daven walked over and embraced Floyd in the warm, crushing kind of bear hug that the boys loved. "Merry Christmas, Floyd. Hey, can you go wait in your dad's office while I talk to him for a minute? It's the one way down at the end of the hall with the green door. Don't stand outside with your ear to this door, okay? Promise me."

Floyd looked to Hank for permission (he knew his father too well to do otherwise), and reluctantly got it. He went out with a sniff, closing the door softly behind him.

Hank glared. "Don't even start on me, Dav. He's my kid and I don't want your opinion on this."

"Actually, what I was going to tell you is that we should wait until 11 for the call, as you said. I'll keep Floyd occupied with my putting green until then. It's only 25 more minutes."

"No, he's going to sit in my office and keep his mouth shut. And tomorrow I'm going to teach him a-"

Daven's office phone rang suddenly, quite loud in the abnormal quiet of the empty office building. They both jumped. Again.

"Sorry," he said, turning around to the phone. "Who on earth is calling me *here,* on a Saturday?"

Hank shrugged. "And on Christmas? No idea."

Daven picked up the receiver. "Yes?"

"Jesus, Dav. Answer your damned cell phone once in a while, will you?"

It was Rupert. Daven's eyes flashed to his phone; the satellite connection was still turned off.

"Rupe, I'm going to have to call you back in half an hour. Hank and I are waiting for an important phone call. Is there an emergency?"

"I wouldn't bloody well call you on Christmas morning if it wasn't. Have you been watching the news?"

"No. What's up?"

"Put him on speaker, Dav," Hank said suddenly, and firmly. There was no disobeying that tone, so Daven hit the speakerphone button and hoped for the best.

"I've got you on speaker. Hank's here. Go ahead."

"Hank, it's Rupe. Listen, one of our double agents was found dead in Colorado. It's all over the news."

Holy mother of…

"Wait," said Hank after a few moments of shocked silence, "was he actually identified as one of our agents?"

Daven felt nearly paralyzed and overwhelmed by anxiety and guilt, until Rupe answered, " *She,* actually. And if they've identified her as a mole, they're not saying it yet."

Despite the fact that he hated himself down to the core for it, Daven found himself incredibly relieved and grateful that the dead agent wasn't his man, but a woman. He would have turned himself in, and Hank would have known his betrayal, and-

"Why is this all over the news?" Hank asked, still reeling and not even thinking to ask who the victim was first.

"Well, because she's one of Colbert's drivers. Found dead with her bike on Seditionists property. And I'm sorry to be the one to tell you this, but it's only a matter of time before they find out what she was doing there. It's been a drop for the past few weeks, and our surveillance video has already been subpoenaed. I think whatever she had was taken by her killer,

most likely an Urbane. It could have even been one of us, if they thought she was one of them.”

“*Fuck me*,” Hank breathed under his breath. “If this happened at the Greeley office, she was carrying something for me.”

“Yep. She’s the only agent we have in Colorado right now. Sorry, Hank. Merry Christmas, huh?’

Daven looked at Hank in complete shock; he had not known of any such operation, nor that any of their agents were in Greeley. It was his duty to know absolutely everything.

“What was she carrying?” Dav asked as calmly and disinterestedly as she could.

Hank ignored him. “Thanks, Rupe. It’s not even 11am and it already feels like a week since I woke up. How come you called the office, though? Just curious. Dav and I both have our new cell phones on us, and this is the kind of thing they are meant for.”

“I did. Yours must be on silent, and his went straight to voicemail like a million times. Listen guys, I’m going to get back to this and get a PR plan together when the inevitable shit hits the fan. Look for an email from me within the next two hours for more details. Call me if you need me…on my cell, of course. That's what it's for, as you said, even though you won't answer it."

Hank pulled his phone out for the first time all morning and dismissed the 17 missed calls from Floyd. "Yeah, mine's on silent. Sorry, we were waiting for a call on Dav's phone. Merry Christmas Rupe, and keep in touch."

Daven seemed frozen in place, so Hank was the one who had to walk around the desk and lean over to hang up the phone.

"Dav," he said gently, "let's call it a day. But first, I'm going to ring the emergency line and see what happens. Maybe our man has been calling all along but your phone's not working."

"Yes, that could be a possibility," Daven blurted as he swept up his phone from the table. "I don't have any missed calls or voicemails, though." He pretended to be flipping through the screens in confusion as he toggled the satellite connection setting back on and prayed for it to connect before Hank could finish dialing from his own phone, which he was busy doing at this very moment.

Hank dialed, paused...hung up, got lost in thought for a few moments, and began dialing again.

"Almost couldn't remember the number. That could be a problem someday. Jesus."

That single slip of memory saved Dav from having an awful lot of explaining to do. In the time it took Hank to re-dial again, and put the phone to his ear, Dav's phone connected to the network and then began ringing.

"Hello?"

"Hey, it's me," Hank said pointlessly, considering they were standing three feet away from each other holding their phones at their ears. "Well, it's working. Maybe it's Rupert's phone, then." He closed his phone.

"That does seem the most logical explanation. I would hate to think we missed the agent's call."

"Dav...you can hang up now, obviously. Maybe it's time to have another espresso, huh? You seem a little shell-shocked."

They both looked at each other quizzically for a few moments, and Daven couldn't help himself from asking the same question that had been previously ignored.

"What was the agent carrying, do you know?"

Hank shrugged. "Depends on the agent. I have a few things in the works."

"Things I didn't know about, you mean?"

"Daven," Hank began in a warning tone, purposely using his full name instead of the nickname to indicate that his patience was nearly at an end. "We've been through this before. We're a *huge* organization. There's things going on with us that even I don't know about, so you shouldn't take it personally. I don't."

"Yes you do, actually."

Hank sighed. "I've said it before, and I'll say it again. You, me, and Rupe together don't possess all the brain power it would require to run this place. If we did, why would we hire anyone else? Do you know how many employees we have right now, besides us?"

Of course he did. "512."

"How many of them do you trust?"

"Seven."

Hank's expression darkened, and he furrowed his eyebrows. "That's....that's not the answer I was looking for. You should have said 512."

"That would be a lie," Daven said simply.

Hank shook his head, and then turned away to gather up all his belongings.

"Time for you to go home, Dav. If our mystery man calls, you have my permission to keep him on the line - in silence - while you race back to the office to verify him. But you're leaving, and so am I."

"Don't forget about Floyd," Daven mumbled. "And take it easy on him. It's Christmas." He was clearly unhappy with his boss right now for several reasons, but Hank didn't have the energy to hold his chief strategist's hand again. They went through this little crisis every once in a while, but it always blew over quickly.

"Yeah, I know. I'm mostly just mad he drove the Thunderbird alone. Damned unsafe."

The three of them walked out together, Floyd perfectly silent as Hank held his arm in an iron grip all the way to the backseat of the car (not the front, which meant he was really in trouble), and drove one behind the other to their respective houses down the street from each other.

Daven was obliged to fight the urge to look at his phone again until he was in the safety and privacy of his home, upon which he sat down at the kitchen table and forced himself to breathe through ninety seconds of calming meditation.

Now...the phone. He was not at all surprised to see 9 voicemails since 8am. Two from Rupe, one from Floyd. Six from an unknown caller. He took a deep breath, cursed himself for being so paranoid, and then dialed into the message center.

CHAPTER FIVE

Bancroft Home

Hank was still furious as he threw the car in park and got out to haul Floyd out of the backseat. His oldest had other ideas about that, though, and quickly emerged from the opposite side of the car. Safe out of his dad's crushing grip.

"Dad, can I-"

"Floyd, it's Christmas day so we're going to put this discussion off until tomorrow. I don't want any apologies right now. In fact, don't say anything. Just get inside."

Floyd stood stock still and looked Hank in the eyes. "I wasn't going to apologize, no matter what you do today or tomorrow. Theo needed you, and you broke your promise."

"So you drove the Thunderbird by yourself and then snuck into my office-"

"And I would do it again," Floyd interrupted calmly, with a dangerously sullen expression. "It's not my fault your phones were off. What if we had a real emergency, dad? Like one of us was dying? Would you even care, then?"

"My phone was on silent for a reason. You have Daven's number, why didn't you call him? He knows never to ignore a call from you."

"I did! Like a million times. It just went straight to voicemail. And you never picked up your office line since you were in his office, and I don't even know his office number so I couldn't call that. This is so unfair, dad. You basically abandoned us. On Christmas day, and I'm going to be the one punished for it?"

Hank said nothing more about the unauthorized drive; Floyd's comments about Daven's phone instantly took precedence. His mind flashed back to what had transpired over the past three hours with the call that never came.

Floyd mistook his dad's sudden silence for penance and strode past him into the house.

Hank didn't even notice. He pulled his phone out of his pocket and dialed the emergency number.

Daven's Townhouse

You have. Nine. New Messages.

First message, 8:01am: "Uh....please tell me you missed my call because you're taking a dump, and not because you're freezing me out. I'll call back in five minutes."

Delete message? 1 for yes, 2 for no. Message deleted.

Message two, 8:07am: "Daven, for god's sake. I called when you told me to, where the hell are you? Are you not picking up because Hank is with you? Get rid of him, we've got to talk."

Delete message? 1 for yes, 2 for no. Message deleted.

Message three, 8:29am: "So this is how you treat your agents, huh? I risk my life for you guys, and you won't even answer my fucking phone call? I'm calling back at 9. You better fucking pick up the phone, Daven. My life is on the line."

Delete message? 1 for yes, 2 for no. Message deleted.

Message four, 8:31am: "Dav, it's Rupe. We've got a bad situation going on. Call me back ASAP."

Delete message? 1 for yes, 2 for no. Message saved.

Message five, 9:00am: "I take it Hank's still with you. Man, if you don't pick up at 9:30 I'm going to...just, pick up the phone!"

Delete message? 1 for yes, 2 for no. Message deleted.

Message six, 9:28am: "Dav, it's Rupe again. I can't reach Hank, guessing he's still out cold from that hangover you wanted him to have. What the hell was that about, anyway? Call me ASAP, our Colorado agent just got zipped. I need to talk to you."

Delete message? 1 for yes, 2 for no. Message deleted.

Message seven, 9:35am: "I'm trying one more time, Daven. If I get zipped before you get the whole story, you've got no one to blame but yourself."

Delete message? 1 for yes, 2 for no. Message deleted.

Message eight, 10:02am: "Uncle Dav, it's Floyd. I'm waiting outside the office to pick dad up. He hasn't called me and Theo needs help. Can you call me right back? If not, I'll come in. I have dad's badge. Thanks."

Delete message? 1 for yes, 2 for no. Message saved.

Message nine, 10:33am: "Fuck you all. I'm calling Rupert. And he's not going to be happy to get this story on top of the other one today. Hope you lose your job like I just lost mine because of our fearless leader's treason. Merry fucking Christmas."

Daven jerked upright and threw down the phone in horror. Shit, had he already called Rupert? Then the phone rang again: the emergency line. Daven blanched, then shakily took a deep breath, said a quick prayer, and hit the answer button.

"Yes?"

"Hey. Long time no talk. It's Hank."

There was a telling pause. "I don't understand. We were just together about 25 minutes ago."

Hank groaned. "I wanted to test this number again. Floyd just told me he's been calling you all morning and your phone wasn't picking up. First thing tomorrow morning I want you and Shane to get on this. Nothing else takes priority, not even the dead woman. We didn't spend hundreds of thousands of dollars on telecommunications infrastructure to be missing calls from agents whose lives are in danger. For all we know, she was calling it, too."

Daven had to fight to remember to breathe again. "I will get on it. First thing tomorrow," he repeated.

"I need you to call around to the field supervisors today and have them check in with our remaining agents, see if anyone else has gone missing."

"Right away. Is Theo alright?"

"I don't know, I haven't gone inside yet. Talk to you later."

Hank hung up and went into the house. Theo was sitting askew on the couch, having cried himself into exhaustion, and Floyd was there with his arm wrapped protectively around his little brother. Hank could not possibly ignore the critically hostile expression his oldest was wearing.

"Floyd," he said sharply, "come with me for a minute. Just want to get this talk over with so we can move on to our Christmas festivities."

"I don't want to talk."

Hank didn't have time for this; he grabbed his son by the arm again and hauled him into the study. Floyd didn't try to struggle, not even when Hank forced him to stand still and look him in the eyes.

"Floyd, I'm only going to say this one time," he said calmly, without rancor. "I shouldn't even be telling you at all, because I don't want you to have dangerous information. There was a woman found dead in Colorado this morning on Seditionists property."

Floyd swallowed hard. "I heard that on the radio station in the car. One of Colbert's assistants."

"His driver, specifically. She was a double agent. For me. That's why I got stuck at the office, okay? That, and one other thing going on that Daven is handling. If I could have gotten away sooner, I would have. We were actually on the way out when you showed up. I did *not* forget it was Christmas. Do you understand?" His tone was very gentle now, and indeed, he was feeling extremely sorry for manhandling one of his children (twice) on Christmas day.

Floyd nodded, expression already less angry. "So...you're going to be working all day, then?"

"No. Rupe is handling this one. I'm only angry about you driving the Thunderbird by yourself. You have a driver's permit that allows you behind the wheel if - and *only* if - an adult is with you. You could have been stopped by the cops and arrested."

"But it was only-"

"Our drivers literally live fifty feet from where we're standing, and I've instructed you a hundred times to use them if something like this happens. You did when Theo broke his wrist, and when the dog needed to go to the vet. There was no excuse for this today, Floyd. None. I know you care about your brother, but you have to keep your head on your shoulders and think straight in times of crisis. I'm very disappointed with you right now."

Ouch. Floyd didn't have an answer for that.....what possible defense *could* he have?

"Okay, dad. I'm sorry," Floyd mumbled contritely. He really was, too.

"I can see that you are. You're forgiven, but I'll still have to punish you tomorrow."

"How?"

"What do *you* think?"

Floyd swallowed hard, then said quietly, "It's so much worse waiting, can't we just do it now? Theody's asleep."

"No," Hank replied firmly. "It's Christmas. Pull yourself together and then come out to open your presents."

Hank left the study and went to pour himself a long overdue glass of whiskey.

"Rupe, it's Dav."

"For the hundredth time, I know. That's what caller ID is for. What's up?"

"An agent called through on the emergency line yesterday and then tried to call it back again this morning. For whatever reason, it didn't forward to my phone. He said he's going to call you, so I was just wondering if you had heard from him."

"But...if it didn't go through, how do you know he's going to call me?"

Shit. "Well, the call itself didn't come through, but the voicemail did. Eventually. I just got it now."

There was a long pause while Rupert moved away from the sound of Christmas festivities, and the other line became progressively quieter until there was no sound at all.

"Rupe? You there?"

"Yeah, I'm here. And yes, I got his call about half an hour ago. You and I need to talk."

"I know. When?"

"Now. You said that your phone wasn't working this morning, which I find really strange. The technology has proven to be extremely reliable."

Daven swallowed hard. "Yeah, I know. Hank wants me to get on it in the morning with Shane. Maybe it was-"

"Dav, *stop*. I know you were hiding this agent's calls. Blocking them, because you were with Hank. That explains why my calls to you didn't go through, either. For hours."

There was nothing to say. Visions of packing up office boxes and being disgracefully escorted out of the building suddenly filled Daven's vivid imagination. Ten years of friendship with Hank and Rupe, and countless hours of hard work with the Seditionists. Wasted.

"If you really did talk to the agent," Dav eventually replied, very slowly, "then you'll know why I did that. But...if you and Hank want my resignation, you can have it today."

Rupe sighed. "Yeah, and I'd be next in line behind you for talking with an unverified asset. This stays between us. What did you think of this agent's claims?"

That change of tack threw Daven for a loop, and he took his phone away from his ear, stared at it quizzically, and then put it back.

"I...I...there's no reason not to look into them. Except that it feels so wrong doing it without Hank."

"You'll have to get over that. This isn't an emotional or subjective decision, Dav. We have to do it. You should know that from the start. To be honest, I'm disappointed you didn't come to me yesterday and tell me this was going on. I could have diverted the calls to my phone and talked to the guy while you waited at the office. At least now I know why you used me to get Hank drunk. This is just shameful all around."

Rupe was clearly angry now, and Dav had to work hard to put that fire out. Fast.

"You're right," he said contritely. "I'm sorry. I shouldn't have condescended to subterfuge."

"No, you shouldn't have, and if you ever do it again I'll turn you in to Hank myself. Now, moving on. Can you talk about 9pm tonight? My family should be asleep by then."

"Yes."

"Good. Talk to you then."

Click

CHAPTER SIX

Floyd was still sulking after dinner despite a couple of impromptu swats to his rear that Hank had administered in the early afternoon for an attitude adjustment. It surprisingly hadn't worked, but at least Theo had been significantly cheered by the quality and quantity of his Christmas presents. It even appeared he had forgotten all about this morning's drama, which irritated Floyd to no end, because now Theo got off scot-free and Floyd was going to be the one suffering tomorrow morning for his brother's tantrums.

"Floyd," Hank called from behind his giant mug as his oldest went around collecting all the discarded wrapping paper and angrily stuffing it into the trash compactor. Theody was already asleep, of course, and didn't have to help. As usual. The kid knew how to get out of his chores.

"Yes, sir?" Floyd replied automatically.

"Did you like your Christmas presents? You haven't said much. Hope you aren't disappointed. Theo seemed to be hurt you weren't excited about the video games he gave you."

"Because they're stupid, and I already had two of them. His lazy ass didn't even bother to check."

Hank was the one who had picked out the games, so Floyd's rude comments were officially the last straw for the day.

"Alright. That's enough. Get in your pajamas and go to the spare room. When I'm done with my coffee, we're going to have a chat. Leave your phone with me."

Floyd stopped what he was doing to hand his dad his phone, then he turned away and rolled his eyes as he trudged upstairs to change.

The 10x10 "spare room" with its bright white walls, white tile floor, and little twin bed pushed into the corner was seriously disliked by the brothers, and usually the threat of being sent there for a few hours was enough to straighten them up. The windows were still frosted due to its former life as a kitchen pantry, and the room was constantly cold due to a problem with the heating unit that had yet to be resolved. But worse than that, it was horribly, incredibly boring. And it made a person think too much. Floyd had nicknamed it "the asylum."

Hank knew full well that sending his boys to their own rooms was the farthest thing from a punishment that he could possibly dream up, so this was the next best thing. He hated having to do it to Floyd on Christmas night, but there was no choice now. The boy needed to settle down and re-center himself.

Hank suspected that Sunday was going to be a colossal headache on many fronts.

"Rupe, it's Daven."

"Yes. *I know* . Caller ID. Remember?"

"It's nine o'clock."

"I know that, too. *Clock*. Remember?"

Daven grunted. "I'm not looking forward to this conversation but it has to be done. But first we have to address one thing. This man is not verified, and we should do that first.

"Agreed. The problem is, he wouldn't give me his code."

Daven paused. "Why not? That's incredibly suspicious."

"Not really. He's never met me and doesn't trust me. Said he would only give it to you directly. You're going to have to talk to him, Dav. There's no avoiding it."

"Didn't you tell him we won't look into his claims until he's verified?"

Rupe sighed. "Actually, he says you promised to look them immediately before he would even tell you the thing about Hank. And he's holding you to it. Did you really say that?"

Dav's mind flashed back to his very first conversation with the agent, at Hank's house during the Christmas party. *Shit.* He definitely had said that. His heart was pounding suddenly.

"What else did he tell you, Rupe? Start from the very beginning. Don't leave anything out, just tell me exactly. Every word."

Rupert pinched the bridge of his nose and took another drink of wine. This was turning out to be quite the nightmare of a day.

"Alright. It wasn't much, but brace yourself..."

Floyd was pretending to be asleep, back to the door, when his dad showed up for "the talk."

Hank didn't buy it. "Sit up, Floyd."

Floyd ignored him, so Hank sat next to him on the bed and gently pulled him upright. He wasn't ready to fight right now, or ever. He wanted to forget this was happening and go to bed. But it had been a long time since Floyd needed *a talk,* and he was really pushing Hank's buttons lately.

"Look," he said, running his hand through his son's perfectly cut hair. "I know it's been a rough day. I just want to say Merry Christmas to you one more time, and see if we can end tonight on a good note. I'll let you go back to your bedroom if you just talk to me for five minutes. *Talk.* Not argue. Okay? Look at me, Floyd."

Floyd didn't look, but at least he responded at all. "Doesn't matter where I am, I'm not going to be able to sleep knowing what's going to happen in the morning."

Hank swallowed hard; he had already been harboring a ton of guilt about that same pending event. But it had to be done; Floyd had put himself in a terrible and risky position by driving the Thunderbird almost 20 miles without a license. Not to mention risking the incredible media circus that would have ensued afterwards by the arrest of a party leader's son.

He needed to tread carefully, so he said gently, "Losing sleep over it isn't going to help matters."

"Do it at midnight, then, so it's technically not on Christmas day. That's only three hours away, I should survive until then."

Hank sighed to himself. "No. But...Floyd, look at me. I mean it."

When Floyd looked up, finally - eyes wet with unshed tears - Hank lost his anger immediately, exactly as he expected. The boy was a master at disarming his father, and they both knew it.

"On Monday, I promise we will go to the DMV and you can test for your provisional license. If you pass, that means you can drive alone, but with no passengers. Not even Theody."

Floyd looked away, starting to sniff. "I don't think they'll be able to get me in so soon."

Hank smiled. "Well, let's just say I have a little bit of influence there. We'll get you an appointment. Whether or not you pass is completely in your hands, though. Tomorrow afternoon we'll go driving around for a bit after church, ok? As long as it takes until you feel ready to kill it on Monday."

"Dad..." Floyd began, a bit miserably, so low that Hank almost didn't hear him.

"Keep talking, Floyd. We're not at five minutes yet."

"You're not going to like what I want to say, though."

Hank smiled encouragingly. "Well, you haven't liked anything I've said so far. Seems only fair you should be allowed to return the favor. I'll even let you cuss, if you feel like it. But no name-calling."

Floyd shrugged. "Fine. I think...it was really shitty what you did today. You broke your promise to Theo. And to me, too, but I didn't care as much as he did. You should have heard him crying, dad. I just...I did what I had to do. I'm not trying to get out of anything for driving the car alone, but I want to let you

know that nothing is ever going to make me sorry for being
mad at you for being a crappy father."

"Floyd-"

Floyd's volume and temper escalated. "We woke up to an
empty house. By ourselves. On *Christmas morning.* You could
have left us a note to tell us there was an emergency so that
Theo didn't freak out. This was the worst Christmas ever and I
just wanted it to be over from the moment it started. Maybe
you could buy Theo's forgiveness with expensive presents, but
you'll never buy mine. Not for this, or for anything else."

Jesus, thought Hank with a bit of wry amusement. *Be careful
what you ask for.*

The tears were falling profusely now, but Floyd did not sniffle
or wipe them away. They just trickled down as silent witnesses
to the young boy's grief. Hank didn't respond right away; he
needed time to collect his wits again. He had no idea of the
depth of Floyd's resentment for him until now...and it stung.
Hard.

In a gentle but firm voice he responded, "Alright, I think I get the picture. And I'm going to make a deal with you. Are you calm enough to talk to me reasonably right now?"

"I don't know," Floyd sniffed.

"Okay. Well, this is what I'm going to propose. I promise you I will always, *always,* let you know when I'm leaving and when I'll be back, and I'll let you know if I'm running late. My purpose for keeping you in the dark in the past has been to protect you. Obviously, that backfired today. I'm also going to give you Daven's office number, and Rupert's two numbers, so that you can reach them in an emergency. I'll make sure to reinforce that they must pick up if you call, so you have to be careful not to use it unless there is a dire emergency and you can't reach me. Okay?"

Floyd nodded silently, still unhappy. "In exchange for what?"

"Never repeating what happened this morning. You know that Daven had a gun pointed at you because we thought you were a burglar?"

"Yes." Floyd shuddered at the memory.

"Floyd, I'm only going to say this once - and I mean it. That's the second time you've shown up at the office without my permission. There will not be a third. You're not to come within a mile of it ever again, unless I take you there myself. If you do, I'm sending you and Theo to boarding school again to keep you safe. This is not negotiable. Do we understand each other?"

Floyd nodded as he wiped his eyes, and they solemnly shook hands to seal the deal. He wasn't upset by the thought of boarding school, considering he'd actually liked it. They had spent three months there while Hank was busy traveling for his re-election campaign last year. Floyd had made friends and been popular. He'd even thought of asking to be sent back...until he remembered that Theo still might never recover from the trauma of being bullied by his own roommates.

"Okay, that part's settled, then," said Hank with finality as he stood up abruptly. "Now for the rest of it. The driving infraction. Since we've talked, and I know how wound up you are about waiting, this crappy father is willing to honor your request to get it over with now if you still want to. You need to sleep tonight, big day tomorrow. But it's up to you."

Floyd hesitated, then carefully slid down onto his knees and bent over the bed. Hank took off his belt with trembling hands.

He *really* didn't want to do this.

Especially because he knew Floyd was exactly right.

CHAPTER SEVEN

Hank had a hell of a time waking Floyd up on Sunday for church. Out of the three of them, only Theo was eager to go, as usual. He shuffled impatiently from foot to foot at the door of Floyd's room while their father poked and prodded at the grumpy teenager.

"*Floyd* . UP. Now. Or else we're going to cancel that driving lesson I promised you, and no appointment tomorrow."

"Don't care," Floyd mumbled. "Go without me."

Theo braced himself, grinning with expectation. He knew exactly what was going to happen next. Hell, everyone did. Even Floyd.

"Ow! Dad, stop," Floyd cried as Hank pulled him bodily out of bed and dumped him onto the floor, all the while unwrapping him from the blanket which was quickly tossed aside. There was no anger or manhandling in the action, just the usual impatient purposefulness. The spectacle was practically a weekly ritual at this point.

Hank was perfectly calm, although much shorter on temper than usual. "If you're not ready and waiting at the door in twenty minutes, my belt is coming back off when we return. Your choice, buddy."

Belt?

Back off?

Theo ghosted out the doorway and quietly ran down the stairs, all trace of amusement gone. He waited in the kitchen, rigid as a statue, shaking a little while his brother and father made themselves presentable. Despite his lack of sympathy for Floyd's inability to get out of bed without being harassed into it, he really hated it when his brother pushed dad far enough to actually be punished. And it was taking less and less these days for that to happen.

Hank and Floyd Bancroft were far more different than alike, but they did share a strong opinion that church was a colossal waste of time. Keeping up the appearance of being a religious family was necessary to his position as leader of the Seditionists, however, the party having more deeply spiritual constituents and leaders than the Urbanes. Daven and Rupert were well-known for being highly devout and vocal about their beliefs, and a couple of years ago they had an enormous fight with Hank at the office because the party was getting bad press about having leaders who couldn't agree on simple religious matters. It wasn't true, of course, but appearances were everything. So after that fight, Hank gave in and went to church.

The press, of course, quickly dropped the story and let them be…as long as he went every Sunday, that is. And he knew they were waiting for him to slip up, watching from their tinted cars across the street. Even being late for services would have caused incredible drama, which was why he was so hard on Floyd every Sunday morning even though he desperately wanted to sleep in, too. 7am services were brutal, even more so on an empty stomach. But that was what their "faith" demanded.

Hank hated the press and church in equal measure.

As usual, when they entered the church Hank turned and waved pointedly at the press cars like he was grand marshal of a parade, plastering a disgustingly wide smile on his face. Watching from inside, Daven sighed and cringed.

"Must you do that every time, Hank?" he muttered in annoyance as he and his boss took their usual pew in the back row.

Hank smiled, but did not look at Daven. "Yep. Just want to make sure they know I'm here. That it's really me, and not some doppelganger. Wouldn't want to cause another media circus, now would I?"

"They know it's you. You're just mocking them at this point," Daven grumbled.

"Not sorry, Dav. Get used to it."

Hank sighed and leaned back against the wall (the very existence of it being why he preferred the back row, although he insisted it was for security purposes). He wanted to close his eyes so badly and take a nap, but Daven would rightly kill him for that. He chuckled to himself at the thought, then picked up on some kind of general disturbance in the crowd. *Oh god.* His sons were seating themselves up in the side balcony, shoving each other for space and bickering loudly.

Everyone below was staring at them, then back at Hank, then up again at the boys. The service was moments away from starting, so Hank couldn't exactly get up to go talk to them.

He kept his cool and turned to speak directly into Dav's ear. "Ask a guard to calm the boys down, please." *Before I kill them*, he added to himself as he looked around the congregation with a slightly humorous apologetic expression.

"Already done," Daven whispered back, having noticed the situation long before Hank did and quietly summoning help from the guards with the radio microphone inside his suit lapel. Avery slipped into the scene to whisper something to the boys, who stilled immediately and dared not look anywhere but at the altar. Hank was immensely satisfied by that, returned Avery's eye contact with a smile and nod, and turned his mind to other things. By the time the sermon started it was already forgotten in favor of worrying some more about the telecommunications problem at the office.

The boys sat rigid in their pews, determined not to make another sound. Like his father, Floyd also immediately tuned out of the sermon and began thinking about other things, like last year when he and Theo slipped away from their guards and hailed a cab bound for Disneyland. The cab driver had recognized them, however, and quickly turned around and delivered them to the bewildered receptionist at Seditionist HQ. Dad was out of town, so Rupert took them home after immediately firing the driver and guards who had been in charge of watching them. He then hired the cabbie to replace the driver, so the man was now enjoying a lucrative salary and had quickly become a favorite amongst the women on the household staff.

Suffice to say, Floyd and Theo learned an unforgettable lesson during the whole affair, both emotionally and physically, and now they obeyed the new guards better than they obeyed their father...a fact which had thoroughly annoyed Hank until he realized he could use it to his advantage, and then it amused him. Avery in particular had absolutely no qualms about stepping in to prevent an escalation, so Hank was glad he had been closest.

Hank himself also obeyed his own assigned guards down to the letter; after all, they were there to ensure his safety at the cost of their own lives. There was no one who respected the black-suited men more than Hank Bancroft, and they respected him in return and took good care of him and his sons.

The sermon dragged on. And on. And on. Daven glanced at the suddenly still man next to him, saw what he was doing between his legs, and resisted the urge to curse. He leaned over to his boss.

"Seriously? Put the phone away."

"Shhhhhh. I'm praying," hissed Hank as he kept his head down and continued to scroll through his emails.

"Hank. Stop."

After waiting in vain for a few long moments, Daven reached over and snatched the phone away, dropping it into his opposite pocket and then folding his hands again in his lap. Hank looked at him aghast, with a dangerous expression he very rarely wore.

"Give it back."

Daven looked straight ahead and didn't move. "No."

"Give. It. Back."

"*No*. Pay attention to the sermon, Hank."

Hank straightened up and looked ahead, feeling like a chastised little child. After pouting for a few moments, he glanced aside to the balcony and caught Floyd and Theo watching him, laughing behind their hands, having clearly seen what Daven had just done. *Shit. So much for setting a good example.*

He gave them a stern warning glance, placing a finger to his lips in a "shushing" gesture.

Then he couldn't help but laugh, too.

Daven rolled his eyes and sunk deeper back into the pew.

Craving

Redemption

The Ways We Heal

CHAPTER ONE

Hank pulled Daven aside after the sermon, moving him gently into their usual after-church chatting place in the corner of the lobby. It was private there, and Avery stood a discreet distance away to ensure their safety.

"Hank," Daven began as he handed over his boss's phone. "I... I'm so sorry. I hope you're not angry with me."

"Not at all. You were right." He dropped the phone into his pocket, struggling not to laugh again. "No harm done. Speaking of phones, are you going to call Shane about the issues you were having yesterday morning? I want a full report of exactly what went wrong and why your phone was not taking calls for several hours. We know it's not a problem with the emergency line, since Floyd and-"

Hank stopped in surprise as Lucas suddenly approached him. It was highly unusual for any of the guards to interrupt a conversation, especially the aloof and distant Lucas. But he had also drilled into all of his staff that they are never to apologize for doing their job, so the man got straight to the point.

"Sir, the boys were fighting again. I've stopped it, but a lot of people saw it. We need to take them to the car."

Hank sighed. "For fuck's sake. Take Theo, but send Floyd to me."

"*Hank!*" gasped Daven as Lucas walked away.

"Sorry, Dav. Still inside a church, I know."

Daven shook his head. "We shouldn't be speaking in here about party business. Especially not this topic. Is there a good time we can talk today? I have something we need to discuss."

Hank nodded. "Your car outside?"

"Yes."

"Let's go there and talk, then."

"Wait, what about Floyd?"

"Oh...yeah." Hank turned around and watched as his son walked up to him with a "who, me?" expression. Hank wasn't buying it, and he gestured for him to walk with him about ten feet away from Dav.

"Can I trust you to sit in the car with your brother for ten minutes without killing him, or am I going to have to take you into the restroom for a chat?" he asked calmly, with a neutral expression. People were watching, after all. They were *always* watching.

Floyd swallowed hard. A *chat* was never actually a chat in this context.

"Theo keeps making fun of me, dad. I have a right to defend myself."

"Making fun of you? For what?"

Floyd looked at the floor. "For...forget it. I'd rather *have a chat* than explain it. I'll meet you in the restroom."

Hank was bewildered and hurt at his son's attitude. "*Stop, Floyd,*" he said as he stepped in front of him to block the path. "What's gotten into you?" he asked harshly. Floyd then looked ready to burst into tears, so Hank put his hands on his son's shoulders and softened his tone. "Hey. Forget it, we'll talk later. Just relax. Let's go to breakfast. Come on."

He put his arm around Floyd and walked back to Daven. "I'll have to call you later, Dav. Floyd isn't feeling well."

With Avery and Daven leading the way, Hank guided his son down to his waiting car. This time, he didn't wave because he forgot the press was even there.

Hank leaned his head into the car. "Hey, Theo. You're going to ride with the guards this morning while I talk to Floyd alone. Come on out."

Theo climbed out, smirking at his miserable brother. Hank saw it and gave him a warning glance, but he still couldn't decipher what was going on between them. He was determined to find out.

It was an hour-long drive to where the Bancroft family had their weekly Sunday brunch with the entire household before the work week started up again. The hotel was located in a poorer section of the city, where most of the servants spent their Saturdays. Every Sunday at 10am Hank rented out a ballroom at the Hilton and had a nice banquet brunch served for the household staff, which was about twenty people, and for their immediate families. It was a rather large affair. A motorcoach was waiting to take the servants back to the house afterwards, but there was no urgent rush to leave since they didn't need to arrive until 3pm to start preparing for dinner.

On Friday nights at 9pm, the same motorcoach arrived at the house and took them into a parking lot in the city where they could be picked up by their families. It was an extremely thoughtful and expensive arrangement, and no one else with such a large household ever did the same for their servants. Hank prided himself on obtaining respect and loyalty by serving up plenty of the same in return. On these days they celebrated birthdays, anniversaries, and promotions for the upcoming week, and Hank always attended even if it meant his travel plans had to be changed. Everyone in the Bancroft household loved Hank and the boys.

The downside was that every Sunday, *everybody* knew where Hank Bancroft and his sons were going to be. That's why their little town car was followed by a van full of security guards - and this time - Theo, too - even though no one else from the Seditionists party was ever invited.

Hank expected Floyd to resent him for forcing him to ride with him alone and talk about his feelings, but he was pleasantly surprised when the boy scooted up next to him and all but *cuddled* with him. Cuddled. *Floyd* . Cuddling. Something was really wrong.

As he put his arm around his son, Hank asked the driver to close the partition window for privacy. Then he handed Floyd a bottle of his favorite iced tea and lemonade drink. Floyd didn't take it, so Hank set it down. His stomach began growling, and Floyd chuckled.

"Oh you think that's funny, huh?" Hank said with a smirk.

"Yeah. Sorry."

"I know what else you thought was funny today."

Floyd chuckled again, but just barely. "Yeah. Uncle Dav taking your phone away. I wish you could have seen your face, dad. It was hilarious."

"I'm sure it was."

"And his face, too. He was so pissed at you."

"Ha. What else is new."

Silence.

"Does Uncle Dav get mad at you a lot, dad?" Floyd sounded like he was falling asleep.

"Yes. Usually when he thinks I'm acting childish. You know he hates that we don't take church seriously. And sometimes we fight about party policy, but that's only because we care passionately about what we believe in. And we don't always agree on everything, and sometimes we don't talk for a while and act like brats. Just like you and your brother."

Silence.

"So now that I've told you what's going on between me and Dav," Hank said, drawing his son closer to him and running a hand through his hair, "I want you to tell me what's going on between you and Theo, so we can fix it."

Silence.

"Floyd?"

Silence.

"Can you promise me you won't be mad at me for what I'm about to tell you?"

Oh, lovely. What now? "No."

Floyd grumbled, "Never mind, then."

"Talk to me, Floyd," said Hank, a little sterner. "I guarantee you I will be mad if you don't let me in on what's going on between you too."

Floyd sighed. "You're going to find out from Lucas, anyway. I hit him because he was making fun of me for not being able to sit still in church. Because my butt hurt, because of what *he did* yesterday morning. I should have never gone to the office to get you. He's stupid and was just being a big baby, and I don't care about him anymore. He can cry for days for all I care!"

Hank was stunned by Floyd's hostility, both in words and action. "You *hit* him? In the church, you mean, just now?"

"Yeah. Well it was more of a shove, I guess. Kind of."

"What *exactly* did you do?" Hank asked calmly, although his heart was pounding out of his chest.

Silence.

"Floyd. Tell me."

"I...I shoved him. He fell down but he wasn't hurt. I also kind of slapped the back of his head. Lucas saw the whole thing, he can tell you why I did it."

Hank was incensed. "I don't care why, Floyd. You're in serious trouble. You should never, *ever* , hit your brother. Period. I've made this very clear to both of you boys throughout your entire lives. And doing it in public makes it ten times worse."

"But dad-"

"Be quiet. I don't want to hear anymore. Sit up and move to that bench."

Floyd peeled himself off his dad and moved to the lengthwise bench of limousine, where he laid down again. "Dad-"

"Quiet. And sit up straight."

"My butt hurts."

"And it's going to hurt a lot more when we get home. Plant it straight down on that seat or else I'll plant it for you."

Floyd sat up, but he wasn't happy about it. Hank didn't care. He pulled out his BlackBerry and called Daven.

"Yes?"

"It's Hank. Sorry we got interrupted. You talk with Shane yet?"

"Just hung up with him, actually. He's going to look into it. Do you have an hour or so to talk later today? I need to bring something to your attention that could potentially blow up into something much bigger, but I don't want to get into it now while you're on the way to brunch. We may need more than an hour, and it's best if we do it in person."

"It can't wait until tomorrow?"

Daven paused. "Unfortunately not. The sooner, the better. And we should meet at the office."

Hank eyed Floyd, his heart hurting from the fact that his boys had gotten physical with each other. "The office should be fine. I was going to take my son for a driving lesson, but that's just been canceled."

"That reminds me, I don't know if you had a chance to talk to Lucas, but nearly everyone saw that scuffle between your boys."

"I'm sure they did."

"You should call him and get the whole story from him before you take action-"

Hank interrupted him rudely. "Dav, this is not your jurisdiction. End of story. I'll call you when I leave the hotel so we can figure out a time to meet today. About *party business*. Only."

He hung up, feeling furious at Daven now, too. Was everyone out to ruin his day, or what?

Twenty very long and silent minutes later, Hank's phone rang. It was Theo.

"What's up?" Hank asked quietly, not wanting Floyd to know it was Theo for fear of a temper tantrum. The boy suspected nothing and barely glanced at him with his red eyes that were still wet but no longer spouting tears.

"Is Floyd okay, dad?"

"Yeah, why do you ask?"

There was a long pause. "Because I feel really bad about what I did, and he was right to be mad. I just feel really bad and I want to talk to him."

Hank's heart dropped. "What exactly did you do?" he asked in a business-like tone.

"He didn't tell you?"

"Nope. Maybe it's best if I hear it from you."

An even longer pause. Floyd's eyes were closed now, but his face was white and he was clenching his fists harder than before.

"I knew you took a belt to him and I was making fun of him for not being able to sit still during the sermon. Because it hurt. As we were leaving the church I picked up a bible and…." there was a choking noise and a cry and at least a minute of nothing else.

Then another voice on the phone. Lucas. "You want me to finish the story for him, Mr. Bancroft? He's lost it again."

"Yes, please go ahead," said Hank tightly, gritting his teeth with keen distaste. The last thing he wanted was his guards involved in the family's personal business.

"As we were exiting he picked up the bible and with both hands took a huge swing at Floyd's rear. Hit him pretty hard. Floyd turned around and pushed him away, and Theo fell. Lost his balance, I think, it wasn't a very hard shove."

Jesus Christ. "And then what?"

"Floyd smacked Theo in the back of the head, not hard, told him to stop. Then Theo picked up the bible again and went after Floyd as he started down the stairs, and nearly hit him with it again but I managed to grab him back by the collar. I'm sorry to tell you almost everyone saw and heard it. There was some commentary afterwards in the lobby, which is why I interrupted your conversation with Mr. Johansson."

Now Hank felt like crying, out of frustration and anger. "I see. Objectively, who would you consider to be at fault in this situation?"

"Theo, no question. It was unprovoked, and Floyd was trying to get away rather than fight."

Hank took a deep breath. "Okay. Thanks. We'll see you at the hotel."

He disconnected the call, then stared at Floyd placidly until he opened his eyes and turned to look. His heart fell when Floyd shied away from him, moving further up the bench.

"Come here, Floyd." He patted the bench gently. "That was Theo and Lucas. I know what Theo did, and you're off the hook. You can lay down." He scooted over the far left to give Floyd room to stretch out, but Floyd didn't move. He looked like the proverbial deer caught in the headlights.

"I'm okay here," he whispered.

Hank waited, but Floyd stayed put. So he got up and clambered over the other bench next to Floyd and wrapped his arms gently around his son and kissed his forehead.

"I'm sorry I didn't let you explain. That was wrong. Next time, I will. I always will from now on. I promise. Okay?"

Floyd sniffled, then nodded. He was a lot more upset than Hank realized, and it was going to take a while for him to recover. Hank was infinitely glad he chose not to spank him in the limo again a little while ago.

A few minutes later, when Floyd was quiet again, Hank let him lay down and put his head in his lap. Then he ran his hand through his hair slowly, gently.

"Floyd?"

"Yeah, dad?"

Hank was a little choked up suddenly. "Yesterday, when you called me a crappy father..."

Floyd started to sit up. "I didn't mean it, I'm so sorry!"

Hank pressed him back down. "Listen. Even if you didn't, you're weren't entirely wrong. I've been thinking, you know? It killed me that you said that, but I needed to know you felt that way. I heard you, loud and clear. And I'm going to be a better father and spend a lot more time with you guys. You have my word."

Floyd said nothing. He was trembling again, and his eyes were closed.

"I can't take back anything I've done or haven't done," Hank continued. "So all that resentment you have towards me is just going to linger unless you let it go on your own free will, when you're ready. I hope it's sooner than later, but I wouldn't blame you if it's never. God forbid."

"What are you going to do to Theody?" Floyd asked quietly.

"First I'm going to paddle the daylights out of him, and then I'm going to have this same talk with him. He won't be very receptive to it, of course, but that's Theo. We'll have to see how it goes. Take it day by day."

Floyd murmured, "You should talk to him first. And *then* paddle him. He learns better that way. Opposite of me."

Hank nodded, impressed with Floyd's sudden wisdom. Why hadn't he himself ever picked up on that distinction before? "You're exactly right. I'll do that. Speaking of which, how's your rear?"

"Hurts."

"I'm sorry. You didn't deserve what Theo did."

Floyd asked hopefully, "Does this mean my driving lesson is back on again?"

Hank laughed. "Yeah, I suppose so. Remind me to have a few drinks beforehand."

Floyd didn't laugh, but he visibly relaxed. After a moment Hank took his hand and squeezed it.

Floyd squeezed back and didn't let go.

They were silent the rest of the way to the hotel.

CHAPTER TWO

Hank was always the last out of the limo when the little caravan arrived at the Hilton, per his bodyguard's wishes. The hotel was kind enough to always offer a private parking area covered by a tent so that the press couldn't hound his every step into the hotel. That's part of the reason Hank was fine with giving them so much money week after week.

"Vance," Hank called out to his driver, who had exited on the other side of the car and was now scurrying around to meet his boss.

"Sir?"

"I need you to take Theo home and stay there. Floyd and I will ride back with the guards. But first go inside the ballroom and eat something; he'll wait for you here."

Vance nodded and disappeared, and Hank grabbed Theo's arm and guided him over to the limo.

"Get in," ordered Hank quietly. The guards that were all standing around waiting for him to enter the hotel looked puzzled, as did Floyd, but Hank ignored them all and climbed into the car after Theo and shut the door behind him.

"You have no idea how much trouble you're in, do you?" Hank asked calmly.

Theo was trembling, just like Floyd had been an hour ago. "I think I know. You're sending me home so I can wait in the spare room for you, and then...then you're going to...."

Hank nodded. "You can go to the kitchen for a bottle of water first, *only,* and then straight to the spare room. Except for calls of nature you will stay in there until I return home. And then yes, I'm *going to*. Big time."

He got out of the car and told Avery to stay with it until Vance returned. Then he gestured everybody else inside the hotel with him, and everyone put on their happy faces for the next couple of hours.

The ride home in the van was completely silent because Hank had received a phone call during breakfast that put him in a scary, snappy mood. Floyd could barely dare to blink after having received a solid smack on the butt for taking too long to leave the ballroom - given right in front of all the guards and some of the hotel staff, no less. Floyd was so humiliated and angry that Avery felt obliged to take him aside to calm him down, and then Hank went after Avery for that, too. When the subdued contingent finally piled into the van, Floyd jumped in first and scrambled to the very back to keep at a safe distance from his irate father.

Floyd had no idea what was upsetting his dad so much. It was extremely rare for him to be so bossy with his guards, and until now he had never once disciplined his kids in public. They were all rather bewildered by the whole affair, but it became clearer once they pulled up to the house and spotted Daven's truck in the driveway.

Hank was the first out of the van.

"I told you I would meet you at the office!" he snapped so loudly that everyone cringed.

Daven responded calmly, "I told you this can't wait. We can drive there together if you want, but-"

"No. My study. Go in. I'll be right there. Floyd!"

"Yes, dad?" answered Floyd in a small voice, and Hank spun around to see his son standing right behind him.

"Go straight to your room and stay there until I tell you to come out. Understand?"

Floyd felt like crying again. "You're scaring me. What's going on?"

"When I tell you to move, you move. Or do you need another reminder?" He raised his hand.

"No!" Floyd ran off, and Hank turned to his four-person security contingent, who were standing in a square around him, looking extremely concerned.

"Everything alright, boss?" ventured Avery in a neutral tone.

"Not even close, but it's not a security matter. Sorry for being an ass. You can return to quarters and relax. I'll call down when I'm ready to go back out."

Hank said nothing more and turned around to go in the house. He held the door open so the guards could go down the stairs to their rooms, then headed straight for the spare room in order to let Theo know he would be a little while longer. He was shocked to find Floyd sitting on the bed next to his brother; the boy jumped up immediately and began apologizing.

Hank was furious. "I said go *straight* to your room. Was I unclear in any way whatsoever, Floyd?"

"Theo's hungry, dad. We've been gone for-"

"Out. Now!"

Hank forgot all about what he was going to tell Theo and followed Floyd out, slamming the door behind them. Then he made a beeline for his study, where his chief strategist was standing there looking like a man who just ran over his best friend's dog.

"*Daven,*" he growled as he strode in and set his briefcase hard down on the table. "There better be a really good fucking explanation for the information we just received from Shane. Start talking."

"Maybe you should calm down first," tried Dav, but Hank wasn't having it.

"Did you, or did you not, *deliberately* turn off your phone while we were waiting for the agent's call to come through on the emergency line?"

"Hank, I know you're upset, but please listen to me first. It's complicated."

"I only want a yes or no answer. *Now*."

Daven took a deep breath to steady himself. "Yes."

Hank shook his head in disbelief. "Alright. You're fired, then. Whatever you choose to tell me at this point is on your own time."

"I'm certainly not going to talk to you while you're this upset," Daven finally declared, firmly but somewhat breathlessly.

"Did Rupert know about this?" Hank demanded angrily.

"Yes…he figured it out when the alleged agent called him directly after he couldn't reach me."

Hank did not expect that answer at all, and it threw him for a loop. His heart fell even further.

"Wonderful. So you were both conspiring against me. On Christmas. Thanks a lot."

Daven flipped open his notebook. "No, actually. We were both doing our jobs. Our charter has a clause in it which clearly states that all-"

"I have that fucking charter memorized, Dav. Don't quote my own words to me."

“Sorry,” replied Daven, truly chagrined. He flipped the notebook shut. “When you are calm, I will explain everything. Do you want me to leave until then?”

“Just a minute,” said Hank as he walked over to the intercom on the wall and hit a switch.

“Theo?”

There was a short pause, then Theo’s small, tremulous voice. “Yes, dad?”

“You can come out now. Make yourself lunch, then go outside with Floyd and play with the dogs. I’m going to be with Dav for a while, then your brother and I are going for a drive. After that, you and I will talk.”

“Yes, sir,” replied Theo shakily. “I’m sorry, dad.”

“I know. Try to relax, buddy,” Hank said softly. “We’ll get through this. See you in a bit.”

“Okay.” Theo’s relief was obvious, and Hank smiled a little. To be eleven years old again…

”Oh, Theo? Can you bring me a couple bottles of water to the study first?”

“Sure, dad. Be right there.”

While waiting, Hank took out his copy of the charter from his desk and ran his fingers over it without seeing any of the words. They had all written it together, ten years ago. When everything seemed exciting and right and purposeful and pure…but now, not so much. How fast life moved sometimes. Yesterday had been normal. Today, Daven had to be dealt with, and then Rupert. It was all over.

Theo delivered the water, and then it was time.

"You better start from the beginning. This time, don't leave anything out. No opinions, just facts. I am calm and will listen in silence until you finish." He sat down and looked up at his friend - former friend? - expectantly.

Daven took a deep breath. "Very well. On Christmas eve, just after I arrived at your house for the party, I received a call on the emergency line…"

"…and then last night at 9pm, Rupert called me to tell me everything the agent had told him, which was exactly what he told me. But the man still refused to give his code number. At that point we made the decision that the alleged agent was untrustworthy and you needed to be informed of the situation immediately, in case there was a plot against you."

“Except it wasn’t immediately.”

“No,” explained Daven patiently. “We hung up at midnight last night. Remember this morning I told you we needed to get together in person today? Had I known Shane would beat me to the punch with the findings about my phone, I never would have waited. Now it looks like I’m covering my tracks, but I’m not.”

Hank was calming down, but Daven was still fired. So very, very fired.

“And how exactly do you expect me to believe you?”

Daven pulled out his phone. “I took measures to ensure you knew Rupert and I were aligned and aware of the seriousness of our actions. Here is an email from me to Rupe at one o’clock this morning with the draft of the memo I wrote you for this very meeting. Here’s the final version, sent at 2am. A copy of which is right here in my hand, by the way, signed by both of us and time-stamped at 6:24 this morning. The original is on your desk right now. You can check our badges. We left the office at 6:50am and have not been back again today. I also FedEx’d a copy to your home after leaving the church, which was dropped off at 8:37am. Here’s the tracking number.”

Hank took all the papers, but said nothing.

"Furthermore," added Daven, "once the decision was made to inform you of our actions, we both wrote our resignations in order to save time. Also time-stamped from this morning and left on your desk."

Hank still said nothing.

Daven continued patiently, "What this all means, Hank, is that Rupert and I took all these actions hours before we even *asked* Shane to start an investigation. So if you still think I'm backtracking now, there's nothing else I can do to convince you otherwise."

"Very thorough," murmured Hank. He didn't want to admit he was impressed, but he was. "I just have one question. Did you know that Shane would be able to tell you turned your phone off? Because one could say you knew you were screwed and are trying to score points by turning yourself in before he had the chance."

"Absolutely not. I was stunned to learn this morning that he was able to do that. Believe me, if I had known *that*, I would've never done it in the first place."

Hank nodded. "Okay. I believe you. Anything else to add?"

Daven took another deep breath. "I'm not trying to get out of being fired, Hank. I accept responsibility for my actions. I should have never turned off my phone, and found another way to speak to the agent. But before I go, I need to say one thing. Your refusal to give me the list of people you met with last Tuesday was the impetus for my decision to keep the details of the call from you. You should have given me the list so I could validate who you're meeting with. That's my job. Or *was*, rather. I would like to know why you wouldn't cooperate with me on that."

Hank was annoyed again. "Because I didn't want to deal with it on Christmas eve. I was tired. I was drunk. I was busy hosting a huge party in my house. The only other person who had access to those names was my secretary, and she was here partying and drunk, too. It had to wait. End of story. Any further questions? Maybe you also want to know what my agent was doing in Greeley when she was killed? Ask Rupert, it was his idea. I'm guessing he didn't tell you that, huh?"

Daven said nothing. What could he possibly say that wouldn't increase Hank's defensiveness and make things worse?

Hank suddenly made up his mind and spoke with a firmness and finality that Daven always appreciated, even if others didn't.

"I don't want to see you again for 30 days. That's how long I'm suspending you. Two weeks for the phone stunt and another two for speaking with an unverified asset. Rupert will also get two weeks for the latter. All unpaid, of course. I'll call him in a moment to tell him."

Daven stared at him in disbelief. "You're not accepting our resignations?"

"Oh, I want to, believe me. But you know I can't. It would destabilize the party and throw our constituents into a frenzy. We're going to have to get through this together and learn how to trust each other again. If possible. I'm not sure how. Time will tell. Give me your BlackBerry and your office badge. You'll get them back on January 25."

Daven handed the objects over.

"I'm so sorry, Hank-"

"*Don't*. Just leave. You're not to have contact with anyone at our office except me and Rupert, and try to keep that to the bare minimum while I stave off the press for the next month. Go."

Daven left the house without another word and drove straight to Rupert's house, his bodyguard faithfully tailing him at a discreet distance.

137

CHAPTER THREE

Rupert had received the grim news of his fate from Hank directly by the time Daven's truck pulled up the drive, followed by the little dark blue BMW that always accompanied him. He was upset, yet grateful not to have been fired, but was more than a little uneasy about all the unanswered questions and implications that had spent two days raining down on his head in a cycle of nothingness and frustration.

 It was likely the agent was a plant...but how did he get the emergency number?

- So it's one of our own agents, since all the others are accounted for.

What if the agent is working with the Urbanes in a plot against Hank?

- What would be the purpose? Hank is free of scandal and on cordial terms with Harmon.

Who would want to kill a double agent on Seditionists territory?

- Maybe it was one of our own who thought she was spying. But there were no reports of that.

If Hank is innocent, why would he not turn over the names of who he met with?

- Remember that Hank has a lot going on in the background that you don't know about.

We shouldn't have speculated at all until this guy was verified.

- We couldn't just leave it alone until he called again. We were obliged to investigate.

...and so on. And so on. And so on.

It was all driving him crazy.

"Sorry to show up unannounced," Daven said apologetically as Rupert opened the door and stepped onto the porch. "Hank took my phone and your number was in there. I don't have it memorized. Do you have time to talk?"

"I do, but he's actually on his way here to take my phone and badge, too. Might make things awkward."

"Oh. Then I'll call you on your home phone later. I need to write it down, though."

Daven pulled out a notebook and took down the number as Rupert read it out, then turned around as Rupe's eyes focused on something else over his shoulder. Daven heard it before he saw it; the noisy Thunderbird roaring down the street, being dutifully tailed by a comically large and shiny black Escalade that wallowed and swayed over the speed bumps like a drunken hippo. As they pulled up, Floyd waved from behind the wheel. The men quickly walked down to the car where it was parking in the street due to Daven's truck and the BMW blocking the driveway.

"Hey Floyd," Rupert called after the engine was shut off. "Looking good, buddy!"

"Hi guys," he replied with a huge grin, but he stayed put. His dad had clearly told him not to get out of the car, or else he would have already been out and giving hugs to his "uncles."

Hank unfolded himself out of the passenger side, then walked up to Rupert without a single glance at Daven. "The house looks good. I like the new color scheme."

"Thanks. The shutters are going to be repainted a shade lighter, though. Came out a bit too dark. And did you notice the driveway?"

Hank looked down at the fresh black asphalt. "Yeah. Looks great. I need to do mine before I sell." He pointed up. "You re-did the chimney, too? Man. Decorative brickwork and everything. Going all out, aren't you."

"Yeah. Got to keep up with all the new money folks rushing into the neighborhood." They both grinned. He meant Hank himself, of course, who had bought the largest plot of land in the neighborhood last year and was almost finished with his new house. The exterior was barely started before all the neighbors started getting catty about it making their own homes look shabby in comparison, and Hank thought it was hilarious that Rupe's own wife was one of the original chief naysayers. That was before she knew it was Hank's. Now everyone knew, of course, because the press had gotten a hold of the building permits.

Daven shifted uncomfortably from where he was observing the disturbingly normal interaction, feeling a bit like he had entered the metaphorical Twilight Zone. But then he spotted Rupe's wife and teenaged children watching from the living room windows, just barely visible behind the glare of noon sunlight. That explained it. Hank had seen them, too, and was being painfully careful to do nothing to alarm them. Or Floyd, for that matter, who had all the windows down in the car and was also watching the scene intently. It was also extremely likely that one or more of the cars on the street had a photographer lying in wait behind the tinted windows, hoping to get a juicy shot to sell.

To that end, Rupert handed his badge and BlackBerry to Hank in two regular envelopes. "See you in two weeks then?" he said lightly, but respectfully.

"At the office, yes. But I still expect you in church on Sunday. *Every* Sunday. Don't skip it again." He was highly annoyed that he had been forced to unfailingly attend per Rupe's insistence, but Rupe didn't always go himself. Like today. If Hank had to suffer, they would all suffer, period.

"Okay. Sorry. Shall I call you at 6pm, or will you call me?"

"I'll call you."

Daven wanted Hank to say something to him, too, but Hank turned back and got into the car, completely ignoring him as if he wasn't even there. Floyd waved again as he pulled out and drove off, and Daven waved back. Hank was watching him coldly through the side mirror.

"Wow," Rupe said gravely, "looks like he is a lot more pissed at you than me. What happened?"

"Sentenced to 4 weeks of being a non-entity, apparently."
Daven was wildly depressed all of a sudden, and Rupert felt
terribly sorry for him. The usual envy and friendly rivalry he
felt toward the man who was best friends with Hank Bancroft
dusted away like it was never there to begin with.

"I'm sorry, Dav. Give him time. It'll be alright."

"Why are you two talking tonight?" asked Daven. "Just
curious."

"I'm the PR guy, remember? He asked me to write a few
paragraphs to explain to the press what happened and wants it
by 6pm."

"What are you going to say?"

"That the Seditionists hold all of their party's employees to the
same standards, and that we violated a longstanding
communications policy. No tolerance even at the highest levels
of leadership. Blah blah blah. I'm not exactly sure how to word
it yet without ruining our careers. He wants it to be completely
transparent, of course. Now I'll also need to explain why you
got a bigger punishment than I did. Any ideas?"

"No idea," grumbled Daven. "The Urbanes are going to have a
field day with this no matter what we say. I'm so sorry, by the

way, for getting you dragged into this. If I hadn't...well, this is all my fault."

"If it helps, neither Hank nor I blame you for my part in this. I spoke with the caller without getting his code first. That was on me."

"Yeah, but if I hadn't ignored his calls, he never would have gotten to you. I resigned, you know, but he wouldn't accept it."

Rupert shrugged. "Yes, Dav, I know. So did I, remember? We literally sat down and wrote our letters together." He shivered. "It's cold out here. Let's talk later, okay? Try not to mope. It could have been so much worse."

"Not by much."

Rupe looked up, waved up towards his house, and sighed. "Hey, lunch is ready, my wife just waved me in. We can put on an extra plate for you. Why don't you come up? Been a long time since we had the pleasure of your company."

Daven shook his head. "Won't be very pleasurable today, I can assure you. But thanks."

"Nah, I think it's exactly what you need. It's my youngest's birthday today, and we just got a dog. Come in and take your mind off all this. At least for an hour. Come on, Dav. They'll be so happy to see you. And I'll have one of my guards follow you back."

"If you're sure?" Dav asked hopefully. Despite his outward reluctance, he desperately wanted to go in and try to enjoy himself before the shit hit the fan with the press. There was nothing to be gained by going home alone to sit around and think about what a mess he'd made of his friendship with Hank.

"Yeah. Come on. Tell your guard."

"Okay. Be right there."

Daven waited a minute for Rupe to go into the house, and then he walked up to the little BMW and knocked on the window. Gordon rolled it down quickly.

"Yes, boss?"

"You can go on home. Rupe's going to have his guard follow me back."

"I can't, sir, it's against the policy."

"I know. Do it anyway. I'll sign a variance form."

Gordon pulled the stack of forms from beneath the seat behind him. He was the only person in the party who used them on a regular basis, because Daven was constantly violating security and transportation protocol. The signed form completely waived the guard's responsibility for whatever happened once it was signed. Gordon used to protest more in the past at being told to leave his boss all kinds of places alone, but now he was quietly resigned to the fact that nobody at HQ really cared that their chief strategist had very little regard for his own personal safety.

Hank should have been paying more attention to Floyd's driving than he was, but he just couldn't focus. Didn't notice the rolled-through stop sign, blowing a short yellow light, and overall lack of signaling. Didn't notice that the Escalade had to commit the same infractions just to keep up with them. He only sat back and told Floyd to slow down or speed up when he needed to. His mind was elsewhere. Completely, totally dissociated from his current task of ensuring his son didn't kill anybody from behind the wheel of the Thunderbird for the past two hours.

He was already regretting being so hard on Daven, and wished he could take back a few things he'd said. The man was loyal to his party to a fault, and Hank knew he really thought he was doing the right thing. If only he hadn't violated two clear policies, Hank could have let him off easier. If he hadn't talked to the agent. If he hadn't turned off his phone.

And that was the big one - turning off his phone. Daven was the emergency contact for all 50 of their agents. The *only* emergency contact they had. It had been a highly irresponsible and indefensible action to shut that channel down, something that anyone one else would have been fired on the spot for, and probably sued into oblivion for good measure.

Hell, maybe he *should* still fire him for that. But he didn't know, and every five minutes his feelings changed on the matter. It was so frustrating. At this particular moment, he just wanted to strangle the man for putting him in a position to mistrust him.

As if he had been reading his mind, the cell phone rang. It was Rupert's home phone number.

Hank sighed heavily. One of the two people in the world he least wanted to talk to, calling him now in the middle of his son's driving lesson. He should let it go to voicemail.

"Floyd, pull over into this parking lot. Leave room for Avery behind us."

Floyd obeyed, and Hank picked up the call at the last second before it went to voicemail.

"Yes, Rupert?" he answered tensely.

"It's Daven. Do you have a moment?"

Fuck, really? We're doing this right now?

"What do you want, Dav?" he asked irritably, noticing Floyd raising his eyebrows out of the corner of his eye. They both knew he had never spoken to Dav so rudely before. And Hank hated himself for it, but he couldn't help it.

"I just realized the emergency line is still routed to my phone. Shane needs to forward it to someone else as soon as possible, until I come back."

You mean *if I let you* come back, Hank thought to himself.

"Who do you suggest?" he asked, forcing himself to be diplomatic now that Daven had just saved Hank's own ass from charges of neglecting the emergency line. *Jesus Christ, Hank.*

"Taylor."

"I will call Shane right now and arrange it. Thank you for reminding me."

He hung up before Daven could say anything else, then dialed Shane.

"Mr. Bancroft?"

"Sorry to bother you. I need you to re-route the emergency line to Taylor right away. Like yesterday."

There was a clicking of keyboard keys that lasted about 20 seconds.

"Shane..?"

"One moment."

Hank glanced sideways at Floyd, who was watching him with an expression of alarm. This was exactly why he never took work calls around his sons.

"It's done, sir. I take it that means you received my report this morning?"

Oh good god, he had never written Shane back. The poor guy must still be... *shit.*

"Um, yes. Are you still at the office waiting for us?"

"Yes, sir. That's what I was told to do, in case you had more questions."

More than six hours ago. Jesus Christ, Hank. You seriously need to get your shit together.

"Shane...fuck. I'm so sorry. Go home. I'll add an extra vacation day to your file. Make it two, and I'll buy you lunch tomorrow. I'm really sorry." His face burned with embarrassment. Goddamnit. Daven or Rupert would have picked up on this if they hadn't been so busy screwing up everything else.

"No problem, sir. It's good I was still here because I couldn't have made the change to the emergency line from home. Does Taylor know about this so she can keep her phone on? I'm seeing it's turned off right now."

"Okay, thanks. I'll call her at home or on her wife's cell. Good work, Shane."

"Thank you, sir."

Hank hung up and Floyd turned to him immediately.

"Dad? What the hell is going on?"

"Just a moment, Floyd," Hank said as movement in the rearview mirror caught his eye. The Escalade idling behind them was now pulling out to the right and sidling up to his door, looming so large that Hank had to look way up at the driver.

"Everything alright, sir?" asked Avery, looking down at him worriedly. "We're not in a great part of town right now and I'd really like to get you headed back the other way."

"Okay. I need a minute to make an emergency call, and then let's head straight home. I want everyone assembled in the conference room downstairs and waiting for us when we pull in."

"Everyone? Theo, too?"

"No, sorry. I mean just the security team. And wait a sec, Floyd's going to join you for the ride back."

Hank turned to Floyd now and said gently, "I have to make a call that you can't be allowed to hear. Go hop in with Avery."

"Dad, you're seriously freaking me out. I ran two stop signs in a row just to see if you'd notice, and you said nothing. You're not even here right now."

Hank hardened his tone. "I do *not* have time for this, Floyd. I'm in the middle of handling an emergency. Get out of the car, now."

Floyd was becoming slightly hysterical. "No. I'm not going until you tell me what's up. I'm freaking out. What happened with Rupe and Uncle Dav? Are they okay? Are we in danger?"

Lucas appeared on the driver side to open the door, but Floyd quickly jammed down the lock.

Losing control of his temper now, Hank smoothly dragged Floyd out of the passenger side of the car, then gently but firmly pinned him against the side of the SUV. He was furious, but kept his tone level and low.

"That's it. You're getting the belt again. I can do it right here over the trunk of the car, or you can get in the SUV immediately and I'll do it at home. You choose."

"You wouldn't do it here," Floyd challenged. "It would be bad publicity."

"I don't see any cameras around here, do you? I'll give you three seconds to decide. One. Two."

"Home!" Floyd blurted, and Hank immediately loosened his grip.

Floyd scrambled away and fled for safety in the far back row of the giant SUV. Hank followed him and stood at the door, glaring at him while he buckled in. Once that was done, Hank slammed the door and stalked off to his car to call Taylor.

The guards said absolutely nothing, of course, and kept their eyes carefully averted away from Floyd. But it was clear what they were all thinking: they sympathized with Hank, but they also felt really sorry for Floyd, too.

Hank was finally calming down as he made his way from the spare room downstairs into the conference room, where all his guards were waiting to hear exactly what the hell was going on with their boss. He had to talk fast; the servants were due back from Eagle Rock at any moment. He looked around to confirm all nine guards were present, and then immediately launched into his explanation.

"I can't give too many details, gentlemen and lady, but the short story is that my leadership team experienced a major hiccup today and we've lost Rupert for two weeks, and Daven for a month, for disciplinary reasons. So my workload just tripled, and I'll be working 24/7 and traveling around to meetings everywhere. It's likely the Urbanes will take every chance they get to follow me around more closely, and will likely be spying a little extra on the boys as well. Not to mention all of you, in order to monitor my movements. We all need to up our game and make things seem as normal as possible until this blows over. It should hit the news tomorrow morning. Any questions?”

Avery spoke up, as he always did. He was extremely good at his job but never failed to bring up particularly painful points of discussion. Hank didn't hold it against him, though. He had never been out of line even once with his concerns.

“This is obviously going to put a lot of stress on Floyd and Theo, as well. Do you expect to spend all day in the office now, and how do you want us to handle them if they start acting out while you're not here? With all the fighting lately, it may become a problem and there might be a point where they have to be disciplined on the spot before things get too carried away.”

There was a slight uncomfortable murmur of agreement among the guards, and Hank groaned internally. Again, a painful point. More so than usual. But absolutely necessary.

“Yeah, thanks Avery for bringing that up.” Hank chuckled lightly, and the guards followed suit and relaxed a little. “The boys are...well, for those of you who haven't already heard, they were fighting in church today in front of the entire congregation. I'm sure it's going to be gleefully reported in the papers tomorrow that Hank Bancroft's bodyguards had step in to keep his sons from killing each other."

He stopped in order to gauge the reaction from the guards, who looked alternately horrified and embarrassed. Just like Hank felt, actually.

Hank took a deep breath. "Look, I'm just as uncomfortable talking about this as you are to hear it. But Avery brought up a good point. With the boys being on winter break and lacking my supervision, they could seriously hurt each other without intervention. I don't want any of you saddled with the task of disciplining them, so other than me remarrying within the next 24 hours, I'm out of ideas. Anyone?"

Everyone laughed uncomfortably.

Brittany, the new female guard, answered quickly. "You could hire a nanny for them. I have some contacts who may know-"

There was a knock on the door, and Hank said, "Sorry Brittany, one sec," then yelled "Come in."

It was Theo. "The staff is here, dad. Waiting for you to let them off the bus."

"Thanks Theo," said Hank kindly as he walked over and ruffled his son's hair. "Go ahead and let them know they can come in, but to be quiet because we're having a meeting in here."

"You aren't going to greet them at the door?"

"How about you do it for me this time? I think you'd be really good at that. Shake everyone's hand and welcome them back, just like I do. Okay?"

"Yes, sir."

"Good boy. Remember to tell them to be quiet. Go on."

Theo shut the door, and Hank turned back around to his guards.

"A nanny is not a bad idea, but it's going to take months to find one and vet her. I think for now, though, one of you is going to have to volunteer to stand in for me for the next four weeks, just to keep them in line until I get home. I'm sorry this is so damned awkward for all of us."

"What if you took one of them to work each day?" asked Avery. "The other one couldn't do much trouble if he's home alone."

Brittany spoke up again. "I think taking them out of the house will help them stop focusing on antagonizing each other. But we should take them to soup kitchens, animal shelters, et cetera. Places that need volunteers. Keep 'em busy all day and do some good. It will be good PR for you to have your boys contribute to the community. Maybe even something like Habitat for Humanity, since Theo likes to build stuff."

The guards all started talking amongst themselves while Hank thought about this option.

"But security-wise, I don't know if that's going to work," he finally responded. "Talk about making more work for you guys, which is what I was trying to avoid."

"I don't mind it," was the general consensus of the guards after several more minutes of discussion.

Then, Avery again. "Just be aware you have them in public again, though. Which means, if they start fighting again, everyone will know it."

Hank made up his mind. "Then they'll do separate things. Focus on what they like to do rather than what works for both of them. Theo can do some kind of building thing, some kind of physical labor, and Floyd can work with kids or the homeless."

Brittany put it, "Or you could just ask them what they want to do. Have them research some good causes and make their own decision about it."

Hank nodded thoughtfully. "I think that's a good idea. Keep them busy all day long, separate from each other, all the way up until dinner time. Everyone ok with that? We'll do it for a couple weeks, until they're in school again. Then back to the old program. Thanks Brittany. Anything else? No? Okay. I better go take care of Theo, then. Poor kid's been waiting all day for his reckoning. See you all in the morning, bright and early."

Hank trudged up the stairs and stopped into the spare room, where he grabbed the paddle he had just used on Floyd for disobeying him in the car (after discovering he wasn't actually wearing a belt and didn't feel like going to find one). He took it with him into his study and reluctantly hit the intercom button to summon Theo.

CHAPTER FOUR

Urbanes Headquarters

Denver, CO

"Holy. Shit. You see the paper yet, Colbert?"

Colbert paused from stirring the sugar in his tea and turned around to peer over his shoulder.

"Hell no, I'm still half asleep. What now? Oh...... *holy shit* ."

They looked at each other, grinned, then read the article in full, twice, not quite believing the implications of the news. "Let me borrow that paper for a minute. Thanks."

Colbert practically bounced into his boss's office, only to find Harmon sitting down to study the exact same article. Damn. He could never beat him to the punch on anything.

"Close the door," Harmon grumbled, "and stop acting like you just won Miss America. It's unprofessional. Sit down."

Colbert felt like a bucket of ice water had been dumped over him all of a sudden. Harmon had that effect on people, but he had never gotten used to it after all these years. No one had, really. He clenched his fists and waited in silence for his boss to finish reading the article.

"So," Harmon said as he set the paper down. "Looks like the first seeds of mistrust have been sown. That didn't take long. Have you been in contact with Yannick again?"

"No, we agreed he should go radio silent for a few days. I have no idea whether or not he actually talked to Daven, but obviously something huge has happened, and you know I don't believe in coincidences."

"And Yannick never confirmed back whether this emergency line was legit or not?"

"No."

Harmon sat back in his chair and drummed his fingers on the table. "I need to know if he spoke to Daven. If the line is still active. Just a simple yes or no will do. I want to know if this" - he jabbed a finger at the newspaper - "is our work, or if they're imploding on their own because of something else."

"I will do my best."

"Also, speaking of statements...we need to talk about Janet. I know you don't want to go there yet, but we haven't said anything publicly about her murder. Are you ready to work on it?"

"Hell yes. I mean, yes. Already on it. First things first, we have to state that we're looking into exactly why she was on Seditionists' property at the time. That's the first thing I want to know, too, but we have to wait for the FBI to do the security footage review."

Harmon said nothing, just… *tap, tap, tap.*

"The first thing people are going to say is that the Seditionists would never be stupid enough to commit murder on their own property, no matter who the victim is. They're going to be saying it's random. Or, that she was a double agent and gotten taken out by one of us. And if we address that publicly, all kinds of questions are going to come up that we can't even start to put answers to yet."

…tap, tap, tap.

"So Zane and I are meeting in a minute to put together some kind of statement, which right now is basically we are investigating the circumstances that led to this tragedy and extend our heartfelt thoughts and prayers for Janet's family and friends . As soon as she's in the ground, though, her family is going to be coming after us for answers."

...tap, tap, tap.

Colbert took a deep breath, feeling dizzy from the implications of what he was about to say next.

"And you're *really* not going to like this, since there's no point in me keeping my suspicions quiet at this point. But I think we have to seriously consider the possibility that she really *was* a double agent. I mean, it's possible when you starting thinking hard enough about it. If so...we fucked up big time, and Bancroft is going to catch on pretty fast. If he hasn't already, that is."

...tap, tap, tap.

Harmon's phone rang, and he leaned over to look at the phone display. A call from...Los Angeles?

Seditionist Headquarters, Los Angeles

Same day

Hank Bancroft stood at the espresso machine in Daven's office, trying and failing to figure out how to work the damned thing. He stopped trying when he heard Daven's assistant talking on the stairs.

"Billie!" he shouted.

Oh god, what did I do? Billie wondered in panic as she exchanged startled glances with her co-workers. She ran up the last few steps and tossed her purse down on her chair, absurdly upset that she hadn't even put lipstick on yet. Damn it.

She hurried in and looked around the office, surprised to find her boss not present. He was usually - no, always, the first one in the office.

"Oh, the espresso machine. I'll get that for you, sir." She hurried up to the machine and hoped she could remember how to do it. Hank made her terribly nervous.

"Wait, first things first. Close the door. And don't call me sir." Hank had walked away now and was staring out the windows into the ocean, just like Daven always did when he was thinking hard. There was a newspaper in his hand.

Billie froze. She had hardly ever spoken to Hank, and only a few times one-on-one when he was looking for Daven and needed her help in tracking him down. Those few times, he had always been very nice. Now...

Hank looked back and barked, "I said *close the door* . I need to talk to you."

"Uh, yes, sir. Mr. Bancroft, I mean…" She was shaking, already wondering if something terrible had happened to Daven. After shutting the door, she leaned against it, back pressing hard into it as if it could shield her from anything bad coming her way.

Hank unfolded the paper and then turned around to lay it out on the desk.

"Have you seen this yet?"

"No, sir."

"Hank."

"Hank." It sounded strange on her tongue. No one called him Hank, even when he wasn't around. Except for Rupert and Daven, of course, and Hank's assistant.

"Okay," he said, his tone softening considerably. "I'm sorry for being short with you. But I have news you need to hear immediately, before anyone else, because they're all going to come up to you for answers and gossip. And I need to make sure you are armed with a proper response."

"Is he alright?" Billie blurted before she could stop herself, the increasing fear of hearing that Daven had died overtaking her usual discretion.

Hank looked at her sideways. "Are you going to stay calm and listen to me, or-"

"Yes, sir."

Hank sighed, deciding not to worry about the 'sir' thing for the present.

"Billie, he violated a major policy and I had to suspend him. Rupert, too, but I'll talk to Ellen about him separately. It's already in the papers because I gave the government a heads-up yesterday, but we haven't made an official statement yet. Are you following?"

Billie nodded.

"Okay. People are going to start asking you questions the moment you find out. The exact statement you are going to make no matter who asks - and I mean *no matter who* - is 'I'm aware of the matter but not authorized to discuss it with anyone outside of Hank's leadership.' Repeat that, please."

"I'm aware of the matter but not authorized to discuss it with anyone outside of Hank's leadership team. Can I say Mr. Bancroft, though?"

"Yes, of course. Repeat it one more time."

Billie did, and he had her repeat it again for good measure. She was much calmer now.

"Okay. I want you to keep doing your job as if Daven was still here, but per the terms of our charter he is not allowed to contact anyone in the party until January 25. He will not contact you, and you're not to contact him. For any reason, I don't care what it is. Same goes with Rupert, although he'll be back on January 11. If you have any questions, ask me."

Billie swallowed hard. "I do have a question, sir. What did Daven do?"

She had a right to know, Hank knew, even as he hesitated. More so than probably anyone else who didn't already know.

"This stays between us. He missed a few calls to the emergency line, and then spoke to an unverified asset, all of which ended up causing a shit show that we're going to spend the few next months cleaning up. Rupert also spoke to the same unverified caller. I really don't know what got into either of them, but all I can say is this happened at my Christmas party, and you know what that was like."

The vast amount of alcohol and good cheer could have clouded their judgment, he meant. Daven didn't drink, as they both knew, but she let it be.

"Yes. I see what you mean. When are we going to make an official statement?"

"In a few hours." Hank was speaking to her much more kindly now, and he regretted having been so rude to her earlier. "Look, I know how much you care about Daven, and vice versa. Just know I had absolutely no choice but to suspend them. They're lucky they weren't fired on the spot. It sucks, but we can't fall apart over this. Our constituents will depend on us to keep on going, business as usual."

Billie nodded, her expression determined and calm. "Ellen is most likely here by now. You should go talk to her right away."

Hank laughed; in two minutes Billie had gone from being petrified and calling him sir, to outright ordering him around. Learning fast.

"Yes ma'am," Hank said with a cheeky grin as he sprang up to open the door for her.

Billie almost died from embarrassment for a few minutes. But then she went in the bathroom to put on her lipstick, and cried her heart out for Daven.

After speaking to Ellen, who didn't take the news as hard as Billie had, Hank locked himself in his office and stared at all the papers Rupert and Daven had left on his desk for him.

The resignation letters, in particular. He should have accepted them. Anyone else would. Why didn't he?

Fuck.

He shoved them aside, then picked up the phone make a very difficult call.

Urbane Headquarters - Denver

"Hank *Bancroft*?" asked Harmon, a bit stunned.

"Yes, it's me. Don't act so surprised, we just talked like a week ago. I need a minute. Are you alone?"

Harmon looked up at Colbert, who shook his head. "Actually, no. I have Colbert with me. Just the two of us. Would you like me to send him out?"

"No. You're going to tell him what I have to say, anyway. Listen, I'm sure you've seen our little fiasco in the papers this morning, but that's not what I'm calling about."

"Okay. Then what-"

"The murder in Colorado on Christmas morning. It took place on Seditionists property, as you know. I want to review the surveillance footage as soon as possible, but I'm being told the FBI is going to give it to you first, and that you will then hand it over to us *at your leisure.*"

"Yes, of course. Our investigation should come first. She was *our* employee." Harmon was staring in confusion and alarm at Colbert, who shrugged back at him.

"I know that. If you're willing, however, the FBI will release copies to us both at the same time once they're done reviewing. You have to grant permission for that, so I'm faxing you the letter to sign and send over to us."
Sure enough, they immediately heard the *beep! OOOEEEEEE! WEOWEOWEOWEO!* of the fax machine under the desk.

Harmon shook his head at Hank's bravado, then remembered Hank was actually on the phone and couldn't see the gesture. So he waited in annoyance for the fax machine to finish its ministrations before speaking again.

"And why would I want to do that, Hank?"

"Because a woman was murdered and it's only fair we both launch our investigations at the same time to get it resolved as quickly as possible and figure out who did this for the benefit of her family. I'm willing to take the fall for it if it was one of mine. And you should be equally willing if it was one of yours."

"So this is basically a PR move."

"Not my main aim, but yes, that too. Look, Harmon, I've got a lot of shit going on right now and have lost my two closest allies literally overnight. I have no ulterior motive here but to get this murder investigation going quickly. But since you're resisting, I'm going to make a very clear threat, and I don't care who knows about it. Hell, I'll tell the world myself. If you don't sign the form, I will personally inform Janet's family that you are not cooperating with the investigation by allowing us to immediately review the tapes to help identify her murderer, which could very well be someone from my own damned party. More likely yours, but that's not the point. Up to you where we go from here. I mean, I wouldn't want anyone to think you're *hiding* something. Do you?"

Checkmate. *Fuck*. Hank was a master. And really, Harmon had already known he was going to lose this battle as soon as it had begun. When Bancroft set his mind to something, he usually got it.

No. *Always* got it.

"I don't have the tapes yet, Hank. But when I do, I'll sign the form."

"No, you'll sign it now. I heard it come in, so I expect it back by end of the day, which means 5pm. Your time zone or mine, I don't care which."

Click.

Colbert didn't want to look at Harmon for fear of seeing him implode on the spot.

But Harmon said nothing. Just...*tap, tap, tap...*

CHAPTER FIVE

Hank Bancroft, leader of the Seditionists Party, confirmed today that he has placed two of his top executives on temporary unpaid leave per standard procedure. On December 26, Daven Johansson, Chief Strategist; and Rupert Aster, SVP Public Relations, reported to Mr. Bancroft that they had inadvertently violated an unspecified internal communications protocol for two phone calls made on December 24 and 25. As the communications involved non-strategic and public knowledge, the executives were allowed to remain after agreeing to a re-training program and reduction in salary. The Seditionists have always held all employees to rigid but fair standards and will continue to do so in the future.

Hank had spent at least two hours staring at the statement Rupert sent him for approval. He hated that it wasn't the truth. Transparency was one of his biggest obsessions, but it wasn't always possible. It felt wrong, but there was no one he truly trusted to bounce it off of for a second opinion. Or third, rather.

Except for Daven. Hank had been resisting the urge to call him all morning long. He missed his right hand man more than he would ever dare to admit. But he was giving in, against his will. Slowly.

Half an hour later, the battle was lost. He picked up the phone and quickly dialed the number that had always been so familiar and comforting. And strangely it still was, despite the circumstances.

"Hello Hank," replied the gruff, sleepy voice. Hank had woken him up. At 11am. That was strange.

"Hey, Dav. You awake? Do you have a minute?"

"Yes, and yes." He sounded wary and suspicious.

"I don't want to fight. Our media statement is due in an hour and I'm really not happy with it. Need your thoughts, if you're willing."

"Of course."

Hank read the statement to him, only realizing afterwards that part of it would be surprising and unhappy news for Daven. He hadn't meant to tell him this way, but it was too late now.

"Shit…we haven't talked about some of this yet. The salary and the re-training parts. I should have told you first."

Pause. "That would have been a better way, yes."

"Sorry. I wasn't thinking. If you're really not okay with this in any way, tell me now."

"Do I have a choice?" replied Daven coolly.

Hank cleared his throat, a bit unsettled by his own thoughtlessness and Daven's edgy replies. It was very unlike him, but Hank probably deserved it.

"Ok. I'm truly sorry, I'm an idiot. But let's stay on topic. What do you think about the statement?"

"Let's just say I completely understand why you're not comfortable with it. Too much spin."

"Yeah. But Rupert thinks we're exposing ourselves to some seriously bad press if we don't spin this enough. He's still pissed about my edits to the last release."

Daven asked Hank to read it again, so he did. Then Daven replied, "Rupert's right, though. You can't tell the whole truth all the time."

Hank couldn't stop himself from firing a bitter shot across Daven's bow . "Yeah. You've had a lot of experience with that one lately, huh?"

Silence from Daven. Hank didn't feel bad about the jibe. At all. There were more where that came from.

"Look," he continued after a moment, "I just can't put this statement out and then sit there through interviews repeating these outright lies. You guys may have no problem with it, but I have a conscience. It's not right, and it's not sustainable.

Daven still said nothing,

"You still there?"

"Yeah. It's funny that you're worried so much about transparency and honesty when you can't even bother to just say how you really feel, instead of hiding behind all this passive aggressive commentary. It's blatantly hypocritical, don't you think?"

Hank was so surprised at this blistering broadside that he actually thought he hadn't heard the man correctly. It took a minute for his brain to process the words and understand their meaning. Such open hostility had never passed between them before. Anger, yes, but nothing even remotely close to this. It hurt.

"You don't want to know how I really feel, Dav," was all he could say. A horribly weak response.

"You're correct, I don't. So let's get back on topic, as you said, and revise this statement so I can go back to bed. I have a suggestion on how to start it off…"

Harmon jumped as his fax machine started whirring and beeping again, and it seemed to take an eternity for the paper to spit itself out. He breathed a deep sigh of relief when he recognized Umber's number as the sender. It was a copy of an unusually lengthy press release from the Seditionists, with a handwritten note on the top.

King Hank the Oversharer strikes again! Game changer.

BREAKING NEWS! Hank Bancroft, leader of the Seditionists Party, confirmed today that he has suspended his two top executives. The official statement is below:

On December 26, Daven Johansson, Chief Strategist; and Rupert Aster, SVP Public Relations, reported themselves to Hank Bancroft, Party Leader, upon realizing they had each violated a critical internal communications policy during separate but related phone calls that took place on December 24 and 25. The executives immediately offered their resignations, which were ultimately not accepted due to mitigating circumstances, and were placed on disciplinary leave for 30 and 15 days, respectively. In addition, Mr. Johansson and Mr. Aster were obliged to agree to an intensive re-training program, permanent reduction in salary, and one-time forfeiture of bonus pay. The Seditionists have always held all employees to rigid but fair standards regardless of position or tenure, and will continue to do so in the future.

He smiled to himself. Hank had to approve that, so he could take it for granted that every single word of the oversharing masterpiece was the truth. But that didn't meant it was the whole story, either. December 24 and 25. So Yannick must have reached either one or both of them through the emergency line, and whatever they did about it (or didn't do) seems to have pissed Hank off royally. Especially Daven, apparently. And Hank hit them really hard in the wallet, too. Ouch.

So they were rattled, then. That was good. Very good.

But it wasn't a game changer. Yet.

CHAPTER SIX

As soon as the press release was out, Hank called Floyd to let him know he was ready to take him for his driving test.

"Where are you guys right now?" he asked tiredly.

"At the animal shelter but we're ready to go."

"Which animal shelter?" Hank asked, embarrassed that he had lost track of his kids. He had no idea where Theo was at all, come to think of it.

"The Santa Monica Humane Society. It's like ten blocks from the DMV."

"Okay. I'll call my driver now and meet you there at 1pm."

Floyd replied, "No, you took the Thunderbird to work so you have to drive it here."

"Oh yeah." Hank rubbed his temples. God, this headache.

"And did you remember to buy Shane lunch?"

Hank paused, completely puzzled by the unexpected question. "Did I what?"

"Buy Shane lunch. Yesterday on the phone, you said you would. Because you forgot about him."

Shit. Hank would have remembered on any other day, or made certain to send himself a reminder. He hated how scatterbrained he was feeling lately.

"Floyd, I'm going to have to hire you as my secretary if you keep this up."

Floyd laughed a little, not sure if it was a joke or not. "I don't think you could pay me enough for that," he replied carefully, hoping the humor wouldn't miss the mark.

Hank laughed, surprising even himself. It was amazing how nice it felt to laugh again. Without Dav and Rupert in the office to keep him constantly entertained, the day had felt like the world's longest funeral so far, and it was only noon.

"Probably not. I'll go see Shane now, then drive the Thunderbird to the DMV. See you soon. I love you, Floyd."

"Love you too, dad."

Hank had Vance drive the Thunderbird while he followed as a passenger in the SUV, stretched out in the back seat. It was nice to be able to indulge for once and hide behind the tinted windows, especially knowing full well the press statement was making its rounds and things were about to get out of control. The last vestiges of peace, and all that.

Of course word had gotten out that Floyd was taking his test today, so the parking lot at the DMV was filled with eager paparazzi who had become so emboldened over time that they openly stood there with their huge cameras and kept each other updated on Hank's movements. Driving a noisy old Thunderbird around town wasn't exactly the most discreet mode of transportation, and everyone got really excited when they heard it coming.

Groaning, Hank slumped even further into the seat and watched carefully as they meandered through the lot to see if the photographers were out for blood after having read the press release. It wasn't clear if they knew, though. Everything seemed normal. No one was overly excited, so maybe they hadn't seen it yet. Good.

Lucas pulled up to Avery's SUV so that the two identical cars were nearly touching, and Floyd rolled down the window to talk to his dad.

"You ready, Floyd? Big day, but you've got this," said Hank encouragingly.

"No. What are all these people doing here? I can't...I don't want to."

"It's okay. They want to see you succeed, too. Don't be afraid."

Floyd quickly clambered out the window and across the gap into the other car, flopping into Hank's lap before he could stop him. Not that he wanted to stop him, of course, but it wasn't exactly a dignified motion. The Thunderbird was parked directly in front of them and already surrounded by cameras being held by disappointed photographers. Nobody wanted pictures of the random driver. They wanted to see the Bancrofts.

Floyd was petrified at the sight of all the cameras clamoring for a shot of him, but Hank had expected them. The party's leader's son getting his driver's license was a big deal in the paparazzi world. Mostly because they wanted to be the first ones to know if Floyd failed, so they could gleefully spread the word. And Floyd knew it.

"Dad. Let's go home."

Hank shifted himself to a comfortable position and held his son like he was a small child, offering the kind of comfort that most boys stopped needing when they turned Theody's age. Neither of his sons were cuddlers at any age, so these moments were few and far between, and a lump soon appeared in Hank's throat that made it difficult to say anything for the moment.

"I don't want my license," Floyd said a few minutes later, his anxiety increasing to levels that would soon be uncontrollable if Hank didn't act fast. "Please. Can we just go home?"

"No. I know that you're afraid of failing, but that's life. We have to take chances or we'll never grow. I'm going to give you a few more minutes to get yourself together, and then we're getting out together so you can do your test."

"But dad, they're going to follow me around the whole time! It's not fair. Why can't we just be normal and do things like this without the whole world wanting to watch and waiting for us to make a mistake?"

Hank didn't know what to say. Floyd had never complained before about being in the spotlight, so this was new. Stage fright, as it were. But then again, the spotlight had never focused on him alone before. And one thing was certain: Floyd was right; they would follow him around and be watching for him to fail. And no, it wasn't fair at all.

"Okay, Floyd. Let me up. I'm going to go talk to them."

"Too late. There's like a dozen people out there and now more are coming." Floyd was looking backwards over Hank's shoulder at the entrance to the parking lot.

"Avery!" Hank yelled at the other car. "Go block the driveway, please. I don't want anyone else coming in here."

"It's a public parking lot," Avery replied, puzzled at the request. "We can't just go-"

"Don't care. Block it anyway."

"Yes, boss. But we're going to get the police called on us."

"I'm sure we will. Go."

Hank watched as Avery drove off and positioned the ponderous piece of machinery directly across the gate to the parking lot, effectively cutting off all cars from entering. Thankfully, the exit was separate and one-way, but he still fully expected to get completely trashed by the press in the next day's papers for abusing his powers to make the lives of his constituents that much harder.

"Floyd, get off my lap. Come on."

"No."

Hank shoved him off, then exited out the driver's side back door. The cameras went completely nuts; there were about 20 photographers now. Hank stayed still to let them take pictures, and then he raised a hand. Everyone fell completely silent and attentive, as expected. He could never deny that it was nice to have that kind of power.

"Gentlemen. My son is here to take a driving test, and frankly, you're scaring the hell out of him. He's fifteen years old and has way too much pressure on him already. Now, he is going to get out of this SUV in a moment and get into that Thunderbird, and drive away with the instructor. Every single one of you who walks away right now without taking a single picture or leaving this parking lot until he gets back will receive a personal invitation from me to attend a press conference today at 4pm. Front and second row seats. Trust me, it's one you don't want to miss."

He turned around and pulled open the door as the men all murmured excitedly among themselves.

"Dad...no."

"It's alright, son. Come out. I've got you." He kept his voice loud enough so the photographers could hear him and hopefully have enough sympathy to keep their damned cameras from snapping every 2 seconds.

"No." Floyd moved away into the back row, out of Hank's reach. There was nothing Hank could do but drag him out, and he wasn't about to do that in front of the entire world. He had to think of something, fast, before they became a laughingstock. He turned back to the photographers.

"Alright, new plan. Everyone who wants to go to the presser needs to set down their cameras down on the ground - right here in front of me - and get back in their cars and stay put. This kid is not coming out until you do that, trust me. So either you get no pictures at all, or you get no pictures and an invitation. Your choice."

There was hesitation, and for one frightful moment Hank thought they were going to refuse en-masse. That would have been extremely embarrassing considering his position. But then...one man set his camera down, and that was all it took. The rest quickly followed, but then they all just stood there, looking dumbfounded.

"Into your cars, gentlemen," Hank snapped authoritatively. "Quickly, if you please. I'll let you know when you can get back out."

They turned away. Hank was keeping a careful eye on Avery's SUV; a line of cars was piling up to get in the lot and all the horns were starting to attract way too much attention to the group.

Hank poked his head back into the car.

"Floyd. *Out*. Right now. Your instructor is here and doesn't have all day."

"I'm scared," he said in a small voice, looking about 8 years old all of a sudden.

"No need. Nobody's going to follow you. I have all their cameras right here. Look. You got to go now, before more show up."

"I know, but..." He seemed about to refuse for good, then suddenly got a spurt of bravado and jumped out of the car. Hank looked around. There was a small crowd, but no one was taking photos. He pulled Floyd into a tight hug and then sent him off with a pat on the shoulder.

"If you don't pass, it's not the end of the world. Just do your best. Good luck."

"Thanks," said Floyd as he climbed into the driver's side. Then they were gone, and Hank let out the breath he'd been holding as he walked over to Vance.

"Nice one, boss," the man said with a huge smile.

"Yeah. Except now I got to invite these idiots to the office." His attention broke away as a man who obviously worked for the DMV came towards the group. All three guards jumped out of the SUV and went to Hank's side.

"Can I help you?" Lucas asked the man rudely, but Hank shushed him.

"I'm sorry we're blocking the driveway," Hank said apologetically. "We'll get him moved right away."

"Thank you, Mr. Bancroft, but I didn't come out here for that."

"Oh? How may I help you, then?"

"Just need to collect the $115 for your son's driving test. It was supposed to be paid over the phone ahead of time, but we can do it here." He held up a bulky credit card reader machine.

Hank flushed ten shades of red as he pulled out his wallet. "Of course. My apologies."

"No worries." The man worked busily at his task while Hank waited patiently. His guards all suddenly turned away, and Hank could see their shoulders quivering with laughter.

When it was done and Hank signed the receipt, he shook the man's hand and made some cheerful small talk, then promised again to move the SUV. The guards then pulled themselves together and were able to look at Hank again without cracking up.

Hank crossed his arms and glared at them. "Stand at attention. I ought to fire the lot of you right here and now. If he had pulled out a gun and held it to my head, no one would have noticed because you were too busy giggling like girls at a slumber party. Totally unprofessional. You're all docked today's pay. Fall out."

He turned away, waved to Avery to move out of the driveway, and climbed back in the SUV. He was furious at his guards, yes, but also at himself for being unable to see the humor in the situation. In the past, he would have been the one laughing the hardest. He had never docked any guard's pay before, either, and already regretted doing it.

God damn you, Daven.

His phone rang very loud in the silent car. The guards hadn't gotten back in yet, and he was glad for it.

"What's up, Taylor?"

"Shit's starting to hit the fan, boss. Your phone hasn't stopped ringing for the past twenty minutes or so. We're all going nuts here."

"I'm sure. Everything set for the 4pm presser?"

"Yeah. Who are we letting in?" Taylor was rapidly pounding on her keyboard.

"Got about twenty photographers in mind, so reserve the first two rows for them. I'll give you their names shortly. Open up the rest of the auditorium to first come, first serve."

"We did that once and people trampled each other trying to get in. You said we'd never do it again."

Hank shrugged. "These are new days, Taylor."

"I think it's a really bad idea, Hank. And it's my job to tell you when I think you have a bad idea."

"Noted. Then give them a numbered card as they pull in the parking lot. Once we reach one hundred, every single car after that gets turned away, period."

"But then we can't control who we're letting in and the room could end up dominated by Urbanes. And the questions you're going to get…"

Hank didn't feel like fighting about this. "They have a press card, they can come in. End of story. Last thing: I don't want any of the questions to be plants. I'm not going to let it be said that we packed the room with our own people in order to avoid uncomfortable questions. Are you going to argue about that, too?"

"No."

"Good. Get this info out on the wires ASAP."

"Okay, boss. It's your show."

"Yes it is. Thank you for remembering that."

He hung up the phone, his irritation with himself increasing by the second, and sat in the car for twenty more minutes, leaning back against the headrest with his eyes closed in order to help stave off the horrific headache that was growing worse in proportion to the number of things he began worrying about.

Hank desperately wanted to talk to Daven. But he also never wanted to talk to him again. He picked up his phone, hoping to see a missed call from the man. Nothing. Of course. Maybe he was still asleep, and would call when he woke up.

Avery poked his head inside the car, jerking Hank out of his very dark thoughts.

"They're coming back, sir."

Hank got out of the car and waited as the Thunderbird pulled up to his feet and parked. As he crossed in front of it Floyd leaned on the horn, startling him out of his wits. Floyd's favorite prank. Hank should have known better.

He broke into a huge grin. "Hey bud. Thanks for the heart attack. How'd you do?"

"I passed, dad!"

"Awesome!" They hugged, and Hank shook the instructor's hand.

"He was flawless, Mr. Bancroft. Not a single point off."

"Good. Hop in with Avery, Floyd. We'll celebrate tonight."

Then, to Lucas. "We'll drive away first with Avery, and Vance can take the Thunderbird. Can you walk around and get the business cards from these guys, and tell them to come retrieve their cameras? Then call Taylor ASAP and give her all the names and numbers from the cards."

"Yes, sir."

"Thank you."

Lucas said quickly, "Sir, I'm really sorry about what happened. We all feel pretty terrible about it."

"Good. That means it won't happen again, then."

Lucas nodded and headed towards the cameras. Hank pulled out his phone, turned the ringer off, and put it back in his pocket as he climbed in beside Floyd.

"Want to swing through Dairy Queen on the way home?"

"Yeah!"

"Avery-"

"This car doesn't fit in their drive-thru, boss. We can hit the Shake Shack, though."

"Shake Shack it is, then. Tell me about the test, Floyd."

His son was beaming up at him, chatting away excitedly, and Hank slid his arm around him and relaxed into the seat.

Floyd was happy, and nothing else mattered right now.

CHAPTER SEVEN

Hank was well aware he should return to the office sooner than he was planning to, but there was no use in rushing back just to sit as his desk alone and be depressed again. But he did need to make Floyd pause for breath for a moment while he made a quick call.

"Hey Taylor. Can you check my fax machine and see if…" he looked at Floyd, knowing he would likely be highly disturbed by any mention of Harmon. "You know, that fax we are expecting by 5pm. Has it arrived yet?"

"One sec."

Hank patted Floyd's leg. "You ate that fast," he said, indicating the double waffle cone that was now dripping all over the place. "Going to have a sugar rush."

"So are you."

"Ha. True." Hank had been so distracted by Floyd's chatter that he didn't notice (or taste) the root beer float he had inhaled in the short time it took to get back to the house. There was a Federal Express truck out front. It must be delivering

Daven's memo. Was he home now, or was he visiting Rupert? *Of course he was home. Where else would he be, anyway? It's not like he had any friends.* Except for Rupert. *You know, because he's literally given up his entire life to work for you.* They could be together right now, talking about him. Saying who knows what?

Maybe even agreeing they don't want to come back to work for me.

"Hank? Hank?" prompted Taylor into his ear.

"Oh. Sorry, bit of a bad connection."

"Nothing yet."

"What?" He'd actually forgotten what he called her about, to his chagrin.

"The fax. I can hear you fine, by the way. I think we should move the press conference to 5pm."

"Why?" Hank asked in a quizzical tone.

"Because that's how long you gave Harmon to respond to the fax. What if he doesn't do it until 4:59pm? Then you've lost a prime opportunity to put some serious pressure on him."

Hank smiled. "This is why you're my right hand man, Taylor."

"Only for now. So that's a yes?"

"Yes," Hank replied, swallowing hard at the jibe. He had always thought of Taylor that way. Maybe he should tell people how he felt about them more often. "Move it and announce it ASAP. Thanks kiddo. You're doing a great job. See you in a bit." He hung up and turned to his son.

"Floyd, do me a favor. Pull the Thunderbird into the garage. I'll take the SUV back to work. Come to think of it...I think I heard a rattle, so you may need to drive it around the block a few times first just to make sure it's running okay."

"A rattle? From where?" Floyd was instantly concerned, but then he saw the mischievous sparkle in his dad's eye and he grinned. "Right. I'll make sure to check it out. Drive it around for a while."

"Ten minutes should do the trick," said Hank firmly. "Absolutely no main streets. *Ten minutes*, tops."

He handed the keys to his delighted son, then hopped out and walked around to Avery's window.

"Follow Floyd around, then come back and get me. I gave him ten minutes, and if he goes on a main street let me know so I can kill him when he gets home."

"Got it, boss."

Hank patted the window frame, then walked up to the house to intercept the FedEx delivery man at the front door, even though his butler was already there to take the delivery.

"I got this, Maurice. Thanks."

He signed for the envelope and then took it into his study. It had to be the report that Daven had sent him yesterday to prove he and Rupert were reporting themselves voluntarily and not as a result of Shane's findings. Hank hadn't yet read the copy of the memo yet, so this was a new, fresh wound that he didn't want to reopen already.

Re-open? Actually, it was still gaping wide. It might never *not* be fresh. There might never be enough healing. The scars would never fade, if they ever formed at all.

God help me...

He didn't have the courage to open it yet and threw the entire unopened envelope into his locking drawer. Then he picked up his secure phone line - the one that nobody could trace back to his home - and started dialing.

Urbanes Headquarters, Denver

"Sir, I have a call for you from Shot One," announced the receptionist quietly over the secure intercom line.

Harmon's head jerked up from the new dress code policy he had been approving. Or rather, not approving. Dealing with any amount of HR nonsense made him feel slightly homicidal. Even enough that a call from his main rival was a welcome distraction.

"Send Colbert in here first, then put it through."

His right hand man arrived and locked the door, then they both took deep breaths and sat down.

"Hello, Hank. Just for transparency's sake, I want to let you know Colbert is with me again."

"Good afternoon to you both. I'm told we haven't received your fax yet."

"Yeah. It's not 5pm. Impatient, are we? Makes me wonder why."

Hank smiled to himself as he picked up a framed photo of himself and Daven at Crater Lake. That was a fun trip, although all the water-skiing had taken a toll on his knees that he hadn't quite recovered from yet. And Daven…he had gotten all drunk and giggly from just two cans of beer and then insisted on busting out the karaoke machine. Rupert was never going to let him forget it for as long as they all lived.

"Not impatient at all," Hank responded pleasantly. "Just concerned that it didn't come through. We're moments away from announcing a press conference at 5pm Pacific, and questions about Janet might come up. I'm just hoping by then to have some guidance on what you would like me to say about the matter, just to ensure we are on the same page."

In other words: *send me the fax, you fucker, or I'll throw you under the bus faster than you can say 'constituent mutiny.'*

"I see," Harmon responded slowly. Tap. "Is this a live broadcast, then?"

"Yes, with a press audience. Your reporters are welcome. There will be a Q&A. I'm really looking forward to being able to say whatever I want, since Rupert isn't around to dictate my every word and slap my hand for saying too much. You know how I can be sometimes."

Tap. Tap. "Silly me. For a moment I thought you were making another threat. Obviously I'm completely wrong, because you would never stoop so low. I would very much appreciate the opportunity to be educated on what your motives are right now, if you would be so kind. Just to 'ensure we are on the same page,' as you said."

"Allow me to offer my apologies," Hank responded politely. "It appears I'm the one who is jumping to conclusions this time by thinking you're trying to somehow slow down the speed of the investigation. I would also appreciate the opportunity to be educated on *your* motives. You know I've always valued the chance to learn something new from you, as rare as that may be."

God damn, breathed Colbert as he eyed his boss warily. How the hell did Hank Bancroft even manage to walk around with balls that size? If he didn't hate him so much, he would admire him.

"Apology accepted, Hank," Harmon responded coolly, after he had taken a moment to gather his wits. "As planned, the fax will come to you at 3pm when my secretary returns from lunch."

"Oh she's already back, I just talked to her. Nice girl, seems efficient. I'm sure she can take care of this for you in no time."

Harmon looked about ready to implode, but he kept his tone even. "Thank you for letting me know. But again, as I said, you will receive a fax at 3pm. Oh, and please extend my congratulations to your son for passing his driving test. We were all rooting for him, you know, even if he does misbehave in church. I'm certain he was properly disciplined and it won't happen again. Goodbye, Hank."

Click. Harmon slammed down the phone and then looked up at Colbert with a dangerous gleam in his eye.

"That fucker! I swear to god, if I ever win an argument with him I might just have a stroke from the shock of it. What do you think he's really up to?"

"I told you. I think Janet was a double agent and he's catching on. And now, after this…I'm almost sure of it."

"*Almost sure* ? No such thing. You're either sure, or you're not. Can't have it both ways."

Colbert said nothing. Once Harmon began to fight about semantics, he was too rattled to reason with any further. Anyone who had brains dared not argue with him under such circumstances.

Tap. Tap. Tap.

Slowly We Rise

The Different Stroke

CHAPTER ONE

BANCROFT HOUSEHOLD

Hank stared at the phone in disbelief for a moment, then took a few deep breaths to calm himself. There was no need to panic; there were a ton of people at the DMV, and by Floyd's glee when he got out of the car only an idiot would be unable to deduce that he had passed the test. And there were dozens upon dozens of people at church who saw Floyd and Theo bickering. Even if no one there was directly connected to Harmon...

No, stop being paranoid. I can barely take a piss without it being reported in the papers the next day.

It was okay.

If not, it would be okay.

Everything had to be okay, because he didn't know what to do if it wasn't.

His heart dropped when he saw an incoming call from Avery.

"What's up, you guys okay?"

Avery sounded embarrassed. "We're okay, but Floyd saw Daven's truck in his driveway and pulled in behind it. He got up to the front door before I could figure out a reason to stop him."

Hank had to almost restrain himself from throwing the phone to the ground in frustration.

"I see. Guessing he wants to tell his Uncle Dav he just got his license. What's he doing?"

"Yes, telling him about the license. I'm with them on the porch. Now Floyd is asking why he's not at work." Avery's voice was very low, he must be standing within a few feet of them.

"Fuck me…I should have thought of that. I'm sorry." At least it was an enclosed porch and no one could take pictures of them. "If it gets awkward, go up and tell him his dad wants him home right away. Be nice, don't give anything away. I haven't told him anything."

"Yes, sir. See you soon."

"You sick, Uncle Dav? If you need some DayQuil or something, we have some at the house."

"No, it's okay, Floyd. Thanks, though."

"Are you growing a beard..?"

Daven smiled. "I was going to because I've never had one before, but it's all scratchy and itchy. Definitely not for me. I don't know how your dad can stand it."

He caught a glance at Avery as the man hung up the phone. There was absolutely no need to explain the look he threw him; they knew each other so well that speech was usually unnecessary for communication.

Daven's ruffled Floyd's hair, then nodded at Avery. "I think your dad wants you home."

Avery nodded. "He does, Floyd. I'm sorry. He's got to go back to work now."

"Come here. Hug," said Daven as he held out his arms. "I'm so proud of you, Floyd-o." He held him much tighter than usual, longer than he normally did, and when they parted his eyes were maybe a little wet.

"Uncle Dav, I...are you sure you're okay? I know Dad hasn't been very nice to you. He's been really bent out of shape la-"

"Let's go, Floyd," said Avery firmly. "Time's up."

"Wait a minute," Floyd responded without looking at him, and quite rudely. Avery blinked; Floyd had never defied him before. "Can I come in and pet Shannon?" Daven's golden retriever, much beloved by the Bancroft family, especially Theo.

Avery stepped forward and put his hand on Floyd's shoulder, and Floyd shook it off as if were a wasp with the stinger deployed. "I said wait!" he shrieked, and Daven stepped in at this point.

"*Floyd* . You got to go. Shannon will be here when you return. She's asleep now, anyway."

Two sudden loud barks from within the house immediately refuted this declaration, and Floyd's expression fell as he realized he wasn't welcome.

"Okay. I get it. Sorry I bothered you." He turned away dejectedly, and Avery placed a hand on his shoulder.

"Don't touch me!" Floyd shrieked again as he violently slapped the man's hand away, shoved him, and hurried off.

Avery turned and looked at his friend with a shocked and apologetic expression.

"It's okay, Avery, not your fault," Daven offered quickly, his voice rougher than usual.

"I'm so sorry about all this, Daven. I really am. I'm sure Hank will come around and we'll get back to normal soon."

"Thanks, but I would advise you not to share that opinion with anyone else. If Hank learns you're sympathetic to me, well…it won't be pretty. You can pretend you hate me, it's ok."

"I don't, and I never will. And I'm sure of that without even knowing what's going on. See you soon, Daven."

"Later, crocodile."

"Alligator."

"What?"

"It's later, *alligator*. In a while, crocodile."

"Oh. Noted." Daven's demeanor was serene, but Avery could swear he detected a trace of sudden amusement as Daven's attention was diverted to the driveway. "Oh, look. There goes Floyd, you better catch him."

Avery cursed as Floyd started up the Thunderbird and peeled out across Daven's beautiful front lawn. Then he jumped into SUV and put the pedal to the metal, but he had the courtesy to back up into the street first instead of tearing up the grass. He tailed Floyd closely all the way home, intercepted him in the garage, then took an inescapable grip on the boy's arm and marched him into the house.

Hank lasted all of five minutes after the call before he gave in and tore into the envelope Daven had sent. There was a handwritten note paper-clipped on the top, in Daven's neat handwriting.

Hank -

I realize that by the time you read this, our friendship will have come to an end - even if our work partnership doesn't. If you fired me, it was likely a bitter and painful conversation that I rightfully deserved, and you should feel no guilt or shame in enacting that resolution. My deepest regret is that my actions were wholly inexcusable and forced you into an impossible situation. Regardless of what you may think of me now, or whether I am to retain the honor of being your employee, please know that I believe in you 100% and will continue to fight for what we have always believed in....even if I have to do it alone.

Daven

PS

Please shred this note after reading.

Hank threw the letter down on the desk and wiped his eyes, fighting back anger and sadness and an overwhelming desire to forgive and forget and throttle and yell and apologize and..

God damn you, Daven.

There was a loud thump and a few whirs from the back wall of his office indicating that the garage door was opening. *Not now. Has it been ten minutes already? I'm losing track of time. I'm losing track of everything.*

Was it even still Monday? It felt like weeks had passed since his confrontation with his best friend less than 24 hours ago. He could still hide in his study for a little while, anyway. It was only 2:30pm and Avery knew never to bother him, that he would come out only when he was ready. Avery would just have to wait patiently, and allow more than enough time for Hank to pull himself together.

Except that today was different. There was a firm knock on his study door.

"It's Avery. May I speak with you, please?"

Hank looked up in confusion. Avery had never once knocked on his study door before. Nobody ever had, come to think of it.

"What is it?"

"I have Floyd with me, and we have a situation."

Good god. What else could possibly go wrong with this shit show of a week?

"Come in," he answered resignedly, his annoyance turning to shock as he saw the obviously strong grip Avery had on his son.

"Stand still," growled Avery as he released Floyd. Again, Hank was shocked. His guards were not authorized to handle his children in this manner, period, so what he was seeing definitely raised his hackles.

"What's going on?" he asked in a neutral tone, eyeing Floyd's defiant expression and trying not to jump to conclusions. Whatever Avery did, it was unfailingly for a very good reason.

Avery spoke calmly and without inflection. "Floyd fought me as I tried to lead him away from Daven, then drove across his lawn and tore it up...and then proceeded to drive along Olympic Avenue for five minutes before I forced him to turn around and come back."

"I'm sorry, but....is this a joke?" Hank asked after an extremely long and uncomfortable silence.

"No, sir," replied Avery, just as tense. "Several paparazzi were parked in front of Daven's, but they didn't follow us as far as I know."

"Oh, I'm sure they saw the whole damned thing," Hank said between his teeth. Floyd was dead. *So dead.*

Another long silence, and then Floyd blurted out, "Why aren't I allowed to talk to Uncle Dav all of a sudden? What did I do? Or what did he do?"

Hank was quite literally speechless for a few seconds, and then he responded coolly, "Don't change the subject. Did you really do what Avery has just described?"

"Yes," Floyd replied immediately. "Because he wouldn't let me talk to him, and then he grabbed me and-"

"I didn't grab him, sir. I barely put my hand on his shoulder to guide him away, and he shoved me and ran off."

"*Shoved*? I barely even touched you-"

"Alright, stop. Both of you." Hank felt like his head was going to implode and explode at the same time, not that such a thing was possible. "Floyd, stay here. Avery, come with me for a moment."

Hank stalked out of the study with Avery close on his heels, and they went into the kitchen.

"Avery, for god's sake. What the hell is this?"

"Exactly what I said, sir. No exaggeration. If anything, I'm downplaying it. And he tried to get away from me again when we got back, that's why I was holding on to him." He stared back at Hank unblinkingly. Undefiantly. Unemotionally. "Can I speak freely?" he added after a moment.

"Yes."

"Don't be mad at me, because it has to be said. You know how deeply he's attached to Daven. I don't want to be in the middle again if you're going to keep them apart. He hates me right now, and we can't have that long-term. Just my two cents, Hank."

And you're exactly right, Hank mused, even as he acknowledged to himself (again) that he was irked about Floyd idolizing Daven so much.

"I hear you, Avery. Thank you. You said Floyd fought you? Explain exactly what happened, please. Every detail. And please know that I'm not upset with you."

Floyd was gone when Hank returned back to the study a few minutes later.

Yep. Dead. Even more dead now, if possible.

He rubbed his temples for a minute or two, talked soothingly out loud to keep himself from screaming, and then looked around his desk. The memo from Daven was still inside the FedEx envelope untouched, but the handwritten letter was in a different position than where he left it. And it was face up. He had set it face down.

He was puzzled for a moment, and then he realized Floyd had read the letter in the past few minutes. *Shit.* It was already 3pm, and Hank really didn't have time for this. He trudged upstairs to Floyd's room, where he found his son listening to music with his gigantic headphones firmly encasing his ears. He was sitting on his bed against the headboard, arms crossed, looking straight ahead at the wall.

Hank strode over and pulled the headphone cord out of the stereo, then took the headphones off. Floyd did nothing.

"Hey," Hank snapped. "Look at me."

Floyd closed his eyes and leaned his head back as if he was relaxing, but Hank could see every muscle tensed up like they were clamping down on his bones.

"Nobody is keeping you from Daven. You jumped to conclusions and-"

Now Floyd turned to look at him, eyes blazing. "I read his letter. You aren't even friends anymore, dad, so don't give me that bullshit."

Before Hank could stop himself, he slapped Floyd full across the face, hard. Then he backed up as Floyd lifted a hand to his cheek and stared at his dad with eyes wider than they had ever been. Shock. Hurt, too, but mostly shock and perhaps a little bit of incomprehension about what had just occurred. His dad had never slapped him or Theo before, nor even threatened it.

"Go to the spare room and wait for me there. I'll be home around seven. If you're not up in three seconds..."

Floyd jumped up, still clasping a hand to his cheek. His eyes were wet and it was only a matter of seconds before the floodgates opened. Hank didn't want to see that, so he left the room and trusted Floyd to do what he was told. Mostly because he had no idea what the hell to do if he didn't.

Hank quickly descended the stairs towards his study to grab his briefcase. "Avery!" he shouted down the other staircase that led to the basement. "Let's head back to the office."

Maurice and the housekeeper were waiting by the door, and now Hank turned to his jumpy butler. "If Floyd doesn't go into the spare room within five minutes, let a guard know to call me. That's all I'm going to say, clear?"

"Yes, sir," said Maurice, his expression clearly indicating he was dying to know what was up. He was, by far, the biggest gossip in the household. Since by law all indentured house servants were unpaid and allowed no material belongings, there was very little else to do but talk amongst themselves, and their imaginations were boundless. That was why Hank never told him much, and why he spent most of his time in his study.

As Hank walked out the front door, Lucas, Brittany and Theo were coming in.

"Hey, Theody," Hank said, enveloping his youngest in an obviously unwanted embrace. "How was the...the...." He realized he still didn't know where his youngest had been all day.

"Fine."

Hank knew that was all he was going to get for now. Theo was stiff as a board, obviously still hostile and distant after being paddled yesterday, so Hank released him and let him go on his way. It would be at least another day before he would look at his dad, never mind engage with him in a voluntary act of affection.

Hank gave up on him and got into the car, dialing Taylor at the same time.

"Hey Hank, I was just about to call you. We got a fax from Harmon at 3."

"Thank god. Finally a piece of good news today."

Taylor took a deep breath. "Not really. I'm sorry, Hank."

"Sorry for what?" Hank asked in a confused tone.

"The fax we got back…it was the form, but it's not completed. Harmon wrote on it instead, and it says…wait, first you have to promise you won't shoot the messenger."

"Promise. What does it say?" Hank demanded.

"It says… *Your request is refused. Please find below a statement which will be released to the press at 4:30pm, should you choose to pursue the matter any further. - Harmon*"

"Holy fucking shit," muttered Hank, absolutely astonished at this turn of events. "Dare I ask you to read me the statement?"

"No."

"Read it anyway."

Sigh. "Here goes: *At 3:45pm Pacific Time / 4:45 Mountain time, we were obliged to notify the FBI of a blackmail attempt made at 12:40pm PST today by Hank Bancroft, Leader of the Seditionists Party, in regards to surveillance tapes seized from their office in Greeley, CO. Details as to the nature of the attempt will remain confidential until such time as the investigation is complete.*"

Hank seriously felt like asking Avery to drive the SUV off the side of the cliff they were currently skirting. Just a few seconds of terror, and it would all be over. He wouldn't have to deal with this, or with Daven. Or Rupert. Or with Floyd, or Theo. Or the dead woman, or the mysterious caller. A quick but messy death would solve it all…

"Hank, I'm sorry. I don't even know what to say."

"Alright. So...it says at 3:45 they notified the FBI. It's only 3:02 right now, which means they haven't actually done it yet. Right? You're sure it says 3:45?"

"Yes, positive. That's strange, maybe a typo?"

Hank smirked. "I'm going to call Harmon and wave the white flag. Put the fax on my desk and lock the door to my office."

"Wait, Hank-"

Hank hung up and dialed Harmon, and told him he was backing off and to not contact the FBI or issue the press release. Hank hated the smugness in the man's voice as he agreed to "cancel the premature press release" due to a "simple misunderstanding." Hank hated groveling and acting like he'd lost a battle, but gritted his teeth and got through it. The reward would come soon.

Avery dropped him at the back door of the building, and Hank raced to his office faster than he ever had in his life. Feeling rather silly, he said a prayer while dialing Stewart, deputy director of political affairs at the FBI.

The man picked up the call on the first ring. Thank god.

"Stewart? Hank Bancroft here. Before I say anything else, please note it is currently 3:10pm Pacific time, 4:10pm Mountain Time. Is this call being recorded?"

"Of course," replied Stewart, his tone indicating how puzzled he was by the urgency in Hank Bancroft's tone. "What's going on, Mr. Bancroft?'

"Have you spoken to Harmon today regarding the surveillance tapes from Greeley?"

"No, last talked to him yesterday. Why?"

"Nobody from the party has contacted you today in regards to the tapes from Greeley, or to speak about my role in requesting the tapes from you at the same time they are released to the Urbanes? No contact at all? Please confirm with a yes or no."

"No. Nothing."

"Then I need your fax number, immediately. Please. One that goes straight to you."

"Yeah, the one on my desk." He gave the number.

Hank smiled and carefully placed Harmon's fax back into the sending tray, punching in Stewart's number and hitting *transmit*.

"Let me know when you get it."

"Okay. It's coming. You mind telling me what's going on?"

"Harmon just tried to blackmail me in order to impede a murder investigation, and I've got it all in his very own writing."

CHAPTER TWO

Seditionists Headquarters, Los Angeles

Monday, December 27

4:00 pm

"Hey. So Floyd tells me you're growing a beard. Couldn't believe it unless I heard it from the man himself."

Daven furrowed his eyebrows. "That's…that's what you're calling me about?"

Hank had to resist the urge to laugh. "No, Dav, it's not what I'm calling about. That was an attempt to break the ice."

"Right. It's actually just two days of stubble. If you're calling about the grass, it's okay. There's no permanent damage."

"No…I'm calling because Avery pretty much called me a dick for what happened between you and Floyd. I shouldn't have put him in the middle, and now I want you to understand something. My intentions were good. I was only trying to prevent awkwardness for you, from Floyd asking too many questions and saying too much. You know how he can be."

"Yes. Gets that from his father."

Hank rolled his eyes. It wasn't the first time they've had the same exchange, so he kept going without acknowledging it. "My point is that I have no intention of not letting him see you. It's just that the timing was really damned awkward, and…well, you should also know that afterwards he went snooping through my mail and saw the note you wrote me. Which, by the way, was very kind. Thank you for that."

Silence.

"At any rate," Hank continued, feeling horribly off-kilter by this stilted and one-sided conversation, "I think that I need to tell him something ASAP, and I want you to think about it and let me know what you would like me to say. I'm afraid that if I do it on my own I'll villainize you, and that's the last thing I want. I'll be home at seven. Call me before then."

Damn it, Hank. Stop giving him orders. He's not your employee right now.

"Take him to the press conference," Daven finally said.

"What?" Hank thought he hadn't heard correctly.

"Take him to the press conference. Let him hear the story from the calm, honest, unemotional Hank Bancroft, rather than the angry father who can't seem to ever discuss things objectively with his sons. Let him make up his own mind for once."

Hank was a bit set back on his heels by that; it was the first time Daven had ever criticized his parenting.

"I...wow. Okay. I'll think about it."

"How is he doing otherwise?"

Hank didn't want to say it, but he really needed someone to talk to. "To be honest, Dav, I haven't spent enough time with the boys and sometimes feel like they are strangers in my house. They're growing up too fast and leaving me behind...I'm sorry, I don't mean to dump this on you. I only called to apologize for having Avery step in like he did."

"I forgive you. And you should forgive Floyd, too. Completely and entirely, no caveats."

"Why would I do that?"

"Because he won't forget it. I should go, Hank. You have to talk to the world in an hour."

Yes, but the only person in the world I want to talk to is you...

"Thanks, Dav. Let's chat again soon."

"Sure. Good luck with the press conference. Stay true."

Those two words were always that last thing Daven said to him before any of Hank's public speaking events: *Stay true.*

Lump, meet throat.

It took Hank a few moments to lay the receiver back on the hook, as lost in thought as he was. Daven had been incredibly candid all of a sudden, which was strangely intriguing. Not the black and white strategist now that he didn't have a job to do. He should open up more often. It was rather...refreshing, even if he did insult him once. Or was it twice?

Hank picked up the phone and called the house.

"Brittany, have Floyd get dressed in his nicest suit and bring him to the office. Tell him he's not in trouble. You'll have to hurry. Thanks."

Taylor poked her head into Hank's office. "Hank, you have a visitor. Really handsome dude, too. Best keep him away from the secretaries."

Hank looked up and waved his hand. "Thanks. Come in, Floyd. Close the door."

Floyd had flushed at Taylor's words, but now he looked as though now he was the one about to get fired from a job. He stood by the door, somewhat petrified, and stared around the office through the glass panel in the wall. He had never been there during the day, and was a bit dazzled by all the activity.

"Floyd. Sit. You're not in trouble. Relax. Grab a water from the fridge if you want."

Hank continued writing out his thoughts on top of the press release as his son declined the water invitation and slowly lowered himself into one of the "electric chairs," as some people called them. He rarely had anyone in his office unless they were in trouble; he much preferred to go around and hang out elsewhere to talk and meet. Especially Daven's office because of that ridiculous fluffy chair that Rupert loved so much. When they all met together, though, the boss always got the chair. Period.

Hank set his pen down and leaned over to grab two bottles of water from his refrigerator, handing one to Floyd.

"Here. Take it with you."

"Take it where?" asked Floyd in confusion. He looked as if he expected to be slapped again.

Hank sat back in his chair and downed half a bottle of water. "To the press conference. I have to talk fast now. The reason I made you leave Daven's house is because I had to suspend him from his job for 30 days. I hadn't told you yet because it just happened. Floyd, I want you to remember that no matter what is said today, Dav is still Dav and always will be. He didn't break the law, just a company policy. Yes, I'm angry with him right now, but my greatest hope is that I will regain my friendship with him after this is over."

Floyd wasn't really comprehending Hank's reasoning at first. "But why am I here?"

"Because your Uncle Dav wanted you to be. Okay?"

Floyd seemed to not understand still, but he nodded. "Okay. Is he here, too?"

"No, but I'm here and will do everything I can to protect his reputation. He means everything to me - to us - but when people screw up this big…it can get really ugly. Maybe even for a long time. I'll need your cooperation and support to help get through this. Do you understand?"

"Yes, sir."

"Okay. You're just here to listen and learn. You can ask me any questions you'd like afterwards at home, although I probably can't answer them."

"Afterwards? You mean, before or after you...*you know*..." Again with the fearful expression.

Hank softened his tone considerably as he set his water bottle down and leaned across the desk. "I'm not going to *do* anything, Floyd. You're completely forgiven...by me, at least. You still need to apologize to Dav and Avery, though."

Floyd looked flabbergasted. "But I don't...why are you..."

Because Daven said so.

"Because I said so. I'm out of time now. Go with Taylor and she'll seat you in the briefing room. Remember you're just there to listen, do not speak with anyone about anything. And most like there will be cameras on you, so don't be picking your nose or anything like that."

That comment, and Hank's unexpected forgiveness, finally broke Floyd out of his shell. He smiled a little and then grabbed the bottle of water. "Does that mean I can't fart, either?"

Hank chuckled. "The microphones are all up with me, so you're safe to fart away. Just make sure you're sitting in between two Urbanes when you do it."

CHAPTER THREE

For whatever reason, Hank never got nervous before or during press conferences. Considering it had recently become a class 2 felony offense for party officers and government employees to lie outright while in the course of their duties, such a public gathering should make anybody nervous. But he liked to theorize it didn't matter; that his lifelong and sincere desire to be honest and transparent soothed his conscience so much that speaking to this room of a hundred people came just as naturally as speaking to anyone else. So when Taylor was working with the A/V guys to do the sound test, he calmly re-read his notes behind the little screen in the corner and waited for the doors to open. Calm as can be. Everything was fine. He had this.

Then the room began to fill up and he recognized some prominent Urbanes at the exact same time he suddenly remembered he had told Floyd that Janet was a double agent. And then, heart racing, he spotted Floyd, chatting animatedly in the corner with one of the most nosy and manipulative reporters the world had ever known. One of Harmon's favorites, actually.

"Taylor!" he hissed. "Floyd's with Hailey. Why aren't you with him?"

"You said to sit him down and-"

"Get him, *now* . Bring him here."

"Okay, sorry." She ran off, and Hank sweated bullets in the horrifying moments it took her to pull his son away from the vile woman. Was it too late? Who knew how long they'd been chatting. Did she corner him outside the doors for the past 15 minutes? Surely Brittany would have pulled him away from her, if so. Where the hell *was* Brittany, anyway?

Floyd suddenly appeared behind the screen, looking scared. "What's wrong, dad?"

Hank took his arm angrily and pulled him further back, so that they were both leaning against the wall and out of sight. "I specifically told you that you were only here to listen, and not talk. That woman you were just chatting with? Basically my worst enemy. What were you saying to her?"

"Ow, dad. Let go, please." Hank did, then Floyd continued, "I was telling her that I was only here to listen and learn, and that I wasn't authorized to speak with anyone but you."

Hank looked at him sideways. "It looked like more than that."

"It wasn't! I had to say it twice. She's so nosy. Then she was congratulating me on my license, so I was just saying thank you and how excited I was to drive. That's all!"

"Hank, 5pm. You're on," busted in Taylor, in that overtly bossy tone that meant Hank was about to make a fool of himself if he didn't do what she said.

"Wait," said Hank and she stopped in her tracks. "Take Floyd to the back corner away from Hailey. Both of you stand there the entire time, do not move...and Floyd? Play deaf if anyone else asks you anything. Not a word. If I see you open your mouth even once-"

" *Okay* ! I got it." He caught Hank's expression and then straightened up. "I mean. Yes, sir."

"Go."

"Aye aye, captain!" That was from Taylor this time, eye roll included. He would have to chat to her about that later. Amazing strategist or not, she tended to be insolent at the worst possible moments. It was especially unwise to do it in front of his very impressionable son.

Hank breathed in deeply and stepped out from behind the screen while the cameras clicked approximately five thousand times. For the hundredth time he idly wondered how many photographers it would take to change a light bulb...

"Good evening. Thank you for joining me." Lighting setups for live broadcasts were always blinding, so he took the opportunity to squint like he was adjusting his eyes in order to watch Taylor and Floyd take up station in the far back corner. There was Brittany, too. Good, although he would be chatting with her later for leaving his son alone with Hailey.

His throat swelled a little after he had automatically looked for Rupert and Daven in the opposite corner, where they always stood, talking together and making notes. Sometimes Rupe would make an obscene gesture at Hank if he said something he shouldn't, or to loosen him up or distract him if he started getting twitchy with the reporters.

Hank knew his audience had always really been his two favorite aides, not the reporters. They were a happy little trio. Now, though, his attention was on...Hailey. All he could think about was Hailey. And how Floyd knew something he shouldn't, and had been talking to her.

And now, for the first time ever, he was completely petrified in front of those microphones and learning really quickly what it was like to feel stage fright. He'd had no idea how much those two men carried him through these moments, and their absence was nearly unbearable.

Come on, Hank. You've got this.

"Ahem. I will begin by reading the statement that was released this morning." He proceeded to read it, but didn't really hear his own words. Why the hell did he tell Floyd about Janet, for god's sake? Oh, that's right. Because Floyd was having a temper tantrum, and you were weak in handling it. *You're weak in handling everything lately.*

"At this point I have nothing to add to the statement, but I will take ten questions now."

In order to avoid bias, he never selected the reporters himself for questions. Upon entering the room, every single reporter chose a numbered clicker from a basket, and there was a green light behind him on the little stage activated by a button he pushed on the podium when he was ready to take another question. The first person to click while it was green had their number pop up on an electronic signboard on the back wall for him to call out.

"Yes, number 47?"

An Seditionist, but an annoying one who pushed all the wrong buttons.

"Mr. Bancroft, regarding these bungled communications. Was there any confidential information that was compromised as a result of this violated policy?"

Bungled?? Go fuck yourself. "No. They would not have a job right now if that was the case. Hence the 'mitigating circumstances' I mentioned. Yes, number 13?"

Hailey, who was usually first to pull the trigger and get on the board. "Your statement says explicitly that you hold all your employees to equal and fair standards, so can you explain why Mr. Johansson received a heavier penalty than Mr. Aster?"

Hank almost laughed, because he had already predicted that would be her question as soon as he saw her in the lobby an hour ago. Everyone knew she harbored a secret crush on Daven...except Daven.

"He made two mistakes, and Rupert made one. I will not elaborate any further." Button press. "Yes, number 4?"

Another tough Urbane. "It seems odd that your two top executives would violate any policy at all, considering you've mentioned before that the three of you wrote them together and all of you have been with the party since day one. Was this violation entirely unintentional somehow, or was it blatant and purposeful?"

Shit. Although Hank had prepared an answer for this question, he was really hoping not to get it. There was an option to decline to answer, and he'd done so numerous times in the past if wasn't legally able to answer. Maybe he should refuse to take any questions at all in the first place, like Harmon always did, but then again...he was Hank Bancroft. Mr. Transparent. Mr. Cool. He *had* to answer.

It was easy to picture Rupert having an anxiety attack in the corner while he picked up his bottle of water to buy time to think some more, praying that whatever he said would be good enough to save his friend's careers. He knew Rupe and Dav were watching right now, from their homes. Waiting for him to give them hope...or to put the nail in the coffin.

Even worse, maybe they didn't care anymore and were looking for new jobs already.

"Right. Difficult but reasonable question. You know I don't spin things, as much as that would help sometimes, but I'm perfectly aware that this answer will sound like spin. And that's the only reason I'll admit that I'm uncomfortable with it.

Yes, they both knowingly violated the policy. It was a difficult situation, and to be perfectly honest, I'm still struggling with my decision to suspend them because I still wonder what I would have done in their place. It's very likely I would have done the same thing. I don't know. There isn't an easy answer. Policies may be written in black and white, but reality isn't. As I said, there were mitigating circumstances. Moving on. Yes, number 98?"

Another no-nonsense Urbane. Great. And then another. Then a softball from an Seditionist. Then, *finally* …the question he had been hoping for all along, from Harmon's other favorite weasel.

"I can take one more question, Yes, number 50."

The man stood up, looking more smug than usual. "On December 25 there was a murder of an Urbane employee on Seditionists property in Colorado. Both parties have been strangely silent on the matter. Was this incident related the suspensions? Please give us an update as to how that investigation is going, and whether or not you are cooperating with Harmon in order to identify the attacker."

The room murmured in approval of the question.

Here goes nothing, he thought to himself. "That was actually three questions, maybe four, but I will answer anyway. First, the incidents with Rupert and Daven are entirely unrelated to the death on our property. Secondly, I have been in regular contact with both Harmon and the FBI with requests to have the surveillance tapes released to us. Unfortunately, I've been unsuccessful so far. I feel strongly, of course, that all three parties should work together and solve the crime as soon as possible in order to provide answers to Janet's family, but I cannot do that without the tapes."

He reached for his water bottle and took a huge swig, knowing that he absolutely, definitely, undeniably should NOT say what he was about to say anyway. Something he had been practicing for an hour to make it sound as natural as possible. If Rupert was here he would likely kick him in the nuts afterwards a few times, and Hank wouldn't even be mad.

Deep breath. Steady. "Therefore, around 3:30pm today I called the deputy director of the FBI for his assistance. For transparency's sake I must admit that this backfired and resulted in me being officially reprimanded for threatening Harmon by saying I would bring his refusal to cooperate with me to public attention unless he signed the waiver to release the tapes. That was inappropriate, and I was instructed to wait silently for further information. Thank you all again for being here, and have a nice evening.”

Urbanes HQ, Denver

“*What. The. Fuck*,” muttered Harmon in shock as he watched Hank Bancroft throw him under the bus on national television. He glanced at his aides to check their reactions. Umber, Colbert all wore similar stricken expressions, Colbert in particular.

“Boss, we need to put out a statement ASAP,” said Umber in a quiet tone. “We’re going to get murdered for this. No pun intended.”

Harmon was expressionless, which - as everyone knew - meant he was in his most dangerous state. “Yes, get me a draft as quickly as you can. Everyone out, please.”

They all rushed out, and Harmon turned down the volume on the television and watched the local news wrap-up the hour. In silence, no captions. He didn’t need them. He knew what they were saying.

Hank Bancroft had won again. His capitulation to the fax earlier today had merely been an act. And Harmon had bought it...hook, line, and sinker.

Tap. Tap. Tap.

Rupert's House

"*What. The. Fuck,* " murmured Daven and Rupert in unison.

There was a long pause, and then Rupert said plainly as he threw up his hands in surrender, "I'm going to kill him. That's it. He's dead. But I need a beer first." He got up and went into the kitchen.

"Get me one, too," shouted Daven as he dropped his head into his hands.

————-

FBI Headquarters, Philadelphia

"What. The. Fuck."

Stewart stared open-mouthed at the monitor in his office for a good five minutes, then brought up his email to send a note to his boss in the Capitol.

He didn't need to, she had already beat him to it:

Stewart, please issue a mandatory in-person summons to Hank Bancroft. I'm available at 8am or 2pm on Wednesday. Let me know you got this.

-Salome

On it.

-Stewart

Thanks. I will summon Harmon, too, if he responds with anything that fans the flames. I'll call you if so. Go home soon.

-Salome

We might as well do it now. I would bet my life right now that he'll fire back with something even worse within the hour.

-Stewart

You're right. Prepare it now and then pull the trigger when I give the ok. Keep in touch.

-Salome

Will do.

-Stewart

Stewart hit send and picked up the phone to dial his Los Angeles courier.

CHAPTER FOUR

Floyd was very quiet in the car on the way home from the press conference.

Too quiet.

Way too quiet.

"What's wrong?" Hank finally asked after about ten minutes of total silence.

"Nothing," Floyd replied. Then he unbuckled his seat belt and started to move to the third row of the SUV.

"Hey," snapped Hank, pulling him back down into place. "Put your seatbelt back on. Stay put."

"It's a red light-"

"*Floyd,* " Hank warned calmly, with an unmistakable edge to his tone. He could see Avery's eyes focus on them in the rearview mirror.

Floyd threw him a look, but snapped the seatbelt back into the buckle and turned to stare out the window. It reminded Hank of the times he would always pout as a little boy when they passed by Disneyland on the way back and forth to their old office in Santa Ana.

"Where do you want to go for dinner to celebrate your license?" Hank asked after a minute, after his annoyance faded away.

"Nowhere."

"I'm not aware of a restaurant called Nowhere. Want to try someplace that actually exists?"

"I don't care."

"Should I tell you we need to have a chat when we get home?"

"Do whatever you want."

Avery's eyes were still on them, so Hank looked right back at him until he looked away. Hank felt absurdly self-conscious all of a sudden, so he dropped the subject when he felt his phone buzzing with a number he didn't recognize. But it was coming from Philadelphia, so he had to pick up.

"This is Hank Bancroft."

"Good evening Hank. This is Salome Danby, director of the Office of Political Integrity under President Rickon. This call is being recorded."

Oh shit. "Good evening," he responded as pleasantly as he could manage.

"Listen, Hank, in the morning you're going to get a summons to meet me and Stewart in Philadelphia on Wednesday. Normally I don't call to give a heads-up, but I wanted to give you advanced notice so you can arrange for your flights and child care. I would advise you to fly private and bring your lawyer."

Hank's throat constricted a little. "Will this...may I assume I can book a round trip?"

"Yes. I am free at 8am or 2pm on Wednesday and you'll probably be here for two hours. Once you receive the officials summons, I expect you to respond immediately with details of your flight arrangements."

"Yes, ma'am. I'll take the 2pm time slot. Thank you for the heads-up."

"I would also advise you to issue no further statements or make any public comments, whatever Harmon says or does at this point. But that's not a gag order and it's completely up to you to take my advice or not."

Her tone was utterly professional and smooth, with a trace of British accent. No indication of emotion at all. Hank wasn't sure if that made him feel worse, or better. He may have been less alarmed if she had screamed at him outright. Kind of like how he felt better when Floyd bitched at him instead of shutting him out.

He turned to look at his son, who was paying no attention to the call.

"Thank you, again. See you on Wednesday."

Then to Floyd, as he poked him hard in the side. "Hey. How do you feel about a little trip to Philadelphia to see Independence Hall?"

Floyd hesitated, and then turned around to stare at him. "That's random, dad."

"Yeah. I have a meeting there on Wednesday and don't see any reason why you and Theo can't come out and spend the day sightseeing."

The boy's eyes suddenly got really big, and he retreated into his shell a little again. "I do. Because everyone will be watching us. Taking pictures. Following us."

Hank nodded. "Yeah, Floyd. In case you haven't noticed, that's the life we've lived for ten years now."

"Well, I don't want it anymore. Take Theo, he enjoys all the attention."

"He's not speaking to me right now, either." Hank's phone buzzed again; a call from Rupert. He sent it to voicemail. "Look, I know it's been a long day. Let's go home and pack. We'll head to Philly in the late morning and go someplace historic for dinner. Near Valley Forge there's an old tavern that was used to store gunpowder during the-"

"I *said* I don't want to go," Floyd growled, throwing his dad a look of pure annoyance and...hatred? Was that really...could it be *hatred* ?

Hank was actually so taken aback by his hostility that he had no reply to make. Seconds later the big SUV pulled up to the front door, and Floyd leaped out and disappeared past Maurice inside the house in a flash.

Hank got out and nodded at Maurice, who was now holding the door for him. "Did Floyd just breeze by you without saying anything?" he asked the man.

"It's ok, sir, he was obviously upset."

"Yeah. On behalf of my son, I apologize for his rudeness."
Hank's blood was up now. Indentured or not, all of his
household staff deserved to be treated courteously. Floyd knew
better. It was time to have a chat.

——

Rupert's House

"Damn. He sent me straight to voicemail," Rupe muttered as
he tossed his phone onto the table.

"I don't know why you expected otherwise. You ever had Hank
pick up when he knows he's pissed you off? Because I haven't."

"No. Never, actually."

Daven took a large swig of his beer. "Honestly, Rupe, I can't
fathom what he was thinking by slandering Harmon like that
on national television. He's out of his fucking mind."

Rupert smiled. "No. It's not slander if it's true. I would have
agreed with you five minutes ago, but I've changed my mind.
He knows exactly what he's doing. Wish I had half the stones
he does and a quarter of his brains."

Daven stared at him for a moment in stunned silence. "Would
you mind letting me in on the secret? It feels to me like he's

deliberately sabotaging himself, so yes, in that regard he knows exactly what he's doing."

"Well, think about it. We know for certain that Harmon is refusing to cooperate with Janet's murder, no matter what he says next. Hank has written proof of it with that reprimand they issued him, and it's going to be published in the weekly FBI digest…is tomorrow Tuesday? Yes, so tomorrow. For the whole nation to read."

"The general public doesn't read that!"

"They don't need to, because the reporters do it for them. And Harmon's party? Janet is one of *theirs*. That's going to throw his constituents into a feeding frenzy because his lack of cooperation makes no sense at all. Why would he block an investigation of his own employee's murder? We should turn on Boswin News just to see what they're saying."

Daven shook his head. "No, you missed something. Janet was one of ours. The faster the investigation moves, the faster that's going to be revealed."

Again, Rupe smiled. "Exactly. This investigation is going to move forward at light speed now, and the faster we are going to be vindicated, because the public will realize that obviously we would not kill our *own agent* on our own property. Not to mention we certainly wouldn't push for a deeper investigation if we did kill her. So the blame will shift to Harmon, who has just been publicly shamed for trying to hinder the whole damn thing. He'll be public enemy number one at just the right time."

"Oh." Dav nodded slowly as the puzzle pieces all came crashing down on him in slow motion. " *Oh.* Holy shit."

"Not only *that*," continued Rupe, "but this takes the attention off of us. Meaning, you and me. Who do you think is going to be the big story tonight? Little us taking a couple of phone calls? I don't think so. We're old news already."

Daven thought about it some more, feeling a little drained now. "You think that he...that he planned all this from the beginning? This chain of events? Or did he just get lucky?"

Rupe laughed. "Are you kidding me? We are talking about *Hank Bancroft*, right? Absolutely planned down to the minute."

"Yeah. I guess you're right. Well, good thing it all worked out. Be right back, need some water. Want another beer?"

"No, I'm good."

Jesus Christ, breathed Daven, as he went back into Rupe's kitchen and rummaged through the refrigerator. His heart was beating strangely now, with a rhythm and power he never felt before. It wasn't remotely pleasant. Sickly, even. And why was that? It shouldn't be. His friend, his boss, just took the nation by storm in just fifteen minutes and rescued his party from a pending debacle. Getting a murder investigation to move faster was no small thing. Making the opposition look like shit, which they were? Priceless.

Yes, quite a feat. He should feel proud of the man. Should be admiring his mentor. Praising him.

But why wasn't he? Hank *was* brilliant in his handling of this. His mind worked in ways Daven could never even imagine.

Amazingly brilliant.

Maybe a little *too* brilliant.

Maybe a little *too* calculating.

But still brilliant, all the same.

And frighteningly dangerous.

And that was why he felt no joy. Daven shut his eyes to the sudden, very belated pains of realization that maybe he had underestimated exactly *how* dangerous Hank Bancroft could be with a mind like that.

He put the bottle of water back in the fridge and grabbed another beer instead.

Bancroft Manor

Hank left his secretary's office after arranging for a charter jet and hotel rooms in Philadelphia, then trudged up the stairs to Floyd's room. His head felt like it weighed 500 pounds right now, easily. How could it only be 6:30pm? This day seemed to have lasted a month already. The last thing he needed was yet another fight with Floyd.

Charter jets were expensive. Hank had a lot of money, yes, but he hated throwing that much away in just a matter of hours. He couldn't even imagine how much Harmon's own personal jet cost every year, but it had to seriously hurt.

When he pushed open the door to his oldest's room he was delighted to see an open suitcase on the bed that was already half-full. Hank walked in.

"I take it this means you changed your mind about Philadelphia?"

"Yes. Because I know Theody will want to go and I don't want to be left here alone."

"Good. But the packing will have to wait. Come with me, let's talk."

Floyd paused in folding a shirt and watched him fearfully. "Are you going to-"

"Nope. Said I wouldn't, and I won't. Let's go into my sitting room."

They went into the little square room off his top floor master suite and sunk into the comfy chairs. Floyd looked around in wonder; he had never actually been allowed on this floor before in the entire ten years they'd lived in the house. It was Hank's private sanctuary, and he chose it for this particular conversation because Daven's house was in full view from where Floyd was sitting.

Sure enough, that immediately prompted Floyd to start talking. "I need to apologize to Uncle Dav," he said softly.

"Yep."

"Do you think he's mad at me?"

"I know for sure he isn't, but that doesn't make your actions any less serious. When do you want to do it?"

Floyd ignored the question. "Dad, the press conference is really bothering me. I don't like the way that you answered some of the questions."

Hank was completely caught off guard by this unexpected statement. "What? Why?"

He shrugged, then pulled his knees up to his chest. "The last one. About Harmon."

Floyd was terrified of Harmon, for some reason. Hank never could find out why; they'd never met before and neither of the boys were allowed to watch regular television or read the political sections of the newspaper. They didn't even have access to the internet yet.

Hank softened his tone. "Should I regret taking you?"

"No, but I wish I hadn't been there. It was the first time I've seen you actually working, you know?"

"No it's not. You've seen me give interviews before."

"This was different."

"Why?"

Floyd looked away, towards Daven's house. "I don't know. It's just…you…"

Hank was fighting impatience now, but he did his best to hide it.

"What, Floyd? Talk to me."

"It's just…I didn't know how powerful you are until recently. How everybody listens to every word you say, and wants to know what you think about everything. They want to know everything about you, and me. When you freaked out on me for talking to that woman, it scared me when you called her your worst enemy. And the photographers, and the guards. How many enemies do you *have*, dad?"

The poor kid was almost beside himself with fear, and Hank's heart shattered into a million pieces. He resisted the urge to go pick Floyd up and put him in his lap.

"I understand where you're coming from. But I didn't mean *enemy* like she's trying to kill me or anything. She's a reporter, and she likes to gossip about me and try to embarrass me. They all do. She won't physically harm me. Or you. I shouldn't have used the word enemy. I'm really sorry that frightened you."

Floyd wasn't convinced. "Dad, I want you to quit your job so we can be a normal family."

"I see. Is that why you've been acting out so much lately? You do realize I've had to punish you more times in the past two months than in the last two years combined?"

"Yes. Because I'm scared."

"We have nine security guards who follow us hand and foot. Nothing has ever happened before, so why suddenly worry now? Don't be scared of Harmon."

Floyd stared out the window again, swallowed hard, then looked back at Hank. "I wasn't talking about Harmon. I was talking about you."

Hank's heart stopped for a moment. This was something he always suspected, but hoped to be wrong about. Even though he knew he wasn't. *Well. Now you know.*

Floyd was trembling. He had been doing that a lot lately, even when Hank wasn't even mad about anything. It had started in November, after Hank belted him for the first time in months for snooping in his office and reading an old article about his involvement in bringing down the corrupt and morally bankrupt Democrat and Republican parties in the terrible years of the disastrous Durdan presidency. That day, Floyd learned that his father, Rupert, Daven, and even Harmon himself would be forever known as part of the hundreds of men and women who tore apart and then rebuilt the nation within two years: *The Seditionists.*

Unfortunately, this particular article had focused on Hank alone, due to an early infamous photo of him on the Capitol steps during Durdan's second inauguration ceremony. It was a dazzling, candid shot of him single-handedly stopping a violent protester with one hand while shooting the finger to the shocked president with the other hand. That photo had instantly become a symbol of the movement, and to Hank's utter horror he soon found his face (and finger) plastered all over posters, t-shirts, and protest signs. For *years.*

Floyd hadn't really been the same since learning his dad was the person in the iconic photo that sparked the Second American Revolution, and Hank really didn't know what the hell to do about it now. He had already explained that he wasn't a leader and was basically relegated to being a bored paper pusher after the image made it too dangerous for him to be out in public, but nothing registered. Floyd was too young to understand the politics of it all. He was only three years old when it all ended. A newborn when the picture was taken. But to him, and to millions of other youngsters as well, his dad *was* the revolution.

"Okay," Hank said, somehow finding the ability to swallow again. "Listen, why don't we call Uncle Dav and ask if you can come over and apologize to him and play with Shannon for a little while."

"He's not there. Wait, aren't you going to tell me to not be afraid of you?"

Hank got up to look out the window. No truck in the driveway. Probably with Rupert, drinking beer and talking about the press conference.

Talking about *him*.

Gently he sat back down directly across from Floyd and put his hands on each of the boy's knees, and looked him straight in the eyes.

"You should not be scared of me unless you're tearing up Daven's lawn or fighting with your brother in church. But you already know I'm going to nail you every time for stupid shit like that, which is my job as your father."

"I know, dad, but it's more than that."

"*And* as your father, I would also give my life for you in a heartbeat. No hesitation. That's also my job. Whether or not you accept it is something you have to decide for yourself. Now go finish packing while I have chef make us some dinner. What do you want?"

"Bacon burger and fries."

Hank patted his knees and stood up. "Okay. Consider it done. Pack warmly, it's snowing in Philly."

Floyd lit up. "Really? I've never been…wait, dad, I don't have any snow boots!"

"Oh, shit. Neither do I. Guess we better go shopping and get dinner, then."

"Can we go to Tropical Rainforest Cafe?"

"I don't see why not. Get dressed."

Hank grinned to himself as he hurried down the stairs to find Theo. There was always a way to get Floyd to do what he wanted, one way or the other.

His phone continued to buzz in his pocket unabated as email after email after email came in. He ignored it, and the battery died 20 minutes later.

Urbanes Headquarters, Denver

Harmon eyed the whiskey bottle on the cart in the corner of his office. Must not drink on the job. Must not drink on the job.

Umber had just arrived and was reading his media statement out loud.

It is currently, and always has been, the policy of the FBI to release surveillance tapes to the most interested party first in any investigation. As the victim was one of our employees, we felt it was our duty to take charge of the investigation. Unfortunately, our motives have been-

"No good," said Harmon. "Start over."

"I thought you would say that, so I already have another draft."

It is the legal right of the Urbanes party to-

"No. Start over again."

Umber pulled out another piece of paper. "Right. Thought you'd say that, too."

Hank Bancroft has not been forthcoming about his motivations in obtaining the tapes faster than the law currently provides for. Until it is clear why his rushing into an investigation in which-

"No. No. No," Harmon exclaimed, pounding the desk. "Not even close. Write this down."

Umber whipped out his notepad, and Harmon spoke slowly enough for him get it all.

"The Urbanes Party intends to press integrity charges against Hank Bancroft for misrepresenting our stance on obtaining the surveillance tapes. Our motivation is, and always has been, to complete the investigation as quickly as possible without interference from external parties. We will not comment further, as anything we say at this point would be misconstrued as spin."

Umber looked at him askance.

"Boss, we can't...we can't say this. We can't accuse him of lying, because everything he said was technically true."

"Did you get it all down?"

"Yes, but...but..."

Harmon stood up and put his jacket back on. "Send it out immediately."

\-\-\-\-\-\-\-\-\-\-\-\-\-\-\-

US Capitol - Philadelphia

Salome Danby was starting to doze off as she watched the wires come through in a jagged pattern on her specialized news monitor. *Come on, Harmon. I know you're going to do it...just pull the damned trigger already so I can go home and go to bed.*

A jangling alert tone perked her back up, and quickly she pulled up the notification feed. Yep, there it was. And yes, he was not only fanning the flames, but throwing gasoline on them.

She pulled her desk phone over and yanked up the receiver, hitting the number 4 on her speed dial at the same time.

"Stewart, you still at the office? Good. Summon Harmon now. I want him here at 2:00pm Wednesday so we can get him and Hank together. President Rickon himself is planning to spank them both and send them running home with their tails between their legs. Thank you."

CHAPTER FIVE

Bancroft Manor

Finally...

Hank stepped away from the window where he had impatiently been watching and waiting for over an hour for the big black truck to appear across the street in the driveway.

"Hey. Sorry to call so late. You have a minute?"

Daven set down his keys and wallet and braced himself for whatever mood Hank might be in at this particular moment.

"Yes," he answered cautiously. He had all the time in the world for the next 29 days, to be precise.

"Thanks. I have a personal matter to discuss with you. Two, actually."

Oh god. I'm fired, aren't I? Either that or he's going to give me hell for spending so much time with Rupert...or both...

"A personal matter?"

"Yeah. Floyd is really sorry for tearing up your lawn today and wants to come over and apologize. I was wondering if you're available around 9am tomorrow for a few minutes."

"But I told you the grass is fine. Can't even tell."

"You do realize I can see your grass from my bedroom, right? Including the tire tracks."

There was a short pause. "I forgot about that. Anyway, it doesn't matter. The landscapers are coming tomorrow to fix it."

"Fine. He'll be paying their bill with his allowance. And I'm not forcing him to apologize, he actually wants to. So can he come over in the morning?"

"Sure. 9am works. And the second matter?"

Hank took a deep breath. "Listen, do you remember when I told you last month that Floyd got into my study and found out way too much about my past? Well, it freaked him out. I don't know what the hell to do. He's terrified of me, Dav. He's barely talking and acts like I'm going to slit his throat at any moment. Because of one damned photo."

"He's always been afraid of you, Hank. Everyone knows that, except you."

"I do know that, thank you. But this is different." Hank paused to get up and make sure his bedroom door was locked. "I was wondering if...this is stupid. You probably hate me right now, right? And I'm sitting here asking you for favors."

"What do you need?"

"Well, it's a big favor. Feel free to say no. I was wondering if Floyd could spend the next couple of days with you. I think it would do him some good to get away from me for a while."

Daven was confused. "And doing what?"

Hank was becoming a bit rattled by the terseness of Daven's tone and suddenly felt like he was talking to a complete stranger.

"Just being with you. Overnight. I have to travel tomorrow and you know how he is about flying. Tonight he had a panic attack at the mall, and it didn't help that all the paparazzi were following us everywhere. It was pretty bad. Anyway, he gave me such lip afterwards on the way home that I had to...this is...this is really awkward. I don't know why I'm telling you all this."

"I'll do it, Hank, but under one condition."

"What?"

"You have to talk to me about Harmon first. I want to know what you're up to."

Hank sighed heavily. "Dav, no. Forget it."

"Hank, regardless of what you-"

"And what do you mean by '*what I'm up to*?' Other than saving your ass, you mean?"

Silence.

Hank continued irritably, "I never would have called you if I thought you'd use Floyd as a bargaining chip. I thought he meant more to you than that. So just forget it. Goodbye, Daven."

"Wait-"

Hank hung up angrily, then laid in bed with his phone on his chest, staring at the ceiling blankly. Sure, he had some serious nerve to pry about Harmon, but what upset him more was that he had basically asked outright if Daven hated him...and Dav hadn't said no.

He hadn't said no , which meant yes.

Hank knew he should apologize for what he'd just said. None of it was true; Daven loved Floyd like a nephew. And he had every right to know why the fight with Harmon had just escalated to new heights. After all, he was still technically his right hand.

But Hank Bancroft was a stubborn man.

Daven kept calling back until Hank blocked his phone number. Then he blocked Rupert's for good measure, and turned over to go to sleep.

A minute later there was a strong knock on his bedroom door that caused him to bolt upright in alarm. No one was allowed to knock on that door, period. That's what the intercom was for. Hank waited in case he had been dreaming, but there was another knock.

"Dad?" It was Theo. Hank jumped up and opened the door.

"What's wrong? Why didn't you use the intercom?"

Theo was upset. "Can you go talk to Floyd?"

"Why? I'm in bed, Theody. It's almost midnight."

"Please. Just make sure he's okay."

Against every ounce of common sense in his body, Hank didn't ask any more questions and followed Theo to Floyd's room.

Floyd was sitting up in his bed, drinking ice water. With one look at his teary face Hank knew something was very wrong. He quickly moved to put a hand on his son's forehead.

"Oh no. You're burning up, buddy."

"I know. I just threw up like five times."

"Your stomach hurt? Like it did last time?"

"Yeah."

"God. Not again. Theody, go get Avery and Brittany. Don't alarm them, just tell them to pull the car to the front door."

"Can I come with you guys?"

"Sure. Hurry up and get dressed."

Palisades Hospital - Los Angeles

Twenty minutes later they arrived at the Palisades Hospital, where Floyd's doctor was thankfully on duty. Since they were the only people there, Floyd was taken in immediately to be seen.

Hank and Theo waited anxiously in the lobby with their guards for what seemed like way too long. Floyd hated being examined in front of anyone, even his own family. He insisted on privacy, and Hank respected that because he was exactly the same way. But it made it all the much harder to wait for the outcome.

"Brittany?" called Hank. "Come here for a second, please."

"Yes, boss?" She moved away from the door and sat down next to him at his invitation.

"I didn't get a chance to thank you for your help at the mall tonight. You and Lucas were invaluable. I was wondering if you would stay with him, if he's admitted."

"Of course."

"Thank you so much. I think that you-"

He didn't get a chance to finish; the doctor called him back to the examining room. It had been almost 90 minutes. Theo was asleep, leaning on Avery. Hank nodded at the man and followed the doctor.

Floyd was laying on the examining table, looking at his dad warily. He had a frightfully pale complexion.

"Is he okay?" Hank asked Dr. Harborough quietly.

"Yes and no," said the pediatrician as she set her clipboard next to Floyd's feet on the bed. "He says he thinks he threw up some blood, and all indications show he was correct. We've been talking about how his anxiety seems to have increased past anything he's felt before."

"Does this mean what I think it means?" asked Hank impatiently.

"I'm afraid so. We'll do one more test to rule out an eosinophilic esophagitis, but I don't think it's that. Looks like we'll have to prescribe him some anxiety meds again."

Hank looked at Floyd, who was now shivering. "Do you have a blanket? And can I talk to him for a minute alone?"

Dr. Harborough reached under into a cabinet and brought out two blankets, which she draped over Floyd herself while Hank just stood there, watching his son closely. The poor kid was still a little green, and his forehead was glistening with sweat.

"Take your time, Mr., Bancroft. Just come out to the desk when you're ready."

The door closed. Floyd was staring at the ceiling now.

"Hey, look at me," Hank started off firmly. They'd been through this a few times before, and his patience was long gone. "How long has your stomach been hurting?"

"Couple of weeks," he mumbled, still staring at nothing.

"And you thought it was okay to go that long without telling me?"

"Mmhmm."

"Ulcers are not a game, Floyd. They're serious business. You promised me last time you wouldn't let it get this far."

Now Floyd looked right at him, expression hard. "It's your fault, so can you at least wait until I feel a little better before you punish me again?"

Hank was shocked. "What? Who said I was going to...okay Floyd, that's it, we got to talk. Man to man. Not here. Home. When you feel better. After I get back from my trip. I can't have you worrying yourself sick over things I did fifteen years ago. This is getting ridiculous."

He got up and left the exam room and went to find the doctor. "If I asked you to admit him again, could you?"

Dr. Harborough nodded. "I was already planning to. Preliminary blood draw shows all sorts of values out of whack. Nothing major, so 48 hours resting and rehydrating should be enough to get him back on track again. And of course I'll refill the fluoxetine. Maybe a little higher dose this time."

"Okay, thanks. He'll need a double room so that his guard can stay with him. Let me go say goodbye."

Hank went back into the room and found Floyd turned all the way around, facing the opposite wall. He picked up the doctor's stool and moved it to where he could sit at eye level with his oldest son. He regretted barking at him a minute ago and made sure to keep his tone calm and kind.

"Theo and I are going to Philadelphia for a couple days. You're going to be admitted now, but we'll pick you up as soon as you're better. Okay?"

Floyd nodded. He didn't mind the hospital at all. It was actually a welcome escape from the life he was growing to hate so much as he got older. This was the fourth time that his ulcers had re-appeared, despite Hank's best efforts to keep the boy calm, happy, and safe.

Hank stroked Floyd's hair. Floyd did not look at him.

"You should go. I'm fine," he said after a moment, pulling back from his father's touch. "Can Theody stay with me?"

"No," replied Hank, pulling the blanket up around Floyd's chin. "Brittany will be here with you. We'll talk in a few days and figure out how to get back to where we were before you saw that photo. I don't want to continue like this. Do you?"

"All I want is for you to quit your job, but you won't listen to me."

"We're not having this conversation again," Hank replied sharply.

"Of course not. It's so much easier to shut me up with your belt."

Hank said nothing more and stood up, knowing that any conversation at this point was useless. Floyd was too wound up to do anything but fight, and any further words would just widen the gap between them.

Theo was awake now and jumped up when Hank returned to the waiting room.

"The ulcers again?"

"I'm afraid so," he responded quietly, giving Theo a quick hug as he did so. "He's going to stay here for a couple of days while you and I go to Philadelphia."

"Can I go talk to him and say goodbye?"

"Yeah, make it quick. Room 4."

Theo rushed back to the exam rooms.

"Hey, jerk."

"What's up, bitch?" replied Floyd automatically as he smiled and struggled to sit up.

"I know you didn't want to go to Philadelphia but this was a little extreme, don't you think?"

Floyd laughed. "Yeah, well you know me. If you're going to fuck something up, do it big."

Theo didn't react. "I asked dad if I could stay here with you but he said no."

"It's okay Theody. Go see the Liberty Bell. Take pictures for me."

"It's just a stupid bell, and it's broken. Have you...are you crying?"

"No. Shut up."

Theo didn't buy it. "Something dad said?"

"I just puked my guts up like five times, Theody. I feel like shit, okay?"

"Okay. Sorry." He sat up on the bed next to his brother. "Lay back down. You're shaking."

Floyd did. "See you in a couple days, then?"

"Yeah. Sorry we're leaving you here."

"It's alright. I don't mind getting away from dad."

Then Theo did something he hadn't done in about three years.

"Move over." He shoved his brother over and laid down next to him.

"Theo! Stop. You're going to push me overboard."

"You're fine." He rested his head on Floyd's shoulder, and Floyd threw his arms around him to hold on for dear life.

"You're too old for this. My ass is hanging off the side," Floyd protested half-heartedly, pulling Theo in tighter all the same. "You want me to sing you nursery rhymes, too?"

"Shut up," Theo giggled.

"So the lab just called and it's definitely *not* esophagitis. So besides the antibiotics, I'm going to go ahead and increase the fluoxetine dose by about 25%. He should still have no side effects at all. Maybe a little drowsiness on the first day."

"Okay. Is he going to have this problem for the rest of his life?"

"Probably. You're not going to like this, but I would like to suggest that you take him to see a child psychologist as soon as possible. That much anxiety in a 15-year old is not even remotely normal."

Hank smiled without humor. "Yeah. We're not exactly a normal family, in case you haven't noticed."

Dr. Harborough shrugged. "You seem way more normal than most of the families I see in here. Theo is the most well-adjusted kid I've ever known, and Floyd would be too, if it wasn't for his crippling fear about your job."

Hank took in a sharp breath. He had told Floyd a million times to never, ever talk about his job. "What? May I ask what he said to you?"

"Yeah, said he can't handle that you're in danger all the time. Surely he's told you that, also?"

"Yes, it's been an ongoing debate. I can't seem to convince him otherwise."

"Well, may I point out that he's not exactly wrong? You don't go anywhere without armed guards, and the poor kid-"

"Thank you doctor. I'll talk to him in a couple of days. What the hell is taking Theo so long?"

Hank stalked back to the exam room and saw his boys lying alongside each other in the bed. Theo was falling asleep, and Floyd put a finger to his lips as his dad came in.

Hank ignored him and laid his hand on Theo's leg. "Up. Let's go."

Floyd protested, "Dad, he-"

"Quiet. Theo, on your feet in five seconds or you're going to get spanked."

"Get up Theo," said Floyd firmly, unwrapping his arms and pushing him up. It was more like fifteen seconds until Theo was out of the bed, but Hank let it go because it was almost 2am and the poor kid was too groggy to obey much faster.

"There's no need to be so mean to him, dad," said Floyd grumpily as he got back under the blanket that Theo had appropriated.

Hank almost snapped at his oldest, but then he relented when he realized how utterly unfair that would be. Instead, he softened his tone.

"Theo, let's get you home and into bed. Go back out to the waiting room for a second."

He left, and Hank walked to the bed to look straight down at his weary son, expression stern but tone as calm as if they were discussing baseball.

"What do you think about coming to work with me when you're feeling better? You can meet everyone, get a better feel for the office. Help me with a few things."

Floyd looked aghast. "Why would I want to do that, dad?"

"Because you seem to think we're some kind of slaughterhouse or something, and that we're running the world, kicking ass, taking names. I'm sorry to say you're going to be really disappointed when you find out how unexciting and normal the organization really is."

"No, thank you."

Hank didn't relent. "And more importantly, you'll see how normal I am, too. Believe it or not, I'm actually a prankster in the office and...shhhh, don't tell anyone, but," he lowered his voice conspiratorially, "your dad is actually *not* a monster. Keep that between us, though." He winked.

Floyd had no intention of giving in. "Right, everything's totally normal. That's why Daven keeps a gun in his drawer and you threatened to send me to boarding school if I get within a mile of the building. Just leave me alone, please."

Hank's response was simply to swallow hard; no possible retort for that one. Floyd had an excellent point. So much for a peace offering.

"Right. Well, I can't argue with you there. I'm going to go. Remember not to talk to anyone about any details of my job. I'll know if you do. Sleep tight. See you Wednesday night."

He turned around and saw Dr. Harborough in the hallway, so he stopped her and spoke in a low voice.

"Who is the best child psychologist in the city?"

———

TWO DAYS LATER..........

PALISADES HOSPITAL

Hank was quite surprised to see Daven sitting worriedly next to Floyd's hospital bed when he arrived back at Palisades. Their eyes locked for a few seconds and Hank's heart leaped a little into his throat, but he pulled his attention away as quickly as he could and focused on Floyd.

"Hey buddy. You feeling well enough to go home?"

"No," mumbled Floyd. Hank was not at all surprised that his son wasn't happy to see him.

"Your doctor thinks you should be discharged. You want to disagree?"

"Yeah. Need to stay here."

Hank got closer to him and felt his forehead. "This isn't a hotel. When they say you're ready to go, we're going. She said she'll be back in half an hour. Promise me you won't fight about it?"

Floyd shrugged noncommittally.

"Need a verbal answer, Floyd."

"I want to stay."

Hank pushed his irritation aside. "We'll see. I'm going to go to the cafeteria and grab a snack real quick. Haven't had dinner yet. Daven, want to join me?"

Dav looked up from where he'd been studying his fingernails, then he leapt to his feet. "That'd be great." He looked over to Floyd, who had his eyes shut again. "See you later, Floyd-o."

"Bye Uncle Dav."

They walked down the hall in silence, a guard in front and behind them. Daven then veered off to the left, but Hank called after him.

"Dav? What are you doing?"

"I'm…leaving? Parked out this door." He pointed behind him.

A group of women at a nursing station was watching them, so Hank forced himself to sound cheerful. "Can you join me for a quick bite in the cafeteria, first?"

"Uh…sure."

They went, still walking in silence, and sat down in a private booth after grabbing snacks and water. Avery was hovering at first, but Hank shooed him away.

"I'm sorry, Hank," blurted Daven, a little desperately. "But Floyd called me and begged me to come, and we couldn't reach you because you were in the air. He tried to call you after you landed but it seemed like your phone is dead. And…it seems my number might be blocked."

"It is," replied Hank calmly.

Daven looked as if he was about to say something about that, but changed his mind. "Okay. I couldn't just say no to Floyd, so I've been here about 4 hours. He was asleep most of the time. I think he just needed a familiar face to watch over him, with Brittany being so new and all. He didn't say much of anything, but you'll be happy to know he managed to apologize for the grass incident before dozing off."

"Good." Hank took a bite of an apple slice. "Did he say anything about me at all?"

Daven looked incredibly uncomfortable all of a sudden. "He did, and I'll tell you if you really want to know."

"Do I want to know?"

"No."

Hank grimaced. "Okay. Never mind. Thank you for coming. I know it meant a lot to him."

"And I'll leave as soon as...wait. What?" Daven cocked his head sideways. "I thought you would be...you're not upset?"

"Not at all." Now Hank chugged down the rest of his coffee, but said nothing more as he wondered why the hell he was drinking coffee at 11pm. There was a long, awkward silence as he pondered the question without any answer except that he was possibly a little jet lagged.

"Ok, well...you're welcome," said Daven eventually, as he played with his tie. The ultimate sign of nervousness.

Hank finished his apple and then leaned forward a little bit, fully conscious of all the eyes on him in the cafeteria. "Trust me when I say that you visiting Floyd without my consent is the very least of my concerns right now. I would have said yes anyway, had you managed to reach me. So don't worry about it."

"Oh. That's good to know. I would hate to think that you didn't want me to see him anymore. You know, considering I treat him as a mere *bargaining chip* and all."

Hank's expression didn't change. "Can we talk business for a moment? Preferably without the passive aggressive commentary."

Says the king of passive aggressive behavior. "Of course," Daven murmured, feeling rather ashamed of his jibe all of a sudden, no matter how well-deserved it was.

Hank signaled Avery over and asked him apologetically to refill his coffee mug. As soon as the man stepped away, Hank took a deep breath. "Before I say anything else, I just need to know if you're really planning to come back to the office in a month, or if you...you know, let's just say I wouldn't blame you if you didn't want to work for me anymore."

Daven looked puzzled. "Do you even have to ask?"

"Yeah, I do, actually. Because I honestly don't know what's going on in your head right now."

"You know how you can find out? Stop shutting me out and talk to me."

Hank could see that Daven was entirely sincere, so he plunged forward. "Okay, good point. I'm sure Floyd told you I've been in Philadelphia. I got summoned there under the pretense of meeting with Stewart to get berated for publicly throwing the FBI and Harmon under the bus. Turns out Harmon was summoned for his own response, and we were hauled in together before the president himself to get our asses kicked for embarrassing the politics community at large."

Daven was completely stunned. "Holy shit, Hank," was all he could say.

Hank added, "Yeah. There's more. We really need to talk, but not here. Can you come to my house tomorrow night?"

"What about Rupert?" Daven asked after a moment. "If this is a serious business matter, he should hear about it as well."

"I don't disagree with you, but…honestly, your opinions carry more weight at the moment. Especially after how much he fought me over that last press release."

"I don't agree at all, Hank" Daven responded, even though he was secretly flattered. "If we're to rebuild trust between the three of us, we need to get past these differences in opinions and just talk to each other plainly in the future. Otherwise…" *this will all happen again….*

Hank nodded. "Okay, agreed. Since his family eats dinner at 6:30, let's meet at 5. I'll leave work a little early and you guys can meet me at the new house."

Daven smiled. "Great. I've been wanting to see it."

"The electricity and water was just turned on yesterday, so I'm rather eager to see it myself. The security gate uses fingerprints, but the bypass code is 40774077."

Of course it was. Hank was a huge fan of M*A*S*H. And there was another reason he wanted to go to that house, too: the long driveway was completely private and solidly gated. Although the top of the house was visible from the street, no one would be able to see any cars that were coming and going, never mind any activity at the front door. For that reason alone, Hank could not wait to move in.

"Okay." Daven wanted to ask Hank to unblock his phone number, but it was perhaps too soon for that. Maybe he would even do it on his own.

"There's one more thing, Dav, before I go back to Floyd."

"Yes?"

"I just...the harsh things I've said to you lately. I'm not even sorry. I'm having some serious trust issues right now. With you, with Rupe, with my guards. With Stewart. With my own sons. Honestly, I don't even trust myself at the moment. This whole thing has just kind of shattered me, and I'm resentful and unhappy, and...a lot of things. But I'm really trying to work through it and get us back to where we were before. I need your patience and understanding."

Daven nodded. "Understood. In the spirit of being completely honest, can I say something a little harsh in return?"

"Sure, why not."

"You've been scaring the shit out of the same people you claim not to trust anymore, Hank. I don't think that's a coincidence."

Hank looked like he hadn't heard correctly. "I...what?"

"You heard me correctly. I would like to posit that maybe your trust issues with everyone else are happening because *they're* starting not to trust *you*. Not your motivations, of course, but your impulsiveness and need to always have the last word. it's dangerous."

Hank was flabbergasted. "That's...that's what you call a *little* harsh?"

Daven took a deep gulp of his own water. "I call it the truth. And if I didn't care about you, I wouldn't tell you this outright and risk you shutting me out forever: you should have never thrown the FBI and Harmon into the fire on national television. It was vain, and aggressive, and altogether indefensible. The Hank Bancroft I want to work for knows when he's getting too smart for his own good."

Hank smiled a little. "Too smart, huh?"

Daven did not smile back. "Yes."

"Even though I got exactly what I wanted?"

"You did? You got the tapes?"

Hank winked. "No. Even better. Harmon was put on a 90-day probation. One more misstep and he's gone."

"But...doesn't that apply to you, too?" Daven was appalled.

"Nope. I just got a warning." Hank grinned. "My first one. Harmon already had two, so that's why I baited him at the press conference. Knew he couldn't resist shooting himself in the foot and earning that final warning."

Daven almost asked if he had planned this all out from the very beginning, from the moment they learned of the murder, as Rupert had said. It now seemed incredibly likely. But he stopped himself when he realized he didn't *really* want to know the answer to that.

An ill omen seized Daven's heart like a claw grip, and he realized he no longer trusted the man who was sitting in front of him, calmly drinking his third cup of coffee at midnight and smiling to himself victoriously.

CHAPTER SIX

Los Angeles

"Okay, wait, Hank...so you're saying you *purposely* earned yourself a warning in order to see if you might be able to take Harmon down with you?"

Rupe was carefully aghast, and Hank sighed as they all climbed the stairs up to the second floor of Hank's new house after just having touring the mostly-finished kitchen.

"Don't be so dramatic. It was a calculated risk to make him behave and focus on other things besides all this back-and-forth aggression between our parties."

Aggression that you started, thought Daven.

"Oh, I like this big landing," Rupert cooed. "Lots of natural light."

"I was going to carpet this area, but it will be hard to keep clean with all the foot traffic. My sitting room is up this staircase," he said, pointing. "It's the only room with furniture so far."

He turned around and yelled down to Lucas, who was still wandering around on the first floor.

"Lucas! We'll be up in my sitting room, all is well. Can you wait in the car, please, or in the pool house?"

"I'll wait in the car, boss," he called back.

"You can see Dav's house from here, too," Rupert laughed as they reached the top of the stairs.

Daven looked out the window. "Just the roof. Guess I won't be sunbathing naked up there anymore."

Normally Hank would make some kind of inappropriate homoerotic joke at this point, but he said nothing, which was somewhat disappointing to the other men.

There were only two chairs in the room - still plastic-wrapped - so after Hank closed the door, he sat on the broad window sill while Dav and Rupe plopped themselves down onto the squeaky, slippery chairs.

"Sorry," he said. "I would take off the plastic, but we still need to paint in here."

"So, you were actually in the same room with Harmon when this all went down with the president?" asked Rupert, whose expression was darkening by the second.

"Yup. Standing right next to him. Alright gents, get comfy. I'm going to tell you everything that happened from the moment we touched down in Philly...So I get to the waiting room, which they call the *antechamber* because they're so full of themselves, and guess who's sitting there looking as smug as a cat in a box? Harmon himself."

Urbanes Headquarters, Denver

"So I just looked straight at him and said, good day, Hank. I'm glad to see you've gained weight since we were last together. I was a little worried about your health for a while."

"So I just laughed. I've gained maybe five pounds since then, all muscle."

"Hank was so pissed. You should have seen his face."

"I got up to shake Harmon's hand and he immediately came over to me and acted like we've been best buddies for fifteen years."

"I didn't think he'd talk to me after the insult, which is what I wanted, but he got up and started glad-handing me until I had to move away. Twice. No sense of personal space whatsoever. He must drive Rupert and Daven nuts."

"So I tried my best to make him as uncomfortable as possible. Taking his hand and then wiping my nose and shaking his hand again. You know how he is with that germophobia. I just kept closing in. And he kept backing up, and I'm trying my damndest not to laugh the whole time."

"Thankfully President Rickon quickly came out and called us in, looking like he just sucked on a lemon, as usual. Salome and Stewart were seated on either side of him."

"They didn't even ask us to sit. Felt like I was in the principal's office again, waiting to get my ass beat."

"The first thing he says is that we have shamed our parties, ourselves, and our constituents in general. Then he gives us a copy of our press releases and has us read them out loud to the entire room."

"Then we had to switch and read each other's press releases to each other. I'm still trying not to laugh. And there was this really long, uncomfortable silence as the president pulled out two books from under his desk. Taking his time flipping to pages he wants.”

“And he hands them to us and makes us read out the entire code of conduct that Hank and I both had to agree to and sign before the parties could be legitimized by President Hannigan.”

“The entire damned thing. Simultaneously. Every freakin’ word. It took an hour. I had to piss half the time.”

“We finally get to the end and then he pulls out the appendix to that agreement, which lists all of the consequences for every possible violation of the code of conduct. Makes us read that one, too, in full.”

“So basically for 90 minutes we’re doing this, and I can tell Harmon has to piss too because he’s getting all fidgety and looks approximately as annoyed as I am.”

“I seriously had to take a shit at this point. And for some reason Hank thinks the whole damned thing is hilarious.”

“Then Salome asked us if there was anything we did not understand, so that she could provide clarification. We both said no, so she handed us a pen and we had to sign the book again with the current date.”

"The president proceeds to remind us that per the terms of our charters, he is technically our boss, and has the power to take disciplinary action if needed...which is needed now, he adds."

"Up to and including removal from our positions. He then issued an order for us to speak to each other every single day for ten minutes at 10am."

"We each have to hand write out the entire code of conduct, terms & consequences, and our own charters, and submit them with 90 days."

"If we don't do it, we lose our jobs. Period."

"Then he issued me a final warning, and gave Hank his first warning. Then he dismissed us."

"And that was it. I ran to the bathroom on one side of the lobby and Harmon ran to the other one. And when we came out, we were told a car was waiting for us."

"The nail in the coffin came when we were made to share a car back to the airport, and there was a ton of traffic on 95 so it took forever to get there."

"We didn't talk at first, until I asked him if he was still friends with Lester Boyd. Turns out they're still in touch. Lester's some kind of school teacher now in Virginia. That surprised the hell out of me, to say the least. Didn't seem he was that type. Anyway, at least we found that common ground to talk about."

"On the way there, Hank asked me about Lester Boyd. I knew they had some kind of falling out ten years ago, but I didn't know they were that close. So I just said he was a teacher. Didn't mention what kind."

"And then we got to the airport. Theo just about wet his pants when he saw us get out of the car together, and my guards probably did, too, but there was no further drama."

Daven looked surprised. "You actually talked about Lester Boyd? Your college roommate who almost shot you the last time you saw each other?"

Rupert's eyebrows raised way up. "Wait, what? I haven't heard this particular story. Do tell."

"Yeah, thanks for the reminder, Dav." Hank rolled his eyes. "As you know, we parted ways after Harmon asked him to join the Urbanes. Lester thought that's where I was headed, too. In the same night, he learned I was chosen to run the Seditionists *and* that we'd been banging the same woman...well, let's just say we had a really big fight about it, among other things.

Anyway. He ended up getting married to one of my old girlfriends later on. I'll leave it at that."

"Sordid. So now you and Harmon are BFFs now, huh?" asked Rupert with a thin smile.

Hank frowned. "Hardly. But I think we came to somewhat of a truce by the time we got to the airport. There's something else, though, and it's the reason I asked you to come over."

Rupe moaned. "Oh god, what now?"

Hank cleared his throat. "He told me this morning on the phone that Colbert suspects Janet was a double agent. Then he said their double agents are so untrustworthy that as of yesterday they're not going to use them anymore, after one went radio silent for a week. He asked me to do the same, in order to *maintain good relations*. What do you think of that?"

Rupert blurted right away, "I think he's lying."

"Absolutely," agreed Daven. "Don't trust him, Hank. Not for a heartbeat. He may not be *employing* them, strictly speaking, but he'll get inside information in other ways."

Hank nodded. "The thought occurred to me afterwards that maybe I should have asked Harmon if that agent was responsible for the calls that got you guys in trouble."

Daven shook his head. "He has no reason to tell you that."

"He fired him for a reason, Dav. And he last heard from him at Christmas, or right before. I don't think that's a coincidence. He wouldn't have mentioned it other-" He paused as a low, jangly noise emanated from his backside. "Hang on, my phone's ringing."

Hank pulled it out of his pocket and was astonished to see Harmon's cell phone number and name in the caller ID. He managed to keep a straight face somehow and stood up to walk just outside the door, then answered the phone cheerfully.

"Hey Theody, what's up?"

"Hank, it's...it's Harmon," said the curt voice on the other end.

"Oh yeah, I know," Hank relied casually. His heart was pounding in his ears.

"Ah, I see. You're not alone."

"Nope."

"I'll make this quick, then. On our call this morning you asked me if I would consider turning the name of our double agent over to you. The one I just had Colbert fire for going silent on us for a week."

Hank's throat went dry. "Yeah, I remember."

"I will tell you his name 24 hours from now if you do me a favor."

Hank felt a bit dizzy and sick suddenly.

"Why exactly are you calling to tell me this now? Could this not have waited?"

Hank heard Harmon take a deep breath. "I needed an unrecorded line. On tomorrow's 10am call, I'm going to ask you if Janet was a double agent. Colbert is going to be with me, listening silently. I need you to not fight with me about it, and just say no. Even if she was."

"Uh. Why?"

"I can't tell you right now. You'll have to trust me."

"Ah. The answer is no, I won't do you that favor. Don't ask me again, Theody."

Hank hung up, rattled to the core. *Fuck...*

"Hank? Everything okay?" Rupe asked in alarm as he saw Hank's flushed cheeks a moment later.

"Yeah, I'm...it's been a long day. Let's get out of here and go back to the house for dinner. I can't think straight anymore."

"Hank, we haven't even-" they both began.

"Let's go anyway."

He hurried down the stairs while Daven and Rupert looked at each other with wide eyes.

"That wasn't Theo," whispered Rupert. "Did you notice the ringtone?"

"No. Why?"

"It was the 'Halloween' theme song."

Dav was still puzzled. "Okay, so..?"

"It's kind of an inside joke. That's the ringtone Hank uses for Harmon. And only for Harmon. I'm telling you, that was *not* Theo."

"What the hell..." whispered Daven.

Never Nothing

Blame the Tide

CHAPTER ONE

Bancroft Manor

With the servants in Eagle Rock for the weekend, Hank took it upon himself to cook breakfast for his sons. Normally they would go to a restaurant on Saturday mornings, but with the recent media circus and Floyd's new unwillingness to go out in public, the whole tradition was suddenly now more of a massive burden than anything else.

Floyd hadn't willingly spoken to his dad since his release from the hospital, and secretly Hank was glad for it. Not that he would ever admit it, of course; but if Floyd wasn't talking, it meant he also wasn't complaining or being insolent. Theo wasn't saying much, either, but that was okay, too. Hank desperately needed the peace and quiet.

Hank didn't bother to wake up his oldest for breakfast. He knew the moment he threw the bacon on that Floyd would rise up like a cartoon and follow his nose down the stairs. Theo was seated at the table, reading a comic book, when Hank's phone rang. Since Daven and Rupert were still blocked, there was really only one person who would be calling him at a time like this. Well, maybe two, but he already knew which one it was.

"Hey Taylor."

"Good morning, boss. I just got a call on the emergency line from an anonymous agent."

Hank turned off the stove and removed all the pans. "Hang on." Then, to Theo, "I'll be right back. Make sure the dogs don't jump up on the counter to get at the food."

He went into his study and locked the door.

"God, I'm afraid to ask. What's going on?"

"As soon as I answered he blurted out that he was the one who called Daven on Christmas eve and Rupert on Christmas day. He won't speak to anyone but you and said he will call in exactly 48 hours. That is literally all he told me, verbatim. I didn't get a word in edgewise before he hung up."

Taylor sounded scared, and Hank knew why. She didn't want to be accused of talking with an unverified asset, like her unfortunate colleagues.

"It's okay. You did good. Speaking of which, I didn't get the chance to ask you yesterday if there is any news about those meetings I had before Christmas? Any clue as to who could have been the secret Urbane?"

Taylor sighed a little. "Well, I've been able to definitely exclude three of them, and I'm focusing on the other two. I promise you I will have a better update on Monday evening."

"Can you come to my new house on Monday morning at 7 for this call? I'll call you tomorrow with the address and gate code."

"Will do. See you then."

Hank's heart was pounding so hard that he felt physically ill and had to sit down for a few minutes. Normally at a time like this he would be rapidly dialing Daven to get his take on the incident, but that was the farthest thing from his mind right now.

He picked up his phone and scrolled through his work emails, then took a peek into his personal email, which was nearly all junk. But there was one message from Rupert's personal email that was two days old.

"Hank, just wanted to let you know Dav and I are going to Maui for a week. Back on January 6. Happy New Year."

Rupert had a little beach house there. It would do both of them a lot of good to get away and have some privacy, so Hank was happy for them, but he still deleted the message without responding. By the time he returned to the kitchen, Floyd was hovering over the bacon and the dogs had been taken outside, where they were busy struggling for custody of a Frisbee, tails banging against the French doors.

"Floyd, sit down. Bacon's not done yet."

"Yes, sir." Floyd turned and sat, then picked up one of Theo's comic books.

"How's your stomach?"

"Fine, sir."

Again with the unnecessary *sir*. Hank resisted a sigh as he pulled the pan back on the stove.

"Theody, why don't you go play with the dogs for a minute. I want to talk to your brother."

"Yeah, right. You guys just want to eat all the bacon for yourselves!"

Hank scowled. "I'm hurt. That's not true. You know we'll save a couple slices for the dogs."

"You suck, dad." Theo grinned and went outside, where he joined in the struggle for the Frisbee.

Hank said absolutely nothing in a test to see what Floyd would do. Sure enough, the boy began fidgeting as he waited for his dad to speak. Then he started drumming the table, which he knew his dad hated. Hank didn't take the bait.

A few minutes passed, and Floyd couldn't take it anymore. Just what Hank was hoping for.

"What is it, dad?"

Hank smiled a little. "Oh good, I'm *dad* again. Thought you disowned me there for a while. Food's done, go get your brother."

Floyd blinked, expecting to have a little more of a talk than just that. Hank turned away and busied himself with the dishes.

Urbane HQ - Denver

Harmon normally didn't work on Saturdays, much less on New Year's eve, but it was a new era. Colbert was obsessed with the idea that Janet had been a double agent, and now Harmon was convinced, too. The possibility was driving him crazy. Her murder had been planned to frame Hank, but now everything could be turned upside down. He wasn't the praying type, but if he was, he would have been asking for the tapes to not show even the slightest glimpse of Yannick.

Colbert was also convinced that Yannick didn't realize he was on Seditionists property at the time. Harmon wasn't so sure. The man had turned before, and could turn again. In fact, considering they hadn't heard from him in a week, that was increasingly becoming a possibility, too.

Harmon took another drink of chai tea and flipped through the final pages of the charter. He had chosen to write that one out first, since it was shortest, but it was still taking far too long. Damn Stewart and his schoolboy punishments.

Colbert walked into his office without a sound, as usual.

"Boss? Got a second?"

"Yeah. Sit down."

Colbert's massive body made the chair creak. "I was wondering...I hope you don't mind me bringing this up again. But I thought you were going to ask Bancroft if Janet was a double agent? You've spoken to him twice since we agreed on that, and-"

"Yeah, I know. But he's not going to tell us if she is. Or was, rather."

"Still might be good to ask. We might be able to figure it out from his reaction."

Harmon set down his pen and leaned back. "Look, I've been thinking. One more misstep and I'm out. You understand that, right?"

Colbert nodded. "Yes."

"So...I'm all but praying the FBI doesn't identify Yannick. If they do, Hank will reveal Janet was double and then it will make even less sense that she was killed by one of their own agents on their own property. And *then* it will become clear that Yannick was also double. Then I'm out of the game. So we're going to leave this Janet issue alone right now and wait for the FBI to hopefully declare it a cold case. So don't ask me again, please. In fact, don't even mention her at all."

Colbert was stone-faced. "I understand. So that brings up just one more question, and then I'll shut up. May I? Thank you. I have a feeling Bancroft set you up with that press conference of his. He wanted you to take the bait.”

“I know, we’ve already discussed this. I was stupid and I’m paying the price.”

“Okay. Sorry. My point is, he wanted you exactly where you are now, and he got it. Which means she was double. Period. What makes you think Hank won't volunteer that information himself?"

"Because he doesn't know what side the killer was on. Are we done now?"

"Yes. That’s the last time I’ll mention it.”

Harmon took a deep breath and calmed down a little. “I actually happen to agree with you, which is why I’m walking the straight and narrow from here on out. It’s time for me to accept I can’t win against Hank Bancroft. Never have before, and he’s getting smarter every time. There’s no reason we can’t just start cooperating with him. It’s not like our parties are that different.”

Colbert was incensed. “Cooperating? You can’t be serious.”

“I am. At least on the subjects we happen to agree with. The government is really our biggest enemy right now, Colbert.

Look at what they're doing with trying to strengthen the felony manual labor laws. It's slowly escalating to cruel and unusual punishment over the years. We've watched it happening and done nothing, because we're too proud to band together and fight back. And that's just one example of where we should be cooperating."

"You're basically talking about rebelling against the government."

"No. It's called lobbying. We would never be doing anything illegal. Speaking of which, if Yannick ever calls back, tell him his services are no longer needed and we'll send him a nice payment for what he's done so far. In fact, why don't you try calling him again today and letting him know."

"I doubt we'll ever hear from him again," muttered Colbert.

"Fine with me. What he apparently did to Daven and Rupert is more than satisfying enough. But I'm telling you, as of right now, this subterfuge stops. I don't want to lose my job. We have to focus on other things from here on out. And you know there's another reason I want to work with Hank."

Colbert smiled. "Ah yes, I wondered when you would quote Napoleon again. It's been at least two days. *Keep your friends close, and your enemies closer*."

Harmon smiled back as he stood up. "Exactly. Here, I'll get some cash out of the safe for Yannick in order to entice him to meet you. Then let him know outright he is never to contact us again or we'll turn him in for his little cocaine trafficking side job."

"You got it, boss. He'll want to see a payment slip to know this isn't a trick. I won't actually give it to him, of course."

"No problem. Fill it out for me and I'll sign it."

"Yannick? It's Colbert."

"What's all that noise?" Yannick asked.

"Just wind. Sorry, I'm driving and the sunroof is open. Hang on." There was a long mechanical sound as the roof closed. "Listen, I just left Harmon's office. He wanted me to pass along a message to you."

"Oh great. What now?"

"He's really happy about the work you did with Daven and Rupert. Wants to send you a nice big payment for it, and an advance for other future services which I'm about to ask you for."

"What services?"

"Among other things, he wants you to call the FBI and tell them you were ordered by Hank Bancroft to kill Janet, because he no longer trusted her as a double agent. With the hope that in doing so on Seditionists property, Harmon would be framed. Obviously you'll have to use a voice changer and everything. I have some other details to share first before you do that, so they know you are legit."

Another long pause from Yannick. "Okay. I'll need authorization from Harmon directly, as you know."

"I have it right here, and the payment as well. In cash."

"Cash?"

'Yes, indeed. Where can we meet?"

CHAPTER TWO

Bancroft Manor

Hank slammed his hand down on the alarm clock and turned over with a grumble. Today was the day their mystery man was due to call, and Taylor was due to the house in an hour. He almost didn't want to know what the strange caller had to say, and the overwhelming desire to quit his job and go live in a cabin in the woods overtook him for the tenth time since Christmas, at least. Nothing really seemed worth living under such stress anymore.

He fell back asleep and was soon awakened by the second alarm that had been set for 6:30am.

La Quinta Inn, Phoenix Airport

Yannick once again opened his wallet and counted the money advance that Colbert had given him to frame Hank Bancroft for Janet's murder. He smiled, and then counted it once more. For this kind of cash, he'd do pretty much anything.

He picked up the phone in his room, connected the voice changer to the mouthpiece, and dialed Stewart in Philadelphia.

FBI Headquarters, Philadelphia

"This is Stewart, how may I help you?"

"Uh, yes. I'm calling in with an anonymous tip in the case of the recent murder in Colorado."

Stewart sat straight up. "I'm listening. Please proceed."

"I'm going to give it to you straight, then I'm hanging up before you can trace me. I'm a professional hit man. Hank Bancroft contacted me and offered me $10,000 cash to kill Janet. I declined, but obviously he got someone else to agree to it."

"I see. And did he give you a reason for wanting to kill her?"

"Yes. He said she's a double agent for the Seditionists, and that I was to follow her to a drop-off spot on their property so that Harmon would be blamed once Bancroft announced she was double. He wanted me to shoot her in the back of the head with an untraceable bullet, which I wouldn't have been able to obtain in time. Hence, my reason for declining."

"Okay. Why are you turning him in and taking the risk of being identified? Your motives for calling me are just as important as Bancroft's are for killing Janet. For example, maybe someone paid you even more money to pin the blame on him."

Yannick hadn't expected that question, but he was a smooth talker and a fast thinker. "If I'm not telling the truth, how could I possibly know she was a double agent, or the details of her execution method? Goodbye, Stewart. Time to do your job and lock him up."

Maui, Hawaii

"Dav…it's almost 4 o'clock in the morning. What are doing out here sitting in the dark?"

"I don't know. Can't sleep. Why are you awake?"

Rupert shrugged in the dark, even knowing the other man couldn't see the gesture. "Same deal, I guess." He sat down, too. "Can't stop wondering if Hank will ever forgive us."

"Well, stop wondering. He won't. My brain is actually stuck on those calls we got on the emergency line. Do you think he's doing anything at all to identify that person?"

"No, but Taylor is. She started working on that before we got…in trouble. All I know is that part of me still believes he was telling the truth, that Hank unknowingly met with an Urbane and paid out money to get something done. He's done similar things before, although none of it has ever been against the law."

Daven sighed. "You mean like the time he paid off Floyd's teacher to tutor him at his house in order to prevent him from repeating 8th grade? Or paid a reporter to destroy camera film on the spot? Things like that?"

"Yeah. Like I said, not against the law, and hardly scandalous."

"No, but not exactly kosher, either. He's done some really borderline shady things. I don't like how he flaunts his ability to charm his way out of trouble. Or the way he plans moves way in advance like a chess master, and I'm referring to the whole thing with Harmon and the FBI tapes. That is a case study in Machiavellian strategy. I know he's never technically broken the law, but Rupe...he's going to cross the line someday, if he hasn't already. It's inevitable. He thinks he's untouchable."

Rupe laughed a little. "Daven, you've known him for over ten years and you're just now realizing this? I knew that from day one. Come on."

Daven shook his head. "No, I knew. But recently...well, he's gone from merely playing with fire to actually burning himself on purpose with that press conference stunt, and I swear to god he enjoyed every second of the smoldering wreckage he left behind. I've never seen him do anything like that before. Have you?"

"No. But he's had a very long rivalry with Harmon, and maybe it just feels good to see the man put in his place for once."

"For *once* ? Hank forced him into a final warning with the president, and he was also the cause of all three warnings before that. He's going to get taken out just like Janet if he's not careful, or maybe locked up, and then his sons...you know what, I'm sorry I brought it up."

"Seriously, Dav? That's what I'm here for. To talk these things out. I'm just trying to play the devil's advocate here."

Daven grumbled, "You're doing a shitty job by just defending him blindly. Don't you realize how self-destructive and dangerous he's become lately? I can't be the only one seeing this. His ego is going to be his downfall, and disaster is just around the corner.'

Rupert said nothing for a long time.

"You still awake?" Dav prompted after a while.

"Yeah. Just thinking about all you've said. Dav, you've never doubted him until we got that call. Never. Did it really rattle you that much? Don't you think it could just easily be something Harmon set up in order to shake our confidence? Hank isn't the only chess master in this game, you know. None of our agents in their right minds would ever refuse to give their identifying code. The only thing that stands to reason is that he wasn't one of our agents at all."

Daven was quiet for a little while, and then he replied, "No, actually. I hadn't given that much thought."

"Well maybe you should, before you keep excoriating Hank any further. Maybe he isn't the only one who is getting exactly what he wants right now. If anything, Harmon is more dangerous now because he's cunning *and* desperate not to let Hank win again. I'd be willing to bet big bucks that Hank is going to step aside entirely at this point and just wait for Harmon to fall on his own sword."

"Yeah. I see what you mean. Thanks, Rupe."

"Sure. Go back to bed. This will all be clearer in the morning."

"God, I hope so."

Bancroft Manor

Taylor's phone rang at exactly 8am, and even though Hank was expecting it, he still nearly had a coronary when it happened.

"Hank Bancroft."

"Mr. Bancroft. I'm using a voice changer, so don't try to identify me."

"Fine. What do you want?"

"I am the person who called Daven on Christmas eve and claimed you met with an Urbane and gave him money to plant an agent in the government."

"Okay. And who are you, exactly?"

"I'm calling to tell you it was someone higher up in your own party who put me up to it. Not Rupert or Daven. But someone within your headquarters."

"I see. And you're an Urbane yourself, I gather?"

"I was, yes. Now I'm neither party. You're all really fucked up, you know that?"

Hank cleared his throat, not sure what to say next. Taylor looked at him and shrugged, her face a picture of blank confusion.

"Right, so...why are you calling to tell me this, exactly?"

"Simple. My loyalties lie to my bank account now, so I want you to pay me a lot of money to tell you who it was that put me up to this. I'll call you back in exactly 7 days from now to hear your initial offer. Expect to negotiate up for a while. Goodbye."

"Wait-"

The line went dead, and Hank wasn't really sure if his heart was still beating or not.

La Quinta Inn, Phoenix Airport

Yannick hung up the phone and grabbed his duffel to make his way to the airport. While he waited at the gate, he made a quick call to Colbert.

"Hello, kind sir. Stewart is aware of the situation. Vacation's over and I'm headed back to Los Angeles now for my drudgery of a day job. Awaiting further instructions….and payment."

Colbert laughed. "Who knew a mere accounts payable specialist could be so treacherous."

"Oh, my friend. I have not yet begun to fight. Just you wait. Talk soon."

Yannick hung up, and then smiled as he pulled out his Seditionists employee ID badge and studied his picture for the hundredth time. Almost five years at the company now, just enough to avoid suspicion. He wasn't sure how long he could play both sides, but it sure was going to be fun while it lasted. And quite profitable, if the past two days were any indication.

January 9

Hank was fitfully resting in bed after the Sunday servants banquet while one of his dreaded tension headaches pounded like a bass drum on his temples. This was disappointing considering it had been an unusually peaceful week, with both of his boys behaving perfectly and the paparazzi mostly leaving them alone. The latter was mostly because business was back to where it had basically been before Christmas, with no new inflammatory press releases or devastating news to report. Even Harmon was being nice on their daily calls, saying nothing that raised Hank's hackles or gave him reason for suspicion. Taylor was still working diligently on all her leads, and Hank was confident they would have an answer to his many questions soon.

He already knew he wasn't going to offer the mystery caller any money, so that point of stress was on the side burner for now. If there really was a mole in the company, which he doubted, he would ask for Daven's help to sniff him or her out. In the meantime, he had to focus on his own overwhelming workload.

Hank was just about doze off, but groaned as his phone began buzzing on the dresser. He would have given anything to be able to ignore it with no damage to his conscience.

"Yeah, Avery. What's up?"

"Boss, sorry to be the bearer of bad news. Your sons just got kicked out of the library."

"Oh god," Hank moaned. "I knew this day was too good to be true. What exactly did they do?"

Avery continued, "They were scuffling. One of them - they won't say who - knocked over a sculpture and broke it. Shattered it, actually. I'm being asked to pay for it on the spot."

Hank closed his eyes and counted to ten in order to compose himself. Boys will be boys, and he had been just as much of a delinquent at that age...but his father wasn't constantly in the spotlight, either. Floyd and Theo knew better than to draw negative attention to themselves, and that's what infuriated him.

"Okay. I hope it's not some kind of Ming Dynasty vase."

"No, but they're asking for almost three thousand dollars, sir."

Hank pinched the bridge of his nose. "And my sons were definitely at fault?"

"Yes, sir. I saw part of it happen, just not enough to conclude which one of them did it."

"Okay. Put whoever is asking you for money on the phone with me, please."

Another pause, some shuffling noise. "This is Tami."

"Good morning, ma'am. This is the father of the boys who broke your sculpture. I'm so very sorry. Will you please give Avery a bill for my records? I'll have him return with payment in the morning."

Her tone was highly skeptical. "*Right*. You'll just voluntarily return with a few thousand dollars sometime tomorrow. I'll just call the police and make a report, instead. Thank you anyway."

"*Wait*." Hank realized with a start that this woman didn't know who the boys were, or who he was. That could be a good thing about 99% of the time, but right now it was pretty much the worst thing. "Ma'am, make out the bill now and I'll be over in twenty minutes with cash. Yes, *cash* . My boys will stay there with their, er, babysitter until I get there. Please don't call the police. You'll understand why when I arrive."

There was a pause long enough to make Hank worry, but then she finally agreed. "Twenty minutes, then. That's all I'm giving you. We close in half an hour," she added firmly.

"Thank you, ma'am."

Hank cussed up a storm as he spun the dial to his safe and pulled out the cash, but his sense of humored returned quickly when he pulled up fifteen minutes later in the Thunderbird with Vance; Tami turned sheet white and grasped onto Avery to keep herself upright.

"Mr. Bancroft. *I'm so, so sorry.* I didn't know that was you."

Hank struggled not laugh at Avery's expression as he pretended to be contrite. "Please accept my apologies for not introducing myself. May I have the bill?"

She handed it over with a shaky hand, eying him like he was a lion about to take down a gazelle. "Do you...I mean, want the evidence, and your boys said they did it, and...if I would have known-"

"Ma'am, it's okay. I promise I don't bite." He pulled open his wallet and pulled out $2,940. "I'd like a receipt, please. As quick as you can. And discreetly, if you don't mind."

"Of course, sir."

Hank walked away and climbed into the SUV where Theo and Floyd were waiting, slamming the door behind him. Avery stayed outside with Vance and moved away to the other side.

"It was me, dad," Theo confessed immediately. "I bumped into it."

Hank was surprised to find he couldn't muster up any real anger about the incident. On the contrary, he felt deeply sorry for his sons. They couldn't get into any kind of trouble without the threat of it being all over the news the next day, and that wasn't fair. Hardly a childhood at all.

But it wouldn't do to let his children think they could act like hooligans just because their father felt guilty for being a public figure. He cleared his throat and affected an angry expression.

"*Bumped* into it. While doing what? Having a seizure?"

Theo swallowed hard. "No. We were, I was...well, it just kind of happened."

"It was my fault," put in Floyd, very quietly.

Hank resisted the urge to ask them no further questions and forgive them on the spot. They wouldn't learn anything that way.

"Rough housing in the library, huh? Are you trying to get yourselves-"

Theo protested immediately, "Dad, we weren't rough housing. Floyd had a panic attack-"

"Shut up, Theody!" hissed Floyd.

"*You* shut up*!*"

"Boys!" yelled Hank. "What the hell? Theo, finish your explanation. Floyd, shut it or else."

Theo was breathing hard. "He *was* having a panic attack, and he kind of shoved me backwards trying to get outside, and I fell into the pedestal that the sculpture was on. It wasn't his fault, he just needed to get some air and he was freaking out."

Floyd was instantly irate. "No I wasn't! We were fighting because Theo was being obnoxious."

"I was not! You were totally freaking the fuck out over nothing!"

"It wasn't nothing!" Floyd objected.

"I was trying to *help* you, you stupid piece of-"

Floyd shoved his brother backwards and Theo shoved back even harder, then they started hitting each other. Hank separated them easily by dragging Theo over his lap on the opposite side of the car.

"Alright, that's settled. You're both getting punished when we get home. You'll go directly to my study-"

"I didn't do anything!" protested Theo angrily, at same time Floyd said, "It was an accident!"

Now Hank's anger was real. "I don't care about the sculpture! The world will be fine with one less crappy piece of art. But I will not abide you being dishonest with your guards and fighting each other, period, and by that I'm referring to what just happened in this car. You know better than that."

They did, too, and they finally settled down with matching guilty expressions.

"Sorry. Do we have to pay you back the three thousand, dad?" Theo asked nervously.

"No. You're both getting paddled after you apologize to Avery, and that will be the end of it. Floyd, are you okay?" asked Hank after a moment, when it appeared his oldest had completely tuned out and was in his own world again.

Floyd didn't look up. "I'm sorry, sir," he said miserably.

"What caused you to panic?"

"I didn't panic."

Theo answered for him. "There was a guy following us around and taking pictures."

"What? *Inside* the library, you mean?"

"No, outside. He was stalking us through the windows."

Hank was not surprised to hear this at all. Goddamned paparazzi.

"Floyd, I'm going to ask you one last time. Are you ok now, or not? Theo, you be quiet."

"No, dad. I'm not okay. I'm a freakin' basket case and you know it."

Damn it. "Alright. So you did panic. It's okay. Anything you need from me before we head home?"

Floyd shrugged yet again, almost appearing not to answer. But then he blurted out angrily, "For the hundredth time, I need you to quit your fucking job! Then I wouldn't have to deal with this shit in the first place."

Hank flinched and nearly snapped back, but managed to keep his cool.

"Hop out of the car, Theo, and get in with Vance. Have him take you home."

"Yes, sir," responded Theo with a stunned expression as he climbed out.

"Yeah, go home and cry to your stuffed animals, Theody," Floyd muttered.

"*Floyd!*" Hank softened his tone and looked down at his anxious youngest son. "We'll talk later. Go."

Theo nodded, chin quivering, as he turned away.

"I want to go home now," Floyd said quietly, still not looking at his father.

"We're going. Just waiting on a receipt. Did you take your anxiety medicine today?"

Floyd nodded. "Yes, sir."

"Okay. Listen up. I've made a decision. You're going to counseling, and no amount of protesting is going to make me change my mind. So don't start. And I'm going to ask Rupert if you and Theo can home school with his kids. It will take you out of the spotlight a little. We've talked about it before, and you didn't seem against the idea."

"I'm not against it at all," Floyd replied. There was nothing he wanted more, actually, and it upset him that he wasn't already homeschooled. "You should know that considering I've asked you about it a million times, but you never listen because you don't care."

"Settle down, Floyd," Hank replied mildly, hoping Floyd would shut the hell up before he took things too far.

"It's true. You never listen to me and only pretend to care how I feel. Theo doesn't care, either. The only person who is always nice to me is Uncle Dav. Forget home school, I want to go back to boarding school so I don't have to put up with this shit."

"If you don't calm down immediately, we're going to have a problem."

"You're already the problem, dad!"

Floyd suddenly burst into tears, and Hank got out of the car in disgust. Tami was just starting to walk back towards the group, and he waited patiently for her to reach him and hand him the receipt.

"Here you go, sir. Again, I'm so very sorry for what I said on the phone."

"Who was the artist of the piece they broke?" Hank asked out of curiosity.

"The original founder of the library, actually. He died last year."

Hank felt extra horrible all of a sudden. "Oh, shit. I mean…forgive me. I can't express how sorry I am. When I return home I'll make a donation to the library in his memory."

"That would be nice. Thank you."

"Sure. Uh. Have a good evening if you can, I guess?" He cringed at his own awkwardness. "I'm sorry. I mean well."

"I know," Tami replied with a thin smile. "Your sons are still being banished from our library for one year, though. Have a good evening, too…if you can." She winked flirtatiously, gave a little shimmy, and then walked away.

Hank blanched, then glanced aside at Avery, who was clearly shocked as well, but in an entirely different way altogether.

"Don't you dare laugh," he muttered out of the corner of his mouth as they stared at the departing woman. "I will kill you where you stand, I swear it."

"Might be worth it, boss," he replied dryly.

Vance had gotten back into the car abruptly and was all but writhing in silent hysterics.

"Traitors, the lot of you," Hank declared with good humor as he turned away. "Let's go."

"Dad," blurted Floyd as his father reappeared in the SUV. "I didn't mean what I said."

"We'll talk later." Floyd nodded and went quiet, so Hank looked at Avery through the rearview mirror as the man got in the car and shut the door. His eyes were sparkling.

"You alright there, Chief?"

There was a strangled chuckle, and then a gravely formal reply. "Yes, sir, I'm fine. Home?" he asked.

"No. Let's stop by Daven's house. But first pull through the Shake Shack so I can use the restroom and Floyd can get some food."

Shake Shack

"Good afternoon, Hank," answered a very surprised Daven. Hank hadn't called him in almost two weeks, and Dav was starting to think he never would hear from him again.

"Are you home?"

"Yes...you called me on my house phone, remember?"

Hank was in a locked restroom by himself, but he still lowered his voice almost to a whisper. "Right, sorry. Floyd really wants to see you. We had a bit of a blowup today. I feel extremely awkward asking, but if you don't have any plans, can he come over for a bit and play with Shannon?"

"Yes. You shouldn't feel awkward, Hank. He's been over here plenty of times before. May I ask what the blowup was about, so I'm prepared in case he mentions it?"

"No, it's best if I don't say anything. Let's just say he's finally entered his *I hate you* stage, so...it's been rough."

"I see. Well, I'm here, so whenever you want to send him over.
I don't really have any food for him or anything though,
haven't been to the store in a while."

"That's okay. We'll drop him off. I'm ten minutes away.
Thanks, Dav. I owe you."

CHAPTER THREE

Daven's House

Daven was waiting outside when Avery pulled up the drive. There were, surprisingly, no cars out front at all, which meant the press had become tired of waiting for something exciting to happen at the Johansson house. So Floyd quickly jumped out, excited to hear Shannon barking madly from inside the house. He hugged Daven briefly and then ran inside.

Hank hadn't been planning to get out of the car, but Floyd had left all the food behind, so other than asking Avery to do it there was no other choice. He grabbed everything and climbed up to the porch.

"Hey," he said, somewhat shyly, unsure of what else to say, and it wasn't because he was upset or anything. It's just that Dav was wearing a very nice suit and looked as though he'd been at some kind of professional function. *Or a job interview.* And Hank didn't want to give away that it was the very first thing he noticed.

"Nice to see you, Hank." He looked over to the car and nodded with a slight smile at Avery. "I was upstairs in the balcony at church with Rupert this morning. We didn't want to disturb you."

"Oh, good. So now I don't have to yell at you guys for not going. Um." He handed the bags over and the tray of drinks. "You said you didn't have food, so we got your favorite burger with onion rings. And a root beer float, of course."

"Oh." Daven looked puzzled as he took the tray and drinks. "That's....really nice. Thank you. Can you open the door for me, please?"

Hank opened the screen with one hand and the front door with the other, but stayed on the porch. Daven did not invite him in, for which he was grateful. The last thing he needed right now was more awkwardness.

After setting everything down in the kitchen, Dav came back to the front door. "Thanks so much, Hank. That was thoughtful. How long do you want him to stay? He's already out in the backyard throwing Shannon's Frisbee. Seems very cheerful."

"Yeah, well that's because he's away from me. I really appreciate this and I'll make sure he doesn't overstay his welcome. Just kind of discreetly call me when you're ready for him to leave."

"I can't," Daven replied evenly. "You blocked my numbers."

Hank flushed. "Ah. Right. Um." He took his phone out. "Let me fix that." He scrolled through the settings for a few long awkward moments before realizing he had no clue how to unblock a contact. Daven realized it shortly after he did and held his hand out.

"Here, I'll do it." He took the proffered phone and quickly completed the task without any trouble, then handed it back.

"I have to leave for dinner in two hours, but that should be long enough. Shannon gets exhausted pretty quickly at her age."

"Right, um...where's your guard?" Hank had noticed the little BMW wasn't in the driveway.

"I gave him the week off."

"Without a replacement? You can't do that, Dav. You should *never* be without a guard. We've talked about this before, about how it blatantly violates our security policies."

"Well," said Daven with a small smile as his eyes swept up and down the street. The very empty street. "It's not like I have anyone after me right now."

Hank tried to ignore the simmering anger that suddenly overtook him. "I don't care. You're getting another guard and that's the end of it. I'm sending Lucas over as a substitute, and you're going to take him everywhere with you. This isn't negotiable."

"Very well." Daven wasn't smiling now, but he didn't protest. After all, with Floyd in his house he should damned well have a guard standing by. Hank called Lucas, who said he would be over in two minutes.

"How was Maui?" Hank asked abruptly as he hung up the phone, trying to shake off his all-too familiar irritation with Daven's disregard for his own safety.

"I wouldn't mind spending more time there, let's just put it that way."

"Hmmm. Rupert comes back to work Tuesday, as you know."

"Yes."

"I..." Hank hesitated, not wanting to force Daven into a conversation he didn't want. But he was desperate for someone to talk to. "Look, I, umm..."

"Come inside, Hank," Dav said abruptly as he turned away.

"No, I don't want-"

"Hank," repeated Daven with more urgency. "Come inside. *Now,* if you don't mind."

Hank was puzzled at first, but then he turned to follow Daven's glance down the street.

"Oh, fuck. Really?" The press were coming; Hank and Dav knew the cars anywhere. It was always the same group who arrived first on a scene, and within seconds the four cars were lined up across the street with telephoto lenses at the ready. The screened-in porch wasn't enough to completely block them, so Hank went in and closed the door behind him.

"God, I'm sorry. Thought we got away from them at the drive thru."

"It's alright. They were following Lucas, I think." Daven waited a minute and then stepped back outside to unlock the screen door and let the man in. He nodded and then silently started to make his rounds about the house, keeping one eye out the front windows all the time.

Daven had the news running in the background in the living room, and Hank happened to glance at it out of the corner of his eye and saw a very familiar sight. Sure enough, it was live video from somewhere outside Daven's house. He dashed over to the remote and turned up the volume.

"-question of what happens when Rupert Aster returns to work Tuesday, and whether or not the trust can ever be regained between them. As you can see, Hank Bancroft clearly doesn't hold too much of a grudge against Mr. Johansson, at whose house he arrived with his son a short time ago after stopping first at the Shake Shack on Pico and Westwood for some burgers and root beer floats, just in time to watch the big game. We'll stay on the scene and go live again when we obtain more information about their dramatic incident at the library only an hour ago- "

Hank muted it angrily as the unexciting footage of him entering the house with bags of food was shown, and then shown yet again.

Daven looked at him askance. *"Dramatic incident at the library ..?"*

"Fuck. There are cameras hidden in the trees outside your house. Probably at mine, too. I'm starting to get why Floyd is having a meltdown every day over this shit." He sat down on the couch and grabbed his float, inhaling almost all of it in one fell swoop before he realized he was making himself at home way too easily. He jumped to his feet.

"I'm sorry, Dav. I...it's been a day. Can I sit for a minute?"

"Of course. Eat, please. At the table though, if you don't mind."

At that moment Floyd came bouncing in through the sliding glass door, Shannon close on his heels. "Uncle Dav, the Frisbee is stuck on the roof of the pool house. I'm really sorry. Does she have another-"

He stopped abruptly as he caught sight of the television. Hank snatched up the remote again and turned it off, swearing under his breath as he did so.

"Floyd-"

"Why is your house on the news?" Floyd almost shrieked at Daven. "Is it because we're here?"

"Yes, they're out front right now," said Daven calmly, throwing a look at Hank that shut him up instantly. "Floyd, settle down, and look at me," Dav commanded in a surprisingly authoritative tone as he reached for the boy and took a hold of his wrists, clasping them to his own chest while walking over to the dining room table at the same time, all but dragging

Floyd alongside him. Hank watched in fascination, far too surprised to say anything.

Daven held fast to Floyd as he sat. Floyd tried to wriggle away once and then stopped. "Breathe. Look at me. You're inside and they can't see through the walls. You're safe. Are you breathing? Steady."

"I can't." Floyd was on the very edge of a panic attack. "Why are they following us everywhere?"

"Because they make lots of money selling pictures of your famous dad," Daven answered matter-of-factly. "It's their job to take pictures. They aren't out to hurt anyone. It's a paycheck. Are you listening? You really need to steady your breathing or you're going to pass out."

"I don't know how," Floyd gasped after a moment, and Daven instantly moved his hands from Floyd's wrists to put one on his lower back, and one over his diaphragm, keeping him standing in place with a tight grip, at perfect eye level where he was sitting on the chair. Hank stood watching, frozen by the couch, remote still in hand.

"Concentrate. Count with me. Breathe in from deep down here (he patted his back) for four counts, then out for four from here (patting his belly)." Floyd tried, messed it up, then tried again. "Good. But you're still breathing too high. Take it lower. One more time. Stop looking at the television, it's off. Look at me. Now breathe in for five counts, and out for five. Okay, again and then we'll move on to six. Floyd, *stop* looking at the TV. Close your eyes."

The repeated this exercise for quite some time until they got to ten. To Hank's utter shock, his son was so deeply focused on his breathing tasks that he'd apparently forgotten about everything else around him. Daven had removed his hands after eight and let Floyd do the rest on his own.

After ten Daven stopped counting, and Floyd's eyes fluttered open and locked on to Dav. He did not look towards the television. Hank still dared not move for fear of breaking the spell, but his thoughts were racing in ten different directions.

Watching Floyd melt under Daven's calm ministrations vividly brought back the deep affection, admiration, and warmth for the man that Hank had been forcefully pushing out of his mind since the incident on Christmas day. There was absolutely no question that the next thing Hank was going to do was to let Daven know he was completely forgiven, and then ask for forgiveness in return. Beg, if needed.

Floyd broke the silence suddenly. He was perfectly calm. "Thank you. Are they still out there?"

Daven swallowed hard. "Probably. Let's find out. Hank, turn on the television again."

Hank nearly dropped the remote in his surprise. "Uh, no. Let's not do that."

"Turn it on," commanded Daven, and Hank only hesitated a second before complying. To his horror, there was the house, still...and the video was focusing on Avery sitting in his car, doing literally nothing of any interest whatsoever. Hank glanced anxiously at Floyd, who didn't seem perturbed at all. In fact, he seemed amused.

"Why are they looking at Avery? He's not even famous at all. I hope he doesn't pick his nose. Can you turn the sound on, dad?"

This was where Hank put his foot down. "No." He clicked off the television and threw a look at Dav that dared him to protest. "We're all going outside with Shannon. Together. We're going to walk right up to their cars, talk to them, get their names, be friendly, let them take pictures of us, and then we're going to come back and eat our cold burgers and melted shakes. Come on. Dav, harness up the dog."

“Uh, Hank….”

Hank went to front door and put on his coat, then held Floyd’s out for him.

“Come on, Floyd. You can walk Shannon. Dav? Harness, now please.”

Floyd walked over and let his dad put his coat on him. Since Dav was moving so slowly, Hank picked up the harness and slipped it onto Shannon, who was now carrying an enormous hot dog toy in her mouth. Hank opened the front door and stepped out, with Floyd close behind him.

“Dad, I don’t like them. Why are we doing this?”

“Because I want them to stop harassing you and Theo, so we’re going to be friendly and try to make peace. All I want you to do is come with me and just say hello. You don’t have to do anything else. Can you do that?”

Floyd nodded, tightening his grip on Shannon’s leash. Hank heard Dav come out behind him and laid a hand on his son’s shoulder as they went down the porch stairs. “Okay. Just relax, buddy, we’ve got this. Just follow my lead.”

Shannon immediately peed in the bushes, and Hank realized with a slight moment of panic that he hadn’t brought a bag.

Daven saw his expression. "She won't poop again yet. By the way, Hank, you are insane for doing this."

"Play along, Dav. We're on live television. Smile."

The trio - or quintet, rather, now that Avery and Lucas had scrambled to join them - crossed the street. Hank could feel, but not hear, the cameras clicking constantly as they went up to the lead car. He kept a hand tight on Floyd's shoulder when he thought he was about to bolt.

"Steady, Floyd," he murmured as he gestured for the man to roll down his window. The man did, but he looked confused and not a little scared.

"Good evening. I'm Hank, this is my son Floyd, and this is Daven. We noticed you're taking pictures of us, so we thought it was only proper to come say hello and introduce ourselves. How's your day been?"

"Uh....fine?" The man set his camera down on the passenger seat. "My name is Hank, too. What's the dog's name?"

"Shannon," answered Daven. "She's friendly," he added unnecessarily as Shannon stood up on her back legs and poked her head in the car while chomping down excitedly on her hot dog. The toy's squeaks practically drowned out what Hank said next.

"Look, you're welcome to take pictures of Daven and me, but I want to request that you stop following my sons around until they're famous on their own accord. I can't imagine you make too much money off of photos of them, do you?"

The other Hank was rendered a bit speechless. "Well, about $50 each, a couple times a month, maybe? Not too much."

"And how about my pictures?"

"A lot more," the man admitted nervously. "Hundreds."

Shannon dropped the toy in his lap, and he picked up the sloppy mess and handed it back to her with a disgusted look on his face. Hank smiled beatifically.

"Well, I will give you $1,500 to stop taking and selling pictures of my boys for an entire year. In return I'll invite you to a private event where you will make even more money off me. I trust you to honor our agreement at all times. Here's my card so you can contact me about receiving payment. Nice to meet you, and have a good day, sir. Floyd, come on. Take the toy away from her."

Dav was horrified as they walked to the next car. "Hank, what the hell? You can't pay off photographers like that! And giving them your cell number, too? What the hell are you doing?"

"Settle down, Dav. It's my secondary cell number that's always dead. Guess I need to find the charger now. Floyd, you doing okay?"

"Yeah."

They walked up to the next car repeated the process. That photographer congratulated Floyd warmly on getting his license, and told a funny story about his own daughter getting hers. They chatted for some time, and Floyd was delighted to pet his English Pointer that was now poking his head out of the rear window.

By the time they were to the fourth car, two more cars had rolled up. Hank hit all of them, and Hank again offered to pay them all off. Dav was still in shock and desperately trying to halt the proceedings, while Floyd was still extremely nervous and shy, but they did the best they could to get through it. Floyd even managed to have a full-on conversation with the last man, whose son he happened to know from school.

When they walked back to the house, Hank made them all turn around and wave to the cars before heading back inside.

Daven was visibly furious, but he kept his tone carefully in check. "Hey Floyd-o, do you mind me taking your dad away to talk to him for a minute? You can go ahead and eat without us."

Floyd was beaming and very visibly relaxed. "Sure. Can I use your microwave?"

"Of course. Hank? I would like to show you something in my office, please. It's rather urgent."

Hank had never seen Daven so angry before, and it was quite disorienting to be the one on the opposite end of the wrath that occasionally existed between them.

"Of all the stupid things you've ever done. Are you *trying* to get yourself jailed?"

"I didn't break any laws, Dav-"

"You most certainly did, and you know it. Bribery, for starters, and setting yourself up in the future for other accusations. Doing all of this on live television, to boot. What the hell are you thinking?"

Hank stayed calm despite the bitter novelty of being yelled at by his subordinate. "First of all, those live cameras have no microphones, so nobody besides us heard me. Secondly, I'm actually going to make them sign a contract before I pay them. All above board and legit. Then, I'm going to work on getting laws passed that prohibit photos of minors being sold for profit. So are you going to calm down, or are we going to have a problem here?"

"We already have a problem! You're totally out of your mind. All but one of those men work for the Urbanes, and you're actually going to literally sign a contract with them and allow them access to you that even our own photographers don't have? You are giving money to these vultures and actually trusting their word? Have you completely gone out of your senses?"

"Daven, that's enough," Hank warned.

"I agree with you there, Hank. This is definitely enough. I was already nervous about everything you've been up to lately, but I trusted you to at least have some common sense. This proves you don't, so I'm done. You'll have my resignation letter this evening by email, and by courier at the office tomorrow. I want you and Floyd to leave my house immediately."

Hank suddenly felt like the floor was collapsing beneath him. He could hardly breathe, and his chest began to burn fiercely.

It seemed almost impossible to speak, but he managed somehow.

"Wait. Dav, please. You're blowing this out of proportion. At least let me explain. Floyd-"

"I don't want to hear it." Daven looked like he was about to throw a punch as he crossed around his desk and pulled the office door open.

Hank swallowed hard, feeling stinging in his eyes. He was *not* going to cry, no matter what.

"I'll go, but Dav...please don't kick Floyd out, too. He did nothing wrong." *God damn it,* he cussed at himself as a stray tear escaped before he could catch it.

"You both have to go," replied Dav, ice cold. "Also, don't even bother blocking my number again, because you'll never get another call from me."

"Okay. I'm sorry you're upset with me. I get it. But I did what I had to do for my son." He strode over to the window and yanked open the blinds. "Look."

Every single photographer's car was gone. Daven was unimpressed. "There will be more in five minutes. All you did was put a band-aid on a gunshot wound. Again, thank you for the food. Now if you don't mind, kindly let yourself out of the house for the last time and lock the door behind you. I'm going upstairs."

Hank didn't respond, he just watched him leave and then stood there a minute to collect himself before going back in the dining room to gather up his wallet and keys.

"Is Uncle Dav okay, dad?" Floyd said between bites of his burger.

"I think so. Where'd he go?"

"Said he had to go upstairs for a while."

Hank cleared his throat. "I think Dav isn't feeling well but he doesn't want to admit it to us. What would you think if we just went ahead and let him rest? I'll clean up all this trash while you finish your burger."

Floyd seemed disappointed, but he didn't argue. Hank carefully picked up every piece of trash and threw it all into the composter, including Daven's uneaten southwest burger and onion rings. Then he drained the root beer float mush into the sink, cleaned the sink, and took off Shannon's harness to hang it up in the closet. The remote needed to go back on top of the television, so he did that, too.

The house was perfectly spotless now. Everything was done. No need to stick around anymore.

“Okay. Say goodbye to Shannon, and let’s head out.”

Floyd stood up and threw his wrappers in the trash.

“Hey, Floyd?” asked Hank, still feeling in total shock by what had just happened with Dav. “I’m so very proud of you for how you handled those photographers. You did good. Thanks, kiddo.”

“Sure, dad. It wasn’t as bad as I thought. They were nice. Except for the third guy.”

Hank smiled a little. “Yeah, he’s a pain in the ass. But he won’t follow you anymore. None of them will.”

Floyd didn’t seemed wholly convinced. “There are so many more, though.”

“Then I better start working on them, too. Come on, let’s go.”

Hank couldn’t help but feel an enormous sense of loss as he looked around Daven’s house for the very last time. Floyd went out first and headed straight to the car, leaving Hank standing in the entryway. He shut off the light, then heard Dav coming down the stairs.

Against every instinct he had to flee and follow Floyd into the SUV, he turned the light back on and waited with heart pounding.

Daven turned the corner, stopping in surprise at seeing him still standing there.

"Did you forget something?" he asked in a totally normal tone, as if he was asking for the time. He had changed into his running clothes and was clearly on the way to the gym downstairs.

"Yeah. I mean, no. Sorry, I'm right now, kind of having a hard time believing this is happening."

"Please leave your copy of my house key on that sideboard," Daven said calmly, nodding to the piece of furniture in question. Without further adieu, he turned and went down the stairs to his basement. Hank stood there frozen for a few moments, then removed the key in question from his keychain and set it down with a soft metallic sound. He couldn't bear to look around the house one more time, so he closed his eyes as he shut the lights off and locked the door behind him.

He opened his eyes to the sight of seven more press cars lined up across the street, exactly as Daven had predicted.

CHAPTER FOUR

Bancroft Manor

Same day

It seemed to Floyd that an eternity or two had gone by in the spare room while he waited his turn for a reckoning, stomach twisting into several varieties of knots the entire time. Surely Theo wasn't getting it *that* bad? They must have been talking a lot, that's all. Hopefully lots and lots of talking. Or maybe his dad just wanted him to suffer, since he knew how much waiting like this tormented his oldest son.

He pulled his jacket tighter and shivered again, then sat on the bed and pulled the heavy blanket around him like a protective barrier and wedged himself against the headboard. He didn't move when his father finally appeared half an hour later and led the still-sniffling Theo to a corner. When Hank looked at him and jerked his head toward the door, Floyd silently rose, folded the blanket back up, and trudged behind him to the study.

"Hey. Sorry it took so long. Theo had a really hard time getting through it."

Oh god. Floyd glanced at the clock and was astonished to see only 45 minutes had passed since he was last in this room.

Hank continued, "I went really easy on him, don't worry. He was just very emotional about the whole thing and needed a lot of time to settle down and talk. He's very worried about you, you know."

Floyd swallowed hard, but said nothing.

"Relax, son. You've got yourself all wound up because you've been waiting, that's all. If I'd known he was going to take so long, you would have been up first. Anything you'd like to say?"

Floyd's tongue felt very thick all of a sudden. "I'm sorry. For everything I did and said today, and…"

"I know. It's okay. The only thing you're being punished for is fighting with Theo in the car and not being honest with Avery, so let's get this over with. If you promise me you'll behave, I'll go easy on you, too."

Floyd nodded, and walked up to the desk to take position. "I promise, dad. Thank you."

After it was done, Hank took Floyd back to the spare room and dropped him off at the opposite corner from Theo with a reassuring squeeze on his shoulder.

"I'll be back in an hour. You know the rules. No talking, no fidgeting."

Two minutes later, Theo tentatively asked from his corner if Floyd was okay.

Floyd's nerves prickled instantly, his irritation at Theody's unflattering description of his panic attack rushing to the forefront again.

"I'm fine, Theody. Heard you were acting like a little bitch, though. What a surprise."

Theo did not rise to the bait. "I'm glad you're okay."

"Yeah? Well I don't care what you think, so shut up and go break another sculpture."

Silence.

Ten seconds later the door opened and Floyd was unceremoniously yanked out of the corner by his very angry father.

"Alright. I've officially had it with you. Come on."

"Dad!" Floyd pleaded in shock as he was bodily pulled down the hall to Hank's study. "What are you doing?"

"You don't remember that I can monitor every room in the house? Really? How dare you make such a vicious comment to your brother at a time like this."

Oh, shit. "I'm so sorry, dad. I have-"

"Pants down and hands on the desk. Now."

Floyd's entire body went numb in a flash. His dad had never believed in spanking on the bare, although Theody got it once when he was eight for starting a fire in the backyard that took out several hedges and a lemon tree. The memory of the trauma his brother suffered on that awful day had haunted Floyd ever since.

Hank took off his belt as he spoke with the deadly calm that indicated he was moments away from exploding. Floyd backed away towards the door.

"*Floyd.* Don't make it worse for yourself."

"Worse?" he cried. "How could I possibly make this worse?"

Everyone hates me, Hank moped as he made himself some tea in the kitchen after returning the inconsolable Floyd to the spare room. Maybe Taylor didn't hate him, or a few people at the office, but there was far more to life than work friends. There also wasn't much to life at all without Daven. The thought of going even one full day with him as an enemy was too much to bear.

So Hank drank his tea, ate a Moon Pie, then took a shot of whiskey and prepared himself for a fight. Daven's phone rang only once, so Hank hung up and tried again, thinking it was a bad connection. This time, it didn't ring at all and went to a generic recording. The third time, too. Puzzled, he started to dial a fourth time, then stopped.

Daven had blocked his number. The realization hit him like the old cliché of stepping on a rake and getting smacked in the face. In disbelief he went to Floyd's room and called him from his son's cell. Certainly Uncle Dav wouldn't block Floyd-o, too?

"We're sorry. Your call cannot be completed to this number. Goodbye."

Then he tried from Theo's phone, and then Avery's, and then the house's landline. All of them were blocked.

Fuck...

He went back to his study and pulled up the live feed from the spare room to check on Floyd. The boys were talking again.

"...wasn't your fault. I'm so sorry, Theody. Are you even listening?"

"Yeah."

"You forgive me?"

"Yeah, but only if you shut up so we don't get in trouble again."

Floyd left his corner and went to lay down on the bed - on his stomach, naturally - and started to sob again. Hank got up and activated the intercom switch on the wall, keeping his eyes on the video feed.

"I'm giving you ten seconds to get back in the corner. Ten. Nine. Eight."

Floyd rose up and dragged himself back into place.

"Thank you."

Hank slammed down the intercom switch, sighed heavily and rubbed his temples for a few minutes. He then called Rupert, feeling absurdly relieved when he actually picked up.

"Hey, Rupe. Got a minute? Or thirty?"

"I'm in the middle of dinner, but I can talk for a few minutes. What's up, boss?"

"Great, thanks. It's been a day, man. I can't even tell you. Have you spoken to Daven recently, by chance?"

"No, I haven't spoken to him today."

"Okay, well...I'm not going to beat around the bush, so here goes. Daven is quitting because of me. I could really use your advice on how to change his mind."

Rupert nodded. "Oh, I see. Honestly, Hank, this isn't the best time or place for that kind of conversation. Can I call you in about an hour, maybe around 9pm?"

Hank tried not to let the disappointment come through in his tone. "Yeah, of course. I'll be up."

He then impulsively called Lucas, even knowing it could easily lead to another fight with Daven if he wasn't careful.

"Hey, are you with Daven?" he asked as casually as he could manage.

"Yes, sir, as ordered."

"Good. Where are you guys?"

"Yamashiro, but we're leaving shortly. He's just now paying the bill."

"Okay, thanks. I just wanted to make sure he's alright, since I haven't heard back from him regarding something urgent we had discussed today."

Lucas said quickly, "Sir, I don't know if you will hear back, to be honest. He's drunk."

Hank thought he hadn't heard correctly. "He's...he's what?"

"Drunk. *Really* drunk, actually. He told me not to take any calls from you, but you're the boss, so I picked up anyway."

"Yeah, good choice. Thanks Lucas. Who are you guys with?" It was a highly inappropriate question, and they both knew it. Lucas had every right not to answer, and Hank was about to take it back before his guard answered anyway.

"Rupert and his family, and some of their friends from out of town."

Rupert and his family.

Rupert, who just told him less than ten minutes ago that he hadn't spoken to Dav today.

Rupert.... lied to him.

Hank felt like an arrow had been shot through his chest.

"Okay, great. That's good, I guess. Just get Dav home safely, then. I won't tell him we spoke, of course. Talk to you tomorrow."

He left his study and went straight to his bedroom, shutting his phone completely off and quietly locking the door behind him.

He forgot all about the boys, who were still obediently standing in their corners when he raced back to the spare room more than three hours later to release them.

CHAPTER FIVE

Tuesday, January 11

For the first time in his life, Hank called out sick from work when he wasn't actually sick. It was 8:00am and the boys were eating breakfast when he finally got dressed and ventured down the stairs.

Theo was startled to see him, and so was the chef, who quickly whipped up another plate for his boss. He took it gratefully and sat down at the table across from Theo.

"Dad? Why aren't you at work? Are you alright?"

"I'm fine, Theody. Working from home today to catch up on some projects."

"Oh."

Hank was determined to eat his meal in silence, but Theo had other ideas.

"Are you and Uncle Dav really fighting, dad?" Theo asked, and Hank nearly choked on his sausage as he eyed Floyd, who looked sheepishly down at his eggs.

"None of your business," he replied sternly.

Theo looked like he was about to cry. "Sorry, was just trying to make conversation. Your phone's ringing."

Stewart was calling. Hank sent it to voicemail. Just as he did that, he noticed a new email notification from Rupert. Unable to resist temptation, he clicked on it even though he knew he'd regret it.

"Hank, what's going on? I waited all night for you to call me back last night. Where are you this morning? Thanks - Rupe."

Hank deleted it, then scrolled backwards through his emails while his heart pounded like a bass drum. Surprisingly, the promised resignation letter from Daven was nowhere to be found. He scrolled through three times just to make sure.

Nothing. What the hell did *that* mean?

"Theo, run up to my sitting room and see if Daven's truck is in his driveway."

The boy complied instantly, and Hank waited for his footsteps to fade before he set his fork down and looked at Floyd.

"What did you tell Theo, exactly? Be honest. I'm not mad."

"That I tried to call Uncle Dav last night but he blocked my phone," Floyd responded quietly, eyes on his plate. "The house phone is blocked, too. And Theo's cell."

"I know. I'm sorry."

"What did you do?" Floyd looked absolutely devastated.

Hank was at least glad the poor kid wasn't blaming himself, but there was very little he could say to make this any better. "Can't say, but I'm working on a resolution. Please be patient."

"What about Rupert? When you are going to ask if Theo and I can home school with his kids? The new semester starts next week."

Oh god....

Theo ran back down the stairs, thankfully saving Hank from having to answer that question. "Dad! Dad!!!"

"What the hell, Theo?"

"Shannon's loose! I just saw her run down the street all by herself! Where's Uncle Dav?"

"Fuck," blurted Hank, and he and Floyd jumped up and ran to front door, with Theo close behind. Sure enough, Shannon was racing down the middle of the street with her leash in her mouth, looking as gleefully joyous and wild as any dog had ever looked. All three of them ran out to catch her, but she dodged them and kept going straight towards Olympic Blvd.

"Boys, back in the house. Now."

Hank jumped into the Thunderbird without a second thought and roared down the street by himself, which he took a moment to appreciate. It was nice to not have guards and drivers clinging to him hand and foot. He picked up the phone and called Avery.

"Hey. Take an SUV down to Olympic and go...right. I'll go left. Daven's dog is on the loose and we're trying to catch her. Yes, I'm by myself. Hurry. Got to go."

Hank drove around for almost two hours with absolutely no sign of Shannon. His phone had long died, so he had almost given up until he turned into a park and saw three adults trying to corner her on a playground. The Thunderbird roared to a stop at the foot of the swings and he jumped out.

"Shannon, come here, baby girl! Come on."

Shannon spied him, and with a burst of energy she snatched up a tennis ball from the ground and ran straight at him. He yanked onto her harness and held on for dear life. It promptly snapped in his hands, and she almost got away again before he grabbed her by the tail and wrapped a strong arm around her torso. The three ladies were clinging on to each other now, staring at him in awe.

"Hank Bancroft! Oh my goodness!" they exclaimed happily. Hank ignored them long enough to get Shannon in the car (making sure all the windows were rolled up and the back doors locked so she couldn't escape again). Then he went over to them and shook their hands.

"Thank you so much, ladies. Thank you very much. We would have been devastated to lose her. I really appreciate your help."

One of the ladies had a camera, so Hank obliged them by taking photos with each of them, and then the three of them wanted a picture with Shannon, and then with the infamous Thunderbird, too. He was desperate to get Dav's baby back to him after secretly enjoying feeling like a total rock star for a few minutes, and was relieved when they finally let him go.

A black SUV had pulled up behind him during the photo shoot. Avery and his sons, of course. Hank waved at them and then got in the car and headed for home, taking different side streets than usual because he wasn't sure exactly how to get to

Daven's house from the park, and Avery honked at him when he took a wrong turn. He quickly flipped a u-turn and went the other way, when suddenly he spotted Daven across the street, climbing down a slope at a different park with Lucas a few feet behind him.

Hank pulled another U-turn, got honked at again by Avery, but ignored it and smoothly raced up an alley alongside the park to intercept the men.

Dav heard the Thunderbird and stopped in surprise as Hank glided up next to him and rolled down the window. "I've got Shannon, she's fine. Hop in and I'll drive you guys home."

Daven crossed in front of the car and leaned in the passenger side to reach back towards Shannon. She dropped the tennis ball into the front seat and barked happily at him, then whined while he rubbed her ears and cooed at her.

"Hank, I can't thank you enough. I don't know what to say. I'll walk her home from here, can you unlock the door?"

"Well, no...her harness snapped into pieces when I grabbed her, and I don't know where her leash went. For an older dog, she's really strong."

"Yes. Do you have a spare leash in the trunk?"

He knew there were a few back there. Maybe three, plus a harness or two. "No, sorry. You can ride with me, or with Avery if you prefer."

"I'll ride with Avery. Thank you, Hank, so much. If you can just wait in the car for a minute when we get there, I'll grab her other harness."

"Yeah, of course."

Hank watched Daven climb in the SUV and felt his heart break almost as much as it had yesterday. He waved to let Avery pull in front of him and lead the way back to Daven's house. When they arrived, Daven harnessed Shannon in the backseat and took her inside with the boys and Avery, who were all delighted at the outcome of the chase. Hank knew he should leave, but Daven's truck blocked him from moving forward in the driveway and Avery's SUV blocked him from backing out of it. Apparently he was expected to awkwardly wait in the car for everyone to decide the reunion was over.

And awkward, it was. Very. After a minute or two with no guard or sons in sight, he got out of the car and went to the front door. Daven let him in without comment.

"Sorry Dav, we'll get going. Floyd, Theo, Avery. Everyone out. Back to the house." Then, quietly but sternly to his favorite guard: "You should have already been outside with me."

"Sorry, boss, I actually thought you were coming in. I guess this makes us even for you taking off on me all alone two hours ago."

Hank fixed him with a ferocious glare. "Do you *really* think it's wise to get smart with me right now?" he snapped, still keeping his voice low.

Avery stepped back a little, startled at Hank's unexpected reaction to what was intended to be a lighthearted remark. "Sir, I....I'm sorry. I wasn't trying to...forgive me."

Hank nodded and reluctantly let it drop. He would have docked a full day's pay for any other guard who left him unguarded for any amount of time, never mind one who talked back to him like that, but he had put poor Avery through enough shit lately. It wasn't his fault Hank's life was miserable at the moment.

Everyone in his group suddenly departed at the same time, which left Hank face to face to Daven at the door. He didn't want to lose what might be his only chance to say something.

"I thought you were going to send me an email last night," he blurted quickly.

Daven ignored the remark completely and scooted past him through the doorway, then waved again at the boys and Avery as they got in the SUV. "Thanks guys. I owe you. Let me pull the truck out of the way for you."

Dav climbed into his truck as Hank just stood there, somewhat dumbfounded and numb. He quickly came to his senses and got in the Thunderbird, resisting the urge to angrily gun it across the perfect front lawn like Floyd had done a couple weeks ago. He would never do it, but had to admit that it would be an incredibly satisfying experience right about now. He even found himself briefly envying his son for knowing exactly how it felt.

When Hank got home he plugged his phone in at his desk and realized with a start that it was almost 10:30am. He had missed his daily call with Harmon. Sure enough, there were three missed calls on his cell. But no messages from him; just one from Stewart.

First things first, however. He hit the intercom button that connected to the security offices.

"Avery, report to my study on the double."

There was a longer pause than usual, then Avery's voice. "Yes, sir, on my way."

Less than a minute later the very subdued head of security arrived. He'd been reprimanded by Hank several times before for various minor breaches of policy, usually related to paperwork delays, but this was different. It was emotional, very personal. For that reason, Avery was incredibly nervous.

"Hey," said Hank quickly as he rose and came around to the front of his desk to lean against it.

"Boss, I'm so very-"

"Correct, I'm the boss, so I'll do the talking. I owe you a seriously huge apology for the way I snapped at you. You didn't deserve it. I mean, nobody does, but especially not *you*. I'm a fucking idiot, and I'm really sorry. Wish I could take it back."

"Uh...well, thank you, sir, but you were right about me leaving you alone like that."

"Yes I was, and I expect that to never happen again."

Avery swallowed hard. "It won't. And with respect, I fully expect you not to take off without a guard again, either. Especially with a dead cell phone. It nearly gave me a stroke trying to find you."

"Deal. Sorry." Hank reached out to shake his hand, and then patted him on the back as he walked him out. "Keep up the good work. I really need you more than ever right now."

Hank shut the door behind him, then raced back to his phone before Stewart could slap his hands for not keeping to the call schedule. Then again, maybe that's what the voicemail was for. He didn't want to know.

"Harmon, fuck, I'm so sorry. You wouldn't believe what I've been doing for the past two hours."

"Let me guess. Chasing Daven's loose dog all around the city and catching him yourself at the park? You're a true hero, Mr. Bancroft."

"Wait...what?" Hank stuttered, alarm prickling the hairs at the back of his neck. "How the *hell* did you know that?"

Harmon paused dramatically. "It was all over the news. There was a live feed of the pursuit, even aired here in Denver. Quite entertaining. You didn't know?"

Hank forced himself to breathe deeply in order to clear away the sudden dizziness. *Fuck.* This was getting out of hand.

"Please tell me you're joking. Because I won't be able to go out in public any more after this."

Harmon paused again, and then laughed. "I'm sorry, Hank. Just messing with you. No, a young lady who took a picture with you sent the story into the newswire a few minutes ago and one of our Denver reporters forwarded it to a few of us. She thought it was cute. You *are* a hero, you know."

"I'm...holy shit. You are a *horrible* person." Relief washed over him like a waterfall, and against his will Hank found himself grinning at the absurd imagery of the whole fiasco being broadcast live. "You got me good, I admit it. Thanks for the heart attack. Jesus H Christ on a pogo stick."

Harmon cleared his throat. "Yeah. Speaking of heart attacks, I got a call from Stewart on Friday. Why did you tell him that I asked you to say Janet wasn't a double agent?"

"Because I don't want to lose my fucking job, that's why," Hank retorted defensively, all amusement over the dog chase instantly forgotten. "You should have never asked me that."

"I asked you for a reason. You know how these things can be sometimes."

"No, I don't know. Because I don't play games."

Yeah...so says the chess grand master. "Fine. Then I'm going to be perfectly upfront. We know Janet was double, and we figured out what you're up to as far as trying to frame me for her murder. I was trying to get Colbert to-"

Hank felt like screaming all of a sudden. *"Frame?* It's not *framing* when you're actually guilty, Harmon. The truth will come out soon enough."

"No it won't. Haven't you read the FBI message this morning?"

Hank turned to his computer and quickly pulled up his email. "No. I've been a little busy playing reverse Lassie all morning with my chief of staff. Hang on."

It was a press release blurb that had been sent to both parties in advance of an afternoon release:

After reviewing all video footage available, as well as extensive forensic testing, we are unable to draw any clues as to the identity of the murderer. Ms. Janet died from a gunshot wound to the head with an untraceable bullet. The case is now considered on hold until new evidence arises.

"You have got to be fucking kidding me," Hank said out loud, feeling his headache arising anew at the back of his head.

"No one is fucking kidding you. That was the FBI's determination, which you *know* I could not possibly influence."

"Even so, you got away with it. Congratulations," Hank offered bitterly.

"Hank, please. If you want to formally accuse me, do so. I'll be happy to prove it wasn't us. But I, for one, would prefer that this incident to be the last one in which we are foes. Think about it. We believe in a lot of the same things, and if our parties unite on those fronts there's nothing that can stop us. We can still fight about the shit we disagree on, because that's our job, but-"

"Wait, what? Are you on drugs?" Hank laughed out loud, not able to believe what he was hearing.

"No. I knew you were going to say that. Actually, I want to meet with you in person this Friday. You and me. Talk some shit out. We can't keep going like this. You know that, right?"

Sounds like every single one of my conversations with Floyd lately, Hank thought wryly.

"Yeah, I've...I know. I hear you, and I don't want to fight either. But Harmon, you can't be serious. You know I don't trust you as far as I can throw you."

Harmon cleared his throat again. "If you prefer, the three of us can meet to talk. I know Daven is not a fan of mine, but his objectivity would be useful to both of us. Perhaps you should ask him for his opinion on this."

Hank laughed again. "Holy shit. You are definitely on drugs if you think Dav is going to go for this. Can I have some of what you're having?"

There was a long pause from the other end of the line.

"I'm trying to make peace, Hank."

"But I'm not. Go fuck yourself."

Hank hung up and reached into his refrigerator for a bottle of whiskey. His phone rang almost immediately, and it was Harmon. Of course. Knowing that Stewart would slap his hand for not obeying the ten-minute rule, Hank reluctantly picked up.

"What now?"

"We still have five minutes, Hank."

"Okay, I'll sing you a song. What would you like to hear? Maybe *I Want to Hold Your Hand* by the Beatles?"

"Stop fucking with me, Hank. I just want you to ask Daven if he thinks it's a good idea for us to meet. That's all. Start small. If he says no, I'll drop it."

Hank looked at the bottle of whiskey, but did not touch it. He felt severely depressed all of a sudden. "Yeah, well. I would, but we're not exactly on speaking terms right now."

"Oh." Harmon sounded puzzled rather than pleased, which was definitely a change. "Well, then we finally have something in common. I'm not speaking to Colbert at the moment, either."

Hank sat up straighter, now highly invested in this surreal conversation. Harmon and Colbert were thick as thieves, probably closer than even Hank and Dav. "Why are you telling me this? And why did I tell you that about me and Dav? I must be on drugs, too."

Harmon actually chuckled a little at that. "Please be serious, Hank. I know you don't believe anything I say, but I would bet my life on anything you say. Your transparency is truly self-destructive. You should channel that trait into other things.

Like cooperation with my party on issues that matter to all of us."

"You aren't kidding about the self-destructive part. What did Colbert do?" asked Hank, genuinely curious now, and all but forgetting he was speaking intimately to the person he hated most in the world.

"Ah, well. Let's just say it's a personality issue. What did Daven do?"

"He didn't do anything. I did. Also a personality issue. Wait, what the fuck? *Why* am I even talking to you about this?"

"Because it's lonely at the top, Hank. And we're as 'top' as it gets. So…"

Yeah, tell me about it…you have no fucking idea how lonely I am right now.

Hank felt his guard lowering even further, and for once he didn't fight it. "Okay, so…you must realize I'm seriously doubting your motives are pure, right?"

Harmon cleared his throat, and now his tone was full of irritation. "Okay, Hank. Let's get real. You want to talk about pure motives? Let's take a look at how many times the great Hank Bancroft has totally screwed me over personally in the past few years in order to advance his own agenda. How much time do you have? Because we're definitely going to need more than ten minutes."

"I haven't-"

"You are a master of manipulation and domination, but you mask it all behind this facade of honesty and purity. And you do hide it well, I must admit. A great talent, light years ahead of me. So I guarantee you that I have far more reason to suspect your motives than you'll ever have to suspect mine."

Hank was actually taken aback by this attack. Not that it wasn't anything he didn't already know...just that he didn't know anyone else knew it.

"The difference between us, Harmon, is that I use my *talents* towards the greater good. You only care about yourself. And that's why I don't trust you. Are we done now?"

"It appears we have reached an impasse, so yes, I'm done. I still have one request. Don't tell anyone I'm having issues with Colbert. I shared that with you willingly in order to open a dialogue. Obviously I'm regretting it now, but what's said is said."

"No need. I won't tell anyone." Hank was actually surprised to realize he meant that. "I would say I trust you not to say anything about me and Daven either, but that would be a lie. I fully expect to see it on the front page tomorrow."

"You won't. I'm sure your boys destroying priceless art at the library is a far more interesting story, anyway."

Hank closed his eyes and took a deep breath. "It wasn't anywhere close to priceless, and I have the receipt to prove it. God. The shit we have to put up with from the paparazzi."

"Yeah. I can't wait for the news of my colonoscopy tomorrow to hit the wires. Look, this may not have been the most pleasant discussion, but I'm still glad we had it anyway. Thank you for your time. Shall we say 10am tomorrow for more pointless bickering, Hank?"

There was a very long pause while Hank looked at the newspaper on his desk that featured a photo of him and Daven cutting a ribbon together at the new container port in San Pedro a few weeks back that was opening today. They were both smiling. Happy. Unaware of the impending disaster that was about to split them apart at the seams.

With equal amounts of hesitation and determination, Hank made the first of many decisions he would come to deeply regret in just four months' time.

"I'll meet with you Friday, but not in Denver. Wheels down in Las Vegas at 9am. I'll pick the meeting place and we'll ride there together with my own guards and driver. That's the *only* way I'm agreeing to it. And you have my word there will be absolutely no tricks or games."

"I'm not happy with those terms, to be honest. But I'll do it," Harmon said in an annoyed tone.

"Good. Since it was your idea, I'll leave it up to you to clear it through Stewart. Let me know what he says so I can make the arrangements."

CHAPTER SIX

Tuesday, Jan 11 - continued

Seditionists HQ

(Rupert's first day back at work)

Taylor sat slumped in a booth in the cafeteria and pecked at her laptop listlessly, only intensifying her activity with a burst of energy as Rupert appeared in the doorway and walked up to stand at her table. So much for trying to deter him from bothering her.

"Late lunch, huh?" he remarked with as small smile. "Got a minute?"

"4pm is still technically not dinner, so yes...lunch. I'm assuming this convo is appropriate for a public space?"

He looked around with his eyebrows furrowed. "There's...nobody here, Taylor. Heard from Hank yet?"

"Not since he told me he wasn't coming in. You?"

"No. I'm on his shit list again, so..."

"Why?" asked Taylor curiously, softening her attitude towards him a bit. "You said everything was fine yesterday."

"It was. But…my first day back, and I haven't heard a peep from him? And my phone is still blocked. He hasn't answered my email. I wanted to tell him what happened last night with Daven before he hears it from Lucas. But I think he already has. In that case, I'm toast."

"One second," Taylor interrupted as she pulled out her ringing cell. It was Hank, but she didn't want Rupert to know, so she cleared her throat and pitched her voice up cheerfully. "Good afternoon, this is Taylor. How may I help you?"

"Taylor?"

"Yes?"

"Doesn't sound like you. I'm guessing you have company. Hey, listen. I'm expecting a FedEx or UPS letter. Just wondering if it came."

"Not yet. Who is it from so I can keep an eye out?"

"Umm. Daven. No one else should be allowed to see it. Isn't the last FedEx at like 7pm?"

"No, 4:30. I'll check and let you know."

"Thanks kiddo. Just so you know, I haven't spoken to Rupert yet, and I'm not ready to."

"Yes, I figured that out. Thank you."

"Call me back after 4:30."

Taylor hung up, carefully set her drink aside and closed the lid to her laptop, then motioned for Rupert to sit down with her. "Okay, I'll bite. What happened last night with Daven?"

Bancroft Manor

For what seemed like the tenth time, Hank erased his email to Daven and started all over again. He had been composing it for almost two hours, and nothing sounded right. It was either too pandering, too desperate, or too cold. So after hanging up Taylor, he decided to go for a walk and went downstairs to the security office to find Avery, and was quite surprised to see Floyd chatted animatedly with Brittany at her desk. He wasn't allowed downstairs, and everyone knew it.

"Hey," he said mildly to Floyd, not wanting Brittany to feel uncomfortable. "When did you get back from the animal shelter? I didn't hear the front door chime."

"Maybe 15 minutes ago, sir," he replied, a little shakily. "Theo is still at the beach clean-up."

Hank nodded. "Okay. Go wait for me in my study."

Floyd's eyes went wide, but he complied without hesitation. Hank then looked at Brittany, who stood up, calm as ever.

"Sir, he was just-"

"Next time he comes down here, you send him back up immediately or I'll want to know the reason why. Are we clear? I've told you this before."

She seemed to take on a sudden defensive posture, and Hank picked up on it immediately and cut her off before she could argue.

"I don't want to hear anything but yes or no," Hank said sternly.

"Yes, sir. But-"

Hank bristled and was just about to bark something at her when Avery walked in, obviously not realizing he would be interrupting anything.

"My apologies, boss," he said, immediately turning to go back out.

"No problem, we're done here." Hank did not look at Brittany again as he left the office. Whatever he had been about to say would have done more harm than good, anyway. Theo was at the top of the stairs when he was on his way back to Floyd.

"How was the beach clean-up, Theody?"

"Good. But I got sunburned."

"In January? Got to love California. Go get cleaned up and rest. Dinner in 90 minutes."

Floyd was fidgeting madly as Hank entered the study and shut the door, immediately speaking as he walked around his oldest and sat down in his chair.

"You know the rule about going down into the basement. Tell me why you broke it."

"I didn't know you'd come downstairs at the same time."

Hank sighed. "Floyd, that's not the point, and that was a piss poor job of avoiding the question. I don't understand why you can't just behave yourself and not break rules. It's simple. Can you explain to me what I'm missing?"

"Yes, sir. You're missing Brittany's birthday." He held up a pink envelope. "Theody and I got her a card and I was about to give it to her. We signed it for you, too, because we knew you'd forget."

Hank felt like throwing himself down the nearest laundry chute. *What an ass, Hank. Good job.*

He collected himself quickly. "You were correct, I forgot. Thank you. But you can't just choose when to obey rules or not. You did the wrong thing, for the right reasons. But it's still wrong. Next time ask me. I would have said yes to this."

"Yes, sir. I'm sorry," Floyd responded politely.

Hank eyed him carefully, sensing something he didn't really like. "Are you feeling okay?"

Other than not being able to sit down for the past 18 hours, you mean?

Hank's phone rang before Floyd could respond, and he went to dig it out of his pocket. "Hang on, Floyd. Yes, Taylor?"

FedEx and UPS just came and there's nothing from the person you're waiting for. But something else did come, and you're not going to like it. I'm in your office with the door closed.

"Jesus Christ, I don't know if I want to hear this. Okay...what now?"

We just received by courier a subpoena from Stewart at the FBI. You have to turn over your phone records for the entire month of December.

"Mine? Like, *mine* , personally?"

Yes, sir. Home, office, cell. Within seven days.

Hank was not exactly stunned by this turn of events, considering everything that had happened in December. He was more curious than anything else, but his conscious was clear enough to keep him from being too alarmed.

"Alright. I'll get on it tomorrow morning with Shane. Thanks, Taylor. See you then."

He turned back to Floyd. "Okay, we're done here. I need to make some calls."

Floyd held up the envelope again. "Sir, may I please take this downstairs to Brittany?"

"That's exactly what you should have done in the first place - ask me. Yes. Go on, I'll see you at dinner."

Floyd went, secretly glad for Taylor having interrupted his dad's anger towards him and redirecting it somewhere else entirely.

Hank hit the intercom to Brittany's office to tell her he was sending Floyd down, then picked up the phone to check the hours-old voicemail from Stewart.

Hank, this is Stewart in Philadelphia. You're going to be getting a subpoena from me today in regards to your phone records for December. This is basically just to continue the investigation on Janet, which I need to discuss with you in more depth. I also need to take a statement from you regarding a deal you allegedly made some photographers yesterday. Hoping you can come to Philadelphia on Friday morning. Call me back at your earliest convenience.

Fuck.

"Hoping you can come" really meant *"if you don't come, your ass is grass."* He was supposed to meet with Harmon on Friday in Las Vegas, and this message was almost ten hours old. He cursed at himself for ignoring it earlier, because now it was almost 8pm in Philadelphia. He dialed Harmon instead.

"Hey. Did you hear back from Stewart about us meeting in Vegas on Friday?"

"Yes, but he said no. I was going to talk to you about it tomorrow on our call."

"Did he say why?"

"No, he was very evasive about the whole thing. I'm in a meeting. Can we talk tomorrow?"

"Yeah, sorry. Bye."

There was another new email notification from Rupert. He set the phone down, then turned to his computer and opened it up.

Hank - we really need to talk. Last night would have been better. Please call me tonight at your convenience. Anytime is fine. Thanks, Rupe

Hank rapidly tapped back a snippy reply:

I'm not available. I hope you enjoyed your dinner at Yamashiro last night. I'm certain Daven did, too. Thanks, Hank

Then he started a new email to Daven:

I did not receive your email last night, or your letter today. Please let me know if you've changed your mind. Thanks, Hank.

Just before he was about to end the work day, he noticed an email from Stewart that he had missed, although it came in two hours ago.

Hank - not sure if you got my voicemail from this morning. Let me know.

This was why being distracted by a runaway dog was never a good thing....

Stewart, I just picked it up. Sorry. I've been out of pocket most of the day due to illness. I will be there on Friday morning. What time? Thanks, Hank

Then he reached down and turned his computer completely off, skipping the shut down process. He knew that would wreak havoc upon booting up next time, but he didn't care. It would be just another irritation in a shitload of irritations for the week.

Twisted Truths

The Fugitive's Scandal

CHAPTER ONE

Urbanes HQ - Denver

Harmon stared at the subpoena for the second hour in a row, feeling the edges of his anger flare up yet again. Colbert was sitting in front of him, running through a minor checklist of weekly tasks.

"You still haven't approved the new dress code policy, so HR is having a fit.....Boss? You ok?"

"I know," Harmon grumbled. "What the hell do you think Stewart is looking for?"

"Don't worry. You never called Yannick. You're fine," Colbert said soothingly. "And I always called him on a secondary phone, so my records would be fine too, if they ever wanted to see them. Can we get back to the checklist?"

"No. It's almost six o'clock. I'm done. So you're certain Yannick is never going to contact us again, right? It was enough money?"

"As I said, the amount we gave him was exactly what he demanded."

"Fine. Then you don't need that secondary phone anymore. Destroy it. Not safe to keep it around."

Colbert swallowed hard, hoping Harmon didn't ask for it on the spot - because he didn't have Yannick's number memorized. Yet. "Will do."

"Where is it?"

"In my safe at home." This was a lie; the phone was in the center console of his car.

"Okay. I'll approve the dress code, even though I didn't have time to read the whole thing. I'm sick of looking at it. We're done, you can go."

Colbert brushed aside his irritation at being dismissed so offhandedly.

Harmon was still angry about their clash last Friday over Colbert's decision to give Yannick and extra two thousand dollars over what was promised, but what's done was done. The money was paid. The man would be quiet, or else he knew the price he would pay.

Well...that's what Harmon thought, anyway. Colbert was still congratulating himself for setting aside $3,000 for future payments to Yannick.

Thursday, Jan 13

Seditionists HQ - Los Angeles

Hank had managed to completely avoid Rupert on
Wednesday, having shut himself behind closed doors all day
by himself. He had so much work to do that it was painful even
making a task list, and something new was added every
minute that caused him a new headache.

What was worse, though, was never hearing back from Daven.
Hank still had no idea what he was thinking or planning to do,
but he was soothed by the fact that Lucas had reported Dav
was spending all day in his office and otherwise acting
normally since the big blowout.

Now it was Thursday morning, and he was due in Philadelphia
in less than 24 hours. It was time for Rupert's reckoning, and
Hank had reserved their most private conference room for the
conversation in order to keep from intimidating the man by
making him sit in one of his "electric chairs" for the duration
of the dressing down.

Hank had woken up abruptly in the middle of the night and
made the decision to fire Rupert, and that was going to be the

end of it. He just didn't care anymore about keeping his two closest allies in his circle. Former allies, rather. It was self-destructive, peevish, and probably the wrong decision, and he knew it. But he would not abide dishonesty in his ranks. There was no choice.

Rupert was waiting in the room when Hank entered, and had a big yellow pad in front of him with several pages of writing already on it. Clearly, he had thought through what he was going to say. But since he still had common sense to spare, he said nothing and waited for Hank to begin.

Hank sat down and took a sip of coffee. "Alright. Let's get down to it. I know you were at Yamashiro with Daven at the same time you told me you hadn't spoken to him all day. I'm interested to hear how you're going to defend yourself from what appears to be a big fat lie. Please proceed."

Rupert blinked, not expecting that cold open. Hank usually eased into conversations like this, no matter how angry he was. "Yes, sir. I'll be equally as blunt in my response. I was not lying. We haven't spoken since Sunday. He said nothing to me at dinner, and in fact, showed up already tipsy and distracted. When I asked him if he was okay, he took a seat at the other end of the table to prevent any conversation with me, and talked to my wife and her friends through all four courses, then paid the bill for everyone and left without so much as a goodnight."

"Oh," said Hank, feeling thrown totally off balance by this development. "That explains a lot."

"And your call during dessert explained a lot, too. When you told me he was quitting, his behavior suddenly made sense. He was looking right at me when I was talking to you, so I didn't want to say anything until we could talk privately."

"I see," replied Hank, with a mixture of relief and new areas of concern. "Has he blocked your phone calls, too?"

"No, but he's ignoring them. Is my explanation sufficient, Hank? I realize you've been angry at me for two days, because I heard Lucas talking to you and put two and two together once you didn't call me back. But of course I wasn't going to put any of this in email."

Rupert was not defensive nor angry, to Hank's satisfaction. He had understood what it looked like from the start. Rupe was going to be forgiving. Thank god...

Hank nodded, then breathed deeply a few times to calm his racing heart. *Count to four. In. Out for four.*

"Yes, it's sufficient. You're correct that it would've been completely inappropriate to email that story. I'm sorry I didn't give you a chance to explain."

"That's alright. I'm used to it."

Ouch.

Hank sighed and found himself suddenly returning to his usual good humor. "Alright. I deserved that. Floyd says the same thing. I haven't received Dav's resignation letter yet, or any response to my questions about it. The last time we talked was when he thanked me for catching his dog, but it seems far-fetched to hope he changed his mind. No pun intended. Anyway, I'm sorry."

"You're forgiven, Hank. For treating me poorly, not for the dog pun - that was inexcusable. Let's catch up later on all this business crap."

"Sounds good. I'm really glad you're back, Rupe. I'm going to sit in here for a while and make a few calls. Shall we have lunch before we start diving into the deeper stuff?"

"Yeah. See you then."

Rupe smiled a little and left the room, and both men went back to work with much lighter hearts.

Friday, Jan 14

Bancroft Manor

Floyd had never felt so low in his life. He was still aching from the belt five days ago, Theody hadn't fully forgiven him for his mean comments, and worst of all…he woke up to learn his dad was traveling. Hank hadn't even bothered to tell his sons where he was going, or when he would be back. Not even the guards left behind at the house knew where he was.

Not only that, he apparently hadn't even asked Rupert about the home school question. Come Monday, it was business as usual at the Brooke school. Which meant photographers stalking him from the fences, bullying from classmates jealous of his dad's money, and most lunchtimes spent with gloomy Theo.

He got dressed and picked up the keys to the Thunderbird, tiptoed past Theo's room, then bypassed the kitchen where chef was cooking and disappeared through an infrequently-used side door into the garage.

————-

FBI Headquarters

Philadelphia

Hank was too anxious to bear for probably the first time in his entire life. Not that that he had never been nervous before. Plenty of times, mostly after press conferences. This was different. He felt a sense of doom that he couldn't shake, and it didn't help that Stewart had been uncharacteristically rude and unfriendly upon his arrival.

If Floyd felt this anxious all the time, Hank would definitely be able to understand some of the very poor choices the kid had been making lately. It was not a fun state of mind, to say the least, and his trains of thought were crisscrossing all over the place.

"Come in," Stewart finally ordered as he threw open the door suddenly, which made Hank jump a little and admonish himself for being a nervous nelly.

As he sat down in Stewart's uncomfortable visitor chairs, he could clearly see a photo of himself, Floyd, Daven, and his two guards and Shannon standing next to a photographer's car outside Daven's house, chatting away.

Stewart turned the monitor all the way around. "What was this about, Hank?"

Hank sat up a little straighter, feeling better now that the ball was in his court. "My son is having some severe anxiety over photographers following us around everywhere, so I made him come with me to meet some of them. To humanize them a little, if you will. It went really well and he's been pretty good about the whole thing ever since."

"Hmmm. Anything else to add?"

"Nothing that I'm obliged to report. Why do you ask?"

"If you made some kind of deal–"

Hank interrupted harshly, "There is absolutely nothing illegal about what I did."

Stewart eyed him. "What you could have done, Hank, is attempt to bribe the press. That's if what I'm hearing is correct, naturally. I'd rather hear it from you, if you don't mind. The entire story."

"That's bullshit," Hank scoffed. "I fully intended to have those men sign an agreement not to take photos of my son in exchange for me paying them the profit they would have made off of selling them over the course of a year."

"You can't do that." He opened up a book and thumbed to the right page, then shoved it over.

Statute 4.2.1 enacted April 2, 1990 - no government or party officer shall attempt to influence freedom or direction of the press by offer of pecuniary considerations, esp. in the form of a payment, material or non-material gift, material or non-material reward, or donation of any kind.

Hank read it.

"Stewart, I repeat: I had no intention of paying them under the table. This was all going to be above-board and transparent."

"I understand that. What you're saying is that you would be *publicly* flaunting the law, then."

"There is nothing in there that says I can't contract them for their services, or lack thereof!"

Stewart closed the book hard and turned around to place it back on his shelf. "Here," he said, shoving a piece of paper at Hank. "I made a copy of it for you for your records. It clearly says you shall not influence the press *by offer of pecuniary considerations* . That says, literally translated: you may not trade money in exchange for influencing the press. Period"

"No money has changed hands. It was just an offer. In fact, none of them have taken me up on it yet."

"Read the statute again," Stewart commanded. "Out loud."

Hank did, and Stewart stopped him on the word *attempt,* at which Hank scoffed. "You can't be serious. My son is having a nervous breakdown because of these clowns, and I'm allowed no recourse? What would you have me do? Blindfold him all day long so he can't see them? It should be against the law to harass them like they do, but I'm the one getting punished. And Floyd, too."

Stewart turned the monitor back to where it belonged and leaned back a little. "Hank, when you took your position, you explicitly agreed to obey all of these statutes. Not just the ones you agree with. The Office of Ethics and Integrity was created at *your* suggestion, with mostly your design…and now you want to defy them? Think about how that makes you look. And how it would make us look if we just disregarded this matter."

"It makes me look like I'm worried for my son's privacy and mental health, actually, and I'm fine with that."

"Does that mean you're fine with going to jail, too? Because you broke the law, like it or not. It's actually a class one misdemeanor, so I could have you put in jail right now for a week. That's the standard sentence if you plead guilty. Longer if you force a trial."

"Do it, then," Hank challenged. "At least it will bring some attention to the issue."

Stewart looked at him askance. "*Do it* ? Really? Is that what Daven would advise you, if he were here? Or are you just recklessly emboldened by being alone with me, because I've always been way too lenient with you in the past?"

Hank started a little; suddenly remembering he had to tell him that Daven quit. That was another statute altogether with worse consequences if ignored.

"Daven and I agreed not to speak again until he returns to work on January 26, in order to avoid more media attention," Hank lied, flushing in shame at the same time. So much for being transparent.

"Okay. Well, I want you to call him now and ask him if you should go to jail, pay the $50,000 fine, or get a warning and public censure. If you two can agree on a solution, I'll agree to it as well."

Shit. He couldn't call, his damned number was blocked. "First of all, Stewart, I will always make my own decisions on those matters. Second of all, it's 6am in Los Angeles. He's asleep."

Stewart's expression was unreadable. "Then what do you choose?"

"I choose to fight this. It's ridiculous."

"Fine. I'll let Salome know. You can expect to hear back from her directly. Do you have your phone records?"

Hank stared at him for a few long moments, wanting to continue the previous conversation, then gave it up to reach down to his briefcase and hand the sealed envelope over wordlessly.

"Thanks." He pushed another piece of paper over to him. "This is just a simple affidavit you'll need to sign to certify the records are accurate. Standard form, nothing to worry about it. I also subpoenaed Harmon's records for our files. This investigation is turning out to be pretty much a dead-end, but there's one important question I have to ask you after you sign."

One more question. No doubt it would lead to another argument. Hank signed the form and handed it over, thankful that he had made no shady calls to worry about. He was secretly relieved, however, that Harmon's calls were going to be scoured as well.

"Yes? What's the question."

Stewart looked anxious very briefly, but then it passed. "Now, I don't want you to jump to conclusions as to why I'm asking. We know that The Seditionists have employed double agents in the past, and that - don't interrupt me, please - we know you do, and it's not illegal. Absolutely nothing I'm about to ask you, or the answer you will give me, will result in any penalty whatsoever. As long as you tell the truth, that is. If you lie, different story."

Hank already knew what he was going to ask, but he didn't jump on it. No use pushing his luck.

"I understand. Will I have the option not to answer?"

"Of course. You always have that option unless required by law. Was Janet a double agent for the Seditionists? I refrained from asking before because that lies outside my jurisdiction, but I'm asking now because nothing about this investigation makes sense, and we could use all the help we can get."

"Yes, she was. Only Daven, Rupert, Taylor, and myself are aware of that detail. I take it back...Harmon knows, too. And Colbert."

Stewart was taken aback by the last part. "What do you mean, Harmon and Colbert *know* ? Last time you and I talked, Harmon was adamant that she wasn't."

Hank shrugged. "Well, something's changed in those ten days. He confronted me about it on our call on Tuesday. I didn't confirm or deny it. Maybe you should ask *him* how they found out. Can I ask you a question now?"

"Uh, sure." Stewart was still a little shell-shocked. Perhaps that mystery caller wasn't lying, after all. Was it possible that Hank could be so devious?

"Did Harmon actually ask you if he could meet with me in person today?"

Stewart nodded. "Yeah. But Hank, you need to watch yourself. I'm telling you this not as your FBI contact, but as a...well, not as a friend, either, since we're not technically friends. But let me put it this way. As a person who wants to see you succeed, I really don't like the path you're on. At all. You're becoming a bit of a rollercoaster, and the tracks aren't even finished being built yet. For the first time...I don't know how to say this, to be honest."

Hank sat up straighter in his chair, all of Daven's harsh words flooding back to him suddenly. Not Stewart, too? He couldn't take any more of the same criticism.

"I'm listening," he prompted. "Nothing you say to me is going to be a surprise, trust me."

"Oh? Why is that?"

"Never mind. Just...go ahead."

Stewart pulled out a binder from his desk. "This is my file on you. It's getting thicker by the day and taking up all my time. Used to be almost empty until last October, when you openly threatened Harmon in a press conference. Remember that? Since then, you've been a total pain in the ass, not going to lie. You're better than this. I realize what went down with Daven and Rupert would drive anyone to distraction, but it's time to get over it and start toeing the line again from here on out."

Hank nodded, feeling significantly subdued and chastised. "Remind me how much the fine is for my little infraction this time?"

"$50,000 if the amount you offered was under that. If not, it escalates into felony territory and mandatory jail time."

Hank did not bother doing the math; he hadn't offered to pay the photographers *that* much. "In that case my fine would be $50,000."

"Okay, and that must come your personal funds. Not party funds. Who has access to your bank back in Los Angeles?"

Hank swallowed thickly. "Only me and Daven. Can I just handle it when I get home?"

"No, not if you aren't the only authorized person on the account. He has to do it, or you have to stay here until he can explain why he can't - such as being out of town. We'll give him a call together and arrange it. Let me get the wire transfer info from our controller. Hang on."

He left the office, and Hank leaned back and stared at the ceiling in a daze. This had all gotten out of control so fast, and Stewart was right. He needed to get it together, immediately. But the problem was that Daven wasn't going to pick up his call. He certainly wouldn't pick up anything coming from Philadelphia at this point, if he truly had decided to resign.

Even if he did, the fact that he had resigned might emerge, and Hank would have a lot of explaining to do. His heart was racing faster than he had ever felt it, and it nearly stopped when Stewart re-entered the room and sat back down.

"Alright. I realize it's early there, but we have to try."

"Stewart, I…he may not pick up. As I stated earlier, we agreed not to speak again until January 26."

"Okay, well try anyway."

Hank dialed Lucas instead, who picked up immediately. "Hey, Lucas. I'm sorry for calling so early. I need you to get Daven on the phone, please."

"Speakerphone, Hank," said Stewart quietly.

Shit. "Wait, Lucas. I'm putting you on speaker. Yeah, sorry. Can you please wake up Daven and put him on the phone? Let him know I'm calling with a personal emergency. Thanks so much."

Hank could barely breathe. He fully expected the man to refuse to take the call, and was started and relieved to hear the low, grumbly voice only a few seconds later.

"Dav? I'm so sorry, I hope I didn't wake you."

"What's the emergency?" he asked testily.

Hank cleared his throat. "Well, I'm here with Stewart in Philadelphia and you're on speakerphone. Let's just say you were right about my offer to the photographers. I've been fined, and I need you to wire money from my personal account so they'll let me come back home. May I ask for your assistance with that?"

There was only a slight pause while Daven took in this unexpected news. "Of course. The bank doesn't open for four hours, though. Can you email me exactly what you need, and I'll head over there and be first in line to take care of it."

Stewart shook his head. "Uh, no. We have to fax it. Is your machine plugged in?"

"Probably not, just send it in like ten minutes and it will be fine."

"Great," said Hank, carefully wording what he had to say next. "Is your cell phone working yet? If so, I'll call you in about fifteen minutes to confirm you received the fax."

"I will have Lucas call you to confirm I received it. Anything else, gentlemen?"

Stewart answered for Hank. "No, thank you. Goodbye."

Daven immediately hung up, and Hank cursed inwardly for losing the call so quickly. Not that Dav would want to spend even one more moment talking to him, of course.

"Alright," Stewart said. "I need to write up a report of this that we both need to go over and sign once the funds are received. So it looks like you have half the day to burn, at least, so maybe go get something to eat. City Tavern is a block away. Be back here by 1pm."

Hank stood up. "Will do. And...thanks for talking me into taking the fine, by the way."

"I didn't talk you into it, you just suddenly came to your senses. Which is good, definitely something I'd like to see more often. And don't think I have no sympathy for the situation with Floyd. I really do, but you did the wrong thing for the right reasons. It was still wrong, though."

Hank smiled a little. "I said that exact same thing, verbatim, to Floyd only a few days ago. I hear you loud and clear. See you in a few hours."

Avery and Hank took a table at City Tavern, and before Hank could even pick up the menu his phone rang with the a theme song. Daven's ringtone. He and Avery both froze.

"Um. Should I step away?" asked Avery.

"No. Hang on. Hello, Dav."

"I got the fax, but I'm calling for another reason. Floyd is here without a guard. He can stay if you want him to, I don't mind. But did you authorize this?"

Hank's blood started to boil on the spot. "No, I did not. Absolutely not." He realized how indignant that sounded, then immediately clarified. "Not because it's your house, of course. It's just that he's not to go anywhere without a guard, period. You're sure he came on his own?"

"Yes. Drove the Thunderbird to my house. I'm not trying to tattle on him. Just telling you where he is."

"I know, thanks. Is he alright? Like, not freaking out or anything?"

"He's fine. Just a bit defensive when I started asking questions. Said you gave the okay, but I didn't believe him and sent him out back to play with Shannon. He even brought us breakfast from McDonalds."

"I'm going to kill him this time. For real. I'm sorry he bothered you, Dav. Shit, I don't know what to do," Hank confessed helplessly. Whatever he did would alienate Floyd even further than he had already pushed him away.

"He can stay until you decide," replied Daven. "Let me know. I've unblocked your number because he didn't bring his phone"

"Thank you. I'm going to have a stroke before the week is out, I'm telling you. I should update my will."

"You'd better hurry, it's already Friday."

Hank groaned. "Shut up. Don't make me laugh when I'm busy throwing myself a pity party. Thanks, Dav. And again, I'm sorry."

He hung up and called a very frantic Brittany, who was already in the car searching for him along, with Vance in a different car.

"Sir, I'm so sorry. He snuck out without activating an external alarm. We noticed the Thunderbird was gone about thirty minutes ago and I've been calling you ever since."

"I know, don't worry. My phone was on silent. He's at Daven's house now. Just stay outside until he comes out. Thanks."

He called Dav back and asked to talk to Floyd.

"Hey, Floyd. I hope you're enjoying the last vestiges of freedom you're going to have for a very long time."

"I don't care. Where are you?" Floyd asked angrily. "You promised you would tell us where you were going all the time, remember? On Christmas Day. You promised."

Hank sighed. "Floyd, I'm technically at work no matter where I am. I'll still be home by 5. What are you freaking out about now?"

"No you're not. The news this morning showed you boarding a plane at midnight. You left last night and didn't tell us."

"Calm down. We'll talk when I get home tonight. Go straight home, right now. If you don't, you're going to be grounded until you're 18, and I'm not even joking."

"Fine with me, I don't care."

"Okay. One more thing. Put your driver's license and car keys on my desk by the time I get home. Goodbye."

"Wait, dad-"

Hank hung up and now Stewart was calling. For god's sake, what did he want already?

"Hank, I just talked to Salome. She wants to see you at 10:00. Think you can be back by then?"

"No problem. See you then."

Salome was very welcoming of Hank's presence, which was quite a surprise - needless to say.

"Hank, I understand that Stewart has spoken to you of the recent behavior that has caused us to become concerned for your welfare, and that of your party. Do you understand where he is coming from?"

"Of course, and I'll take the advice to heart."

"Good. I'm hopeful that the return of Daven will settle you down a little bit. I must say, from my point of view, it appears you've somewhat gone off the rails without his guidance. But maybe that's an inappropriate thing to say."

Hank smiled a little. "It's not wrong, to be honest."

"Right. Well, the reason I wanted to see you now is because Stewart passed along your request to meet with Harmon in person. You are free to meet with him as you wish, in any location at any time. You must split any cost of meeting between you down to the cent and send copies of the paid bills to Stewart. Flights, meeting room, etc. That's my only caveat. There is no need to ask us again."

"Right," Hank replied, faltering a little. "Well, considering we're both under FBI investigation, I just thought it was better to be safe than sorry and ask Stewart about the first meeting. Which he denied, by the way."

Salome nodded. "I denied it and am under no obligation to explain why. But that's irrelevant now and as long as you two can keep from strangling each other on sight, be my guest. And yes, the investigation is still ongoing. That's also why I'm concerned for you. It would truly be in your best interests, Hank, to heed Stewart's advice to toe the line. What do you have to say about that?"

"That he's right, of course."

"Yes, he is. I'm going to go ahead and let you go home before we receive the funds. To do otherwise would show a lack of trust between us, and that's the last thing I want right now."

She stood up and offered her hand, which Hank shook warmly. "Thank you. No offense, but I hope to never see either one of you again."

"I share the same sentiment. Safe travels."
As soon as he was in the car to the airport, Hank called Daven.

"Still two hours until the bank opens," Dav grumbled upon picking up the phone.

"I know. They're letting me go home anyway. Look, Dav, there's no easy way to say this. I royally fucked up in so many ways that I can't even process it all. I don't even care if I lose my job over this. The only thing that I can't handle is losing our friendship."

"Hank, I've already decided-"

"Don't say no yet," Hank pressed. "Just...please give me a chance to apologize first."

Daven paused. "I wasn't going to say no. I was going to say I've already decided we should talk about this. But I'm driving to Las Vegas immediately after I do your transfer at the bank. I'm afraid our in-person conversation will have to wait."

"Maybe not. What are you doing in Vegas?"

"Well, it's technically Henderson. I'm going to watch my brother's house on Lake Las Vegas while he's on vacation."

Hank paused. This was a sticky predicament regarding security; if he wasn't going to quit his job then he'd be required to take Lucas with him. If he was going to quit, he'd feel no obligation to take him...

"Are you taking Lucas?" he asked carefully.

"No."

Shit.

"Okay. Dav, we...I will meet you there, if that's okay. I won't even bitch about you not taking Lucas. Just give me an hour. I don't want to intrude on your vacation any longer than that."

There was a very long pause that made them both uncomfortable, and finally Dav asked how Hank was going to get there.

"I'm on a charter plane, we'll change course. No big deal."

Daven finally gave in. "Alright. Who do you have with you?"

"Just Avery."

"Okay. I'll come get you guys at the airport. Which terminal - Signature, or Atlantic?"

"Signature at Henderson Executive Airport. Much more secure there. I'll call you back soon with an arrival time."

"Alright, Hank. See you soon. Safe travels."

CHAPTER TWO

Friday January 14 - continued

FBI Headquarters, Philadelphia

An hour after Hank Bancroft had left her office, Salome Danby was sitting in front of Stewart, listening incredulously to his newest theory on what exactly the leader of the Seditionists had been up to since Christmas.

"It all stands to reason, Salome. I don't care what that mystery caller said, Hank Bancroft did *not* offer him money to kill Janet. However, the caller knew she was double. *Knew* with certainty . And at that point there were only four people who did, all of them Seditionists."

"Okay," said Salome. "And?"

"Well, what I think is that Harmon and Colbert figured it out after that press conference in which Hank threw Harmon under the bus by revealing he wasn't cooperating with the investigation. In reality, Hank wasn't concerned about being blamed, because Janet was one of his. So he backed Harmon into a corner with the certainty he would fight back. Which he did. And then we played right into Hank's hands by taking that tape away from both of them."

"I'm not following your line of thinking, sorry," Salome admitted. "Are you saying Hank falsely pinned the murder on Harmon?"

Stewart paused to think for a moment. "No, not at all. I'm saying Hank's main aim was to…let me put it another way, sorry. My thoughts are all over the place. He *wanted* Harmon to figure out she was double."

"For what purpose?"

"To shut Harmon out of the investigation by angering him and making him shoot himself in the foot. Hank played us like a fiddle, Salome."

Salome wrung her hands together a little under the desk. "No, I can't accept that. I'm sorry, but I don't believe this was all orchestrated from the beginning. I think Hank spontaneously threw that line out at the press conference without thinking. We all know that he's not any better than Harmon at keeping his big mouth shut."

Stewart shook his head. "I completely disagree, with respect. The reporter who asked that final question was obviously a plant. Hank had his answer at the ready, and I swear to you he was almost triumphant when we called him out. Did you see any regret at all? Because I didn't. The way the whole thing went down, it was almost too perfect."

"That reporter was an Urbane, Stewart."

"Exactly. An Seditionist would have been too obvious. We have to consider he was paid off."

Salome didn't say anything for quite a long time, and they both sat back and silently tried to piece together all the ill-fitting pieces. The only obvious answer was that the Urbanes were behind Janet's murder, but there was no proof.

"Alright," Salome finally said. "Then how did your mystery caller know Janet was double? And how did he have Hank's cell phone number?"

Stewart shrugged. "I don't know yet. But I've got our auditors working on his phone records right now, and hopefully we'll have some answers shortly. My initial theory is that someone on Hank's team has turned, but...again, only four people knew she was double. It could just as easily be someone that Harmon recruited to lie, and the info just happened to be accurate. I don't know for sure at the moment."

"This is giving me a headache," Salome muttered, "and it's just more argument towards President Rickon's stance that double agents should be illegal. I think we should revisit that idea."

"I'm in agreement with you there. Whatever is happening, though, I guarantee you Hank is 100% convinced Harmon is guilty. He would never do any of this to frame an innocent man...which means Hank himself was not involved, and the caller was lying to us."

"Past good character isn't permissible evidence for innocence. You're jumping ahead here. I think it's time to wiretap him. Do you agree?"

Stewart did not agree, actually, but he also knew his liking for Hank had been influencing him too much already. Not just lately, but over the past few years in general.

"As a matter of course, yes, but...I think that's pointless, to be honest. Everyone with a brain knows better than to not conduct illegal activity on the phone, and Hank has a bigger brain than anyone. Even if he doesn't act like it sometimes. I'll bet you he thinks we already monitor him."

Salome nodded. "Probably. Just one last question for you, to which I already know the answer. Why do you think there has been no pushback from his constituents about the murder?"

"Simple. They trust him.”

“Exactly, Stewart. They trust him implicitly, and he knows it. Hell, even I trust him. Every gut instinct tells me to stop trying to figure this all out and just accept that he wasn’t behind the murder. We have to have better proof than that, though. When trust turns blind, it also turns dangerous. So you and I need to stay on him and keep talking about this with me. I’m going to meet with the president today to get the wiretap order expedited. Thanks for your input.”

Henderson, Nevada

Hank had very little idea of what to expect from Dav, except that whatever he did would be a surprise of some sort. Even after ten years, Hank still was totally wrong sometimes when predicting what direction the man would take on any given topic. So when the black truck rolled up to the plane, he felt himself getting more anxious by the second. Maybe Dav was just going to step out long enough to hand him the resignation letter and then get back in to drive off into the desert and disappear. It would be just like him, too.

Daven stepped out and waited for them to come down the stairs. It was strange to see him so casual in jeans and a leather jacket in the middle of a weekday, and Hank was glad that he changed on the plane into a similar outfit.

Avery took the wheel of the truck while Hank and Dav got in the back seat.

"Good to see you," Hank said casually.

"Thank you."

No 'nice to see you too,' eh? So that's how we are going to do this.

"Avery," called Hank, "can you pull through somewhere for food? I'm starving. Dav, any preference? We departed Philadelphia so ahead of schedule that that the catering got left behind."

"In-N-Out? There's one right before we get on the freeway. Avery, just keep going straight up St. Rose for now. Take a right. No, not here...next light. Yes. Just keep going for a few miles, then left on Eastern."

"How have you been, Dav?" Hank asked nervously after a minute.

"I'm fine. Forgive me for being so blunt, but what the hell is going on with Floyd? I tried to catch up with him, but it was like talking to a complete stranger."

"I know the feeling."

"None of my business, of course, but I care about him so I wanted to see if there's anything I can do to help."

Hank cleared his throat and thought about what he wanted to say. He didn't want to share too much, but maybe if he made him feel a little sorry for him, their upcoming conversation might be that much easier.

"Still afraid of me, unfortunately. But he said some awful things to his brother on Monday. Treating him like shit, and I called him out on it and…well, let's just say he's still feeling the consequences every time he sits down. He's been angry at the world ever since, although he's never been more polite to me in his life while he continues to break every rule he can, left and right. The worst being today when he showed up at your house alone, that is."

Was that today? Jesus, it already felt like a lifetime ago.

"I feel bad for getting him in trouble," Dav admitted. "Who was supposed to be guarding him?"

Hank shrugged. "Don't feel bad for one second longer, because he won't blame you for anything. There was no guard on him at 5:30am, so nobody got fired this time. He snuck out the side door to the garage, which I will of course be arming in the future. Anyway, he's going to have a hell of a price to pay when I get back. And no, I'm not going to go easy on him, so don't ask. I just can't seem to get through to him lately."

"Well," Dav answered philosophically, "sounds like you have to change tactics, then. Maybe he's outgrown corporal punishment. Sorry, none of my business."

"No, it's okay. I think you're right, in any case. I'm going to take his driver's license away for a while, for starters."

"Maybe you should shred it."

Hank gaped at him. "What? Wow, that's...that's cold. I don't think I'm *that* cruel."

"It's not cruel. In fact, my father did exactly that to me and my brother when we kept blowing our curfew night after night. I'll never forget it. Total kick in the pants. Set us straight for a long time."

"Jesus. I don't know, I mean…" Hank thought about it, then decided against it. "Floyd would have another nervous breakdown if he had to take a driving test again."

"He wouldn't have to. You can just get a replacement issued when you're ready for him to drive again. Anyway, I'm sorry for putting my two cents in when you didn't ask. I just think anything is better than trying to beat him into submission."

Hank gasped. "I don't *beat* him, Dav! For god's sake." He felt Avery's eyes on him in the mirror suddenly, and his stomach turned a little at the ugly memory of Monday's incident.

The car was silent until they got to In-N-Out. The drive-thru line was a mile long, so they skipped it and opted for the nearby Del Taco instead and pulled over in a corner of the parking lot to eat.

"Did you bring Shannon?" Hank asked between bites of burrito.

"No. She's at Malibu Pet Retreat for a few days. I just wanted to be alone."

"Understandable," Hank replied. This conversation was becoming awkward with Avery being in full earshot, so Hank said nothing more except small observations about the scenery until they arrived at the house.

As they went in, Avery disappeared around the back of the house to check it.

They went into the kitchen and Daven pulled two beers out of the fridge. "Hank," he began somberly as he handed one bottle to Hank, "you should know right off the bat that I actually still want to go back to work. But I have conditions which I don't think you'll agree to, so I've been hesitant to talk to you."

"I see. So that's why I haven't received your resignation letter?" Hank asked once his heart had started beating again.

"Yes. I couldn't bring myself to finish it. I was going to this morning, but then you called me from Philadelphia and told me about the fine. Must say that made me feel a little more validated about my stance on what you said to those photographers."

Hank bit back a rude retort and took a huge swig of his beer. He replied calmly, "You would have been even more satisfied if Stewart put me in jail for a week, I'm sure. Which he would have if you didn't come through with that transfer. By the way, I haven't thanked you for that. So, thank you."

Dav looked at him askance. " *Satisfied* ? About you being in jail? Is that really what you think?"

"I do, actually," Hank challenged.

"You're wrong. If that were the case…look, I told you on the spot you were breaking the law and begged you to stop, and you completely disregarded every single word. You also disregarded me about not throwing Harmon under the bus - also on live television, may I add. If I wanted you in jail, I would have kept my mouth shut on those two occasions, and several others. But you didn't hire me to keep my mouth shut."

Hank knew he had to back down a little. Dav was right. "You're correct, I didn't. But-"

"No *buts*. To be bluntly honest, Hank, I can't stand by and watch while you sabotage yourself trying to take down Harmon. Because that's all you been letting me do lately is stand by and watch you do whatever the hell you want regardless of what Rupe and I think. *That's* why I quit. So unless you agree to take our counsel from here on out, I'll stay quit and you can find another person who doesn't care about you half as much I do, but will do whatever you want as long as he keeps getting a paycheck."

Hank felt vaguely nauseated all of a sudden. "Hold on, let's not get emotional. I want to talk about this in a way that benefits us both, and neither of us are at our best when we're angry."

"But I am angry. And frustrated. You don't seem aware that your actions lately are throwing red flags up left and right. You could have gone to jail today. You probably should have, to be even more blunt. Maybe that would set you straight."

Hank turned and threw his bottle into the trash, fighting down his natural tendency to snap back when attacked like this. "Okay. That's enough," he said calmly. "I get it. Let's go take a walk along the lake and talk. Not argue."

Colbert's Car - same day

"Yannick...pick up the phone, my man. Need to talk to you."

Colbert huffed and then snapped the phone shut again. He hadn't heard from his contact since making the payment, and the thought of what that could mean was getting his stomach completely twisted up into knots. Had the man turned again, or was he legitimately too busy to talk? Maybe he just decided to take the money and run.

But he wouldn't do that, though. He knew Colbert could turn him in to Hank Bancroft in a heartbeat, even if it meant taking down Harmon, too.

Lake Las Vegas

"The very first thing I want you to know, Dav, is that I'm no longer fighting with Harmon. He'll bring himself down eventually, I'm certain of it. In fact, we've been talking cordially every day for almost two weeks, as you know. Per Stewart's orders, I mean."

Daven seemed to not believe him. "You all of a sudden just decided to drop the whole Janet thing and become friends with Harmon? Why?"

"Not friends. Allies. The FBI forced me to back off, and I did. Our first few conversations were rough, but after they declared it a cold case we came to an understand and want to cooperate."

"On what, exactly? I can't believe what I'm hearing."

Hank smiled. "I know, I can hardly believe it myself. We haven't agreed on what to cooperate about yet, but...okay, I can tell by your expression that you don't believe me."

"I...it's not that I don't believe you. This is just all rather sudden and somewhat wild news. Trying to take it in."

Hank flipped open his phone and dialed Harmon. "Well, I'll have to prove it to you, then."

"Hank. What's up?"

"Hey. I...uh, I'm with Daven and you're on speaker. Wanted to see when we could reschedule our meeting in Las Vegas. I got the okay from Stewart and Salome to set a meeting anytime in the future without needing their permission."

"Ah, thanks for that. Well, I'm on vacation next week, so that's too bad. It will have to wait until the following week."

Hank glanced sidelong at Daven. He was indeed incredulous.

"Well, I have a crazy idea, if you're up for it. I'm in Las Vegas now and could fly to Denver tonight for dinner."

There was a short pause. "I would, actually, but we're having a blizzard and the airports are closed."

"Oh. Well, I'll meet you whenever the weather allows, I guess."

Harmon let out either a long sigh, or a very long breath that he'd been holding. "I'm vacationing in San Diego until next

Sunday. If you want to drive down and have dinner there, I can do that on…hold on.”

Hank waited patiently and watched Daven’s expressions change rapidly while Harmon checked his calendar.

“Wednesday night works. My kids are taking in some boy band concert that night.”

“Sure. It’s a date. I mean…you know what I mean.”

“Yeah, let’s not move to first base yet, Hank. Just you, or both of you?”

Hank looked at Daven, who shook his head.

“Just me, since Dav isn’t back in the office until the 26th. We’ll talk more Monday to set up the details.”

“Yep, 10am. Thanks.”

They hung up and Hank looked at Daven with a triumphant glow, barely able to keep from laughing at the man’s face. “See? Told you. I’m honestly trying to redeem myself, Dav. I really am. This is the first step among many.”

Daven was not at all amused. “I’ve been telling you to meet with him for *years* , Hank. And then when I tell you *not* to meet with him because he had our agent murdered, that's exactly what you do? What are you up to now, exactly?"

Hank's heart fell to the ground. " *Up to* ? I'm not up to anything except trying to move forward and cooperate on issues we have in common. What are you implying, exactly?"

Daven looked out at the lake for a while as they continued to walk. "Hank, you must know that your mind is....nothing. Sorry. I'm having some trust issues right now, considering everything that's happened. Do you want to hear my conditions for coming back to work for you? Maybe that will help clarify my point of view before I say something I'll regret."

Hank swallowed hard. "Alright. What are they?"

"The first is that you start taking Rupert's PR advice seriously and agree to a script before the cameras start rolling. No improvising. Nearly every time you do, we end up with a crisis."

"I think that's exaggerating a little, but I can work with that. What's the next one?"

"Secondly," Daven continued somberly, "you always said our team was a democracy. You, me, Rupert, and sometimes Taylor. Since October or so, you've been autocratic and dictatorial, not wanting or taking any input to make decisions. That's not going to work for me anymore."

Hank nearly stopped him at that, but he calmly asked, "Alright. Also an exaggeration, but we can hash that out later. Anything else?"

"Yes. The most important one. I'm your chief of staff and I expect you to treat me as such. You used to, but since last year you've been making up your mind and making decisions long before asking for my take on things, if you even bother at all. So I'm constantly chasing you for answers and sometimes don't even know what's going on at all. Like Janet being in Greeley on an errand for you. Nobody bothered to tell me, really? Why did Rupe get involved? That's my department. I can't work like that anymore. I won't do it. You need to include me in all your decisions that affect the party, period."

"Okay. That is definitely true, and I apologize. To be fair, I have one condition for you. If you can't meet it, we'll have to say goodbye and good luck right now."

Daven looked at him searchingly. "Just one? What is it?"

"You don't ever bring up anything that has happened between us in the past few months to me ever again. I know I've fucked up, I'm paying for it with my happiness as well as my bank account, and I don't need a constant reminder of how the mighty have fallen. And I will do the same for you. No holding grudges bullshit from either of us. Are we agreed?"

Daven smiled a little. "Hank, you're the king of holding grudges. I expect you to still be commenting on my minor failings 8 years ago while we're on our respective deathbeds. But yes, I agree anyway. You haven't said whether you'll agree to my first two terms yet."

"Yes. I agree. No improvising. No dictatorship. No big solo decisions."

"Good. That's settled then. And I want to be at all future meetings with Harmon."

Hank could hardly believe what he was hearing, and seeing. Daven smiling and agreeing so easily to completely reverse his decision of four days ago? Would wonders never cease?

"Okay. You're absolutely sure you want to come back?"

"Yes. Are you sure you want me back?"

Hank felt like crying. "Fuck, yes. Damn, I thought..."

Daven got very serious suddenly. "Oh. You know what, Hank? I'm really sorry, but I forgot my fourth term. It's actually more important that all of the other three put together. Could be a deal breaker if you can't agree to it."

Oh god…… "Okay. I'm listening, but-"

"I want photographic evidence of that god-awful fluffy chair being gone from my office before I come back. If it's not, I'm going to go join the Urbanes and work for Harmon, swear to god."

"Oh, forget it then. Deal's off." Hank grinned, still not quite believing his good fortune. "I don't know what to say Dav, honestly. I actually thought this would be our last conversation ever."

"It almost was. I'm really tired, Hank. How about I drive you back to the airport and call it a day."

"No, call us a taxi. We'll be fine. Get some rest."

"Okay," said Dav as he rubbed his eyes and yawned. "You're right."

Before he could say anything else, Hank pulled his friend into a tight hug. He was glad that Dav didn't pull back; in fact, he hugged him back just as hard.

"Welcome back, Dav. That stupid chair is history, I promise."

"Thanks. Burn it for good measure. Preferably in Rupert's front yard."

Philadelphia

"Hello Stewart, it's Salome. Really need you to speed up the review of those phone records so the president will approve the wiretap order for Hank. When can you let me know if you find anything even remotely suspicious so we can move forward?"

Stewart cleared his throat as he looked at one particular number highlighted in yellow. Four times over two days.

"I already have, actually. On December 19 and 20, Hank made three calls to and received one from an unknown mobile phone with a Denver area code. It's completely untraceable because the number was deactivated on December 26."

Salome paused, not really happy about that development. She wanted Hank to be innocent as much as Stewart did.

"Right. I would definitely ping that as highly suspicious, especially considering the time frame. We'll get on it. Thanks, Stewart."

CHAPTER THREE

Friday afternoon

Henderson, Nevada

As the taxi alternated between crawling and idling in traffic to Henderson airport, an idea that had been brewing in the back of Hank's mind for some time finally leaped to the forefront again and demanded attention. He dug out his phone and took a deep breath before dialing.

"Captain Ketch - quick question. Can we stop off in Palm Springs on the way home? I know you need time to file a flight plan and all."

"We'll only need 30 minutes, Mr. Bancroft. What is your ETA?"

"Probably about 45 minutes, so that's perfect."

"Consider it done."

Hank stared morosely at the passing scenery in silence. He had never been a fan of the desert, but there was no denying the late afternoon winter sun washed all the dreary tan rocks into mesmerizing shades of orange and purple.

"Boss," said Avery, drawing Hank abruptly out of his thoughts. "May I ask why we're going to Palm Springs?"

"No. Please excuse me for a moment, I need to call my assistant."

Avery nodded and turned his attention to the rain that was just starting to hit the windows.

"Hey Olivia, it's Hank. I need a few things, please. Can you have a car meet me and Avery at Palm Springs airport in about an hour and ten minutes or so? I'll probably need two hours, round-trip." He glanced sidelong at Avery, not wanting him to hear the next part but knowing that lowering his voice would insult the man, besides being futile. After all, they were sitting two feet apart. "The second thing is I need to get an appointment at Palms Elite for a quick tour. The person I spoke to last time was named Anna. If she's there, that's great. I don't want any fanfare at all. Once that's all done, can you please call our office movers and have them take away the white chair in Daven's office? I don't want it within a hundred miles of the place. Great. Just let me know when everything's done. Thanks, kiddo."

He hung up and ignored Avery's curiosity. Hank, as always, was fiercely protective of family matters and shared nothing with his guards unless he absolutely had to for the boys' safety. Even so, everyone in the household knew father and son were not on good terms right now, a fact which caused them untold stress without actually affecting them directly.

Avery knew full well that "Palms Elite" was a boarding school for high schoolers, which mean Hank was possibly planning on separating Floyd from Theo. Once again, he found himself secretly pissed off at Hank for being way too hard on the poor kid, not that he could ever say such a thing. He'd tried to intervene between them once at a hotel after Hank lost his temper, and it nearly got him fired. So Avery kept his mouth shut and watched the storm as it rolled in over Seven Hills.

"Floyd, we just landed in Santa Monica. I want you in my study in fifteen minutes. Did you put your car keys and license on my desk?"

"Yes, sir," Floyd responded somberly. "It's almost 7:30. You missed dinner."

"I'm aware of that, thank you."

"You said you'd be home by five," Floyd added flatly.

"Floyd, it's best to just stop talking. Fifteen minutes," repeated Hank firmly before hanging up. Brittany was parked next to the terminal in her own blue Prius.

"Where's the SUV?" he asked in surprise as he descended the stairs.

Brittany waited until he came closer to her before answering. "On its way to LAX with Lucas, as a diversion. I waited 20 minutes and left behind him. Nobody followed me here, thankfully."

Hank stopped in his tracks, adrenaline suddenly rushing at full strength. "What's happened?"

Brittany responded almost timidly, fully expecting him to shoot the messenger. "Word got out that you were in Philadelphia today, and there was a breaking news story. It's probably best if-"

"If I call Rupert, yes. Okay, let's go. Thanks for coming to get me."

He dialed Rupert, who picked up before the phone rang even once.

"Hank, I know you've had a hellishly long day and this is the last thing you want to come back to. But people are throwing a fit about you trying to bribe the press. Their words, not mine. We'll need to make a statement."

"No," Hank replied firmly, feeling like he was about to have a stroke.

"No...no what?"

"I'm not making any statement right now. It's Friday night. Let's revisit this on Monday. I have to get home to my son."

"Understood, but we really should get on top of this immediately. Waiting is a mistake and will only bring about more questions."

Hank was about to bark at him to back off, but then he remembered his promise a few hours ago to Daven. He had sworn he would start listening to Rupert again, hadn't he? Yes, he had, as much as he didn't want to. *Damn it.*

"Alright. Draft something and...can I stop by your house to talk about it? It will have to be fast."

"Of course."

"Okay...Brittany, to Rupert's house, please."

————

Hank stared down at the press release without being able to take in the words. He was too tired, and the couch in Rupert's office was too comfortable to resist. He leaned back, took a long drag of Rupert's third-best brandy, and closed his eyes.

"Read it to me, please. Sorry for asking."

"No problem. *Hank Bancroft, party leader of The Seditionists, readily acknowledges that he inadvertently violated Federal Statute 4.2.1 which was passed to prevent party officials from influencing the press. Mr. Bancroft's only intention was to stop photographers from continually harassing his young sons as they go about their day. The mandatory fine has been paid to rectify the error, which will not be repeated in the future. No payments or contracts have been made, or will be made, to any of the photographers involved.*"

"Read it again."

Rupert did, and Hank thought about it for a while. "I mean, photographers will probably be annoyed that I said they're harassing. But it's the truth."

"Yes, the whole truth and nothing but. As usual."

Your transparency is truly self-destructive, Hank.

Hank jumped. Those were Harmon's words, and he had just heard them clearly...in Harmon's voice.

"You okay?" Rupert asked in a tone of confusion or concern - probably both - after Hank suddenly bolted upright and shook his head like a dog.

"What? Yes, sorry. I just...I'm tired."

He set down the brandy gently but didn't say anything for a long time.

"Boss?" Rupert prompted after a few very long minutes. "Do you have any feedback?"

Hank cleared his throat and brought his attention back to the present. "I think what you wrote would be perfect, normally, but not this time. Let's shorten it down to the bare minimum."

"Seriously?" Rupert replied in surprise. "I think that's the first time I've ever heard you say that."

"Yeah. Meet the new Hank."

"I like the old Hank better. Really been missing the dirty jokes."

Hank ignored that, not being in the mood for lightheartedness. "Here's what I want it to say... *Hank Bancroft, Party Leader of the Seditionists, confirms he violated statute 4.2.1. and has paid the associated fine. No further statements will be made, nor any questions answered, on this personal matter. ”*

Rupert wrote it down and then read it back, tone full of wonder.

“Send it,” ordered Hank flatly. “Don't argue with me.” Of course, as soon as he said that he had a major pang of guilt for managing to break his promise to Daven so soon.

Rupert gulped. “I wasn't going to argue, Hank. But maybe it was a mistake to rush into this. Want to think about it and we can revisit it in the morning?”

“Nope. Send it. Also, I finally have some good news, for once. Daven and I hashed it out today and made peace. He's going to come back to work. One of his conditions was that I remove your favorite chair from his office, which I've already done. So don't bitch to me about it on Monday. And don't ever mention it to him, either.”

Rupert nodded. “Alright. I surrender. The poor man was tormented long enough. Thanks for stopping by, Hank. I'm not kicking you out or anything, but you seriously need to go home. You look half-dead.”

"I am. But I don't want to go home."

"Oh. Why?"

"Family issue." Hank was no more open about this subject with Rupert and Dav than he was with his guards. Even less so, maybe. "I visited Palms Elite this afternoon, and it might be a good fit for Floyd. But maybe not. This is incredibly awkward to ask, but what would you think of adding Floyd and Theo to your kids' home school classes? Would it even be feasible?"

Rupert didn't hesitate. "If it means you not separating the boys, we will absolutely make it happen no matter what."

"Thank you. I have to give it some thought." He hauled himself off the couch.

"He's a good kid, Hank," Rupert said tentatively, knowing he was wading into dangerous waters. "But if you're serious, you should ask Taylor about Palms Elite. She went there, you know."

"I didn't, actually. Thanks. See you Monday."

"You mean Sunday, unless you're planning to skip church?"

Hank groaned a little. "Oh god, no. I've officially had enough scandals for the week. See you Sunday, then."

It was 9pm by the time Hank got home, and Floyd's nerves were frayed almost beyond repair when his dad finally arrived. The door shut quietly, but to Floyd it sounded just like the lid of a coffin closing. After one look at Hank's face he didn't dare complain that he'd been standing in one spot for well over an hour.

Hank didn't really care that Floyd's expression looked like he was preparing to be executed. This was the end of the line, and that was that. He silently picked up Floyd's car keys and, for dramatic effect, took his time casually locking them up in the safe.

Then, the bombshell.

"Look to your left. See that shredder in the corner? Plug it in, and then put your driver's license into it."

"Dad! No. Please. I'm sorry-"

"No, you're not. Nothing you've said or done recently is even remotely sincere." Hank pulled a brochure out his jacket and handed it to Floyd. "I toured this boarding school today and started an application. I want you to seriously consider attending on your own accord, rather than me forcing you. It's actually a really nice place and you might be happy there. One of my employees attended and you can even talk to her if you'd like."

Floyd looked about to pass out from anxiety. "Without Theo?"

"Yes. But if you don't want to go, shred that license and you'll start homeschooling with Theo on Monday. Can you answer this right now, or do you need more time to think about it?"

"I need more time, please," Floyd whispered, single tears spilling down both cheeks.

"You have until 3pm on Sunday. Take this, and choose wisely." He held out the driver's license to his trembling son, who reluctantly accepted it as if it were a live grenade. "Goodnight, Floyd."

Hank walked out passed his stunned son and slammed the door behind him.

CHAPTER FOUR

Rupert's House, same evening

"Hey Dav, it's Rupe. Call me back when you can. This is the fourth message since yesterday, and I'm getting really"-

BOOP, BOOP

Rupe held out his phone to check the incoming call, then sighed in relief.

"Hi."

"Sorry, Rupert," said Dav, sounding winded. "Didn't get the phone...in time...saw your messages...been busy."

"Are you alright?" Rupe asked in alarm.

"Just finished a run...did you need something urgent..."

"Yeah, your advice on a press release. But maybe when it's a better time to talk?"

Daven couldn't possibly pass up the opportunity to see if Hank was holding to his promise from earlier today, so his curiosity immediately overruled the dire need to take a shower.

"Now is fine. Press release on what?"

Rupert explained the issue and read the two different versions while Daven listened in silence.

"So," he asked after a moment, "did Hank actually ask for your counsel on this one?"

Rupe laughed. "Not at first. You know how he's been. But I politely persisted, and he caved and came over to my house without any further argument. I guess this latest trip to Philadelphia might be making him think twice about the way things have been between all of us lately."

Daven found himself immensely satisfied by that, and a small smile started to cross his lips. He would never say it was his doing, of course. That might break the spell.

"What about the shorter statement? Are those his words?"

"Completely his words. Hell should start freezing over at what I'm about to say next: I don't think he's being transparent enough. Which is funny, because I would have given my right arm to be able to say that for the last ten years. But now that it's happening, I don't like it, and neither will our constituents."

"Agreed. Did you tell him that?"

"Not exactly. He shut me down when I started to protest."

There was a pause while Daven pulled out his keys and let himself inside his brother's house, then he said sternly, "It is exactly your job to tell him that, so you need to tell him. That statement is not going to fly. I have a suggestion on how to expand it just a little."

"Okay...go for it. Then I'll suggest it to Hank. Pray for me."

————

Bancroft Manor

"Hank Bancroft, Party Leader of the Seditionists, confirms he violated statute 4.2.1. in order to protect the privacy of his young sons and has paid the associated fine. No further statements will be made, nor any questions answered, on this personal matter."

Hank tapped his toothbrush on the counter while he thought about the additional verbiage. Rupe was nervous, because he had never gotten comfortable with disagreeing with Hank, even after all these years.

"Boss, you know I'm all for less transparency, but not total obliqueness. We can't just go from one extreme to the other in the space of a week."

"Did Daven put you up to this? Because that totally sounds like something he would say."

"No, but it *does* sound like him. Guess he's finally rubbing off on me." Rupe hated lying, but he and Dav had agreed they would not tell Hank they worked on it together, just to be safe.

"Dad?" said Floyd from the hallway.

"Hold on, Rupe. Floyd, go back to bed," he called. "Unless someone is dying, I don't want to talk right now. Especially to you."

There was silence, and eventually the sound of footsteps retreating, so Hank went back to Rupe.

"Sorry. Yeah, send it out at 7am tomorrow. Might as well get a jump on the weekend. Did you talk to your wife about the homeschooling thing?"

Rupe had heard what Hank just said to Floyd, and it made his heart hurt. "Yes, and she's actually excited about it. She loves Floyd. We all do."

"Thanks again. I'll let you know by Sunday night what I've decided."

———————-

Hank skipped breakfast on Saturday morning and went straight to his study, where he worked almost all the way through lunch. Twice his second cell phone rang in its drawer, but he ignored it. The third time, he could no longer resist the urge to find out who was trying to reach him. It had to be one of the photographers he had been trying to pay off, because no one else really had the number.

"Hank here. Who is this?"

"Good afternoon, sir. You gave me your card on Monday and said to call you if-"

"Sorry friend, I can't hold up my end of the deal."

There was a light chuckle on the other end. "Well, I can. Actually, I can do better than that. I have a contact in the government who wants to help you settle this matter lawfully."

Hank furrowed his eyebrows. "I don't know what you mean."

"Do you remember three years ago there was a bill in the house to prohibit photographers from making money off of photos of minors?"

"Of course I do. It was my measure, and it flopped because of people like you. What do you want, exactly?"

"I want to get the two of you connected. He's fairly powerful and has a lot of influence for matters like these. In fact, his partner can-"

"Let me guess. I give you money, you give me his name?"

Again, another light chuckle. "Of course. Off the records, naturally."

"Naturally," Hank replied sarcastically. "Because this couldn't be a trap or anything, right? How gullible do you think I am?"

"Gullible enough to think Harmon is your new best friend all of a sudden. It's a good thing that the meeting in Las Vegas fell through, before you sold your soul to him."

Hank's heart almost stopped at that, and the ensuing silence was deafening.

"Who the hell are you?" he finally demanded.

"I'm a disgruntled employee of the Urbanes, Mr. Bancroft. All I can say is that you need to watch your back. That advice is a freebie. Future guidance will cost you. This isn't a trick. I just want to use my position to make some extra cash, and then disappear into the night one day when I have enough to manage on my own."

Hank pulled his phone away and looked at the number on the screen. It was indeed from Colorado, but it being most likely a mobile phone, that didn't really mean anything. The man could be across the street for all he knew.

"Give me a name to call you by, even if it's not real."

"Christian."

"Okay, Christian. Listen up. I'm going to take your *free* advice and be careful with Harmon. But that's it. We're done. Now here's my free advice to you: Don't ever call me again unless you want to go to jail."

"You're welcome, Mr. Bancroft."

The line went dead, and before Hank could even process what had just happened, there was a knock on his study door.

"What?"

"Dad?" It was Theo's voice through the intercom. "Can I come in, please? I have food for you."

Still somewhat in a daze, Hank hit the button that unlocked the door and Theo let himself in. He was carrying a plate in one hand, and a bottle of Root beer in the other.

"I told you I wasn't hungry," Hank replied irritably, and the stricken look on Theo's face brought him down to earth instantly. He should have remembered it was his youngest's job to make lunch today. "Sorry, I'm...thank you, it looks delicious. What are you and Floyd up to this morning?"

"I don't know. He won't leave his room. I'm going out with Brittany soon to get school supplies but he said he won't be needing any. What does that mean?"

"Did he go to breakfast?"

"No. Or lunch. He threw it in the trash when I took it up to him."

Hank rubbed his eyes, not wanting to know how red they were. "Theo, do you want to home school with Rupert's kids? I asked him yesterday and he said they'd love to have you."

"Oh. So that explains Floyd's comment."

"Not really."

"What?"

"Nothing. Think about it and let me know by tomorrow night, okay?" He took a bit of the grilled cheese sandwich, which was delicious.

Theo looked worried. "Does that mean I would never see my friends again?"

"Probably. But it also means you would be out of the spotlight and not subject to the hundreds of rules that get you guys in trouble."

"I've never gotten in trouble!" Theo protested. "Well, just once, but I was like seven and it wasn't my fault."

"I didn't mean it that way, Theo. I just meant...see, you *should* be able to get in trouble. Live a normal childhood. Break a sculpture in the library without it making the evening news. Right now, you turn in your homework late and everybody within a hundred miles knows it. It's not fair."

Theo said nothing, so Hank took another bite of the sandwich. "This is awesome, Theody. What do I have to bribe you with to make me another one?"

Ah, there it was...the cheeky grin Hank had been missing so much lately. "Let me get one of those new frappuccinos at Starbucks while I'm shopping with Brittany."

"Done. But only the decaf version, so that you're not climbing the walls later."

"Deal." Theo laughed and left the study to go make another sandwich, and Hank felt better for a moment. But only for a moment, because his second cell phone was still sitting on the desk, staring at him accusingly in its silence. Whoever the caller had been, he knew about the meeting in Las Vegas and that was enough to confirm he was an Urbane, because no one except Daven had known about it on his side.

Hank went to the wall and hit the intercom button to Floyd's room.

"Yes, sir?"

"I understand Theo made you lunch and you threw it in the trash right in front of him without eating it. Is that true?"

Silence. That was all the confirmation Hank needed.

"Go down to the kitchen right now and apologize," he ordered tersely. "It better be sincere."

"Yes, sir," Floyd replied wearily.

Hank angrily snapped the connection closed and turned his attention to all the email he had been neglecting since Friday morning, having spent the entire day running around Las Vegas and Palm Springs. There was one from Harmon, which surprised him. He couldn't recall ever having received an email from the man before.

Let's meet at Cafe La Maze at 7pm next Wednesday in San Diego. I have a private dining room booked under the name Hank Tallmadge. Please confirm. - H

Hank looked at his second cell phone again, uneasiness rising rapidly in his chest. He knew he should call Stewart for guidance, or at least tell Daven or Rupert about the call and get their take on it. But for now, he did nothing and moved onto the next email, which was thankfully a routine approval request from Rupert.

Rupe/Taylor, this is not approved. No more media appearances until after Daven returns. Thanks, Hank.

And then the next email, which was from Stewart.

Hank, just received the 50K. Receipt attached. Call me first when you need clarification on this statute (or any other statute) next time. - Stewart

Prick, thought Hank as he printed the receipt and filed the email without replying to it.

Then, the next one:

Mr. Bancroft, this is Yannick down in accounting. I received an inquiry today from a photographer requesting a payment from you for services requested on Monday. His name is Mark Colin and he says you verbally agreed this morning to send him $1,500 but he is unable to contact you directly. Please confirm if we should process. Thank you - Yannick

That made Hank sit straight up in his chair, nerves tingling again.

I made no such promise and we will not be issuing any payment. Thank you for checking. - JW

Luna Coffee Shop - Pasadena, CA

Yannick pulled his scarf a little tighter around his neck and adjusted his sunglasses as he waited at a sunny table near the door and nursed his coffee. He had studied Colin's photo several times, but his photographic memory wasn't very good and he wasn't sure he'd recognize his visitor. So he had asked the man to carry a rolled-up magazine in his right hand to make him easier to spot.

Almost half an hour after the agreed meeting time had passed, and Yannick was about to leave when he spotted the older man walk in purposefully, heading straight towards him. He sat down and seemed unconcerned about fitting in or ordering any coffee first.

"Could you be any more late?" muttered Yannick.

"Probably. Parking is a bitch in this town." Colin responded with a grin.

Yannick shoved an envelope over to the insolent man. "Take this and put it away without counting. $3,000 cash, as agreed."

Colin did, and Yannick leaned back in relief. "As I said on the phone, if your name is spotted on any photos of the kids-"

"I know, I know. Is he paying off everyone this way? Because I wasn't going to take him up on the offer until you called me."

Yannick nodded. "Next year the payment will be double, if you don't break the agreement. Sign this form so he knows I gave you the money."

"He doesn't trust you?"

"Oh, come on. You know he doesn't trust anyone. Sign and take the receipt so I can get out of here, please. I have a party to go to."

"And this is legit? Why did he send you?"

"Do you see his signature down here? Yes, it's legit. It's personal money so we aren't exactly writing checks from the office. I'm just an accounting flunky who happened to be free this morning. You don't exactly say no to Hank Bancroft when he asks you for a favor."

"I'm sure. That's pretty much why I'm here, is it not?"

"You could say that."

Colin signed, and Yannick stood up and put the paper and receipt carefully back into his notebook. "Pleasure doing business with you. Until next year."

Yannick went back to his car and dialed Colbert.

"Three photographers down, three to go. Harmon better give me a nice bonus for this one, considering the risk of doing this in my own hometown."

Colbert chuckled a little. "Oh, don't worry. The reward will be plenty. He's going to be very pleased with you once he gets those receipts back."

"Understood. My next meet-up is in two hours, then the last one is at four. Then I'm having some serious drinks after that. On you, of course."

"Naturally."

CHAPTER FIVE

Bancroft Manor

Saturday Evening

Man had never invented a more useful thing than a Jacuzzi bathtub, at least in Hank Bancroft's opinion. It could refresh a mind, body, and soul all in one fell swoop, almost without fail.

Except for today, which was a Jacuzzi fail kind of day. Even his best whiskey wasn't helping, which was even worse. He probably should feel guilty for avoiding Floyd, but his conscience was kept in check by the fact that he was only protecting his son by taking more time to calm down. Not that he'd succeeded yet. It had been over a year since Floyd's last attempt to dodge his guards went so wildly wrong. Would the boy ever learn his lesson?

An hour of soaking in the tub did nothing, so Hank finally got out and got dressed to head downstairs to Avery to let him know the family would be going out for dinner soon.

--

Theo huffed and reach out to pull Floyd's blanket off of him. "Come on, you can't just mope all night. Let's watch a movie."

Floyd snatched the blanket back and pulled it up to his chin. "Stop it, Theody. I have to tell you something," he blurted suddenly. "You know I'm really sorry for what happened at lunch, right? Do you forgive me?"

" *Yes* , I said I did. What-"

"I'm really sorry." Now the waterworks started, and Floyd didn't try to hide it. He was absolutely miserable for a hundred reasons, although Theo was only aware of a few of them. "I've been...such a *dick* lately. I don't know what's wrong with me. Everyone hates me. Even Uncle Dav."

"What makes you say that?" Theo asked in surprise.

"Why else would he turn me in for going to his house?" Floyd sniffed. "Of all people."

Theo smiled a little. "Because he knows dad would kill him if he didn't."

Floyd felt on the edge of a nervous breakdown suddenly. "Dad's going to take away my license, and he wants to send me to boarding school in Palm Springs. Alone."

"No, he doesn't," Theo scoffed.

"Yes, he does." Floyd reached over to his nightstand and handed his brother the brochure. "Look. He said he already put in an application."

Theo flipped through the colorful booklet wordlessly, then said after a minute, "Floyd...it kind of looks...awesome. I want to go!"

"You have to be thirteen. And I know it looks amazing," Floyd admitted reluctantly. "I want to go. But not without you."

"Yeah, right. That's the reason you *want* to go. I'm not stupid"

Floyd snatched the brochure away and sat up angrily. "How can you say that?" he exclaimed hotly.

Hank chose this unfortunate moment to emerge from the third-floor stair landing, where he could hear the boys clearly arguing. He quickened his pace to reach Floyd's room.

"Are you kidding?" Theo retorted. "What the hell is wrong with you? You've been trying to get away from us for months."

"No I haven't. Shut up."

"You shut up!" Theo shot back. "Dad's been on your case forever for being a dick to me. You should go. It would make two people happy, at least. Me and dad, because we won't have to put up with your shit anymore."

Floyd was devastated and angered by this attack, and he lunged forward to knock Theo to the ground. Not hard, but it was enough. In return, Theo jumped up and shoved Floyd into the wall just as Hank appeared in the doorway.

"Stop!" shouted Hank as he dashed in and grabbed them by the upper arms, jerking them roughly to their feet. "Theo, I'm incredibly disappointed in you."

"He shoved me first!" Theo retorted.

"I don't blame him. What you said was downright cruel. Your brother was trying to make amends and you just...you know what, I can't do this right now. Get in your pajamas and go to bed."

"But it's only six o'clock-"

"Exactly. And you'll go hungry tonight, too. In bed, *now* !"

Hank turned to Floyd after Theo had made his sullen exit. "He was right about one thing, Floyd. You *have* been a dick, there's no denying that. But the fact that he didn't accept your apology doesn't diminish your efforts to make it right. I'm proud of you. Are you listening?"

Floyd nodded and wiped his nose, amazed and warmed by what he was hearing. His father hadn't told him he was proud of him in…well, forever. "Yes. Thank you, dad. Does this mean you'll stop ignoring me?"

"I've been *avoiding* you," corrected Hank, "because I was afraid I'd lose my temper and need to calm down some more. Still mad, you know."

"I know. But can you just *not* be mad anymore? Because I can't handle you both yelling at me." Floyd wiped his eyes again, and Hank's heart softened a little. But he still wasn't ready to forgive. Not even close.

"We'll talk tomorrow. Right now, we need to have dinner. What do you want?"

"Nothing. I'm not eating until you forgive me."

Hank's eye twitched a little in annoyance at that. "Fine. Go to bed, then. We'll see how you feel at breakfast."

Floyd was unable to fall asleep with such an early bedtime, so after an hour of tossing and turning he snuck over to Theo's room to check on him. He was wide awake, too.

"Hey, Theo," Floyd whispered. "I can't sleep."

"Why not?"

"It's too early. Why aren't you asleep?"

"Maybe because my ass is on fire and I'm starving?"

Floyd's heart fell. He had been hoping their dad wouldn't be too hard on Theo, but as usual, that hope was in vain. "Sorry. That's why I came over." He pulled a Snickers out of his pocket and shoved it into his brother's hand. "Here. Don't tell dad."

Theo sat up and tore the wrapper off like he hadn't eaten in a month. "Oh my god, thank you."

Floyd waited in silence while his brother pondered the treat, and his heart fell a little for the third time today as he watched the 11-year old's joy in the dim light of the moon. They may not always get along, and they were so utterly different in almost every imaginable way, but...

"I can't eat this," Theo said suddenly, and he handed it back to Floyd. "Dad said I have to go hungry tonight. But thank you. I really appreciate it."

"He'll never know."

"Yes he will. And my butt's already blistered from being a dick to you, so I need to be good."

"Oh, so you admit it?" replied Floyd with a cheeky grin. "That you were being a dick, I mean?"

Theo wanted to laugh, but he wasn't in the mood. "Yeah. I'm sorry for being mean. I wouldn't be happier without you. Dad, maybe, but not me. Definitely not me. I don't want you to go."

Floyd swallowed hard and felt his eyes stinging. Before he could reply, his heart lurched at the sound of his dad's voice from the doorway.

"Floyd. *Out* ."

Hank crossed his arms as they reached Floyd's room and the teenager got back in bed. "What were you doing in Theo's room?"

Floyd wanted to lie so badly. He never wanted to lie so much in his life, actually. But he didn't.

"I went to check on him, then I gave him a candy bar because he was hungry."

"Did he appreciate it?"

Floyd hesitated in surprise, not expecting that line of questioning at all. He held up the Snickers. "Yes, but he wouldn't eat it. Didn't want you to be mad. Dad, I'm sorry. Please don't be upset at him, he didn't ask me for anything."

Hank took a few steps towards his nervous son and took away the candy bar. "I would never be upset at you for caring about your brother, but this is the last thing you should be giving him. He's hyper enough already."

"Sorry, dad."

"Listen, Avery ordered enough food for three because I forgot to tell him you guys were in bed. Want to come down and join me? It's from Cheesecake Factory."

Floyd nodded, although he wasn't actually sure if he did or not. "Only if I can take a plate to Theo, though."

Hank gave in, just as Floyd expected. He couldn't justify starving his boys no matter how mad they made him. He had made them skip breakfast or lunch once in a while if they were really getting on his nerves, but never dinner.

"Alright. Come on."

CHAPTER SIX

Rupert's House

"Rupe, you can't be serious! You agreed without asking me? Like four kids aren't enough already?"

"I know, but the way he was talking to Floyd, I just…I couldn't help it. I'm sorry." Rupert put his arms around his wife. "You know Hank will pay for all of their supplies, and do whatever he can to support this. We can't let the boys be separated. You're so good at this home schooling thing, and they will feel so lucky to have you. I would hate to think you don't want to teach them."

"I'm not upset about teaching them. I'm upset you agreed to it without a word to me, and not only that…why *exactly* do you idolize Hank Bancroft, again? I've never understood it. He treats his kids like shit, and with the way he's been treating you and Daven recently-"

"Millie, stop. I'm not going to fight with you again. I told you, we got through it. We're good. He's even back to taking my advice, although I'm not sure how long that will last." He hugged his wife tighter and kissed her a few times on the neck.

"I'm sorry I didn't ask you first," he murmured into her hair. "I actually didn't think he was serious until all of a sudden it became a critical turn in the conversation."

Millie sighed, giving in quickly to her well-meaning husband. She never could stay mad at him for long.

"Alright. You meant well, but next time you'll be removing my foot from your butt if you do something like this again. I'm serious."

"I know. Thank you." Rupert kissed her again, then twice more.

Father and son didn't say anything notable through dinner, but while Hank was unpacking dessert from the to-go bags, Floyd suddenly let his guard down.

"I want to go to the boarding school, dad," he blurted quickly.

The knife that had been sinking into the disgustingly sugary Reese's Peanut Butter Cup Cheesecake halted its course abruptly.

"Are you sure?" Hank asked, his throat suddenly dry as sand.

"Yes, sir. I'm really sorry for what I did. It won't ever happen again."

"Apology accepted. You can pack in the morning, then. Your suitcases are in the pool house."

Floyd studied his dessert for a moment. "You ordered my favorite cheesecake! It's not even my birthday."

"Close enough. And now since you won't be here for your birthday, we'll just celebrate it early."

Floyd looked almost ready to cry as he picked up his fork. "Thanks, dad."

"You're welcome."

Until this moment, there was nothing more that Hank wanted than getting Floyd out of the house, but suddenly he hated himself inside and out for making that stop in Palm Springs.

Sunday

It was such a relief to be back together with Rupert and Daven that Hank could almost forget the misery of being in church. The world felt so much safer and smaller when he was sandwiched between them, although the desire to chat them up the entire time was nearly irresistible. It took all of his willpower to keep his mouth shut.

The sermon happened to be focused on the obligations of parents to discipline their children. It couldn't have been a more timely lesson, but it was also spectacularly uncomfortable under the circumstances. Hank felt Floyd's eyes on him from the balcony in several relevant places, but he succeeded in not returning the eye contact until the very end.

...our own failings can be given retribution through trying to prevent our own behavior from happening again. But that can be destructive if not acknowledged and controlled. Parents, if you are hard on your children, be certain you are acting with compassion instead of guilt. Children, if your parents are hard on you, I would also ask that you act with compassion instead of anger. Discipline is love, and lack of discipline shows an unforgivable careless attitude towards your future.

Hank turned his head to look at Floyd, who locked eyes with him.

To be grateful for correction is to acknowledge and know you are loved, and being loved by others makes it that much easier to love yourself. So appreciate the opportunity to make things right, and know you have already received a gift...a chance to be forgiven.

The sermon ended a few moments later. Hank swallowed back his emotion, stood up quickly and made a beeline for the lobby, totally ignoring Lucas's mad dash to catch up with him.

Floyd was the first one down the stairs, and he ran up to his father and threw his arms around him.

"I'm sorry, dad. I love you," he murmured into his jacket.

Hank pulled him into the little alcove behind the stairs, then hugged him back tightly. "I love you too, Floyd. It's okay, shhh."

Theo now appeared, bewildered at what he was seeing. He was too young to understand the depth of what had occurred, and all he cared about at the moment was breakfast. Hank threw a look at Brittany and she shooed Theody away and out into the car. Avery then took her place, shielding them from view entirely from the rest of the congregation.

"Floyd," Hank said gently after a minute. "Are you alright?"

"Mmm," mumbled Floyd; his face being smashed into Hank's chest didn't allow for much more of an answer than that.

"What?" Hank pried him off and looked at him up and down. His expression was peaceful.

"I'm fine."

"You sure?"

Floyd stood up straight and nodded at his father. "I'm sure."

Hank smiled a little. "Okay, kiddo," Hank replied after a moment as he patted Floyd's shoulder and gripped it for a few seconds. "We got to get you home to pack. We'll leave for Palm Springs at 3pm."

Hank turned around to Avery, who was trying his best not to show his concern for Floyd.

"We need to make a brief stop at home to drop Floyd off, then to the brunch. Give me a minute."

He walked over to Dav, who was standing alone. There was no sign of Rupert, who must have bolted at the first opportunity in order to watch a game.

"Dav, are you heading home?"

"Yes."

"Can I ride with you? Need to talk, and it's rather urgent."

"Sure. Come on."

Hank directed Avery to leave for the house and then got in Dav's car, immediately instructing Lucas to roll up the privacy window.

"Listen, Dav...I...this is tough for me to admit, but I've seriously fucked up. Again. Need your advice."

Daven looked instantly concerned. "What?"

"Well, yesterday I got a call on my second cell from an Urbane who wants me to pay him for some information. But that's not what I'm upset about. He knew I was going to meet Harmon in Las Vegas, and..."

"And what?"

"He told me very seriously to watch my back and not get friendly with Harmon. He's obviously trying to worm his way into my good graces and help himself. But I believed him anyway."

Daven thought about it for a moment. "So what did you do?"

"Nothing, at first. Told him to lose my number. Wait, forgot to mention that Harmon asked to meet me in San Diego on Wednesday, by the way."

"Okay. I don't see the part where you did anything wrong."

Hank closed his eyes for a moment. "Yet. Not finished. I couldn't sleep after that warning. It got to me, bad. Like, paranoia-off-the-charts bad. So at like 3am I wrote to Harmon and basically told him to fuck off, in so many words. Told him I wouldn't meet with him, now or ever."

Daven froze, his face draining of color. "Hank, what the hell."

"I know, Dav. I know."

Daven looked away, and Hank could feel the disappointment radiating off of his friend.

"What exactly did this caller say? Tell me everything."

Hank repeated the story of how the caller at first said he was a photographer, then a disgruntled employee, then just a man who could help him get in touch with someone in the government, while Daven listened with a pained expression.

"Okay, Hank," he said, with a slight edge to his voice. "There's nothing wrong with heeding his advice to be careful with Harmon. I don't think you're wrong to be paranoid. But...first of all, get rid of that damned phone. Never answer it again because all the wrong people now have it in their hands, and who knows what they're up to now."

Hank nodded, realizing that was excellent advice. "Okay. I will. Destroyed as soon as I get home."

"Secondly, you need to apologize to Harmon and meet with him in San Diego. Thirdly, you have to tell Stewart. This person could be the same guy that's been calling the emergency line since Christmas. And lastly…you're really not going to like this one, to be honest."

Hank closed his eyes in pain. "I already don't like *any* of this, so why stop now?"

"You need to seriously consider getting rid of all our double agents. I can only-"

"No."

"Hank, you-"

"I said no. End of discussion."

Daven turned bodily towards him, expression hard. "No, Hank. I don't accept your *end of discussions* anymore. I thought we talked about this; it was one of my conditions of coming back to work for you. So yes, we *are* going to discuss it. With Rupert, in fact, the day I return to the office. I'll have him send a meeting invite."

Hank was speechless. He wasn't used to Daven talking back to him, to say the least, and was so confounded that all he could manage in return was a deadly glare.

"You can glare at me all you want, Hank. It doesn't change the fact that you agreed to this."

Hank finally nodded and looked at his BlackBerry. Calmly he said, "I'll send the invite now. Rupe and I are open at 4pm that day."

"Thank you," Daven replied coolly. "And you need to apologize to Harmon and agree to meet with him. Whether it's in San Diego or Las Vegas or whatever, I don't care. Just do it."

Hank's nerves were shot, and he didn't have any fight left in him. "You're right. I will. But I'm not going to tell Stewart about the call yet. I want to see what Harmon says about it first."

Daven nodded. "Agreed."

Hank took a bottle of water out of the console and downed half of it in one gulp, suddenly overwhelmed with the idea that maybe it was a really bad idea to have agreed to let Daven and Rupe have so much control over his decisions. They weren't exactly on the same page lately.

"Dav," he said quietly, almost sadly. "I am the final say, and always will be as long as I'm in charge. I hope you know that whatever I decide in the future, with or without you and Rupe...it's always with good intentions. *Always.*"

"I know that, Hank," Daven replied quietly.

"That's reassuring," Hank sniped facetiously.

Daven did not respond, and they said nothing more on the way to the house.

Keep the Faith

The Distant Connection

CHAPTER ONE

Hilton San Diego & Urbanes Headquarters

Monday Morning

"What the hell do you make out of this email Hank sent me on Saturday night?"

Colbert flinched, glad that Harmon wasn't in front of him to see the gesture. "So it's *Hank,* now. Not Bancroft?"

"Just read it. Says he doesn't want to meet with me anymore."

While the line went silent, Harmon got up and went to raid his hotel's mini bar, although it was only 11am. He didn't really care about the clock, anyway, seeing how time didn't care how he felt towards his again-bitter rival.

Colbert read it twice, and then smiled to himself. "What got his hackles up, I wonder?" Secretly he was glad for the tiff, but he'd never say that. The thought did briefly occur to him that maybe one of the photographers Yannick paid off had somehow gotten back to Bancroft, but then he dismissed that fear. It would make no sense, considering they thought the money was coming from him in the first place.

"Hell if I know. He's supposed to meet me for dinner in two days. No idea what caused this total turnaround, and he didn't call me at 10am this morning. I won't tell Stewart, though. Not yet. If you think of anything that could have caused this-"

"I'll let you know, boss. Try to enjoy your vacation in the meantime."

"Yeah. You hear from Yannick again?"

"Not a peep," Colbert lied, having just hung up with him moments before Harmon called.

"Good. Well I'm off to see some damned aircraft carrier or something. You know how my son is crazy about boats. Keep in touch."

"Will do."

Colbert hung up and tried not to laugh out loud. Then he went back to studying the government's many regulations on what exactly constitutes sedition and treason.

Seditionist HQ

Also Monday morning

"Rupe, don't give me a hard time about this one," Hank complained pre-emptively.

"Actually, I was going to agree with you," Rupe responded quietly from his spot in one of Hank's "electric chairs." It always unnerved him to be called in the office like this, but as far as he could tell, he hadn't done anything wrong. Neither had Taylor, who was equally anxious about the reason for this summons.

"Me too, boss," Taylor chimed in. "Changing the emergency number is not a big deal. I say we do it now, especially if someone got a hold of it as you suspected. I see no downside to it."

Hank rubbed his face. "Or maybe it's a moot point altogether, because Daven wants to get rid of all double agents," he blurted suddenly, feeling the rush of irritation surge back up again as he thought about it. "What do you guys think about that? Don't look at each other, look at me. Tell me honestly."

Rupert shook his head. "I don't know offhand. What's his reasoning?"

The fact that Hank didn't know for once what Daven was thinking did absolutely nothing to soothe his increasingly bad temper. "You tell me. You've been talking to him a lot more lately than I have."

Rupe felt his own blood starting to rise, but he would never argue with Hank in front of Taylor. "We didn't talk about that, though. Never even came up. I'm not sure what-"

"What else have you been talking about, exactly?" Hank demanded, and Taylor jumped a little.

"Mostly sports, Hank. And your new house, like everyone else in the neighborhood. It's looking quite formidable in its final stages," Rupert replied easily in an effort to diffuse his boss. Obviously something was bothering him that he didn't want to talk about, and although this mood was rare, everyone knew meetings like this inevitably ended in a nasty fight. Rupert was determined to avoid that at all costs.

Taylor took a deep breath. "Mr. Bancroft, I believe it's because Harmon has claimed he no longer uses double agents. We know Daven doesn't like to look bad in comparison to the Urbanes, especially after Janet's death. It's only a matter of time before they find out what she was, and they're going to sing it out the world."

Hank looked at her for a moment, his anger put aside as he realized he hadn't exactly been forthcoming with Daven's second-in-command. "They already know, Taylor. I confirmed it some time ago." He looked over at Rupert with a hard expression. "Don't even give me-"

"Hank, how could-"

"*Don't,* " Hank repeated, and Rupe closed his mouth hard. "What done is done, and I've already gotten my ass handed to me about it from Stewart and Daven about it. So just *don't* ."

Taylor looked back and forth between the men. "Then why haven't they made it public yet?"

"Because," Hank replied with a huff, "they're goddamned guilty of her murder, that's why. If I hadn't been banned from talking about it, I would announce it myself."

"Let's not and say we did," Rupert replied after an awkward pause. "Hank, why don't you just tell us what's really bothering you? I assure you we are here to help."

Hank tapped his fingers on the desk and counted to twenty before he responded. "I suspect Harmon is working with a double agent, that's what. One of ours." He looked at Taylor. "And I'm pissed at you for not yet being able to identify who the Urbane was that that I allegedly spoke with before

Christmas eve. You had three names, and you can't pin any of them down as suspicious?"

Taylor looked crushed. "No, sir. We talked about this, and how I believe the caller was lying."

"That's not good enough," Hank barked rudely. "Prove it to me. You only have a theory, but nothing to back that up. At least nothing you are willing to stand by for more than thirty seconds at a time!"

Rupert stood up between them as if to physically break the tension. "Alright, let's take a break. Taylor, give us a minute, if you please." He glanced at Hank, daring him to contradict.

Taylor left, and then Hank stood up, too. "You need to go, too."

"Not going to oblige at this particular moment, but I will shortly," Rupe responded calmly as he sat back down. "Your theory on Harmon working with a double agent is important and I want to hear what you have to say about it. Please tell me your thoughts."

That did the trick nicely, and Hank crossed back to his chair with a resigned sigh and picked up a newspaper. "I should have never sent Floyd to that damned boarding school," he admitted bitterly. "Did you see the paper this morning?"

Rupe sat up straighter. "What? No."

Hank's eyes narrowed. "You're the PR guy. It's your goddamn job to be on top of these things before I am."

"You need to calm down," Rupert answered quickly as he reached across the desk to grab the paper that Hank flipped over to him. "You know I was with my son at the doctor this morning and just got here a few minutes ago."

Hank nodded contritely. "Sorry. That was uncalled for."

Rupe took a deep breath and looked at the bottom of page 2. It was a photo of Hank with a private plane - the one that Stewart had forced him to take to and from Philadelphia - and the caption read: *Henderson, Nevada. Hank Bancroft caught wasting his constituent's money on short hops to scout elite private schools for his son, where he was spotted on a joyride to Lake Las Vegas and enjoying a scenic stroll around the lake with his favorite shunned right-hand man, Daven Johansson. One must wonder what the bill looked like for this excursion, and perhaps demand to know who paid for it.*

Rupert took a deep breath. "What the fuck?" he wondered in awe. The media had been unkind to him before, but this was a spectacular new low. "Who the hell wrote this?"

"Anonymous," growled Hank. "But I guarantee you it was goddamned Hailey Hendricks. It gets worse. Read the front page."

On the front of the politics page there was a distant, grainy picture of father and son carrying suitcases under a palm tree, accompanied by a bitter caption: *Hank Bancroft drops his oldest son off Sunday at the most elite and stuffy boarding school on the West Coast, showing his constituents that if you can't solve your problems buying off photographers, you always have other options to throw your money away! Perhaps here young Floyd will learn there are actual, real-life consequences to vandalizing libraries and fighting in church, since his father seems equally as incapable of controlling his sons and his executives when required.*

Rupert was so offended that he didn't know what to say, but Hank had several choice words as he snatched back the paper.

"Fucking Hailey, I'm telling you. And Harmon is orchestrating this. Daven is coming back to work *now* . I'm not waiting until January 26."

"Stewart isn't going to like that," Rupe breathed heavily.

"Fuck him, too." Hank picked up the phone and dialed Dav, who picked up milliseconds before it should have gone to voicemail. "Hey. I need you back to work ASAP. Taylor's not cutting it and shit's hitting the fan. Can you come in tomorrow?...Why not?...I don't give a damn what he thinks, it's my decision. Dav...you know what, come in tomorrow, or don't come in at all ever again. Yes, I'm serious."

He slammed down the phone.

"Hank, stop it," warned Rupert sharply. "We've been through this before. The media will have their fun vilifying you for a few days, and then they'll get bored and move on. You're giving them exactly what they want right now."

Hank threw him a dangerous glare. "I'm telling you, Rupe. Harmon is working with someone on our side, but I don't know who. We need to find out."

"What makes you think that?" asked Rupert angrily. "You haven't said a thing to try to convince me of that, not even one *single* thing. Help me out here."

"I don't know, Rupe," Hank admitted. "I just have a feeling something's rotten in Denmark."

"Quoting Shakespeare, eh? Must be serious, then."

"I am serious. There's something else I need to tell you, and Dav. But you're both going to think I'm out of my mind."

Rupert cocked his head. "I won't, Hank," he replied seriously. "Promise. What is going on?"

Hank reached back to his bar and grabbed a beer as he took deep breaths to calm himself. "It's just that....well, Theo was on the house phone this morning while I was getting ready for work. Calling Floyd to see how he was doing, because he couldn't find his cell phone."

"Okay."

"And he said he heard a strange click."

"....oh."

"Yeah. And when I called Daven just now, I heard the same thing. I've only heard it once before, and that was a few weeks back when Stewart told me that a call between us was being recorded. Rupe, I think my calls are being monitored. Wires tapped. Whatever they call it. Why would that be? They - meaning the FBI - have to find cause for that. Get a warrant, et cetera. They can't just do it willy-nilly."

Rupert let out a low whistle. "Okay, well...how about this, you call me tonight to talk about Theo's first day of homeschooling and you listen for the click. If you hear it again, you might be onto something. For the record, I don't think you're crazy."

Hank laughed without humor. "Well, you have more faith in me than I do at the moment."

"I've always had faith in you, Hank. But to be perfectly honest, that's not going to last long if you don't pull it together and stop losing your shit without much provocation."

Hank eyed him sternly, then put his beer back in the fridge without opening it. "You're telling me to apologize to Taylor, aren't you?"

"Yes. And Dav. And Harmon, but don't hate me for saying that."

Hank grimaced. "I don't hate you. Obviously I owe you an apology as well."

"No, I'm good. Just...for god's sake, be careful about what you say on your landlines from now on. And don't miss any more calls with Harmon."

"Agreed. Thanks, Rupe. I got this. Let's get back to work. Ask Taylor to come in here, please."

FBI Headquarters, Philadelphia

Monday Evening

"Salome, he didn't make his daily call to Harmon today. But if we call him on it, he'll know we're tapping his lines."

"Are you sure?"

"Yes, because Harmon hasn't reported it to me himself."

"That's strange. Maybe he called from his cell phone?" Salome sounded as distracted as she was; stepping into her dress for a date was infinitely more difficult with a cell phone in one hand.

Stewart mulled that over for a while as he doodled in his notebook. "No. Hank's too careful for that. The Seditionists record everything, and he wouldn't want to go off the grid and have a secret conversation, as it were. You know how much he hates taking business calls on his cell."

Salome shrugged. "True, but he's done it before. Ask him about it when you next speak, but don't call him specifically for that. I'm not going to let him get away with disobeying the mandate, period."

Seditionists HQ

Hank stared at his desk phone for another fifteen minutes without moving, then reached for his cell to call Dav.

"Hey, Dav. It's been a hell of a day. I'm headed home. Wondered if you want to come over for dinner with me and Theo."

Daven sat up straighter at his desk, surprised and alarmed. Hank had never invited him over on a Monday night, which had always been his fiercely-protected family evening.

"Everything okay, Hank?"

Hank held back a grimace. "Yeah. Floyd, you probably already know...he's at boarding school."

"Yeah, I read about that."

Groan. "Theo and I could really use the company to distract us from Floyd's absence. Not that you're just a distraction, of course."

"Sure, Hank. What time?"

"In an hour. Chef's already preparing the food. You still vegan?"

"Yes. Don't forget my tofu scramble and kale salad."

That was an in-joke between them; Daven was as carnivorous as anyone could possibly be and barely touched anything that resembled non-meat. Hank smiled briefly, then got serious again.

"You got it. Dav...please forgive me for being a dick this morning. I got my ass handed to me by Rupert about it, and he was right to say I was completely out of line. Those two little blurbs in the paper set me off like you wouldn't believe."

"I believe it, actually. Your boys are supposed to be off-limits."

Hank looked up to see Avery's face hovering behind the glass panel. It was time to go.

"Can you come back tomorrow? Please?"

Daven hesitated. "Did you clear it with Stewart?"

"No."

"Then, no."

Hank sighed. "Fine. I'll call him now. Stay on the line." He had all but forgotten how to conference call, since his assistant always did it for him, but he somehow managed to hit the right combination of buttons and was relieved to hear the phone ringing to his FBI contact.

"Dav, you on the line?"

"Yes."

"Good evening, this is Stewart."

"Sorry to call you so late. This is Hank Bancroft and Daven Johansson."

"Yes, Hank?" Stewart sounded irritated.

"Listen, I want to run something by you real quick. I need to bring Daven back into the office before January 26. Like, tomorrow. A lot going on. Do you see any problem with that, from your point of view I mean?"

There was a slight pause. "Not our jurisdiction at all, but thanks for asking. You may have to answer to your constituents, though. My guess is they'll be really happy he's back and not give you a hard time about it. Glad you called because I have a question for you, actually. Did you have your daily call with Harmon today?"

Hank hesitated, wanting so badly to lie. So much that it physically hurt. "No. There was...no."

Stewart's tone hardened. "You were given a mandate. Do we need to summon you again to drive the point home?"

Hank swallowed hard and flushed, hating being treated like a little boy about to get hauled over a knee, especially with Daven listening in.

"No."

"Call him now so I can honestly tell Salome you two spoke today. She's going to ask me in the morning. Call me back and let me know it's done."

Hank sighed, a little too loudly for Stewart's liking.

"Hank? Would you prefer that I just-"

"No, no, sorry. Will do."

"Good."

He hung up, and Daven breathed out his own sigh. "Jesus, Hank. Are you trying to get yourself-"

"No, I'm not. Listen, are you in for coming back to the office tomorrow, or not?"

"Yes."

"Okay, then I want you on this call with Harmon, and all future ones as well. I'm going to dial him in. Wish me luck."

San Diego

Harmon lifted his head from the pool chaise lounge to peek at his vibrating phone, again. Literally the last person in the world he wanted to speak to, period, was calling him for the third time in a row. He put down his margarita and flipped open the phone angrily.

"I'm on vacation, Hank. What do you want?"

"Uh…Harmon, I'm sorry to bother you. I've got Daven on the line with me, just so you know."

"Okay. I repeat, what do you want?"

Hank cleared his throat and clenched a fist. "Well, since you told Stewart I didn't call you today, I have to call you now and be nice for ten minutes. What are you doing?"

"None of your business, and I didn't tell Stewart anything. Haven't spoken to him in days, and I was perfectly content not hearing your voice today, either."

"Oh." Hank would have looked at Daven quizzically, but he was by himself in his office, so he had to content himself with just staring at his hands. "Sorry for making an assumption. Anyway-"

"Did you tell Daven about that friendly little email you sent me Saturday night?"

Hank swallowed hard, knowing that he was going to hate himself later for groveling to this man. "All about it, actually. Even read it to him. He was appalled, as I'm sure you've guessed. We'd like to come down to San Diego on Wednesday to have dinner with you, if the invite still stands."

"It doesn't. What else would you like to talk about, Hank? Maybe a movie you've seen lately? One you haven't paid for in a cheap motel, that is. Eight minutes left."

Fuck.

"Harmon, this is hardly constructive," Daven responded, and Hank's heart lurched in dismay; he should have instructed the man to keep his mouth shut.

"Uh, Dav, it's alright."

"No, it's not," Daven replied easily. "Harmon, you were right to be angry about the email. We all know that. So that's at least one thing the three of us have agreed upon already. I'm sure there's more where that came from, but we'll never know if we don't talk. You agreed to meet with Hank for a reason, and vice versa. Do you even remember what it was?"

"Of course I do. And it's no longer relevant."

"Why?" asked Daven, genuinely curious.

Dav, I'm going to freakin' kill you where you stand, Hank thought to himself angrily.

Harmon paused. "Because…he obviously doesn't trust me, and I don't trust him. He doesn't even trust *you*. So what's the point?"

Hank broke in now, sweating profusely. "I do trust him, actually. But you're right that I don't trust you, Harmon. I'll tell you exactly why, and what led me to send that email, but only if we meet on Wednesday."

"What's that supposed to mean?" Harmon demanded.

"I mean," replied Hank quickly, "there was a reason I went off on you. A call I received with specific information, probably damaging to both of us, but you'll never know about it if you don't agree to meet. Period."

There was a long pause, and Hank could hear the other two men breathing heavily.

Finally, Harmon responded. "I don't believe you," he replied simply.

"Fine. I'll let Daven say it, then, since you have no reason to distrust him. Dav?"

Slight pause, then Dav's gravelly voice. "He's telling the truth, Harmon. We need to talk. But perhaps not in San Diego, since you're with your family on vacation."

There was another pause, very long this time, and the sound of poolside calypso music invaded the line for about thirty seconds.

"Alright," agreed Harmon, albeit reluctantly. "Cafe La Maze at 6:30pm this Wednesday. It's a private room on the third floor. Come without your guards."

"No. My guards follow me everywhere except the bathroom," Hank retorted. "And sometimes even then."

"Of course. I meant no guards in the room while we're meeting," Harmon amended. "I don't talk in front of servers, either. Period."

"Neither do I," said Hank. "No problem. See you then. And I'll ask Stewart if we can cancel our calls for this week. He probably doesn't know you're on vacation."

"Okay, thanks. See you guys Wednesday."

The noisy line suddenly cut off, and Hank was left on the line with Daven.

"Hank…I'm so sorry. You're going to yell at me, aren't you?" asked Dav in resignation.

"No, actually," Hank replied, and he was surprised to realize that he had forgotten his earlier anger altogether. "You did good, Dav. Really good. Still want to come to my place?"

"Yes. You have to call Stewart back first."

"Ok, I will in a minute." Hank took a deep breath, slightly shaky but calm. He felt emotional suddenly. "Hey, and…thanks for agreeing to come back early. I can't do this job without you. I don't *want* to do this job without you."

Daven swallowed hard. "I wouldn't even want your job at all, Hank. It's a lot. The shit you put up with, and…I'm just really sorry about everything I did to make it harder for you. I hope you'll forgive me someday."

Hank laughed a little, though nothing was even remotely funny at all. "You know me, the world record holder for grudges. But I meant what I said to Harmon. I do trust you. Just…don't give me another reason not to, ever again. Because honestly I won't come back from that a second time."

“Okay,” Daven replied quietly. “Deal. I better get up and get dressed.”

“You still in your flannel jammies?” Hank asked cheekily.

“They’re not flannel, they’re…Hank,” Daven stopped himself and blushed as he realized he’d honestly answered the teasing question, and now his boss knew he was still in his pajamas after 5pm.

Hank laughed. “It’s alright, but I have to admit I’m just a little jealous. Yeah, put on some real clothes, please. See you in about twenty-five minutes.”

It felt good to hear Hank laugh, and Daven was pleased, even if it was at his own expense. As usual.

CHAPTER TWO

Hank knew they had made a huge mistake leaving so late in the day for San Diego, and the terrible traffic confirmed his worst fears. They would probably be late for the dinner with Harmon...no, strike that. They would *absolutely* be late. But Hank wasn't willing to call him yet, and he turned to Daven to voice his frustration that the afternoon strategy meeting had gone over by half an hour.

"I told you multiple times to end it, Hank," was Daven's bland reply. As usual, he refused to apologize for something that wasn't his fault. Hank admired that in him immensely, but something in him wanted an apology anyway at times like this. It wasn't fair, and he knew it. So he let it go and fumed silently to himself as they rolled through Dana Point almost an hour later than scheduled. Theo was riding along in the backseat, so there wasn't any opportunity to talk business. Both of them were secretly glad for that, although they wouldn't admit it.

Hank's phone rang with a Palm Springs area code, and his heart lit up like a Christmas tree. He hadn't talked to Floyd yet since dropping him off at the new school, and neither had they exchanged any emails. Even Theo was rather silent on the matter; it almost seemed as if Floyd had temporarily ceased to exist.

"Hank Bancroft," he answered lightly.

"Good afternoon, sir, this is Silas at Elite Palms. I'm your son's headmaster."

"How can I help you?" Hank's heart was now racing instead of glowing. "Is he alright?"

"Yes, sir. Perfectly fine. He got himself into a bit of trouble today, however, and normally I wouldn't bother you with calling for something so minor. But our administrative officer says that you may have neglected to sign the corporal punishment opt-in form, and I just wanted to check that it was intentional. Again, I'm sorry to bother you."

"It's alright, thank you for calling. Is he with you right now?"

"Yes, sir."

"Okay. Please hold for about 3 minutes, okay? Don't hang up."

Hank took a deep breath to calm his nerves, muted his phone, and tapped on the black glass, which immediately rolled down.

"Yes, sir?"

"Vance, I need you to pull over and have Avery follow us. Somewhere private."

"Yes, sir."

Theo tapped his dad on the shoulder, his face twisted in worry. "Everything okay, dad?"

Hank smiled. "Yeah. You know Floyd, probably couldn't keep his big mouth shut. It's fine. I just want to talk to him in private for a minute, okay?"

Two minutes later the cars pulled into the far reaches of a hotel parking lot, and Hank ordered everyone out and into the other car. Once he was alone, he unmuted his phone.

"Silas? I'm sorry about that. Had to, uh, clear the room. Look, I didn't miss the form. Perhaps I should have written *void* on it or something. Sorry about that."

Silas cleared his throat. "Okay, sir, so just want to clarify that you're opting *out* of corporal punishment?"

He sounded surprised, so Hank couldn't resist asking, "Yes. Is that unusual or something?"

"No," Silas replied, "it's becoming less common, but...I only called because your son is the one who thought it was wrong. He seemed certain. Wouldn't accept anything else."

Hank smiled to himself a little. Floyd should have been relieved, but he knew his dad too well.

"I see. Can you put him on the phone, please? I'd like to get the story from him directly."

"Dad," said Floyd a moment later, in a very shaky and fearful tone. "I'm really, really sorry. It was my fault and-"

Hank hardened his tone, although he felt no anger at all. "Floyd, stop. We can exchange greetings first, you know. Haven't spoken in days. Besides this, how are you, son? Liking the school so far?"

"No. Well, not at this moment, but I had been until today," he answered tersely, his tone indicating tremendous levels of stress.

Hank gave up on the greetings attempt. "Okay, just relax. Tell me what happened."

"I ditched class to go back to my room."

"Why?"

"Dad...there was...I had a missed call from Theo, and I was afraid something was wrong with you. I had to call him back right away. I'm sorry. And then..."

"What?"

"Well, I intended to go to class after that, but I got sick. You know what I mean."

The ulcers again. Hank's heart fell to his knees, and anger rose in his throat because this meant Theo was in trouble, too. But that was another story.

"Are you taking your medications?"

"Yes, dad. I'm fine now."

"Put Silas back on the phone."

"Okay, I'm sorry. Here he is."

Hank sighed and tried to phrase his next statement in a way that wouldn't make it sound like the tyrant that he really was on the inside when it came to protecting his sons.

"My son is not getting punished for this, period. He suffers from severe anxiety because of my job, and it leads to issues with his stomach. My other son is at fault here, and I'll deal with him."

"Sir, honestly I did not know that until just this moment. I would have never called you if I knew that."

Now it was Hank's turn to be surprised. "He didn't tell you what was going on?"

"No, sir. He told a...well, a different story than that." Silas sounded horrifically embarrassed, and Hank felt sorry for him suddenly, especially because he had forgotten all about it himself, and there was no way anyone at the school could have known. His anger faded away rapidly.

"I'm sorry," Hank apologized sincerely, hoping he hadn't completely offended the man beyond repair. Then his next words caught in his throat a little as he realized how long it would be before he saw his oldest again. "Let me rephrase and soften what I'm trying to get across. Because of Floyd's, uh, medical issues, I don't want him punished without me being notified *first*. Please call me anytime you need to. You won't be bothering me, I promise. He's my first priority. Can you please put him on the line again?"

"Sure. Here you go."

"Dad, I'm really sorry," Floyd blurted. He was, or had been, crying at some point during this call.

"Calm down and breathe," Hank replied gently. "You tell Silas what you need to tell him, okay? He's there to take care of you, and you need to let him. I'm serious. You understand me?"

"Yes, sir."

"Good. Next time you lie, I'm not going to be opting out of anything. Did you actually talk to Theo?"

Floyd sniffled. "Yes, sir. He just wanted to ask me how I'm doing."

"Okay. We'll talk on Friday night. I have to go. You going to be alright?"

"Yes, sir. Love you, dad."

"Love you, too. Behave yourself."

He hung up and then got out of the car, which caused Avery to leap out of the passenger side of the other SUV to intercept him.

"I need to talk to Theo alone. Send him over, please."

He got back in the car, and a few moments later Theo joined him solemnly. Once the door closed, Hank angrily lit him up.

"Why'd you disobey me, Theody? I specifically told you not to call Floyd during school hours, yet I just learned that not only did you do that, but you managed to panic him and-"

"Dad, stop! I know. I'm sorry." Theo looked about to burst into tears. "I know what I did, please don't yell. Did Floyd get in trouble?"

Hank ignored that. "You and I will be having a chat when we get back to the hotel after dinner. Until then, I don't want to hear another word from you. Nothing whatsoever. Got that?"

Theo nodded, looking completely petrified. "But did Floyd-"

"Quiet. Get in the back row and don't fuss around." Hank got out of the car again, and this time Avery was already waiting a few feet away. "Let's go," he snapped as he caught Daven's eye through the windshield.

They all piled back into the car, and Hank irritably dialed Harmon. He didn't pick up.

"Harmon, it's Hank. Look, I'm really sorry. Had an incident with my son that caused us to stop on the way down, and with traffic like this we're definitely going to be late. I don't think we'll get there until 7:30pm. Call me back. Thanks."

"Everything okay, Hank?" asked Daven very quietly.

"No. Floyd had a freak out and then Theo lied to me, and…" he stopped when he saw the shocked look on Daven's face. "Sorry. Never mind."

"It's okay. You can-"

Hank's phone rang; it was Harmon calling back already. "Sorry, hang on. Yes?"

"Hank, it's no problem. I'll change it to 7:30. Where are you staying?"

"Hilton Torrey Pines."

"Uh….that's where I'm staying. Awkward."

Hank wasn't sure if he should laugh or not, but the remark and teeny-bopper tone was so uncharacteristic that he couldn't help but crack a smile. "Uh, yeah. Guess I should have asked you first. Well, I've got my son with me so I'll need to change it. No offense."

Everyone knew Hank's children were terrified of Harmon. Even Harmon himself. Nothing was worth the risk of running into him.

"None taken. I recommend the Lodge at Torrey Pines up the street. That's where I normally stay on business. It should be available for just tonight. Ask for Brian, he's the evening VIP manager."

Hank found himself blushing hotly, and even squirming under these strange circumstances that had just turned Harmon into his own personal travel agent. "Okay…thanks. I will give them a call."

"No problem. You need to cancel your Hilton reservation though. See you at 7:30."

Hank hung up the phone and the entire car was silent for a long time, because he didn't feel like explaining to Daven what had just happened, even though the man was throwing him curious looks for almost an hour.

Eventually Hank asked, "Vance, how far away are we from the restaurant?"

"About 15 minutes, boss."

"Thanks. Theo?" Hank turned around to look at his subdued youngest son. "Sit up."

"Why are you guys having dinner with Harmon, dad?" Theo responded immediately, his tone angry. He had obviously been wanting to ask the question for a long time, and jumped at the first chance he had.

Hank raised an eyebrow at him while simultaneously berating himself for letting it slip who he had been calling. Damn it. "What have I told you a thousand times before, Theo? Say it."

"Don't ask questions about your work," Theo muttered.

"Thank you. You're going to eat with Vance and the guards because we don't have time to stop at the hotel. While you're waiting for your food, I want you to go into one of the private phone booths and call the Lodge at Torrey Pines and get four rooms with two beds each for tonight under Avery's name. Ask for Brian directly and don't talk to anyone else. I'll give you my credit card. And once you have that done, call the Hilton and cancel our reservations under Avery's name. Okay?"

"Yes, sir." Theo was utterly gloomy, which didn't surprise Hank at all, but he still felt compelled to give the boy something to do to keep his mind off his troubles.

"I'll write down the numbers for you when we get to the restaurant. Then I want you to call Floyd and find out when he's available Friday night for both of us to call him together. Maybe ask him what he wants for his birthday so we can go out shopping for him this weekend."

Theo only became gloomier at that, so Hank gave up the half-hearted attempt to cheer him.

"Also...no dessert or sodas tonight. Only because of the sugar. I can't have you bouncing around the hotel room all night. We're leaving at 5am."

Theo rolled his eyes dramatically. "Oh my *god!* Okay."

Daven grinned sideways Hank, who winked back at him. Then his son laid down again, and the rest of the ride was peaceful.

Palms Elite

After Silas hung up the phone, he turned to his new charge and laid a wary eye on him.

"This could have all been prevented if you had just told me the truth, son."

"I'm not your son," Floyd replied defensively as he wiped away the last of his snot and tears.

"Right, you're not. My apologies. But you are my responsibility for the next five months, and I intend to take your welfare very seriously. Do you need to go to the medical center?"

Floyd shook his head no. "I just want to call my brother."

Silas smiled a little. "Nobody's stopping you, son- er, Floyd. This isn't a prison. Go call him all you want."

"I can't. There are five other people in my room. Can I call him from your office or something?"

"Oh, I see. You want special treatment."

"Yes," Floyd replied defiantly as he raised his chin with pride. "I'm a Bancroft, I can't just be blabbing out family business all over the place."

Silas resisted the urge to laugh. "Floyd, literally every boy here could say the same about their own famous family. You'll have to cope somehow, and I promise you'll survive. Now get going, I have work to do."

Floyd flushed with the grim knowledge that the very first time he ever tried to throw his name around, he failed miserably. Now he knew why his dad generally refused to do it...it was terribly embarrassing to get shot down in flames like this.

"Mr. Rawson, I'm sorry," Floyd said quietly. Humbly. "I didn't mean to be like that."

"It's okay," Silas said kindly. "Everyone tries that here at least once. Welcome to the club. The only special treatment you're getting is my extra attention to your medical issue, which is more important. I fully expect you not to hide any problems from me again."

"Yes, sir. Goodnight."

"Goodnight, Floyd."

Cafe La Maze, San Diego

In just the last twenty minutes or so, Daven and Hank had grown incredibly nervous about dinner with Harmon, and as they climbed the stairs to the third floor Hank stopped and turned to Dav, lightly placing a hand on his chest to halt his ascent as well.

"I know you already know this, but it's really important that we appear to be completely unified. If you disagree with me on something, keep it under wraps until later. And I'll do the same for you. Agreed?"

"Of course. But Hank..."

"What?"

"Have to admit that I'm really nervous you're going to say something you shouldn't. In fact, I know you're going to. But please don't."

Hank smiled a little. "We talked about this already, remember? I'm going to be a good soldier. But how about this. If I say something you really think is beyond all reason and logic, kick me or something. Grab my leg. Let me know *discreetly* so that I can change tack. Okay? I don't want this to be a disaster for either of us."

Daven frowned. "You want me to communicate my dismay by playing footsie under the table?"

"Yes. We can take it back to my hotel room later if it really turns you on. Now let's go, we're already an hour late."

"For god's sake, Hank," Daven muttered in resignation as he trudged up behind his boss.

CHAPTER THREE

Cafe La Maze, San Diego

Daven hadn't seen Harmon in person in several years, and it appeared to him that the man had not aged one day since then. Or maybe just being on vacation was doing him some serious good. He tried not to stare as Hank shook hands first, and then he quickly lost the staring battle when he was next. His dislike for Harmon had certainly grown by leaps and bounds since then, that much was for certain.

"Daven," cooed Harmon in an overly-friendly manner, "you look much younger in person. But the TV adds years and pounds to all of us, I suppose."

"Nice to see you, too," a visibly insulted Dav snippily answered the backhanded compliment.

Hank butted in quickly before any permanent damage could be done - or at least, he hoped.

"Let's uh, let's sit down and take a look at the menu. I'm starving." He elbowed Dav threateningly, and then threw a wary glance at Harmon's guards, who were staring him down like he had entered the room with a live flamethrower. Avery was doing exactly the same to Harmon, and Hank didn't like it one bit.

"A moment, please," Hank said apologetically as he aborted his attempt to sit down and gestured to Avery, then followed him down the hallway to the edge of the stairs.

"Hey," he whispered sternly. "I really don't like the looks you're giving Harmon. Cut it out and go have dinner."

"I hate this whole situation, Hank," Avery replied in a sullen tone. "Are his guards leaving, too?"

"Yes, and I swear to god if there are is any confrontation whatsoever between you guys, I'll hand down some serious consequences."

Avery looked as hurt as a kicked puppy. "I wouldn't do that, sir."

"I know *you* wouldn't. Not sure about Lucas. These guys are thugs and will absolutely try to start something if given the chance, I've seen it. Don't give in. Warn Lucas and Vance. And even Theo, if you please."

"Yes, sir. But I'm not leaving you alone in this room with them. I'll leave after his guards go first."

Hank took a deep breath. "You'll go now, and-"

"No, sir."

"Avery."

"I said no, sir. Period."

Against his inclination, Hank relented without another word and walked back to the dining room. The man was doing his job exactly as he'd been trained and knew full well he was in the right. And now Dav was throwing eye daggers at Harmon, too. This was going to be a long evening.

"Harmon, I think we can dismiss our guards now," prompted Hank lightly, and the other man nodded and looked at them, pointedly including Avery in his sweeping glance.

"Of course. Gentlemen? You may go."

Avery, of course, would never take an order from Harmon if his life depended on it. He didn't move a single muscle until Hank finally ordered the same, and even then he waited for the other men to go first, holding the curtain aside as they passed through to the stairs. Hank kept a watchful eye on the proceedings and could only finally breathe again once the door had shut without any sounds of a scuffle or argument.

Harmon smiled slightly.

"Don't worry, they've been thoroughly warned to be on their best behavior. Your man seems just as unhappy to be here as mine are."

Hank nodded and sat down, feeling the blood rushing into his limbs again as he picked up his menu. "Well, I guess it's nice to find some common ground right off the bat. Shall we start with a drink or five, gentlemen?"

———

In order to stop the one-sided exchange of murderous looks from his chief of staff to Harmon, Hank had to kick Daven twice under the table before the first round of drinks even arrived. He finally got the message and joined in the small talk, albeit reluctantly and with no enthusiasm. Harmon was showing no signs of aggression whatsoever and seemed to be trying really hard to be agreeable, so Hank quickly became thoroughly embarrassed by Daven's surly behavior.

After they had ordered their appetizers, Hank pushed away from the table and stood up. "Apologies, gentlemen. It was a long drive and we didn't make any pit stops. Please excuse me for a moment. Dav, can you go down and check with Floyd to make sure the hotel reservations are taken care of?"

"Of course," Dav replied quickly, jumping to his feet and hurrying to open the curtain for his boss. He didn't bother to correct him that it was Theo who was downstairs, not Floyd. Hank must really be rattled to mix up his sons like that.

As soon as hit the bottom of the stairs, Hank latched on to Daven's upper arm firmly and all but dragged him into a nearby empty storage room he had noticed earlier.

"Hank, what the-" Daven squeaked in surprise as his boss slammed the door shut and released him.

"*Daven*," Hank growled, using his full name and dragging out the syllables for added emphasis, "if you were one of my sons I'd be taking my belt off right now to correct your manners."

"*What?*"

"If you can't simmer down and represent us properly, I'm more than happy to ask Vance to take you to the hotel because you're completely embarrassing me so far."

Daven was equally indignant now, but for entirely different reasons. "Did you even notice that his guards are carrying like five guns a piece? And there are four guards for one person, and only two of ours for *three* of us?"

"Of course I did! It's a power play. That's Harmon in a nutshell. If you can't handle it, just go and I'll manage this alone. I mean, what do you think is going to happen? They're going to start a shootout in the middle of a restaurant and assassinate us? This isn't the mafia, Dav, and we aren't mortal enemies. Settle down."

Daven didn't look remotely convinced, and indeed, he wasn't. "Fine. But we're not staying at the hotel Harmon recommended. I mean it, Hank. I'm putting my foot down."

Hank blinked, realizing that was actually a reasonable demand, which calmed him. "Okay. If that's what it's going to take for you to relax-"

"That, and you not telling him where we're really staying."

Hank was tired, and he didn't want to fight with Dav again. They had barely recovered from the last blowout, after all.

"*Fine,*" Hank relented. "You pick the hotel, then. Don't tell me. If I don't know what it is, I can't possibly tell Harmon, can I?"

Daven hesitated, then agreed with a quick nod.

"Go coordinate with Theo, *discreetly.* Then get your ass back upstairs and behave yourself, or we're going to be having a very difficult conversation on the way home tomorrow."

"Yes, *sir*," Daven fired back bitterly. He hated being talked to like a bratty teenager, and thankfully Hank caught his error instantly.

"Sorry, Dav," he added hastily. "I'm...I should have phrased that differently."

Daven took a deep breath, then replied steadily, "Yes. But you're right, I need to calm down."

"Please do. We'll get through this as long as we stick together. Okay?" Hank clapped him on the shoulder and ran back up the stairs, realizing as he sat back down that he still had to piss. Badly. *Fuck.*

"Sorry, didn't mean to leave you sitting alone."

"That's alright. You done ripping Daven a new one?"

"What do you mean?" Hank lifted his huge wine glass and took a long swig to hide his expression. So much for hoping Harmon couldn't read him as well as he thought he could.

Harmon smirked slightly but didn't press the issue, thankfully. "I'm glad to see you two are on speaking terms again," he replied simply. "I'm still battling on that front with Colbert. Good man, really smart, but he rubs me the wrong way on an hourly basis."

"Hmm," Hank replied noncommittally, thankful for the distraction of his phone jangling loudly. It was Floyd, so he sent it to voicemail and then shut off the ringer.

"Sorry, forgot that was on. Listen, I regret this meeting got off to a rough start. Daven doesn't care for the manner in which your guards are armed, and I have to admit that I share the same concern. It's a bit unsettling."

Harmon actually laughed at that. "Ah. I see. Well, to each his own. You haven't been attacked. I have."

"I know."

"Not that I'm afraid of *you*, by any means. But San Diego isn't exactly an Urbane town."

"I know," Hank repeated, feeling suddenly ashamed of having mentioned the guards at all. Harmon had been attacked and nearly killed at a restaurant just down the street almost two years ago by a rogue extremist claiming to be from Hank's own party. Of course Harmon would be worried for his safety, and rightly so. *Smooth move, Hank...you daft idiot.*

Daven came back in the room, thankfully, and Harmon paid him no attention as he seated himself again.

"Hank, I'm under no illusions that this is going to be an easy discussion. Part of me…most of me…doesn't even want to be here right now. I want us to start off by you telling me exactly what led you to flip out on me last Saturday. You said you received a phone call?"

Hank glanced at Daven, who was calm again and wearing a blank expression.

"I did. One that I probably should have shared with Stewart, but we can debate that later."

"Okay. And?"

Hank hesitated and took a few sips of wine. "I know you're aware that I was accused of trying to bribe some photographers. They were all Urbanes, and I had given them a secondary number of mine to call. Anyway, moot point now, but on Saturday a man called me and said…"

He paused for some time as two ladies appeared with the appetizers and more wine was poured.

When they left, Harmon said with a small smile, "Don't stop now, you've got me on tenterhooks."

Hank swallowed hard. Nobody touched the food yet. "He said he got my number from one of those photographers. He knew about our planned meeting in Las Vegas, and told me not to trust you.”

“Okay. Which you already don’t. Then what?”

“Then…” Hank snuck another peek at Daven, who seemed unperturbed by what was said so far. “Well, first he offered to give me the name of someone in the government who could push through one of my measures. For a price, of course.”

“Which one?”

“It…it’s not relevant. I’m getting to the important part.” Hank took a very deep breath, knowing there would be no turning back after this. “He said he works for you, and that he wants me to pay him for insider information so he can leave politics for a new life. He’s not an Seditionist, either. Hates both of us.”

Harmon flushed and set down his wine glass. “Well. Fuck.”

“Yeah.”

“Did you get his number, by chance?”

Hank nodded.

“Okay. What do I have to do in order to get that number? Speak plainly.”

Hank reached into his pocket. "Nothing. It's right here." He handed him a slip of paper with the number, then held his breath until he was quite dizzy from the stress of giving over valuable information without getting anything in return.

Harmon looked at it for a long time, but there was no recognition. At least not any visible signs.

He set it down, then reached over to the appetizers. His countenance was suddenly grumpy and very typically Harmon.

"Alright, Hank. What are you playing at this time?" he asked somewhat rudely.

Hank gulped the last of his wine. "Excuse me?"

Daven put in, "He's not *playing* at anything. What are you implying?"

"Dav," Hank muttered, then to Harmon he replied steadily, "I just wanted to give you a show of good faith to prove that I'm serious about us establishing a cooperative and mutually beneficial relationship."

"It's definitely a *show,* for sure. This could be completely fabricated to trap me into something, and knowing you, I would most likely bet on it."

Hank raised his eyebrows, then calmly helped himself to some calamari. It was just as likely that Harmon was trying to entrap *him* with the call, but he didn't say that out loud.

"Well, you were right that this wasn't going to be an easy discussion."

Daven was all but writhing in his chair, and Hank threw him another *settle down* look.

Harmon chuckled a little. "But if not, I have a traitor in my midst, eh? Big shocker."

"You should be able to narrow it down easily enough," Daven mused thoughtfully, wisely heeding Hank's unspoken warning. "How many people knew about the meeting in Las Vegas?"

Hank was shocked when Harmon laughed again.

"This fellow who called you may not be as connected to me as he seems. My assistant, who has since been replaced, accidentally sent a company-wide email about the meeting, and I have 415 employees. Any single one of them could have told anybody in the world. But I assume you already knew that."

Well, shit, thought Hank. So much for impressing him with an intelligence freebie.

"I didn't know," he replied in a normal tone, fighting back the angry defensiveness that was shoving its way to the forefront of his mood. "But now you have a phone number to go on, at least."

"True. Thank you for that. I didn't mean to sound ungrateful."

"No problem," Hank answered gloomily. "Anyway, his rather frantic insistence that I not trust you or meet with you set me off. I sincerely apologize for that email I sent afterwards. My rudeness was uncalled for."

"Understood and forgiven."

"Thank you."

The conversation halted for several minutes as they all sampled the food, although Hank's appetite was long gone and he had to force himself to pretend to be enjoying it.

"What measure?" Harmon eventually asked, breaking the silence abruptly.

"What?"

"What measure did he offer to help you with? The government contact, I mean?"

"Oh. I've been trying for years to introduce legislation to make it illegal to profit off photos of minors. He wanted me to pay him for an introduction to someone who would help push it through. I have to admit that I seriously considered it for a minute."

Harmon refilled Hank's wineglass for him as he spoke. "Yeah, don't do that. Seriously illegal. Colton Gamble is who he meant. I will introduce you two by email tomorrow." He winked cheekily at Daven. "For free."

Daven was nearly as astonished as his boss at this unexpected generosity. "Why?" he asked suspiciously.

"Because such a law would also benefit my son, of course. Floyd and Theo aren't the only ones being harassed by those vultures. Hell, I'll back it myself, too. You should have come to me sooner, Hank."

"Thank you," Hank responded blandly, feeling out of sorts by the way Harmon was completely dominating the discussion and making him feel like a misguided child.

"Speaking of vultures," Harmon continued pleasantly, "I'm curious why you didn't invite Rupert to this dinner."

Hank flushed hotly at the reminder that there was no one who hated Harmon more than Rupert, and the feeling was unequivocally mutual. In fact, it was exactly like how Colbert hated Hank, and vice versa.

"I would assume for exactly same reasons you didn't bring Colbert," Hank replied politely.

"Ah. Touché."

Harmon was enjoying himself far too much; probably because his incessant ping-ponging between friendliness and contempt and back was making the other two men twitchy. Daven cleared his throat abruptly, and Hank idly noticed he hadn't touched his own wine. Smart man.

"Something on your mind, Daven?" asked Harmon with a completely straight face.

"Yes. Hank's mystery caller apparently knows Colton Gamble. Does that help narrow down his possible identity any further?"

It was an excellent question, and Hank was annoyed at himself for not thinking of it first. He was too busy being distracted by Harmon's jabs.

"Hardly," Harmon replied sullenly. "Colton was one of my employees for five years. Very popular. Left about a year ago, and I've had very few new hires since then. A handful, at the most."

Well, shit ...again.

"So now that we've had an exchange of valuable information, we're even," Harmon continued casually. "We got off to a good start, as agreed, so now it's time for the more difficult part of the discussion."

A good start. Hardly. Hank gulped again, but this time it was water. "Very well. Anything in particular?"

"Yes. I want to know what it will take for you to stop throwing me under the bus at every available opportunity. I know perfectly well how you forced me into my final warning with the FBI. That really was some exquisite orchestration, Hank. My congratulations to your success." He raised his glass in a mock toast.

Hank flinched, but forced himself to stay utterly diplomatic. "That was never my intention."

"Sure. The second thing I want to discuss is how to get you to agree to recall all of your double agents. Permanently."

Daven looked ready to pass out from the strain caused by this sudden change in direction. Fortunately nobody could say anything for several minutes as the main courses arrived and plates laid down and cleared away.

When the room was quiet again, Hank spoke up. "On the first point, if it's an apology you're looking for, I'm afraid you're going to be rather disappointed. I did what I had to do in order to protect the integrity of the investigation into Janet's murder."

"Of course you did," Harmon replied pleasantly. Too pleasantly.

Way too pleasantly.

"Hank," said Daven suddenly, sounding a bit strangled. "May we speak in private for a moment?"

Hank looked at Harmon, who nodded slyly, and the two friends got up and left the room again.

"Hank-"

"Hang on, I seriously have to piss. Just give me a second."

"Okay. I'll just wait here, then."

When Hank re-emerged, they went back into the empty storage room.

"Hank, I was right. This meeting was a mistake. He's making you look like a fool."

"Oh, thanks a lot. Appreciate that."

Dav met Hank's eyes, searching for any trace of mischief or humor in them, and found none.

"Dav, he's practically begging for a truce. He knows he's fucked with me working against him. We could take massive advantage of this. I'll say yes - make him grovel for it first, though - and then use this favor as leverage in the future to force him into cooperation on bigger matters."

Dav felt a little sick. "Sounds like the old diabolical Hank. You're trying to not be that person anymore, remember?"

"Think about it. The leverage we would have!"

"I *am* thinking about it. This is *Harmon* we're talking about. His only concern is protecting himself. And you're literally letting him get away with murder if you agree to not push back on the Janet investigation. He must be caught and punished, Hank, or else you're seriously disgracing her memory to help advance your own interests."

Hank was shocked and hurt by this callous assessment of his intentions. " *Our* interests. And 'disgracing her memory,' Dav, seriously? It's completely unfair to place all that on my shoulders, especially after I fought so hard for justice!"

Justice . Daven still had serious reservations about the whole debacle, but he dared not reopen that old wound. So he said nothing, which to Hank was far more telling than an actual reply.

"Okay, let's not go there again. But you're still for getting rid of our double agents, correct?"

"As much as I hate to side with Harmon on anything, yes I am."

"Okay. I trust you feel that way for a very good reason, and I'll tell him that I'll seriously consider it, but it's not going to happen. You know that, right?"

"So you're just making that decision now, without any further discussion?"

Hank held firm, even knowing he was breaking his own promise not to make big decisions without the input of Dav and Rupe. "Yes. Are you going to be able to live with that?"

Dav nodded, but his chest felt tight. "Not happy about it, but you're the boss."

"Is that a yes, or a no?"

"Yes, I can live with it."

"Good. Thank you. There's one more thing, and I don't want you to read into it or get all flustered. When we're wrapping up this meeting, I will ask you to go downstairs and have Vance pull the car around. Just go, without argument. Okay?"

Dav suddenly looked as dismayed as a cat being forcibly bathed, and Hank suppressed a frustrated sigh.

"Why? You...you *want* to be alone with him?"

"Just for a minute. There's something I have to tell him that's highly confidential. Just do it. Okay?"

Dav shrugged. "Obviously I have no choice."

CHAPTER FOUR

The second half of the dinner was similar to the first half, and Hank was becoming thoroughly worn out by his complete inability to read Harmon. He considered himself a master people reader and therefore wasn't used to this situation, nor was he used to anyone being able to read himself as annoyingly accurate as Harmon could.

It was incredibly strange that they had the opposite experience with each other over the phone, where Hank always had the upper hand and could correctly anticipate Harmon's every response. In person, however, he felt utterly blindfolded and clumsy. It wasn't like this back when they were last together in Philadelphia a few weeks ago, nor the time before that.

How the tables had turned, and Hank had no clue why that was.

Soon after dessert was finished - probably too soon - Hank decided to call it a night, citing their extremely early departure time back to Los Angeles.

"Daven, will you kindly go ask Vance to pull the car around? I'll be down in a minute."

"Yes, sir," he replied formally, to Hank's quiet relief, and all three men stood up at the same time. Harmon was the first to extend his hand.

"Good to see you again, Daven. Until next time."

"Safe travels."

Then he was gone, and Harmon turned to his rival with an audible sigh.

"Having that man in the same room increases my blood pressure by about 30 points. Does he have that same effect on you?"

Hank shook his head. "Quite the opposite, actually. That's why I insisted he be here."

They sat back down, and the old Harmon Hank was used to suddenly revealed himself.

"So. That conversation was more difficult than I anticipated. But I think we found common ground on a few surprising points, and no surprises on those things we've always disagreed about and will continue to clash over."

Hank took a deep breath, steeling himself for what he was about to ask.

"Right. Uh, there was one subject I didn't bring up because it's rather testy. Daven and I have clashed on it a number of times before. Are you aware that our government is planning to bring back public flogging?"

"Yes."

"May I ask how you feel about it?"

"Against it, as you are."

Hank was confused for a moment. "How did you know I was against it?"

"I wouldn't expect anything less. But that's not even the worst of my worries. Are you aware that it's been proposed that indentured minors should be castrated at age 16, and muted at the first sign of dissidence after age 18?"

Hank gasped, feeling truly sick to his stomach suddenly. "What? No. Holy fuck. What kind of country are we becoming? When did this come up?"

"Yesterday. You really need to join the public policy briefing calls once in a while."

Hank took another huge swig of the wine he'd been avoiding for the past hour.

"I will from now on. Rupert always does them, but we haven't connected in a couple days."

Harmon shrugged. "Might want to hurry. The measures will probably be on the March 1 ballot. You know as well as I do that once something passes, we can't touch it with a hundred-mile pole. If you want to work together on those two new issues, I will, but I'm not stupid or reckless enough to dare protest what is already law, so we have to move fast."

Indeed, even openly discussing fighting a passed law was nearly treason in itself, and it was deeply ingrained within both men that such matters were utterly beyond their control for ten years, after which new measures could be proposed to replace them. After all, the laws had been passed with the votes of their very own constituents in the first place. If things went south, the failure lay on their own shoulders for not leading their parties in the right direction.

"Well," Hank said, sweating a little, "Yes, I absolutely want to work together with you on it. But I might have a slight problem. Daven and Rupert don't feel the same way I do about such matters. And you know that my constituents overwhelmingly favor more severe measures for criminals than I do. Than *we* do, rather."

Harmon nodded. "Yes, I know, and that's why I'm continually surprised that your super delegates keep electing you."

That wasn't meant as an insult or a slight, Hank knew. It was simply the truth. He thought for sure he would never be elected again after several ugly, public feuds with his delegates - and even his own executives - over the more severe indentured servitude measures. But somehow, he was still here and more popular than ever. It defied logic.

"So…are you saying you want to work with me even against the wishes of your chief of staff and PR guy?"

Hank shook his head. "Of course not. I would prefer to try and align them with me. If I can't do that…I don't know what to do then. I can all but guarantee there's going to be a huge fight. My constituents can be huge assholes. So can my executives. Lately I feel like…like I'm leading the wrong party, to be honest."

He stopped himself cold, not even being able to register the horrible words from his own mouth. While that's exactly how he'd felt for several months since the October 1994 vote had gone awry, he certainly had not meant to admit such a thing to anybody. He'd barely even accepted it himself, so why the hell did he just blurt it out to *Harmon,* of all people?

Jesus fucking Christ...

Harmon must have been incredibly surprised by such an admission, but he didn't change expression at all. "I'll pretend I didn't hear that. I know what you really meant. I clash with my own constituents sometimes, too."

Hank stood up, heart pounding. "Fuck. Too much wine," he lamely declared. "I need to go. The bill is paid, right?"

"Yes. Just relax."

"This dinner was a mistake. This meeting. We're never doing it again."

"Hank, don't panic. I know what you meant. I'm not going to-"

Holy fuck, Hank whispered to himself as he left the room abruptly and all but flew down the stairs to the safety of his entourage.

"Which car is Daven in?" he asked Avery, who was waiting stiffly at the exit.

"The front car."

Hank got in the rear car, where Theo was sound asleep on the front bench. He climbed over him and into the back row, noting that Harmon's five guards were all out front, watching the party's departure closely and with some apparent amusement.

"Let's go, Vance. Quickly, but don't peel out."

"Yes, sir."

"Everything go okay, boss? A little concerned about this hurried departure."

"Uh, yeah. Thanks Avery. I just realized how late it was getting, that's all."

Hank went to take off his tie, but his hands were trembling too much to manage, so he gave up and leaned back with his eyes closed, trying to breathe again. Avery was watching him through the mirror, but Hank couldn't see the deep concern and alarm on the man's face.

Your transparency will be the death of you, Hank...

CHAPTER FIVE

On the way to Carlsbad, same evening.

"Sorry, dad," Theo said sleepily as the car pulled onto the freeway with a lurch.

Hank opened his eyes to find Theo peering cautiously through the headrest at him.

"Sorry for what?"

"Stealing your seat."

"Don't be silly. Where are we staying, anyway? Do you have your seatbelt on?"

"Yeah. The Omni in Carlsbad."

"Good. Nice place. As soon as we get upstairs I want you in bed."

"So...we're not having a *chat*, then?"

Hank was so wildly distracted and depressed that he couldn't even recall what his son had done wrong, and he wasn't about to ask.

"No. You're forgiven."

Theo's surprise and relief was palpable, and he melted into the words and laid his chin on the seat, looking backwards at his dad with curious, wide eyes. "Thank you. Are you okay?"

"Yup. Just a little too much wine making me queasy."

"Gross. Don't barf on me, dad."

Now Hank smiled as he reached out to ruffle Theo's mop of hair. "I won't. Did you enjoy your dinner?"

"Yeah, and Vance let me have a bite of his cake."

Hank eyed his driver in the rearview mirror. Normally the man's semi-horrified expression would make him laugh, but not now. Nothing on earth could make him laugh at the moment.

"It's not nice to tattle, Theo."

"Just being honest."

"No, you're being a tattle-tale. Don't be that."

"Okay, sorry. Oh I forgot to tell you, Floyd tried to call you but I told him you were busy. He wants us to call him at six on Friday."

Now he had Hank's full attention. "You didn't tell him who we were with, did you?"

"Of course not, dad. I'm not a tattle-tale."

Hank grinned. "Of course not." He saw Theo shiver and immediately took off his own jacket. "Here, put this over you. Vance, can you turn down the a/c a bit? It's January, you know."

"Sorry, sir. About the cake, too."

"No harm done."

Theo laid back down and was soon asleep again. They arrived at the hotel about twenty minutes later, and Hank climbed back out over his youngest, poking him as he went.

"Hey, you're too old to carry. Up."

Theo didn't respond, so Avery reached in and lifted him out, still partially covered in Hank's jacket. Daven then appeared, dutifully rolling his little royal blue suitcase that went everywhere with him. He silently followed Hank and Avery to the elevator, obviously hoping to hear how the meeting ended.

"Thanks, Dav. You did good tonight," Hank said graciously after the elevator doors closed.

"You, too. Your restraint was…admirable."

Admirable, indeed. Up until the last 30 seconds, anyway.

"And exhausting. We'll talk tomorrow on the way home."

Hank always insisted on connecting rooms to their guards, and was relieved to see that Theo had arranged for exactly that even though he forgot to mention it. Of course. He was a good kid, and smart.

Avery carried Theo to the bed and covered him up just as Hank collapsed into his own bed.

"Aren't you going to tuck me in too, Avery? Tell me a bedtime story?"

The big man grinned. "There once was a man from Nantucket, who told the big boss to go f-"

"Alright, alright. Forget it. Go to bed."

Avery laughed and disappeared into his room.

Despite Hank's exhaustion and the effects of the wine, he never managed to fall asleep.

There was so much to think about and do before the March 1 vote. He couldn't believe such drastic, draconian measures would actually pass. But then again, his constituents were pretty harsh on criminal behavior. They could afford to be, what with being mostly affluent; nearly all upper and upper-middle class. People like that didn't care about the welfare of lawbreakers and the disadvantaged. It was Harmon's party who probably wouldn't support the laws - almost certainly wouldn't - and Hank took a brief moment to pray that for once the man's greater number of constituents could outvote his own. That happened rarely, but it wasn't so uncommon that it was impossible.

The problem was that a good ten percent of the nation's citizens were independent, unaffiliated voters of all walks of life. They usually sided with the Seditionists because of Hank's popularity and clean-cut reputation. Almost *always* sided with them, in fact. While that could be a good thing when Hank wanted certain laws passed, it was the opposite when he was personally against his own constituent's wishes. And that's where things could - and had - gone seriously wrong. In fact, since the previous May, the independents had been voting for all the measures he didn't support, at least privately. But he supported them publicly, because that's what his constituents wanted. That's what he was elected for. He had to do his job. Had to speak the words written for him to fight for laws he didn't want.

Hank Bancroft was a conflicted man, and his secret hypocrisy was wearing him thin. After nine years in this position, and especially with increasingly harsh measures passed against people who couldn't fight back, his bleeding liberal heart had started to beat strongly again. And if these March 1 laws went through, it couldn't be ignored any longer.

Then again, it was probably already starting to show itself. He hadn't been kind to Daven and Rupert since the October vote; in fact he hadn't been himself ever since last summer, when they first showed their support of deeply conservative measures that he didn't expect them to ever consider. It was then that he had begun quietly turning against his own constituents. Against his own party.

He hadn't told anybody that, of course. Until tonight. And then he told the worst person possible.

For the vast majority of citizens, the system worked and the laws were inherently good - free healthcare for all and mandatory mental health facilities and homeless shelters in every town over a certain population being a good example of many. That was because they all voted for these things - *all* of them, and that was Hank's doing.

He was very proud of the one passed measure he had personally written and introduced. Because low voter turnout had resulted in the disastrous Durdan presidency that led to the Second American Revolution, citizens 19 years and older of The Reunited States were now required to vote by phone on major laws on the first of every month, except January. Implementing the intricate voice recognition technology had cost a bloody fortune, but it worked incredibly well. Those who did not vote without being excused were heavily fined and sentenced to 100 hours of community service. So far, less than one percent of the population had been noncompliant, which meant 99% of the nation phoned in 6 times a year to vote. It was rather astonishing when compared to the dismal 12% turnout in November of 1980.

Mandatory voting had one major downside, and that was the effect of inequality in social status on passing laws. Convicted criminals and Bonded Retainers could not vote at all, for life - no matter how long they had been free or what their crimes were, and they were a significant population. This resulted in a law that prohibited appeals in death sentence cases. Fifteen years ago, before Reunification, those appeals were automatic, but citizens had become tired of paying for criminals to live on death row for 50 years. They had jumped at the chance to change it. Especially the Seditionists - who were not at all concerned with the welfare of such individuals. Hank was thoroughly ashamed of backing that measure, but he would have been mutinied out of office if he didn't. So his popularity grew as "Death Row" was phased out and executions became mandatory within 7 days of the sentence.

Another law he opposed was the one that prohibited day laborers coming from across the border in Mexico. As he had predicted, crucial farms and fields in Texas and the southwest states were soon plunged into dire straits due to lack of workers. A near-famine soon followed, but the law could not be repealed for ten years. Hence, the hasty introduction of indentured servitude for criminals more than a hundred years after it had been phased out after the Civil War. No one was proud of the arrangement, and it was little better than slavery, but it worked to feed the country again. Convicted men and women could choose "service," or prison. They almost always chose indenture, which by unintended consequence had already fixed the prison overpopulation problems that had plagued the nation ever since the War on Drugs had begun. In fact, it had put the much-despised private prison industry out of business completely.

Again, Hank's popularity wildly increased as he mourned the win.

But then the slippery slope got greased even more, the nation lost its compassionate side over time, and it soon got proposed that children of convicted felons also became indentured. Despite the fact that Hank *and* Harmon had firmly and publicly opposed it, the measure passed in October. Both of them had a brief but massive downturn in popularity for that.

Some things you just couldn't control.

Hank turned around on his side and watched Theo sleep for a while, and by the time his 4:30am alarm went off, he already knew he wouldn't be running for reelection this fall. He had enough money to live off already without ever having to work again, and he already had bought floor plans for a big cabin on a lake near Yosemite for retirement.

Why wait until then?

So that was that. The decision calmed him, and he woke Theo up with a smile on his face and a lightness in his heart that he hadn't felt for almost a year.

"Daven," said Avery quietly as they waited in the car for Hank to appear at the valet stand with Lucas. "I wanted to ask…I mean, is Hank alright? I was really worried about him last night, and I haven't seen him this morning."

Dav cocked his head. "Why do you ask?"

"He didn't look well when he got in the car afterwards."

"Too much wine, I'm afraid. He usually only gets drunk once a year, on Christmas."

"I know, but it wasn't that. Panicked, more like. I almost asked if he'd seen a ghost. I'm sorry. It's none of my business. But if Harmon said or did something to him, I'm going to...I don't know what I'm going to do, but something."

Daven took in the words bitterly, but tried not to jump to conclusions. Now he really needed to know how the meeting ended. He was going to *demand* to know.

"You're right, it's none of your business, so you're not going to do anything about it."

Avery swallowed hard. He rarely talked to Daven, and that was exactly because the man had no problem being abrasive if he felt it was warranted. Like right now.

Jesus, what a dick. "Right. Sorry."

"No problem," Daven replied pleasantly. "If you can roll up the window after we pull away, I'll get to the bottom of it. Thank you for telling me."

Avery looked back at him in surprise. That was Daven, ice cold one moment and totally fine the next.

"Yes, sir."

"Don't call me sir."

Hank suddenly appeared and Dav was relieved to see him make his way back to Avery's SUV after ushering the still-sleepy Theo to the other car.

Daven was astonished to see him in a good mood as he jumped in and spread out in the front row with a big sigh.

"Good morning, Hank."

"Top o' the morning. Ouch. I shouldn't talk so loud. My head. Avery, can you pull through somewhere for breakfast? McDonald's or whatever."

"Yes, boss. Shall I roll up the privacy glass?"

"Not right now. Thanks. Dav, can you hand me the blue blanket in the very back row?"

"It's in the other car," replied Avery quickly as he opened his door. "I'll get it."

He was gone in a flash, and Daven seized the moment to question his boss. "How did the meeting end? Did you say whatever you wanted to say to Harmon?"

Hank nodded, but kept his eyes on Avery. "Yes, and we're fine. We're good."

Daven thought about Avery's description of him as *panicked*. "Hmmm. And he didn't...like, threaten you or anything? Or try to pull something while I was out of the room?"

"No, Dav. Everything's fine. Don't worry about it." Now he turned around to look at his friend. "Why are you so upset? You look like someone just ran over your dog."

"It's just...I couldn't help but notice you seemed a little alarmed afterwards. That's all. I just want to make sure you're okay."

Avery opened the door and handed the big cashmere blanket to Hank, who folded himself up in it and leaned against the window, grumbling to himself. Daven wasn't even in the same damned car last night, how could he know what...

Oh. Of course. Avery.

"Sorry, I'm really tired. Going to take a nap. We'll have to continue this later."

"Okay. But we should talk before we get back to the office."

"Hmm. We'll see."

"Did you not sleep well?" Daven pressed. "Was it something Harmon said?"

"For god's sake, Dav! Stop. I'm fine. Avery, did you forget how to drive?" he snapped.

"Sorry, boss." Avery looked straight at Daven as he turned around and quickly backed out of the driveway, raising his eyebrows slightly as if to say, *See? Told you so.*

Daven shrugged and picked up his Blackberry. There were at least two new messages from Rupert inquiring about the meeting, but he skipped over them both and went straight to the one with the subject: *Draft: Proposed Media Statement supporting the Public Flogging initiative.*

CHAPTER SIX

Thursday morning

Hank never managed to fall asleep in the car, either, but he stayed leaning against the window and kept his eyes closed in order to avoid conversation with Daven, who was catching up on his email with a deep frown on his face. He wasn't really worried at the moment about what had happened between Hank and Harmon in the final minute of their meeting. It was the draft media statement from Rupert that was bothering him. Thinking Hank was sound asleep, he asked Avery to roll up the privacy glass and then quietly picked up the phone and called Rupe as they passed through Marina del Rey on the office.

"It's Daven."

"Yes. I know. Caller ID, for the millionth time. Where are you guys?"

"About twenty minutes away from the office. Lucas is on the way to your house with Theo. I just read your draft statement and can tell you right now Hank's going to hate it."

Pause. "Can you be more specific?"

"Well, for one thing, he's totally against this measure. The draft makes it sounds like he's all but gleeful to be supporting it."

"I know, but that's the job. And he's the only one who's against it."

"That doesn't matter, Rupe. He's the boss."

"Right you are, but he doesn't make *those* decisions. Our constituents do. Our delegates do. He's going to have to suck it up."

Daven sighed. "Rupe, you didn't copy him on the draft and I'm assuming that's because you don't want to fight. But that's exactly what's going to happen. Tone it down and resend it, and copy him."

"Excuse me? You're not my boss, Daven, so don't order me around. I'll speak to Hank directly when you guys get here."

"I'm just trying to prevent-"

The line disconnected and Daven all but threw down his phone in frustration, not noticing that Hank was watching him curiously.

"Did Rupe just hang up on you?" he asked after a moment, and Daven jumped.

"I'm so sorry, Hank. Did I wake you?"

"Nope. What's going on?"

Daven explained the conversation, and Hank's expression darkened. On one hand, it was great to know that Dav was maybe starting to sway to his side regarding the public flogging issue. That was unexpected. On the other hand, now he had to deal with an argument between two men who had never argued before, at least not to his knowledge. Perhaps it was just a one-time thing. He hoped, anyway. It was the last thing he needed right now.

"Okay, sorry Dav. Totally unacceptable for him to hang up on you. I'll deal with that. You just carry on as normal."

"I can handle it, Hank."

"I'm his boss, it's my responsibility. Just because we're all friends doesn't mean-"

He stopped talking in surprise as Avery rolled down the privacy glass all the way.

"Sir, we're getting pulled over. Roll down your windows."

That was law when a car had tinted windows, so Daven and Hank immediately complied on both sides of the car.

"What happened?" Hank asked as he reached all the way over to the passenger side.

"I changed lanes without signaling."

Hank said nothing, although his irritation almost made a rude comeback irresistible.

The police officer cautiously approached the car and peered into the back seats.

"Good morning, officer," Daven and Hank said together.

"Good morning Mr. Bancroft, Mr. Johansson."

He proceeded to Avery. "You changed lanes without signaling, son. Right in front of me, too. What's the deal?"

"The man on the blue motorcycle, sir. I thought he was going to veer into my lane. I was wrong."

While this discussion was taking place Hank had of course noticed two photographers across the street taking pictures of the scene, and all but prayed the officer would issue a ticket so there wouldn't have to be an argument about it.

"Alright. I saw him too, he was all over the place. So I'm going to let it slide this time."

"Officer," said Hank quickly from his spot next to the window. "Please issue the ticket anyway, or else I'm going to be nailed in the press for acting like I'm above the law."

"You kind of are, sir," said the officer with a small smile. "I'll get in a heap of trouble if I ticket you."

Hank swallowed hard. That shouldn't be true, but it was. "But...you'd be citing him, not me. Please just do it."

The officer shook his head and tucked his ticketing pad back into his jacket. "An honor to meet you, Mr. Bancroft. Mr. Johansson. Have a nice day."

He went back to his car and sped off in the opposite direction, and it took the rest of the drive to the office for Hank's heart to slow back down to normal again. He already could picture the scathing headlines the next day in the paper's political section.

Damned if you do, damned if you don't.

"I'm really sorry about that, sir," said Avery after Daven got out of the car when they arrived at the office. "But I figure the press would be a hell of a lot worse for you if we killed somebody."

"It certainly would," Hank mused. "Thank you for putting it into perspective." He aborted his attempt to exit and stayed in the car, leaving Daven looking at him in confusion as the door shut again. "And I'm sorry for barking at you earlier today when we left the hotel. But I need to ask you something. Did you tell Daven I was acting strange after the dinner ended last night?"

Now it was Avery's turn to swallow hard. "I didn't use the word strange, sir. I said...that you looked unwell and I was concerned for you."

"Is that all?"

"I think...I think I used the word *panicked* ."

"Okay. That explains a lot." Hank glanced out at Daven, who was still standing there waiting for him. "Avery, I'm only going to say this once, and I mean it. If you *ever* do that again, you're off my team. You have a problem with me, or any concerns, you ask me directly. What you said to Daven is going to cause a problem between me and him. I know you meant well, but never again. Understand?"

The huge man looked about ready to cry, and Hank pushed aside the instinct to feel bad about being so harsh. He was absolutely right, and he wasn't going to back down.

"Yes, sir. Understood. I only asked him because he cares about you just as much as I do. There was no harm intended at all."

"I know. But you have a duty of confidentiality to me." To drive the message home even further, he took the man off duty for the day. That would sting worse than any words could. "Go home, and send Brittany back to pick me up at noon."

He got out of the car before Avery could answer and rejoined Daven. "I'm going to cut the day short, but we need to talk for a few minutes. Your office. I'll meet you there in ten minutes."

He headed to the cafeteria and got some coffee and a bagel, and headed back upstairs with a heavy heart. There was nothing more he hated than conflicts with his friends, and it hurt him to know that Rupert had treated Daven so poorly this morning.

Daven was waiting by the window in his office, and Hank walked in and shut the door behind him.

"Dav, I just had it out with Avery for telling you I was panicked when we left the restaurant last night. He knows better than that. I'm sorry he upset you for nothing."

"So he was wrong?"

"I wasn't panicked," Hank said, taking a huge bite of his bagel. It took a minute to get it down his throat so he could continue, but that allowed him more time to think. "Harmon pisses me off. I was angry that he was enjoying toying with us. You commended me on my restraint but I don't feel like I should have been so restrained. We looked weak."

Daven shook his head. "I disagree. No offense, but you look awful. You should go home."

"I haven't slept."

"I can tell."

"I need to deal with Rupert first, then the auditors. After that I'm gone. Where's the draft of the media statement?"

Daven wordlessly handed him a printed sheet of paper, and Hank looked around for the big fluffy chair to collapse into. *Oh...it's gone. That's right.* He settled into the ugly modern couch instead, and drank down the rest of his coffee as he read the statement. Daven was right. He hated it.

"Okay, this sucks. Look, I know we've clashed over this topic before. But let's put that aside."

"As I said earlier, I'm changing my mind about it. You should know that Rupert strongly supports it, though, and I don't even need to mention that all the delegates are highly enthused about it." He shuddered. "Public flogging. What a way to set our country back 150 years."

"You mean 23 years. You won't believe this, but it actually wasn't banished in Delaware until 1972, although the last incident took place in 1952. I've studied this topic way too much. There's a reason we outlawed it the first time. At least Harmon learns from history; he said he's going to oppose it."

Daven shrugged. "I wouldn't expect anything else. His constituents would drag him out of office kicking and screaming if he supported it."

Hank grimaced. "You mean like ours will with me, if I speak against it?"

Dav nodded, his face just as grave.

"Fuck," Hank sighed as he tossed the paper on the coffee table and laid down on the couch. "I don't even care, Dav. Let them."

"Hank. You really need to get some sleep before you talk yourself into walking off the job."

Too late...

"Hang on." He sat up and took his vibrating phone out of his pocket. It was Floyd's school again.

"Hank Bancroft."

"Mr. Bancroft, Silas Rawson here. Floyd's fine, don't be alarmed."

Don't be alarmed? Seriously? "Okay. What's going on?"

"He didn't show up for class this morning so I went to check on him and he was packing up all his stuff. Wants to go home, and I'm afraid he's rather dead set on it."

"That sounds like anything but *fine* to me. I take it he's in his room now?"

"Yes, sir."

"I'll call him. Thanks." He hung up and turned to his chief of staff. "I got to go to my office, Dav. I'll let you know when I'm done dealing with Rupert."

Hank trudged to his office and shut the door, paying no attention to the line of people waiting outside to have a word with him.

Floyd picked up on the first ring. "Dad?"

"Floyd, what in the holy hell are you up to now? You're not leaving, so forget it and go back to class."

"Dad, please. I hate it here!"

Hank acted astonished, though he was far from it. "What? Why?"

"Because Theo's not here. Because you're not here. I hate it. I have no friends."

"You've been there *four days*. Give it time."

"This was a mistake. You let me choose to come here, so why won't you let me choose to leave?"

Floyd had a good point, that much was certain. And if he was totally honest with himself, Hank knew this was going to happen all along. Counted on it, actually.

"Alright son, listen up. Four days is not enough to fix everything that's been wrong in the past three months. You're going to stay there, and you're going to shape up, and-"

"Dad!"

"-and if I get one more call about you skipping class-"

"Dad, please," Floyd pleaded, the words issuing forth in a rapid tumble. "I'm miserable. I haven't eaten in two days, my stomach is killing me, this is the wrong place for me. I'm in the wrong school, with the wrong people, everything is just wrong. I quit. I'll be good, I promise. Please come get me. I'll never give you a reason to be mad at me again, I swear. Whatever you want."

"Floyd, you can't quit. It's not a job." Hank breathed deeply, suddenly feeling completely sympathetic for his oldest now that he heard the tears catching in the poor boy's throat. If anyone knew what it was like to be in the wrong place with the wrong crowd, it was Hank Bancroft.

There was silence on the other end of the line for a long time, during which Hank hit the concealed button on his desk to summon Dav. That was how he sometimes got out of meetings that went on too long, and he thought it was sly but the whole office had caught on to the tactic a long time ago.

"You still there, kiddo?"

"Yeah, dad. I miss you," he said softly.

Well, so much for Hank's resolve. Poof. Gone.

"Miss me? I thought you hated me lately. And Theo."

"I thought I did, too, but I don't. I'm sorry I've been a di...that I've been acting up so much. I'll never do it again, I swear."

Daven peeked through the window and Hank crooked his finger to signal him to enter.

"Floyd, hold on for a minute. Just...don't hang up. Hold on."

Hank put his son on mute. "Close the door. Dav, I have a really awkward favor to ask you. Feel free to say no."

"Okay. What?"

"You don't have any meetings today, right?"

"No."

"Can you and Lucas go get Floyd from school in Palm Springs? You're listed as his second guardian so they'll release him to you, but not to my guards. I'm too fucking tired, and I've got that mandatory 11am meeting with the auditors from the FBI."

Daven was instantly concerned. "Sure. Is everything alright?"

"Yeah. Poor kid is homesick. You guys will have to take the Escalade so there's room for all his suitcases."

"Sure. Leave right now?"

"Yeah, if that's ok. It'll take about three hours each way."

Daven nodded. "Sure, Hank. Anything for Floyd."

Hank felt a catch in his throat suddenly, and his heart was all but glowing. "You're a good man, Dav. I'm...thankful for your friendship. And for caring about Floyd. Thank you."

Dav nodded, again. "Are you alright?"

"Yeah," Hank said with a smile. "Getting my boy back when I thought I was going to lose him? Everything's great. I'm going to let you surprise him with the good news. Hurry back, alright?"

"Certainly. See you at the house."

Hank picked up the phone again. "Hey, Floyd. I'm going into a meeting and I want you to just relax and breathe. Do your meditations. Take your medications. Do what you got to do to chill out, okay? We'll talk later about possibly bringing you home at spring break. I can't promise anything."

"*Spring break?*" Floyd moaned. "But I'm ready now, dad. I'm packed."

"Floyd. We will *only* talk if Silas can confirm for me that you went back to class right now and stayed there all three hours. Period. Otherwise, forget it, we aren't talking about a thing. Understood? Call me at lunchtime."

"Yes, sir," Floyd replied miserably, and Hank smiled a little himself.

"Good boy. Talk to you then."

He hung up and dialed Silas.

"Silas, I lost the bet. He lasted three days less than I thought he would. I'm really glad you talked me into paying only one week's tuition."

Silas laughed a little. "Oh, that's alright. He's a good kid. No harm done and we've enjoyed having him. So you're coming to pick him up?"

"No, my brother Daven is on his way." Hank stopped himself in surprise; he had never referred to Dav as his brother before and wasn't sure why he did so now. It was strange that it didn't feel awkward at all. "He and my guard, Lucas, should be there by noon or so. Don't tell Floyd. They're going to surprise him, but I want his ass back in class now until lunchtime. He knows, but can you make sure?"

"Of course."

Hank was happy as that call ended and another rough chapter in the book of Floyd was coming to an end. He missed his kid more than he'd ever confess, although he'd admittedly been too occupied to think about him much lately.

Now to deal with Rupert. He walked over to the man's office, once again ignoring the line of people waiting to talk to him. Normally he'd never be so rude, but this wasn't a normal day.

"Hank, welcome back," said Rupe as he pulled a piece of paper off his printer. "I was just about to bring you the revised version of the media st...is something wrong?"

Hank sat down at one of the chairs in front of the desk, which he never did. "First things first. As predicted, Floyd's time at Elite Palms has come to a premature end."

"No problem. Millie's ready for him. I'm glad the boys won't be separated anymore."

"Good. Thank you." Hank hardened his tone. "Now for the part where I get bitchy, and you shut up and listen, and then quickly agree to everything I expect to happen in the future."

Rupert's eyes went wide with alarm; Hank had never said such a ruthless thing to him before.

"Yes?"

"I overheard the conversation you had with Dav. Two big things wrong with it. Number one, if he tells you to do something, you do it. He's always done what you tell him without hesitation because he understands you both work for me, not yourselves. So don't let your pride get in the way of the job again. Got that?"

"Yes, Hank," Rupe replied quietly.

"Second thing. You hung up on him. Totally disrespectful and I won't have it. Have I ever hung up on you mid-sentence, even when I'm completely pissed off beyond all proportion to reality?"

"No, come to think of it."

"Exactly. Some lines we just don't cross, and that's one of them. You know that, we've discussed this before. I'll admit I did it once to Dav, but I spent a week apologizing for it. Next time it happens, you're out an entire paycheck. I'm dead serious."

"Understood, Hank," Rupert said placatingly. Hank was more furious than he'd since him since the Christmas debacle, but he was speaking in a near-conversational tone and was completely in control otherwise. It was terrifying somehow.

"Thank you. Then this matter is closed and won't be brought up again. Let me see that revised press release, please." He held his hand out, but Rupe froze.

"Hank, please let me say something first. I know that you're fundamentally against this law. After speaking to Daven I've changed the wording quite a bit, to make it much less...enthusiastic. But you must know that our party needs to support this." Hank nodded, so Rupe took a deep breath and handed over the new draft, which Hank read several times before commenting.

"Rupe, this is really good. It think you nailed it."

"What? Really?" Rupert did not expect that reaction. "I thought you...you.."

"No, you're right. Our party needs to support this. It's who we are. It doesn't matter that I'm personally against it." He handed the paper back. "Don't release it yet, though. I got word that the law might be on the March 1 ballot, so I'd like to wait a little longer before proceeding with an endorsement. Things change fast around here."

Rupert nodded. "Of course. That makes perfect sense."

"Hmm. Thanks again for taking Floyd into the home school. I'm leaving at noon because I didn't sleep last night. We'll catch up tomorrow."

Hank went back to his office and fired up his email program.

Harmon: how sure are you that this public flogging measure is going to be on the March 1 ballot? Need to know so we can align our messaging. Get back to me ASAP please. Hope you're enjoying the rest of your vacation. -Hank

Hank went into his bathroom to calm his nerves, and it took some time to get back to the point where he could be seen in public again without raising eyebrows. He must look terrible.

By the time he got back to his desk there was already a reply.

Hank, my contact says it's certain. I'm planning to release our statement around February 18. May I assume you will still be opposing it, and the others we discussed?

Oh shit, here goes, thought Hank. Into the belly of the beast we proceed.

Yes, exactly as discussed. Talk to you on Monday, 10am PST.

Hank felt sick, but he was committed now. If he couldn't persuade Rupert and Daven that opposing the two measures was best for the party, then fuck it. He was going to oppose them anyway with a live press conference before they could stop him, and damn the consequences.

He reached over and pulled the heavy carved stone paperweight into his lap, slowly and idly tracing the lettering with his fingers as he always did when he was uncertain about a decision. The quote always helped him settle down and re-center, and he always felt better afterwards:

There comes a time when one must take a position that is neither safe, nor politic, nor popular, but he must take it because conscience tells him it is right.

9 781801 934701